SINS OF THE FATHER

Kitty Neale was raised in South London and this working class area became the inspiration for her novels. In the 1980s she moved to Surrey with her husband and two children, but in 1998 there was a catalyst in her life when her son died, aged just 27. After joining other bereaved parents in a support group, Kitty was inspired to take up writing and her books have been *Sunday Times* bestsellers. Kitty now lives in Spain with her husband.

To find out more about Kitty go to www.kittyneale.co.uk.

D0036970

By the same author:

KITTY NEALE

Sins of the Father

AVON

A division of HarperCollins*Publishers*
1 London Bridge Street,
London, SE1 9GF

www.harpercollins.co.uk

This Paperback Edition 2016

6

First published in Great Britain by
HarperCollins*Publishers* 2008

A catalogue record for this book is
available from the British Library

ISBN-13: 978-1-84756-349-1

Set in Minion by Palimpsest Book Production Ltd,
Falkirk, Stirlingshire

Printed and bound in Great Britain by
Clays Ltd, St Ives plc

MIX
Paper from
responsible sources
FSC™
www.fsc.org **FSC˚ C007454**

With thanks to my literary agent, Judith Murdoch, and the wonderful team at Avon/HarperCollins. Also my thanks to Clifford Wherlock for his memories of London bombings during the Second World War.

For Ann Jones

A dear friend who speaks with the wisdom of angels. To me she is more than a friend. She is a kindred spirit, who, despite time and distance, is always in my heart. This one is for you, Ann, with all my love.

Prologue

The woman stood outside the train station, a leaflet held out in appeal, whilst a high wind fought to snatch it from her hand.

'Please,' she begged, 'have you seen this little girl?'

As had so many others, the man ignored her plea, brushing her aside as he hurried past. Rain began to fall, small spatters at first, but as heavy clouds gathered it became heavier, soon soaking both her hair and clothes.

It didn't stop the woman. Nothing would. Clasping the rest of the leaflets close to her chest, she tottered forward, thrusting one towards a young woman emerging from the station wearing a straight red skirt and pointy-toed shoes.

'Please, have you seen this little girl?'

The woman took it, her eyes showing sympathy as she said, 'Sorry, no.'

'Please, look again.'

The young lady lowered her eyes to the picture, but then, needing both hands to open her umbrella, she shook her head, the picture falling onto the wet pavement. She wrestled the wind to keep the umbrella over her head, her grip tight and knuckles white as she bustled away.

The woman watched her for a moment, but then her eyes came to rest on the leaflet lying wet and forlorn on the pavement. A gasp escaped her lips. The eyes of her child seemed to gaze back at her, rain spattering the picture as though tears on her cheeks. She shivered with fear, vowing silently, Oh God, I have to find you – *I have to*.

She straightened her shoulders, desperation and determination in her stance. Another train disgorged its passengers, and as they streamed from the station she saw a tide of faces. Hand held out, she once again proffered her leaflets.

It was dark before she gave up, uncaring that she was soaked to the skin and almost dead on her feet as she trudged home.

The house felt empty, desolate, as she walked inside, the plush décor meaning nothing to her now. She was alone. They had all gone, but it didn't matter. The only one she cared about was her daughter.

With hair dripping onto thick, red carpet and

wet tendrils clinging to her face, she wearily climbed the stairs to her bedroom, peeling off sopping clothes before throwing on a pink, quilted dressing gown. Tears now rolling down her cheeks, she flung herself onto the bed, clutching a pillow to her chest. It had been three months and she feared the police had given up, but she wouldn't. She would die first and, if anything, death would be welcome.

It was her fault, she knew that. A sob escaped her lips. Money had become her god, but the means of procuring it had put her little girl in danger. Her stomach churned, as a wave of fear overwhelmed her. Something dreadful had happened to her child.

Why had she let money become an obsession? It had begun in childhood – and her iron will had grown from the desperation to lead a different life from the one her mother had suffered. But there was more to it than that. It was also men! Her need to make them pay – her need for revenge.

And they *had* paid, and she *had* made her fortune, but at what cost? *Oh, my baby! My baby!* The money was meaningless now. She'd burned it all, given up every last penny, but still they hadn't found her daughter. What more do you want from me? her mind cried, eyes heavenward.

She sobbed, unable to stand the fears that plagued her. She forced her thoughts in another direction. To the past, and to where it had all begun.

1

Emma Chambers pulled the threadbare blanket up to her chin, only to have one of her three sisters tug it back. The attic room was freezing. In the far corner was another straw-filled mattress, this one crammed with her four brothers. One of them turned over, breaking wind loudly, whilst another, the eldest, snored sonorously.

The house stirred, awakened from its slumber. Faint sounds reached Emma's ears: a door closing, a cough, and then the sound of creaking rungs as her father climbed the ladder. Through the piece of material slung across the attic to divide children from parents she heard her mother's soft groan and sensed her dread.

At sixteen years old and living with little privacy, Emma had no illusions. Her father was drunk, his feet stumbling on the rungs, and that meant the scant money he may have earned as a builder's labourer had already lined the local publican's pocket. The King's Arms stood on the corner of their street in Battersea, South London, acting as a magnet for her father. It was rare that he was able to pass it without going inside.

There was more noise now, impatient curses as he finally made it through the small, square opening, his footfalls clumping across the wooden planks. Then came the sound of his boots hitting the floor as he flung them off, followed by the swish of clothing. Emma tensed, fearing for her mother, and shortly afterwards the nightly argument began.

'Come on, woman!'

'No, Tom.'

The sound of a slap, a sob, and then his harsh voice: 'You're my wife.'

'The baby's nearly due. Can't you leave me in peace?'

'Leave it out, you've weeks to go yet. Now come on, Myra, lift your nightdress.'

'I don't feel well. Can't you do without for one night?'

'No, I bloody well can't.'

It started then, the grunts, the groans. Emma wanted to scream, to run round to her parents' side of the attic and drag her father away from her mother. He was an animal, a pig, but she knew from past experience that it would only make things worse. Better to do nothing, to just pray that it would be over quickly and that her mother would be all right.

Emma held her hands over her ears, hating the sounds, and as one of her sisters turned over, she found herself without coverings again. Her stomach rumbled with hunger. There had been only cabbage soup for dinner, and so it wasn't surprising when one of her brothers loudly broke wind again.

Food had preoccupied Emma's thoughts more than anything during the past week, but the thought of her dad's pay packet today had cheered her up. Now, though, there'd be no bread to supplement their meagre diet, and though she tried to still it, hate surged through her – hate for what her father had become.

Emma fidgeted again, trying to find comfort on the lumpy old mattress whilst wondering what had happened to the father she had known before the war. Yes, he'd been taciturn, but he'd also been loving, with an innate kindness. She could remember sitting on his knee, his affectionate cuddles, but the man who'd returned after the war, though looking the same, was a stranger – one who was short-tempered, hard and embittered.

A chink of moonlight spilled through a small hole in the roof, one that let in rain, and Emma frowned. They hadn't always lived here. Before the war their home had been several streets away, in a comfortable if not large house, where at least her parents had a separate bedroom. The front door had opened straight on to the pavement and she had fond memories of playing with her friends, chalking numbers on the paving slabs for games of hopscotch.

The war had changed everything. At first they'd been fine, children untouched by the distant fighting, but gradually the air raids had started to hit London, increasing in frequency until it seemed that bombs fell night and day. Many of Emma's friends had been evacuated to the country-side but a few remained, her special friend next door, Lorraine, among them.

One morning they returned from the bomb shelter to find her friend's house flattened, and theirs so badly damaged that it was too dangerous to go inside. All that remained of the wrecked house was the staircase, leaning from the adjoining wall, the steps now leading up to open sky. They had stood, mouths agape, too shocked at first even to cry.

It was the last time Emma saw her friend, the family going to live with Lorraine's grandparents in another borough. Unlike us, Emma thought. Her mother's parents had died, and her father's now lived in a tiny one-bedroom flat, a reserved old couple that they rarely saw. There were aunts, but they had moved away from London at the start of the war. Emma recalled her mother's distress because they had no one to take them in. With so much property destroyed, accommodation had been hard to find, but then they'd been offered this attic flat, and, with no other option, her mother had taken it.

Still uncomfortable, Emma shifted on the mattress. Some people had profited by the war, their landlord amongst them. He'd been clever, buying up property when it was cheap, willing to take the risk that the building would remain standing. This house, and others in the street, had originally been divided into two flats, but the landlord had converted the attics to shoehorn in as many families as he could, raking in extra rent.

She knew her mother had expected to live here only as a stopgap and planned to move as soon as something better became available, but then the war ended, her father's army pay ending with it when he was demobbed. If he'd returned the same man, they would have been all right, but now he drank heavily, lost job after job, and here they remained, the rent sometimes unpaid and on catch-up, her mother's dream of a nicer home unfulfilled.

Emma's stomach growled with hunger again. Huh, they'd been better off when her father was away. At least his army pay had been regular, but now . . .

There was a loud groan, a familiar one. Sighing with relief, Emma knew that her father had finished. She yanked on the blanket again, snuggled closer to her sister for warmth and, knowing that her mother was now safe, she finally fell asleep.

Emma found herself the first awake. As quietly as possible, she crawled from the mattress, but as soon as she left the warmth of her sisters' bodies her teeth began to chatter. God, it was freezing! She moved to the ladder, climbed down to the room below and, after lighting a candle, she cupped the flame as she hurried downstairs to the middle landing. There was only one toilet, shared by all three tenants in the tall, dilapidated house. Alice Moon and her husband lived on this floor, but there was no sound from their rooms. Pleased to find the smelly toilet free, Emma was soon hurrying back to the top-floor flat.

She kneeled in front of the hearth, lighting what little kindling they had, soon holding out her hands greedily to the tongues of flame that licked merrily up the chimney. For a moment she was mesmerised by the sight, but then, with an impatient shake of her head, she covered the flames with a few lumps of wood that Dick, her eldest brother, had procured from somewhere. There were nuggets of coke left, again obtained by Dick and, fearing they were stolen, Emma hastily shovelled them on top of the smouldering wood as if this small act could protect her brother. She frowned, knowing that though she

6

shouldn't encourage him, unless Dick was again lucky in his gatherings there was little chance of getting more fuel.

What sort of man had their father become? What sort of man let his wife and children go hungry and cold whilst he poured ale down his throat?

When the fire was a manageable glow, Emma hung the kettle over it to boil, her mouth drooping despondently. Her mother loved a cup of tea, saying there was nothing like it to perk her up, but there was none left. As though it were her own, Emma felt her mum's disappointment.

Stretching her arm up to the rafters, Emma took down a bundle of dried nettles and, as the kettle boiled, she made the infusion, just in time to see her mother's swollen legs coming down the ladder.

Myra smiled as Emma gave her the tin mug, her hands wrapping round it in pleasure. 'You're a good girl.'

As her mother lowered herself onto a stool, her stomach looked huge and cumbersome. Yet the rest of her was thin, too thin, her arms and legs like sticks. She was only in her mid-thirties, yet she appeared old and worn beyond her years.

In the flickering candlelight, Emma saw her grimace of pain. 'Are you all right, Mum?'

'Stop fretting, I'm fine,' she said, taking a sip of the nettle tea.

'Do you think there's any money left?'

'I looked in his pockets before coming down and found none.'

'How could he?'

'That's enough! It isn't your place to question what your father does. You know as well as I do that he hasn't been the same since coming home from the war. He had a terrible time and it changed him.'

'Mum, you can't keep using that as an excuse! It's been three years and he rarely has nightmares now. If you ask me, he should count himself lucky. At least he's in one piece, which is more than you can say for Mr Munnings next door.'

'Enough, Emma! I know you'll soon be seventeen, but you're getting too big for your boots lately and talking about things you don't understand.'

Emma hung her head, her face hidden by her long, wavy blonde hair as she mumbled, 'If he's blown his money on booze again, what are we supposed to do for food? The rent is overdue too, and I can't see the landlord being fobbed off anymore.'

'You always worry too much. We've managed before and we'll manage again. We've still got some potatoes, and perhaps Dick will earn a few bob on the market today.'

'Without flour there'll be no bread.'

'Then we'll do without. Now come on, buck

up. And talking of potatoes, you can peel some spuds and I'll fry them for breakfast.'

Emma did as she was told, finding as she dug in the nearly empty sack that most were sprouting roots and had turned spongy with age. She sorted out the best of them and, with her hands in the sink turning blue in the ice-cold water, she surreptitiously watched her mother.

There was another small grimace of pain that she tried to hide, but Emma saw it and suspected the baby was coming. This would be her mother's ninth child, and it had been a difficult pregnancy, one that seemed to drain her of energy.

The racket overhead started then, the sound of her siblings waking, squabbling, and then her father's voice rang out.

'Shut that fucking noise!'

There was instant quiet for a moment, but then one by one they came down the ladder. First to emerge was Dick, the eldest boy at fourteen years old. In his arms and clinging to his neck like a little monkey, he held the youngest boy, Archie, who at two hero-worshipped his big brother. Next came thirteen-year-old Luke, the quietest of them, a thoughtful, introverted boy, always the odd one out. He was handsome, almost beautiful, and his pale, blue eyes seemed to hold a strange, deep knowledge. There had been odd occasions when Luke had unnerved them, once predicting that their mother was carrying a boy, and as though he had the ability to see into the future, he had told them in advance when their father was arriving home from the war. Emma loved Luke dearly and he was her favourite brother.

He was followed down the ladder by eleven-year-old Susan, and then there was a lull.

'Where are the others?' Myra asked.

'Still asleep,' said nine-year-old Bella, the last to appear, clutching her peg doll and pretty as a picture with blonde hair and wide blue eyes.

Ann, at six years, along with three-year-old James, had arrived after their father had been given leave during the war. They were always the last up every morning, but they'd show their faces as soon as the smell of food wafted into the attic.

All the children made for the fire, pushing and shoving each other to get close, whilst Myra smiled serenely at her brood. She had a look about her; one that Emma was familiar with, a look that always preceded labour.

'Come on, Em, get a move on with those potatoes,' her mother said.

'They're ready.' After carefully slicing them, Emma got between her siblings to place the frying pan on the fire, adding, 'Get dressed, you lot, or you'll get no breakfast.'

There was grumbling, but all except Dick did her bidding. As the eldest boy, Dick thought himself too old to be given orders, but now, seeing how pale his mother looked, he lifted up Archie, saying with a frown, 'I'll see to this one.'

'You're a good boy,' Myra said, but then with a small cry she bent forward, arms clutched around her stomach.

'Mum! Mum! What's wrong?' Dick cried.

'I . . . I think the baby's coming,' she gasped, but then, after taking a few deep breaths, she managed to straighten, her eyes encompassing them all. 'It'll be a while yet so there's no need to look so worried. In the meantime, Emma, you'd best get the kids fed. And you, Dick, be prepared to take them out for a while later, and . . .' Her voice died as she bent forward again, this time unable to suppress a scream.

Emma's face blanched. She'd seen her mother in labour before, and had even watched some of her siblings being born, but this time she knew it was different. 'Mum, what is it? What's the matter?'

'I dunno.' Despite the freezing room, perspiration beaded Myra's brow. 'Oh, God!' she suddenly cried. 'Quick, Emma, run downstairs and fetch Alice!'

Emma fled the room, almost falling down the stairs in her haste. She hammered on Alice Moon's door. Come on! Come *on*, her mind screamed as she hopped about in anxiety, relieved when at last the woman appeared.

11

'Please, come quick, it's my mum.'

'Stone the crows,' Alice said, her voice thick with sleep, 'what's all the fuss about?'

'Mum's in labour, but something's wrong. She's screaming, Alice!'

At last the urgency in Emma's voice registered and Alice's sleepy eyes cleared. Shoving Emma aside, she rushed upstairs, oblivious to the fact that she was still in her long flannel nightgown.

Alice Moon took over. She urged the children out, sending them down to her flat with Dick in charge, and unceremoniously got Tom Chambers up to help his wife back to their attic bed.

For three hours Emma crouched beside the mattress, her hand numb with pain from her mother's fierce grip, and her legs cramped whilst Alice tried to help with the birth.

'Myra, I'm sorry, love, but I've got to have another go at turning it.'

There was no reply, just a groan, and Emma's heart thudded with fear. The last time Alice had tried this, her mother's screams had been horrendous. Please, she willed, please let it work this time.

Alice bent to her task, her face grave, and then the screams rose again, echoing in the rafters.

'No! No! Don't,' Myra cried.

Alice shook her head in despair. 'Tom!' she yelled.

His head appeared at the top of the ladder. 'What do you want now?'

Alice stood up and, though she spoke quietly, Emma heard every word. 'She's bad, Tom, real bad. You'd better get the doctor.'

'Leave it out, woman! She'll be all right. You've birthed the last three kids and there's never been a problem.'

'For God's sake, man, will you listen to me! It's a breech birth and I can't turn the baby. She needs help, she needs the doctor.'

'He won't come without his fee.'

'For Christ's sake, Tom, wake up! You don't have to pay the doctor now, not since this National Health Service was introduced. Now get a move on or you could lose your wife. I don't care how you do it – bloody drag him here if you have to – but get him.'

Emma didn't hear her father's reply. Her eyes were wide with horror. Blood was pumping from her mother's womb, soaking the mattress. 'Alice! Alice!'

The woman turned at her cry. 'Christ, she's haemorrhaging. Quick, Tom, before it's too late!'

But it was too late. By the time a disgruntled doctor climbed the ladder, Myra Chambers and her baby were dead. Emma was still sitting by her mother, refusing to accept that she was gone, and only when her father touched her shoulder did she react.

'Don't touch me!' she yelled. 'This is your fault! Why couldn't you leave her alone? She'd still be alive if you hadn't filled her belly again!'

Emma cringed then, braced for a clout. She had dared to speak up, to shout at her father, but instead he stared at her, white-faced, his eyes avoiding the lifeless body of his wife, and beside her the baby, pitifully small and wrapped in a rag.

'You . . . you . . .' he spluttered, but then his body seemed to fold. He staggered across the attic, then clambered down the ladder.

Still Emma didn't move, Alice unable to cajole her away. It was only when Dick came to her side, crouching down and placing an arm around her shoulder, that she broke. The anger seeped away to be replaced by a surge of grief that almost choked her. She sobbed, and turning, clutched Dick, finding that his tears mingled with her own.

'Come on, Em,' Dick urged. 'Alice needs to see to Mum.'

Emma dashed tears away with the heel of her hand, but looking at the poor worn-out body of her mother, anger arose again. 'He killed her, Dick.'

'Don't be daft, Em. Alice said that by the time the doctor got here it was too late.'

'I'm not talking about the doctor. It was Dad who killed her.'

'You're talking rot. Of course he didn't.'

Emma was too emotionally drained to argue. She forced herself to her feet, cramped legs screaming with pain, and with a last look at her beloved mother, she allowed Dick to lead her away.

'You'll have to tell the kids, Emma,' Tom Chambers said as Emma climbed down the ladder.

She looked at her father's red face, crumpled in grief but, instead of sympathy, she felt nothing but contempt. 'Why me?'

'It'll be better coming from you.'

Anger still stemmed her grief and, unable to bear the sight of his face, Emma left the room, slamming the door behind her as she went down to the middle landing. For a moment she paused outside Alice's door, her temper diminishing as she wondered how to tell her brothers and sisters. Somehow she had to hold herself together for their sakes. Taking a great gulp of air, Emma went inside.

'Has the baby been borned?' asked Bella. 'Is it a girl, Emma? I hope it's a girl.'

'What's up, Em?' Luke asked, eyes perceptive as he studied her face. Luke the quiet one, the intelligent one, so sensitive that their mother always said he was like a cuckoo in her nest. At that thought, a sob arose that Emma was unable to stifle and, holding her hand across her mouth, she looked wildly across the room at Alice.

'Shall I tell them, love?' the woman asked gently.

15

For a moment Emma was tempted, but then Luke was by her side, his soft eyes now wide with fear. 'I knew when Alice came to fetch Dick that something was wrong. What is it? Is Mum all right?'

Emma could only shake her head, but Luke immediately realised the implications, his face blanching. 'Why didn't I see this coming?'

Unable to answer, Emma's eyes flicked around the room at the others all looking at her worriedly. God, how was she supposed to tell them? How could she break the awful news that both their mother and the baby brother had died? Only little Archie seemed oblivious, absorbed as he gnawed on a crust of bread.

Emma crossed the room and, sitting down, she pulled James onto her lap, beckoning the others to her side. With her eyes heavenward for a moment she prayed for inspiration, but her mind remained blank.

'Why is Luke crying?' Susan asked.

Emma looked at Susan, poor plain Susan, who always seemed to have a runny nose and caked eyes. She was the sickly one, lacking the resilience of her siblings, and, like all of them, as thin as a rake. Susan's bony knees showed beneath a thread-bare skirt as she moved closer. Taking her hand, Emma struggled to answer her question. 'Luke's crying because . . . because . . .' It was no good, the words wouldn't come, and once again Emma's eyes flew to Alice.

With a small, sad shake of her head, Alice took a deep breath. 'Listen, pets, I'm afraid your mother and the new baby have gone to heaven. They're with the angels now.'

Susan was the first to speak, her voice high. 'You mean . . . you mean our mum's dead?'

'Yes, love, I'm afraid so,' Alice said.

A loud cry pierced the air and, as all eyes went to Bella, Alice quickly drew the child into her arms. Susan too began to cry, and it was Luke who comforted her, whilst Emma struggled to answer Ann's questions.

'What does she mean, Em? What's dead?'

'Mummy was ill and she didn't get better.'

'What? Like Mrs Dunston's dog?'

The Dunstons lived on the ground floor, the only ones to have use of a small garden at the back of the house. 'Yes, love, that's right.'

'They buried him in the garden. Is that what they'll do with our mum? I don't want them to do that to our mum,' she cried, tears filling her eyes.

'They won't, darling.'

James suddenly squirmed on her lap, and looking at everyone with obvious bewilderment, he too began to cry. 'Want my mummy. Want Mummy.'

It was too much for Emma, her tears spurting as she pulled James close. For several minutes they remained like that, clutching each other and crying, none of them aware that little Archie was sobbing too, obviously affected by their grief.

The door opened. Dick came into the room and immediately swept the toddler up into his arms. 'It's all right, Archie. It's all right,' he consoled.

Many minutes passed, but at last their tears subsided.

They were still clinging to each other, until Alice gently pushed Bella away, patting her head as she said, 'I'm sorry, pet, but I'd best go back upstairs. You lot stay here for a while, and if you're hungry there's more bread and a pot of jam in the larder.'

Food, Emma thought, feeling sick at the thought, but then James squirmed in her lap again.

'Want jam,' he said.

Emma wiped his snotty nose before standing up to place him in her seat. She then went to the larder, but as she cut several slices of bread, her eyes alighted on a newspaper lying on the table. Just below the banner she saw the date, 7 December 1948, and knew it would be etched on her mind for ever. It was the day their mother had died, their cornerstone was gone, their lives changed. What was going to happen to them now? The thought forced its way to the front of her mind. The task of looking after her brothers and sisters would fall to her now.

Oh Mum, how am I going to cope?

2

On a balmy Sunday morning in June, Alice Moon sat quietly across from her husband, the words she had rehearsed sticking in her throat. Would he agree? God, she hoped so. They had a strong marriage, and she was thankful every day that Cyril had been demobbed in 1945 without a scratch to show for the years of fighting.

Oh, it had been awful without him, and many times she had feared for her own life as bombs rained down on London. Like Myra, she had refused to leave, but felt the children should have been evacuated. Instead, when Myra moved into the attic, Alice had spent night after night helping her to get the kids up when the warning sirens pierced the air, all of them half asleep as they hurried to the nearest shelter. It sometimes felt like a miracle that they'd all survived when so many houses and factories in the area had been flattened. Alice shuddered at the memories, glad they hadn't ever had to shelter in an underground station, as many people had during the raids. In Balham it had been dreadful, and she was still haunted by what happened in 1940. A high-explosive bomb hit Balham High Road, penetrating the booking hall at the underground station. It had ruptured a large water main, along with the sewer, causing water, mud and gravel to pour down the stairs onto the platform, where about five hundred people were sheltering. Her friend Doreen Broker had been killed, along with sixty-four other poor souls.

Who'd have thought the war would last so long? Cyril had only been on home leave twice in six years. It had been the same for Tom Chambers, but Myra had been lucky, Tom leaving her pregnant on both occasions.

Tears welled in her eyes. Lucky! How could she think that? The poor woman was dead now, and those kids left without a mother. Surreptitiously wiping her eyes on the corner of her apron, she took a deep breath, hoping against hope that she could do something for at least two of them. 'Cyril.'

He looked up from his newspaper, expression impatient. Cyril's time on the Sunday morning crossword was sacrosanct and she'd disrupted his concentration. 'What?'

Now that she had his attention, Alice was

determined to plough on. 'I'm worried about poor Emma.'

'What? Emma upstairs?'

'Who else do we know called Emma?' Alice asked. Not waiting for a reply, she added, 'She's not coping with the kids.'

'Well, that ain't surprising. Bloody hell, seven of them, and noisy little sods they are too!'

'That's just it. I think she could manage the older ones, but little Archie is nearly three now and James four. They're too much of a handful for her.'

Cyril shrugged, his eyes going back to his newspaper. 'They'll soon grow up and join the others at school.'

Alice stiffened, determined to keep his attention. 'Tom Chambers isn't any help. When he's not at work, he's in the pub and rolls home drunk all hours.'

'Have a heart, Alice. The man's just lost his wife.'

'Huh! He's been like it since he was demobbed. As for losing Myra, it's been six months now, and if you ask me, things can't go on the way they are.'

'He had a rough time of it, and Tom's one of many who can't pick up the pieces. Anyway, I reckon you should keep your nose out of it. What goes on upstairs is none of our business.'

'Myra was my best friend, and for that reason

I think it *is* my business. I've been trying to help Emma as much as I can. In fact, to give her a break so she can keep up with the housework and laundry, I've been looking after Archie and James for a few hours every day, but it's rotten for her in the evenings too. She never gets the chance to go out with her friends now, and from what she's told me, they've all drifted away.'

'I don't see why the older lads can't look after the younger ones now and then.'

'Since when have lads taken on babysitting?'

Cyril pursed his lips. 'Well, it's good of you to help her out, but I hope you're not suggesting babysitting in the evenings.'

'No, of course not.'

'Good, and don't go wearing yourself out looking after Archie and James during the day.' On that note he seemed to lose interest, his eyes going back to his crossword.

'Cyril Moon! I'm not an old woman! I'm only thirty-eight and quite capable of looking after a couple of kids. In fact, I enjoy it.'

'All right, there's no need to shout.'

'Oh, I'm sorry. It's just that I want to put something to you and I'm all of a dither.'

His head tipped to one side, brow creased. 'Well, you'd best spit it out.'

'It's like this. You see, I've been thinking . . .' She hesitated, trying to find the words.

'Go on.'

With a spurt, Alice said, 'You know I love kids, Cyril, but we ain't been lucky, have we? We've tried and tried, and though the doctor said there's no reason why I can't fall, well, it hasn't happened.'

'We needn't give up, and anyway, it's fun trying,' he said, winking lewdly.

Alice had to smile, but then her face straightened. 'Cyril, fun or not, we've been married fifteen years and it's time we faced the facts. We're never going to have kids of our own.'

His lips pursed. 'Yeah, maybe you're right, but never mind, love. We've still got each other.'

'I know we have, but as I said, I've been looking after little Archie and James, and I've grown very fond of them. I . . . I was wondering if we could take them on.'

'Take them on! What do you mean? Surely you're not talking about adoption?'

'Well, not right away, but maybe later, if they settle with us.'

'No!' he said emphatically. 'I don't fancy taking on another bloke's kids.'

'Please, Cyril.'

'No, and that's final!'

At his tone, her expression became a contrived one of despair.

'Alice, don't look at me like that. Surely you

don't seriously expect me to take on Tom's little brats?'

'They aren't brats!' Alice cried, jumping to her feet. 'They're lovely little boys who need love, attention, and a stable home. We can give them that!'

Cyril voice hardened. 'Pack it in, Alice. Doing your nut ain't gonna make any difference. I said no, and that's that.'

Alice flopped back onto her chair and, throwing up her apron to cover her face, she began to cry, sobs shaking her shoulders. She should have known he wouldn't agree, but as minutes passed, a hand touched her shoulder.

'Come on, don't take on so. Surely it doesn't mean *that* much to you?'

'Oh, Cyril, you have no idea how much I've longed for a baby, ached to hold our son or daughter in my arms. It's never going to be, but whilst looking after the boys I really have come to love them. Archie is like a little monkey, and likes nothing better than to be cuddled. He used to latch on to Dick, but now that the boy's working, he's turned to me. James is cheeky, but not in a bad way, and he's gorgeous, with his blond hair and grey eyes.'

'Dick! Working? This is the first I've heard of it.'

Alice mopped her eyes. 'He was fifteen in March

and has got himself a job on the market, working on Charlie Roper's stall.'

'Has he now? Well, he'll do all right with Charlie, but the lad would have been better off learning a trade.'

'Yes, maybe, but as an apprentice he'd only be paid peanuts, and though he doesn't earn a great deal on the stall, it's been a godsend. They couldn't cope without it.'

Cyril returned to his chair, his expression thoughtful, and Alice knew to keep her mouth shut. She sat quietly, her breath held and fingers secretly crossed as she watched his face.

At last he sighed and their eyes met. 'All right, Alice. If it means that much to you, we'll give it a go with the kids. Mind you, don't count your chickens yet. I can't see Tom wanting to give them up just like that.'

Once again she jumped to her feet, kissing Cyril on the cheek. 'The pub isn't open yet, so he's sure to be in. I'll go and have a word with him now.'

'You do that, but as I said, don't count your . . .'

But the door had already slammed shut, Alice not hearing the rest of her husband's warning as she hurried upstairs.

Tom couldn't stand the noise and had chucked the kids out. At last the room was quiet. Only Emma remained, perched on a low wooden stool, her face set in concentration as she endeavoured to sew a patch onto a pair of trousers. He glanced at her and the pain of his loss was like a blow to his stomach. Christ, she was so like her mother, with the same golden blonde hair and vivid blue eyes. As if sensing his scrutiny, Emma raised her head, lips curling in distaste as her cold gaze met his. He seethed. She should show him some bloody respect, but instead she hardly spoke to him, her hatred like a living thing, that filled the room and tainted the air.

Tom looked away from Emma, tempted to give her a good hiding, but he knew it would only make things worse. She wasn't a child now, she was seventeen, and if the girl took it into her head to walk out, he'd be in a right old fix. Christ, he needed to get out of there – he needed a drink, but with little money left this week he could afford only a pint. He sank back in the chair, berating his life, thoughts drifting.

They'd been happy once, him and Myra, but then the war had started and he'd been called up. As his mind took him to the front, Tom shook his head, not wanting to think about it, yet still the memories invaded. He didn't want to remember the sickening things he'd seen and done. Yet as always, even as he struggled to forget, the first horror returned to haunt him. He was in a landing craft, nerves taut as they waited to beach. The young chap next to him was in the same state, shaking, his eyes wide with fear, and they'd started to talk, inane chatter just to break the tension.

When they'd hit the beach, the shout went up to disembark and, lugging their packs, they surged forward. Tom didn't know how far he had run when the bloke next to him suddenly spun, a look of shock on his face before he fell. Until that moment he hadn't realised how frail the human body was, but as the soldier clutched at his stomach, guts spilling out, his screams combined with the sound of explosions and gunfire. Tom shuddered at the memory, recalling how he'd been paralysed with shock, unable to move, horrified to see the soldier's dying moments.

Bullets raked only inches away and at last he moved, diving to the ground, terrified as he used the young man's body as shelter. It was like a living hell; the thunder of mortars, machine-gun fire, the stench of cordite, shouts, yells, cries as more bodies fell to the ground. He had no idea how long he had lain prone behind the soldier's body, hands over his ears as shell after shell exploded, but then a corporal hauled him to his feet. Tom had seen the look of disgust on his face, and then he'd been shoved forward.

'Get moving,' the corporal had shouted and, feeling like a coward, Tom had followed the command, bent double as he raced up the beach, more and more soldiers falling beside him. He'd lost it then, firing his weapon without thought, determined to kill or be killed.

That moment had changed him, and as the weeks went by he had hardened. He would kill, feeling nothing, becoming an animal with only one thought – survival. One enemy soldier had actually begged for mercy, but, grim-faced, Tom had shot him, uncaring of the blood that spilled from his body.

When the war ended, he no longer felt human, returning home to find that many streets and buildings he'd known were gone, bombed to oblivion. He'd tried – oh, how he had tried – but soon after his return the memories began to haunt him until, day and night, he relived the horrors of war. It had been years now, but still they plagued him. When would they stop? When would he find peace . . . ?

There was a tap on the door. Alice Moon poked her head inside and Tom welcomed the interruption.

'Can I have a word?' she said.

'Yes, come on in.'

'Hello, Emma,' Alice greeted as she crossed the room. 'Doing a bit of sewing, are you?'

'Yes, but I'm still useless at it.'

'You'll learn.' As her eyes raked the room, Alice added, 'Where are the youngsters?'

'Dad made them go out to play.'

Alice's lips tightened momentarily, but then she focused on Tom. 'Do you mind if I sit down?'

'There's only a stool.'

'That'll do me,' she said, making herself comfortable. 'Look, I won't beat about the bush. I've seen the way Emma struggles to look after the kids, and to help her out I've had the two youngest for a couple of hours in the afternoons.' Shifting a bit on the stool she rushed on, 'I've grown fond of them, Tom. They're lovely boys, and Cyril and I would like to take them on permanently.'

There was a stunned silence, but then Emma's voice rang out. 'Alice, it . . . it's good of you, but we can't let you take James and Archie.'

'Shut your mouth, girl. This is my decision, not yours,' Tom barked.

'But, Dad—'

Tom felt his face redden. 'I said shut up!'

'Now then, Tom, there's no need to shout. It must be a shock for her, but listen, love,' Alice turned to Emma. 'They'll be better off with Cyril and me. I love them and we can give them a good home. They'll want for nothing, I'll see to that.'

'Oh, Alice, I know your place is like a palace compared to this, but Dad can't break the family up.'

Tom surged to his feet. 'I'll do what I bloody well like.'

'Please, Tom, calm down,' Alice cajoled. Then she spoke softly to Emma again. 'It's for the best, love. I'm only downstairs and you can see the lads whenever you want.'

'Hold your horses, Alice,' Tom protested. 'It's me you should be talking to, and I ain't said you can have them yet.'

'Surely you can see the sense of it? Emma is run ragged.'

Tom flopped onto his chair again, running a hand over his chin. There was no denying that it made sense. With the others at school, Emma had only James and Archie to worry about, and without them she could go out and earn a few bob, if only part time. After all, the girl had turned seventeen in February and it was about time she earned her keep. The rent owed was piling up, he knew that, and he doubted the landlord would put up with it for much longer. Tom knew he should pull himself together, cut down the booze, but he had a craving inside, eating away at him and driving him to the pub whenever he earned a few bob. A wave of self-pity washed over him. Bloody hell, no wonder he'd turned to drink! Any man would. He'd fought a war, and instead of things getting better, they were still stuck with bloody rationing. Work was tight, and on top of that he'd lost his missus. All he had left was a horde of bloody kids that drove him mad with their constant noise.

It was the thought of having two less to worry about that made Tom's decision. Looking up, he nodded at Alice. 'All right, you can have 'em, but I can't give you anything towards their keep.'

'None's expected, Tom.'

'Right, that's settled then.'

'But, Dad . . .' Emma protested.

'If I hear one more word from you, my girl, you'll be sorry. I'm doing what I think is best and that's that.'

'She's bound to be upset, Tom,' Alice placated.

'Do you want the kids or not?' he said, his tone threatening. He could change his mind, and Alice knew that.

She nodded. 'You know I do.'

'Right then, when do you want to take them?'

'I'll have to get beds first. After all,' she chuckled, 'I can hardly stuff them in with me and Cyril. I'll buy them tomorrow, so how about Tuesday?'

'Yeah, that's fine with me. It'll give Emma time to prepare them, not that I think they'll mind. After all, as you said, they'll only be downstairs.'

Alice rose to her feet, her voice high with excitement. 'Thanks again, Tom. I can't wait to tell Cyril.' She then turned to Emma and her face straightened. 'Oh, love, don't be upset. They'll be fine with me, I promise.'

'Leave her to me, Alice,' Tom said, pleased when the woman left. He'd soon sort Emma out and she could start looking for work. Dick was already earning a fair few bob on the market, and with his daughter bringing in money too, things would finally start looking up.

Emma sat quietly. She should be heartbroken, but instead was disgusted with herself for feeling relief. When Dad told her to look for work she'd felt a surge of excitement. God, it would be wonderful to get out of this flat, to find a job, if only part time. She'd be earning money, her own money, and maybe she could find a way to go out a couple of evenings a week. She missed her mates, missed sharing confidences, having a laugh, talking about boys, fashions, the latest records.

Nowadays she felt like a staid old woman, her life revolving around cooking, cleaning and taking care of the kids. Once again Emma felt a wave of excitement. With Luke coming up to his fourteenth birthday, maybe he could see to the others after school, and then she could work full time. Come to that, he could see to them during the school holidays too. Without James and Archie, that left only the girls, and they wouldn't be much trouble. Well, Susan maybe, with her constant moaning and petty illnesses.

Emma's mind continued to whirr, wondering what sort of jobs might be available. The sound of footfalls on the stairs interrupted her thoughts and she looked up with a start when Dick walked in.

'Hello, love.'

Their father offered no greeting, and Dick ignored him, saying to Emma only, 'Watcha,' before looking round the room and adding, 'Where are the kids?'

'Playing outside. Didn't you see them?'

'No, but I saw a gang running wild on the bombsite and no doubt our lot are with them. Hang on, where's Archie?'

'He's playing outside too.'

'What! But he's only a nipper.'

'He'll be all right. Luke will keep an eye on him.'

'I still think he's too young. You should have kept him in, Em.'

'It wasn't me who chucked him out.'

Dick's expression soured as he turned to look at his father, but the man rose to his feet, saying, 'I'm off out. You can tell him about the kids, Emma.'

'I suppose the pub's beckoning,' Dick said, his voice thick with sarcasm.

'Watch your mouth! Money's tight and I'm only having one pint – not that it's any of your business.'

'How come you're skint already?'

''Cos I had to stump up some of the rent arrears.'

'If you paid the rent every week it wouldn't mount up. I'm not surprised that Mr Bell put his foot down.'

'I told you to watch your mouth. Like Emma, you're getting too big for your boots and I ain't standing for it. Now as I said, I'm off, and I suggest you keep your opinions to yourself in future. I'm the man of the house, and don't you forget it.'

As the door slammed, Dick said, 'What's this about the kids?'

'Alice Moon came to see Dad. She's grown fond of James and Archie. Dad has agreed that she can have them permanently.'

Dick looked thunderstruck. 'But he can't do that!'

'I felt the same way at first, but since then I've had time to think about it. The boys will be better off with Alice. She'll look after them and they'll have the life of Riley. Not only that, they'll only be downstairs so we can see them whenever we want.'

'It still ain't right.'

'Without James and Archie to look after, I'll be able to get a job. I'd like that and I'll be able to put some money in the pot too.'

Dick sighed heavily. 'Yeah, I suppose you're right, but I'm gonna miss the little tykes, especially Archie.'

Emma pictured her youngest brother's cheeky

face, and knew she would too. Dick sat on the only chair they had, the one vacated by their father, and his eyes closed. He's tired, Emma thought, and it isn't surprising. To earn a few bob extra Dick had taken a shift at the Sunday market, rising at five. Sighing, she went back to her sewing, her thoughts drifting again.

Emma felt a wave of guilt. It would have broken her mother's heart to see the family torn apart and maybe she should have fought more to keep James and Archie. Yet she couldn't help feeling excited. Working in a shop would be nice; especially a clothes shop or jeweller's. Distracted, the needle pricked her finger and she let out a small yelp, lifting it to her mouth to suck the blood. She hated sewing. In fact she hated all housework. It was never-ending, the washing, ironing, cooking, cleaning. Her eyes widened in realisation. The work would still have to be done, but how was she going to keep on top of it if she was at work all day? For a moment Emma was flummoxed, but then straightened her shoulders with determination. The rest of them would have to help, to muck in and do their share. She'd give each of them a job, one that, depending on age, they'd be capable of doing.

A small smile played around her lips as she settled back again, ignoring her pricked finger as she finished off the patch. Susan wasn't too bad with a needle and could do the repairs from now on. It was time to sort them out, to move on. For the first time since her mother's death, Emma felt like living again.

3

Things didn't work out quite as Emma expected. Far from being upset, James and Archie were happy to live with Alice.

'She's nice,' James said. 'She plays with us, cuddles us, and we've got our own beds. I like it downstairs.'

Emma lowered her eyes, suddenly realising how much she had neglected them. She'd been busily wrapped up in housework with the ironing sometimes taking hours to complete, let alone the laundry and trying to mend clothes that were nothing but rags for the older ones to wear for school. She should have paid them more attention, but instead had given them bits and bobs to play with, old cotton reels and paper to cut into shapes, getting increasingly annoyed if they tried to distract her. When their mother was alive, they may have lacked money, but they had never lacked love. The housework would be abandoned if

Archie or James wanted a cuddle, and when the others came home from school, she had listened patiently as they chatted away.

Everything had changed when she died. Now, when the kids came home Emma was often cross with them for getting under her feet, happy for them to play out on the streets until dinner was ready. God, no wonder they were running wild.

With a small groan, Emma hugged herself. She'd been so wrapped up in trying to run the home as her mother had that she'd forgotten the most important thing. Love. No wonder James and Archie were happy to live with Alice, going downstairs on Tuesday morning without demur. Alice had been wonderful, letting them run upstairs to Emma whenever they wanted, but the novelty soon wore off and for the rest of the day their trips grew more and more infrequent.

'I want to live with Alice too,' Susan said, breaking into Emma's thoughts.

When Emma looked at her sister she saw Susan's mouth drooping despondently, the child close to tears. Time to turn over a new leaf, she thought, and smiling softly, she rose to stroke Susan's hair. 'Oh, love, I'd miss you something rotten. What would I do without you to cuddle up to at night?'

Susan managed a small smile in return, but she obviously wasn't completely mollified. 'Alice's flat is much nicer than ours, and I bet she buys loads of stuff for James and Archie. It ain't fair, Em.'

'Once I get a job we'll be able to have new things too. I'll be able to save up to buy us some decent clothes, and this winter I promise you'll get a nice new coat.'

'Me too?' Bella cried, followed by an echo from Ann.

'Yes, you too,' Emma placated, 'and what about you, Luke? What would you like?'

Luke's head dipped to one side. 'Well . . . if we've got the money, I'd like a cat, a ginger one. I like cats.'

'We'll see, but don't forget that in future when you come home from school, you'll all have little jobs to do.'

'We know,' Luke said.

Emma held out her arms to her youngest sister, gratified when Ann ran into them. 'When I'm not here, be a good girl and do what Luke tells you.'

Ann's head burrowed into Emma's chest. 'All right, Em.'

With a small sigh Emma closed her eyes. She hoped they'd be all right. Alice had agreed that they could run to her if there was an emergency, and that had eased her mind. Now all she wanted was to find a decent job, something she intended to do as soon as the kids left for school in the morning.

* * *

39

At five thirty the next morning, Emma heard Dick stirring, and she too rolled carefully off the mattress to follow him down the ladder.

She hated lighting the fire during the summer months, but without it she wouldn't be able to boil a kettle or cook anything for the kids' breakfasts. As soon as these tasks were completed she would thankfully douse it, and it wouldn't be rekindled until she had to cook dinner.

'You don't usually get up this early,' Dick said as he went to the sink for a sluice down, afterwards drying himself on a piece of rag.

'If I get a job today I'll have to get used to it. There'll be loads to do before the kids go to school and I might as well start as I mean to go on.'

'Loads to do? Such as?'

'Well, after sorting the kids I'll need to prepare dinner in advance and it takes a while to get the vegetables ready. Then I'll have to cook them, at least partly, finishing them off when I come home.'

'Yeah, I suppose so. I'd best get a move on or I'll be late.'

'What about your breakfast?'

'Charlie always gets me a bacon roll from the café and a nice big mug of tea too.'

'He's a good boss, you're lucky.'

'Yeah, he ain't bad, but he's a bit of a slave-driver at times. Still, it could be worse. See you later,' he called, the door shutting behind Dick before Emma had time to reply.

Emma's stomach rumbled. A bacon roll! What she wouldn't give for a bacon roll. One day, she thought, cheering herself up. If she found a good job they could all have bacon again. She went to the sink, pulling the metal bucket out from underneath and picking out vegetables to use in a stew. God, she was sick of vegetable stew, sick of eating the same thing every day. With her first pay packet she'd grab the ration book and head for the butcher's. At the thought of meat, her mouth salivated.

When the kids got up, chaos reigned. As though to show their displeasure at this change of routine, all except Luke played up. Susan said she felt ill, but when Emma felt her forehead, there was no sign of a fever. Used to Susan's wily ways to get out of school, Emma ignored her whines as she encouraged them to dress, sad that despite her best efforts they still looked like a band of ragamuffins.

She made the porridge, handing each of them a bowl, but when Susan sat on the floor, taking her first mouthful, she grimaced. 'It's horrible, Em. Ain't we got any sugar left?'

'No. You had the last of the sugar that Alice gave us yesterday.'

'I can't eat it without sugar.'

'Then you'll go hungry,' Emma said impatiently.

Susan pouted, took a few more mouthfuls, but abandoned the rest. The others ate without complaint, and at last they were ready for school.

'Now then,' Emma said firmly, 'off you go. I'll be looking for a job today and may not be here when you come home from school. If that's the case you all know what you have to do.'

'Don't worry. I'll look after them,' Luke said.

'I know you will,' Emma said, smiling at her brother, 'but don't forget what I said. Don't try to light the fire. I'll do it when I come home.'

Luke nodded, but as Emma looked at the girls she saw the confusion and uncertainty in their eyes. Remembering her determination to turn over a new leaf, she hugged them one by one, saying reassuringly, 'You'll be fine with Luke and . . . and I'll see you later. Be good at school,' she added as they reluctantly shuffled off.

The door had hardly closed when Emma heard her father coming down the ladder. He scratched his head, then a fit of coughing racked his body.

'I don't suppose there's any tea going?' he croaked.

'Since when have we had money for tea? I used to dry nettles for Mum, but you never drank it.'

'I can't stand the stuff.'

Emma said nothing. She hated talking to her father and avoided it as much as possible. Instead of sitting down he went to the sink, gulping down a mug of water before sluicing more over his head. Emma left him to it, climbing the stairs to the loft again.

She needed to get ready, and hoped the clothes she had sorted out the night before would be all right. She'd carefully ironed a blouse, but the pattern had almost faded, the material worn thin. The skirt wasn't too bad, though you could see a line where the hem had been taken down, which no amount of ironing could hide. She had no stockings, but hoped nobody would notice, and lifting her hand to touch her hair, wished she had something to pin it up. It felt stiff, lank, but without soap she'd only been able to rinse it with cold water. Pulling at the tangles with her fingers, she did the best she could, then returned downstairs.

The room was empty, her father gone, no doubt late for work again. This was a common occurrence and he was always getting the sack, now travelling to a building site in Chelsea after losing a job that had been just round the corner.

Oh, she didn't want to think about him. Today was a new beginning for her, and after a swift look to check that the fire had been doused, Emma hurried out, running down the stairs with her heart full of hope as she headed for the nearest row of shops.

Later that day, Emma was trudging to the market, footsore and near to tears. When she thought about the reception she'd received, her cheeks reddened with humiliation. She'd gone into a dress shop in Falcon Road first, her eyes lighting up when she saw the lovely garments hanging on rails. There were pretty pastel dresses, nipped in at the waist with matching belts, and she itched to touch them, to feel the material, but had resisted, going up to the counter wide-eyed with eagerness to ask if they had any vacancies.

'Miss Fisher,' the young and very smart girl behind the counter had called.

'Yes, can I help you?' a slim, middle-aged and sophisticated woman asked as she came out from a back room.

'I . . . I'm looking for work,' Emma stammered.

'I'm sorry, but we already have a cleaner.'

In her innocence, Emma had smiled, 'Oh, no, I haven't come for a cleaning job. I'd like to work in the shop.'

'You must be joking,' Miss Fisher said, eyebrows rising haughtily as she eyed Emma up and down. 'We have very high standards here, and I could hardly offer you employment looking like that.'

Emma had seen the smirk on the young sales

assistant's face, and flushed, but, fighting to hide her humiliation, she'd kept her head up. 'Fine, I wouldn't want to work here anyway.' And on that note she'd turned on her heels, shutting the door firmly behind her.

Blimey, what a couple of snobs, Emma decided as she'd walked away, refusing to let this encounter stop her. Yet by the time she had tried a few other garment shops the penny had well and truly dropped. Compared to all the sales assistants' attire, her clothes looked awful, scruffy. No wonder they wouldn't employ her. She'd tried a grocer, a baker, a haberdashery shop, but she'd received the same reception time and again.

The colourful stalls failed to lift Emma's spirits as she reached the market. It was buzzing with noise and several traders raised their hands to wave at her.

'Watcha, gorgeous,' called one. 'If I wasn't a married man I'd come out from behind me stall to give you a smacker.'

Emma forced a smile, but it failed to reach her eyes. She didn't look gorgeous. She looked a mess.

'What's up, Em?' Dick asked as she approached his stall. 'You look a bit down in the mouth.'

'I'm too scruffy to get a job in a shop,' she told him.

'You look fine to me.'

'Don't look so downhearted, girl,' Charlie, the

stall-holder, consoled, and, holding out a mug, he added, 'Here, you can have me tea. It'll buck you up no end.'

Emma gratefully took the mug, the strong tea tasting like nectar as she gulped it down. It did make her feel better, invigorated, but she still had no idea where to try next for a job. 'Thanks, Charlie,' she said, handing him the empty mug.

Charlie Roper was a nice man, but showing his age now, his gnarled fingers gripping the mug. 'Try the factories, love. There's Tate and Lyle's round the corner, for a start.'

She lowered her eyes. She didn't want to work in a factory, but there didn't seem to be any choice. 'Yes, I'll do that.'

As customers approached the stall, she called a quick goodbye before moving away.

At four o'clock, Emma was on her way home, her cheeks burning at the memories. Even the factories had turned her down, saying there weren't any vacancies for unskilled workers, but at least this time she believed them, believed that her appearance hadn't made any difference. She'd been led through countless factory floors to foremen's offices, seen women working on machines, their hair in turbans and clothes covered by overalls. Sometimes the noise was deafening and she wondered how they put up with it, but by this time she would have taken anything.

Emma was still brooding when she finally reached her street. It was treeless, grey and dingy, but she was used to the scenery. A few children were playing marbles in the gutter, and a couple of little girls were arguing over a skipping rope made from an old clothes line. Emma hardly noticed. She went into the dilapidated house where she lived and climbed the stairs wearily to the attic.

As she walked into the room the children clambered around her. 'Did you get a job, Em?' 'Where will you be working?' 'Will you be earning lots of money?'

Impatiently brushing them aside, Emma looked around and her temper flared. 'Look at the state of this place. You were supposed to do your jobs, but this room hasn't been touched.'

'We've only been home for five minutes, Em,' Luke said. 'We were just about to start.'

'Oh, I'm sorry, love,' Emma cried as she flopped onto a chair. 'I shouldn't be taking it out on you, but I've been walking for hours.' She pushed off her shoes, massaging her aching feet.

'Did you get a job?' Susan asked again.

Emma tried to sound more assured than she felt. 'No, not yet, but don't worry, I'll try again tomorrow.'

'Come on, you lot,' Luke said, sounding older than his years. 'Let's get our jobs done. Emma's worn out and needs a rest.'

The tears broke then. Oh, Luke was such a good boy, so thoughtful.

He rushed to her side and his arm snaked around her shoulder. 'What's up, Em? Do you want me to get Alice?'

'No, I'll be all right. I'm just a bit tired, that's all.' They were all looking at her worriedly and she fought to pull herself together. 'Go on then, get on with your jobs,' she urged, pleased when they all did her bidding. She had told them she'd try for work again tomorrow, and she'd do just that. But where?

4

After trudging around Fulham the following day, Emma had paused on Wandsworth Bridge on her way home, staring down into the grey, murky water of the River Thames as a coal barge passed below. It was hopeless, nobody wanted to employ her, and she had hated telling the kids that she still hadn't found work. It was her appearance, she was sure of it, especially when even an iron-monger had given her the cold shoulder.

Now it was ten o'clock on Friday morning, but instead of going out to look for work again, she was slumped on a stool at home. Her father was growing impatient, telling her to look harder, but then the door was flung open as James rushed into the room.

'Alice sent me up. She wants to see you.'

Emma forced a smile as she rose to her feet. James looked lovely in his new clothes. He was wearing grey shorts that just reached his knees, a pristine white shirt, and he even had a pair of little slippers

49

on his feet. She may have had doubts about the two youngest living with Alice, but seeing how well James looked, any lingering reservations were dispelled.

'What does Alice want?'

'I dunno. She just said to tell you that the kettle's on.'

A cup of tea, Emma thought, appreciating the woman's kindness. With James in the lead she went downstairs.

'Blimey, you look a bit fed up, love. What's the matter?' Alice said as she walked in.

'I've been looking for a job, but nobody wants to take me on. I look too scruffy to work in a shop and the factories haven't any vacancies.'

'You're such a pretty girl and we can spruce you up to look like a princess, more than fit to work in a shop. Come on, get this cup of tea down you and then we'll start with your hair.'

'Look, Emma,' Archie said, holding up a little wooden boat. 'Ucky Cyril made it for me.'

'*Uncle* Cyril, not *Ucky*,' Alice chuckled.

'I've got one too,' James said, joining Archie on the floor.

As the two children played with their boats, Emma watched them for a moment, noticing how clean and shiny their hair looked. She took a gulp of tea.

'Unlike those two, it'll take more than my hair to improve my appearance, Alice,' she said.

'Don't worry. I'm sure I can find you something decent to wear.'

Alice had a lovely curvaceous body and Emma doubted she could fill her clothes. Her own bust was small, her hips tiny in comparison, and she was at least two inches shorter.

As if sensing her thoughts, Alice grinned. 'I used to be a lot slimmer than this and I've kept the clothes I used to wear back then, hoping I'd get back into them one day. Come on, I'll show you.'

Emma placed the cup on the table, then followed Alice into her bedroom. Unlike her family's attic room, this one was lovely. Instead of mattresses on the floor, there was a real double bed with a wooden headboard and flowery spread. Emma's eyes took in the two double wardrobes and dressing table, a pink glass trinket set arranged prettily on top. With so much furniture the room looked stuffed full, but to Emma it was beautiful.

Alice opened one of the wardrobes and when Emma saw the rail of clothes she gasped with envy. Alice rummaged past a couple of plain, linen dresses, finally pulling out two blouses and a skirt. 'Cyril is always moaning that I never throw anything away, but I knew these would come in handy one day. Here, try them on.'

'Oh, Alice, how can you afford so many lovely things?'

'My Cyril earns a decent wage on the buses and

there's only been the two of us until now. I wanted kids so much, but they never came along. I think I shopped as a kind of compensation. Of course, during the war there wasn't much on offer, only drab clothes, but I still managed to indulge myself. Since clothes rationing ended, I must admit I've gone a bit mad.' She smiled softly. 'It's different now. The boys have changed our lives, and Cyril is growing as daft about them as me. Now come on, Emma, try these things on.'

Emma slowly undressed, ashamed that Alice was going to see her old and tatty knickers. She didn't have a brassiere, but with her small bust it didn't seem to matter. As Alice turned away to pull open one of the drawers in her dressing table, Emma hastily put on the skirt and first blouse. The light blue cotton skirt flared from the waist and felt a little loose. It was also a couple of inches too long, but she didn't care. It looked almost new and felt wonderful. The white blouse with its Peter Pan collar was loose too, but it smelled fresh, of something flowery, and so soft against her skin.

'They don't look bad,' Alice said. 'You'll just need to move the button on the waist and take it up. I've found some underwear too. This bra might fit you.'

'I . . . I don't think I need a bra,' Emma said, feeling her face redden.

'Of course you do. You can't go around without

a bra on at your age. Now come on, put your own stuff back on and we'll have a go at your hair.'

'You won't be able to do anything with it.'

'Of course I will, but first we'll give it a good wash.'

Emma was apologetic. 'I've tried to make it look nice, but without soap it dries all matted.'

'Oh, love, I'm not saying you aren't clean. I know you do your best, but as you say, it needs to be washed properly. Come on, I've got just the thing, and then I'll give it a bit of a trim.'

It was over two hours later when Alice finally sighed with satisfaction. 'There, you look smashing,' she said.

Emma stared at her reflection in Alice's mirror, hardly able to believe her eyes. Her lank, dull blonde hair was now shining, and sat on her shoulders in a profusion of waves. She still had her old clothes on, but she intended to alter Alice's skirt as soon as she went upstairs.

'Oh, Alice, I can't believe it's me,' she cried, her eyes fixed on the mirror.

'You're not just pretty, Emma, you're beautiful, just like your mum,' Alice said, her eyes suddenly moist. 'I was going to suggest a bit of make-up, but with such lovely skin you don't need it. A touch of lipstick is enough. Blimey, anyone would be mad not to give you a job now.'

'I hope you're right,' Emma said, finally tearing her eyes away from the mirror.

James and Archie had been so good, but were now demanding Alice's attention.

'They want their lunch,' Alice said. 'They never stop eating. My Cyril thinks they've got hollow legs.'

'I'm sorry, Alice.'

'Sorry! What have you got to be sorry about? It's a pleasure to see them stuffing their faces. I just wish this flaming food rationing was over with. It's a bloody disgrace. It's years since the war finished. Anyway, pop into the bedroom to get your things, and don't forget the underwear. I might have another skirt – I'll dig it out – but for now I'd best sort these two lads out.'

Emma smiled her thanks, and left Alice's clutching her new clothes. She couldn't help thinking that their own flat looked so bleak in comparison to Alice's, but sat on a stool, relieved that she had enough cotton left on the reel to complete the alterations to the skirt. The fire was still partly alight, enough to heat the iron. After pressing the hem, she put the skirt on, tucking the prettier of the two blouses inside.

There was no mirror to see how she looked, but Emma felt sure she was smart enough to get a job now. It was only when putting on her shoes that a frown creased her forehead. Worn down at the heels and scuffed, she knew they spoiled the outfit, but they were the only pair she had, and would have to do.

Her heart felt lighter and excitement mounted. It was after one o'clock, but she'd walk to Clapham Junction. There were loads of shops there. Surely one of them would have a vacancy.

Emma was about to leave when the door opened, Susan walking slowly into the room.

'What are you doing here? Why aren't you at school?'

'I've been sick and my teacher sent me home.'

Emma felt Susan's forehead, and for once believed her. She felt hot, her skin clammy. 'All right, love. Let's get you into bed.'

'You look nice, Emma. Where did you get those clothes?'

'Alice gave them to me.'

Susan was about to speak again, but then her hand flew to her mouth as she retched. In a flash Emma rushed her over to the sink, her nose wrinkling as her sister emptied her stomach. At least, Emma thought miserably, none of her sister's vomit had marked Alice's clothes.

Emma bathed Susan in cool water and then put her to bed where she fell asleep almost immediately. By the time Luke and the others came home from school, she was a lot better, but still lying lethargically on the mattress.

Emma came down the ladder. 'Susan's in bed.

She's been sick and was sent home from school.'

'Serves her right,' Luke said.

'What do you mean?'

'When we pass the market on the way to school, she's always scrounging stuff. She puts on a sad face, tells the stall-holders her mum's dead, and nine times out of ten they give her an apple or something.'

'She does what?' Emma was horrified. 'But an apple wouldn't make her sick.'

'I know, but she's done it so often that I think the stall-holders have got wise to her. She didn't get anything from them this morning so she tried it on with the butcher. He was just opening up, and when she pulled the stunt he shoved a pie into her hand. She stuffed it on the way to school and the greedy cow wouldn't even give us a bite. Still, she got her comeuppance. I reckon it must have been bad.'

Emma still couldn't believe her ears. 'How long has this been going on?'

'Since just after Mum died. It started when Charlie asked us how we were doing and it was obvious he felt sorry for us. He gave us an apple each and it must have given Susan the idea.'

'I'll give her a piece of my mind when she gets up,' Emma said, but then heard a knock on the door. She went to answer it, her face paling when she saw the landlord.

Mr Bell was in his mid-forties, tall and thin,

with a shock of dark, wiry hair. To Emma he was a toff, well spoken, well dressed, and he always carried a briefcase.

He gazed at her for a moment, his eyes puzzled, then said, 'Is that you, Emma? I hardly recognised you. You seem to have grown up overnight.'

She felt gauche, unsure of herself and stammered, 'My . . . my dad isn't home from work yet.'

'Didn't he leave the rent with you?'

'No, but he'll be here in a couple of hours.'

The man sighed heavily. 'Very well, I'll be back later.'

'Thank you, Mr Bell.' Emma said, relieved to close the door on the man and the predatory look she had seen in his eyes.

An hour passed and when Dick came home, his eyes widened. 'Blimey, Em, you look nice,' he said, passing her a bag of vegetables.

'It's down to Alice,' Emma told him, eyeing with appreciation the carrots, onions and potatoes. 'There's plenty here for another stew tomorrow. It's really good of Charlie to give you the leftovers.'

'They're too soft to put out again tomorrow, and they'd only be chucked away. Anyway, don't change the subject – why are you all dolled up like a dog's dinner?'

'I was going out to look for a job again but Susan was sent home from school.' She then went on to tell him why, his disgust equalling her own.

'Well, stone the crows,' he said. 'I'll have a few words to say to that little madam.'

'Me too,' Emma said, relighting the fire to finish off the dinner.

Another hour passed, one in which they both gave Susan a telling-off, and then Emma looked at Dick worriedly. 'Mr Bell is sure to be back soon and I don't think I'll be able to fob him off again. I hope Dad isn't blowing his wages in the King's Arms.'

Dick's expression soured as he rose to his feet. 'I'll drag him out of there if I have to.'

As Dick made his way to the pub, he found himself thinking about his boss. Charlie Roper was the antithesis of his father, and a man he respected. Charlie had never married and, as far as Dick knew, had no family, but he had taken him under his wing, treating him almost like a son. Yes, he was a hard taskmaster, but he expected no more from anyone than he did from himself.

Charlie liked the occasional pint but, unlike Dick's father, he knew when to stop. The man was hard-working, up at the crack of dawn every day, in all weathers, but never complained, despite the cold affecting his arthritic fingers. Charlie had fought in a war too, albeit the first one, and he'd had it rough, fighting in the trenches and telling Dick stories of rats the size of cats. Yet unlike his father, Charlie never bemoaned his fate, or used it as an excuse to drown his sorrows in drink. Dick scowled, hating his father's weakness, determined never to follow in his footsteps.

When Dick reached the pub, he flung open the door, searching for his father through a fug of stale cigarette smoke. An old boy was pounding out a tune on a wonky piano, the melody unrecognisable to Tom, and at a couple of tables he saw men playing cards. He pushed his way forward, finding his father standing at the bar, lifting a pint of beer to his lips.

Tom's eyes narrowed when he saw Dick, and above the babble of voices he snapped, 'What the hell are you doing in here?'

'The landlord's after the rent money.'

Tom's eyes flicked to the group of men who were drinking close by. 'Keep your bloody voice down!' he hissed.

Dick glared at the pint glass in his father's hand, knowing it wasn't his first and uncaring of who might overhear. 'Mr Bell will be back soon and wants his money.'

'So what? He'll get it when I'm good and ready. Just tell him to sod off.'

'Tell him yourself.'

Tom's lips tightened in anger. 'Watch your mouth, son. Now bugger off or you'll feel the back of my hand.'

'I ain't going anywhere unless you come with me.'

There was a titter of laughter, a man saying, 'It sounds like your young whippersnapper's laying down the law, Tom.'

Tom's grip was tight on his glass. 'That'll be the day,' he quipped. 'In fact, I think I'll take the lad home for the hiding he deserves.' He then lifted his pint, gulping it down and slamming the empty glass on the bar before glaring at Dick and adding, 'Right you. Home – and now!'

Emma heard footsteps on the stairs and her father's yelling before he shoved open the door, his eyes dark with anger as he glared at Dick.

'You've got a bloody nerve, kicking up like that in the pub. I didn't know where to put my bloody face.'

'Can you blame me? If I didn't drag you out, the rent wouldn't be paid – again. Mr Bell isn't going to put up with it for much longer.'

'I paid some of the arrears last week. Anyway, Bell's all wind and water. He's always threatening to chuck us out, but we're still here, ain't we?'

'One of these days you'll push him too far.'

'I'll handle Bell, but if you ever show me up again in my local, you'll live to regret it.'

For a moment they eyed each other like combatants, but it was Dick who finally turned away.

For a moment Tom continued to glare at his son, but then his eyes lighted on Emma. He paled, shaking his head as though to dismiss the sight. 'Christ, you gave me a turn. You look just like your mother. Where did you get those clothes?'

'Alice gave them to me.'

'Have you found a job?'

'Not yet. Susan was sent home from school and I had to stay with her.'

'Bloody kids,' he muttered, flopping onto his chair. 'You'd better find a job soon, my girl.'

Shortly after there was a tap on the door and Emma went to answer it.

'Is your father home now?' Mr Bell asked.

'Yes, I'll get him.' But when she turned round, her father was already on his feet.

'I'll speak to you outside,' he told the landlord, stepping into the hall and pulling the door closed behind them.

They heard raised voices and Dick put his fingers over his lips, pointing to the door. It hadn't closed properly, so both of them moved to the small gap, listening to the conversation.

'I can't pay all the arrears today, but you'll get the rest next week, I promise.'

'You said that last week, and the week before. I've been lenient, but there are still eight weeks outstanding. Either you pay me in full now, or I'll be forced to evict you.'

'Have a heart, Mr Bell. Since my wife died things have been hard, but my daughter is looking for work now. As soon as the girl gets a job there'll be more money coming in.'

'Emma? Are you talking about Emma?'

'Yes, that's right.'

There was silence for a moment, and then a cough. 'What sort of work is she looking for?'

'She'll do anything, shop work, a factory.'

Again there was a short silence, and then Emma's eyes rounded like saucers when Mr Bell spoke again. 'I too have lost my wife, Mr Chambers, and since then my house lacks a woman's touch. I've been considering employing someone as a cleaner-cum-housekeeper and, as Emma is looking for work, maybe she'd like the position.'

'What sort of pay are you offering?'

'It will depend on how many hours she works but approximately one pound ten shillings. If you're agreeable a portion of that could be stopped each week to pay off the arrears.'

Without thought, Emma flung the door open. 'Dad, I don't want to be a cleaner!'

Mr Bell looked at her briefly, but then his eyes narrowed. 'Well, Mr Chambers, if Emma isn't prepared to work for me, I must insist that you now pay the rent in full.'

'I haven't got it. I can give you this week's rent and a couple of bob off the arrears.'

'No, that isn't good enough.' He then opened his briefcase, taking out a sheet of paper. 'This is an eviction notice and states that you must vacate the premises in one week's time.'

'Wait, hold on. What if Emma takes the job?'

'As I said, the arrears can be deducted from her wages. However, this doesn't mean that I'll allow any further to accrue. I'll expect the current rent to be paid on time, each week, without fail.'

'Agreed. Right, she'll start on Monday. I'll leave you to sort out the details with her.' On that note Tom Chambers turned to go back inside.

Dick held the door open, saying to his father, 'Hang on. Emma said she doesn't want to be a cleaner.'

'She'll do as she's bloody well told!'

Emma saw her brother's face darken with anger and broke in quickly, 'It's all right, Dick. I don't mind.' In truth she hated the idea, but there was no choice. If she didn't work for Mr Bell they'd all be out on the street.

'Are you sure, Emma?'

'Yes, I'm sure,' she said, and as Dick withdrew, he left the door ajar.

She turned to face Mr Bell and for a moment his eyes roamed over her body. There was something in his expression that made her shiver, but then he spoke brusquely.

'Right, Emma. As I said, I need someone to

look after my house. Here's my address, and I'll expect you on Monday morning at eight.'

She looked at the piece of paper he handed her. 'Er . . . I'm not sure where this is.'

'My house faces Clapham Common, and isn't far from St Barnabas' Church.'

Emma swallowed. It was a long walk. Nervously she asked, 'Could I start at nine? I . . . I'd like to get the children off to school before I leave.'

For a moment his lips tightened, but then he nodded. 'Very well. I'm not a hard man, or a hard employer. I'm sure we'll jog along nicely.'

He reached out to pat her arm, and Emma shivered again at his touch.

'Goodbye, my dear. I'll see you on Monday.'

He smiled again, this time warmly, and Emma relaxed a little. Maybe it would be all right. She could cope with housework. After all, she'd had plenty of practice.

'I start on Monday,' she told her father as she went back inside.

'Good. Get the dinner dished up and then I'm off out again.'

As Emma spooned the stew onto tin plates, she consoled herself with the knowledge that at least the family were safe from eviction. Then another thought struck her and she smiled. Once the arrears were paid off she could leave. After all, what would there be to stop her?

5

On Monday morning Emma was frantically trying to get the children off to school. Susan was unusually compliant, but after the telling-off Emma and Dick had given her, it wasn't surprising.

'Come on, off you go,' Emma urged. 'I won't be home until after five o'clock, so do as Luke tells you, and don't forget your little jobs.'

'Don't worry, I'll see to them,' Luke said, and Emma smiled gratefully, again thankful that he was such a sensible and intelligent boy. As they all trooped out she watched them for a moment. Surely, even after Mr Bell taking some of the arrears out of her wages, she'd have enough left to start buying them all some decent clothes. She cast a quick glance around the room, making sure the fire was doused, and then five minutes after the children, she left for her first day at work. It wasn't what she had hoped for, but even so, she felt a spark of excitement to be out of the dismal flat and facing something new, albeit someone else's housework.

The June day was warm and Emma's feet were already aching from the long walk as she approached Mr Bell's street, but she couldn't fail to notice the difference. The air here was cleaner than at home, with no taint of smoke from factory chimneys. The houses she walked alongside were large, immaculate, smacking of wealth, and on the opposite side was Clapham Common, a wide expanse of green grass and trees.

She passed St Barnabas' Church and soon after was standing outside Mr Bell's house. Like the neighbouring ones, it was huge and four storeys high. Emma took in the lovely, mellow red-brick façade and, her heart jumping with nerves, she tentatively walked down a drive lined with huge rhododendron bushes. There were bay windows on the ground floor, and a wide stone staircase leading to the front door. For a moment she halted, floundering. Should she use the front entrance or look for one at the side? Unsure, she decided on the front, hand trembling as she rang the bell.

When the door opened, Mr Bell stood there, a wide smile on his face. 'You found it then,' he said unnecessarily.

'Yes,' she murmured, shocked that he had answered the door himself. Surely in a house this size there were other staff? Mr Bell gestured her inside. Her eyes rounded as she followed him into a large hall with a sweeping, carpet-covered staircase. They almost popped out when she was led into a huge, plush room with wonderful views across the Common. The furniture looked sumptuous, large sofas with mahogany side tables, these covered with a thin layer of dust. Huge gilt-framed paintings lined the walls, and inlaid cabinets held beautiful porcelain figurines.

'This is the drawing room,' Mr Bell said, indicating that she should sit down, waiting until Emma perched nervously on the edge of a gilt and brocade chair. 'I'm afraid I have to go out on business this morning,' he continued, 'so I'll leave you to find your way around. You'll find all the cleaning materials you need in a room just off the kitchen, and a Hoover.'

'A . . . a Hoover?'

'It's a machine for vacuuming the rugs.'

Emma swallowed deeply, in awe of Mr Bell and his beautiful house. Her voice quavered as she spoke. 'Is . . . is there anyone to show me how to use it?'

For a moment he looked nonplussed. 'Well, no, I'm afraid you'll be on your own. I did have a daily, but she proved to be untrustworthy. When my wife, Isabelle, was alive, we kept a couple of staff, but when she died I let them go.'

Emma knew that, nervous or not, she would

have to speak up now or she never would. 'Mr Bell, this is a huge house and I don't see how I can manage to clean it on my own.'

'Oh, don't worry, Emma. On this floor you will only have to clean this room, along with the dining room and my study. Oh, and of course the kitchen, which is at the back of the house, with a laundry room and scullery. On the first floor I use the front bedroom and bathroom, but the rest of the bedrooms are closed and can be left.'

Emma's shoulders slumped with relief, but then she sat up again as Mr Bell continued.

'As for the Hoover, I'm sure you'll work it out. I think you just plug it into the wall, and off it goes.' Mr Bell glanced at the ornate clock on the huge mantelpiece. 'I'm sorry, but I really must go now. I should be back before you leave but, just in case, you'd better have these.'

Emma took the large keys that he proffered, and as he hurriedly left, she relaxed, a small smile playing around her lips. If he was out all day, it wouldn't be so bad.

Rising to her feet, she went to explore the house.

When Emma found the kitchen she gasped at the size and range of equipment. It looked unused, everything covered in a thin layer of dust. She soon found a room with mops, buckets, dusters, brushes, and what she could only imagine was the Hoover. She eyed it warily, gulping at the thought of trying to use it. With a small shake of her head she grabbed a duster and polish, deciding as she went back to the drawing room to leave the funny-looking machine where it was for the time being.

To Emma's surprise, she found herself humming as she cleaned the room. She polished the furniture, bringing the dark wood to a beautiful shine, and found that she actually enjoyed the task. As well as the ornaments in cabinets, there were others on tables and ledges, which she moved carefully, dusting them with trepidation before gently replacing them on the surfaces.

When Emma came to the bookcase, she looked at it in awe, her eyes flicking over the titles. Oh, how wonderful to have so many lovely books to read. Reverently taking one out, she was unable to resist opening it, her eyes scanning the first page. Oh, Mr Bell was so lucky, his rooms full of so many treasures that she could only ever dream of owning.

At last the room was done, and though it looked lovely, Emma knew that the effect was spoiled by the huge, dirty rug and dusty parquet flooring that showed around the edge. Maybe she could take the rug outside and beat the dirt out of it? Yet to do that she would have to move the furniture and roll the rug up, an impossible task on her own. With a sigh Emma knew she had no choice. She fetched the Hoover, finding it cumbersome to carry, her hands shaking as she found a socket and plugged it in. The noise of the engine when it started up almost made her bolt, but then she got the hang of it, after a few minutes finding it simpler than she'd anticipated. In no time Emma was switching it off, and after she'd mopped the parquet flooring, the room was finished.

Oh, everything looked lovely, a picture, but it had taken her hours. There was still the dining room, hall, stairs, kitchen and study on this floor, but Emma's throat was parched. With hair lank and wet with perspiration, she went to the kitchen, gulping down a couple of cups of water. For a moment she sat at the kitchen table, her eyes roaming the room. Every surface was grimy; the racks of saucepans dull from lack of use. Like the drawing room, this would take many hours to clean.

Emma fidgeted. She needed the toilet, and had seen one just off the room where the cleaning materials were kept. It was a bit damp, musty, and unused, probably for staff use, she guessed, seeing a small window festooned with cobwebs. She heaved a sigh. It needed a good clean, but it would have to wait.

The hall and stairs didn't take as long as the drawing room, but it was now almost two o'clock. Emma was on her knees, on the last stair, when she heard a key in the lock, her eyes flying to the front door.

'Emma, you look so hot,' Horace Bell said as

he stepped inside. 'I can see you've been busy, but I really think you should have a rest now.'

Surprised by the concern in his voice, she stammered, 'I . . . I'm all right, but I'm afraid I've only managed to clean the drawing room and hall.'

'Emma, I don't expect you to do everything in one day. Go through to the kitchen and make a cup of tea. I think we could both do with one. You'll find some biscuits in the pantry too.'

Emma didn't need telling twice and hurried away. She placed the kettle on the stove to boil, and then searched the cupboards, disconcerted by the large array of china. Which set should she use? Taking out the simplest cup she could find for herself, she laid a tray with a gold-rimmed set, and side plate for Mr Bell. The tea and biscuits were harder to find, but eventually she found the walk-in pantry, her jaw dropping when she saw the contents. There were glass jars filled with preserved fruit and jams, along with tins of meat, fish and soups. There wasn't any fresh produce, but Emma found a tin of milk along with another tin of shortcake biscuits.

So much food! With rationing, how had Mr Bell obtained it all? When he spoke from behind, she almost jumped out of her skin.

'Have you found everything you need, Emma?'

'Oh, yes, sir. Well, except I haven't found any sugar.'

'Sir! You don't have to call me sir. I think you'll find sugar in there,' he said, pointing to an earthenware jar on one of the shelves. 'I don't take sugar in my tea, but you are welcome to use it.' His eyes then roamed the shelves and he heaved a sigh. 'We have several fruit trees in the garden and when Isabelle was alive our cook preserved the fruit and made jam. Nowadays I dine out, and they haven't been touched. If you can make use of anything, Emma, take what you want.'

'Really, sir?'

'Yes, really, and please, I told you not to call me sir. There's a lot of tinned produce, far too much for me, most of it coming from tenants in lieu of rent. Despite the war years and rationing, as you can see, my wife hoarded food.'

Emma felt as though she had died and gone to heaven. She grinned with delight. Bottled fruit, jam and meat, real meat, even if tinned. 'Oh, thank you, sir, I . . . I mean, Mr Bell.'

'It's only going to waste so there's no need to thank me. When the tea is made, bring it through to the drawing room.' On that note he left the kitchen.

Emma was still smiling as she brewed the tea. Mr Bell's kindness was so unexpected, and to think she'd been nervous about working for him! She arranged some biscuits on his plate, carrying the tray through and laying it on a side table.

'Well, Emma, I must say you've done wonders with this room.'

She smiled with pleasure. 'Thank you. I'll have my tea and then start on the kitchen.'

'Very well, but as I said, you don't have to do everything in one day. I'll be going out again shortly, so keep the keys in case I leave before you arrive in the morning.'

Emma nodded, pleased that she was going to have the house to herself again. She ate some biscuits, savouring the buttery flavour, and then drank her tea, still sitting at the kitchen table when Mr Bell stuck his head around the door.

'Goodbye, Emma. I doubt I'll be back before you leave.'

''Bye, Mr Bell,' Emma called, but the man had already gone.

Horace Bell was smiling with satisfaction as he left the house. He'd hardly noticed Emma before, but overnight she had grown up, turning into a beauty. One look and he'd been smitten, not only by her glorious looks, but by her obvious shyness and innocence. He had plans for her, but he'd take things slowly. He knew that Tom Chambers was unlikely to pay the rent each week and that suited him, the man unaware that he would be playing into his landlord's hands.

God, Emma was lovely, but so young. He'd have

to move carefully, gain her trust and liking before making a move. Nevertheless, when the rent arrears mounted again, he would hold all the cards and, knowing how much her family meant to Emma, he doubted she'd say no.

Horace's lips tightened. Things would be different this time, and he would hold the purse strings. His wife, Isabelle, had property when they married and, due to his business acumen, more had accrued over the years. They raked in profits that Isabelle had enjoyed spending, her dress allowance alone enormous. She'd been far too generous with the staff, something he didn't approve of, and after her death he'd been determined to cut down on household expenditure, getting rid of the lot of them. Money was to be accumulated, not frittered away, and nowadays his bank balance was a testimony to his thrift.

He continued to walk; after all, it was good exercise and why waste money on transport? It was half an hour later when he turned into Mycroft Road. His mistress lived here, and she had suited him well, playing the role of a meek and biddable woman perfectly. Yet though he had his needs, he resented the expenditure. As Joyce opened the door, her smile was inviting, and Horace smiled back. He'd continue to keep her for now, but if his plans worked out, he'd have no further use for a strumpet. None at all.

6

Over three weeks had passed, and Emma was thinly slicing a large tin of Spam. She served it with fried potatoes mashed with cabbage, and as they all ate with relish she knew that afterwards they would be having the last of the preserved fruit. It had been wonderful to bring the food home, but the stock in Mr Bell's pantry was growing low.

She would have to break it to them, but dreaded it. If her father let her keep more of her wages, she could buy extra food, but he insisted that she stumped up all but a few pence. Mr Bell had been true to his word, taking only five shillings each week towards the rent arrears, but gone too was her dream of fitting them all out with new clothes.

Emma had planned to leave once the arrears were paid off, but she had grown to love her job. With her employer out most of the day, she would fantasise that the house was hers – that instead of occupying a cramped and spartan attic, she lived in luxury. The upstairs bathroom had been a revelation, with hot water flowing from the taps. Many times she'd been tempted to take a bath, but the thought of Mr Bell arriving home unexpectedly held her back. Lately she was getting to grips with the laundry cupboard, finding that when she went to get clean sheets for her employer's bed, most of the linen had yellowed with lack of use. It had been a bit of a job to master the washing boiler and the mangle, but she had done it. Now each day fresh white sheets billowed like sails at sea on the washing line in the back garden.

As the weeks had passed she gained in confidence, and now when taking a break, she would sneak a book from the shelf, unable to believe that there were so many to choose from. They were all classics, but reading Charles Dickens had become a passion. At the moment she was engrossed in *Bleak House* and sometimes had to force herself to return to the chores. There had been times when she'd been tempted to sneak a book home, but knew that in the attic there'd be little privacy to read it, and anyway, she was fearful that her siblings would get hold of it, ruining the beautiful leather covers.

Nowadays, when Emma dusted the beautiful ornaments, or tackled the laundry or ironing, she did it pretending that she was a lady, the bubble only bursting when Mr Bell came home. Emma had now seen how the other half lived and realised the stark contrasts when she returned to the attic rooms. After Mr Bell's spacious house, the cramped conditions were emphasised, along with the smell of poverty. It bred in her a feeling of discontent, a yearning for something better, not just for herself, but for her brothers and sisters too.

There was a babble of voices and, seeing that everyone had finished their dinner, Emma spooned the last of the pears from the jar, saying as she handed them out, 'Make the most of them. There aren't any more.'

'But I thought you said Mr Bell had loads of stuff in the pantry?' Dick said.

'He did, but with feeding seven of us, it's soon gone down. All the fruit has been used, and though there are still some tins of Spam and corned beef, they won't last long. It's been lovely having this extra food, but we'll be back to vegetable stew soon.'

'Charlie is giving me a rise next week, and if Dad puts his hand in his pocket, maybe we could have meat regularly.'

'Yeah, and pigs might fly,' Emma said bitterly, 'but it's good of Charlie to give you a rise.'

'Yeah, he's a great bloke.'

'Dad isn't home yet so can I have his pears?' Susan asked eagerly.

'I want some too,' Ann said.

Now that James and Archie were living downstairs, Ann was the youngest. Like Emma and Bella, she was pretty, but in a less obvious way. Her hair was brown, as were her eyes, but unlike Susan, she was a loving child and the least trouble. Emma smiled at her, saying firmly, 'Neither of you is having Dad's share. He'll be hungry when he comes in.'

'Huh, I doubt that. I expect his belly will be full of ale as usual,' Dick snapped.

'It ain't fair,' Susan grumbled. 'Bella will get round him as usual, and he'll give her some of his pears. He always does.'

Emma closed her eyes against her sister's words, but knew they were true. Bella's was a doll-like prettiness. She had already learned to manipulate her father, becoming his favourite. Dick and Luke could be wheedled round too, the males of the family unable to resist her delicate looks. Emma rose to her feet, took the last two halves of pear from the jar and cut them into pieces before sharing them out.

'There, are you satisfied?' she said impatiently.

Dick ate his, then said quietly, 'Emma, can you ask Mr Bell how much is left owing on the arrears?'

'He only discusses the rent with Dad so it's unlikely he'll tell me. Anyway, why do you want to know?'

'I've heard about a job in the café. The pay isn't bad, and you'd like the old girl who runs it. Mrs Bright is a good sort and has a heart of gold. If the arrears are nearly paid, you could go for it.'

'It sounds all right, but to be honest, I don't mind working for Mr Bell. I never dreamed I'd enjoy cleaning, but the house is lovely and with most of the rooms closed up it isn't hard work.'

'From what you've told me about the place, the man must be worth a mint. Rumour has it that he owns lots of property, raking in rent from all of them.' Dick's eyes flicked around the room. 'If this place is anything to go by he's tight on repairs too.'

'I don't think he's poor, that's for sure, but I don't understand why he got rid of the staff when his wife died. He doesn't own a car either.'

'Well, going by the state of this place, I reckon he's a skinflint and doesn't like spending his money.'

'I doubt that, especially as he's been so generous with the food from his pantry.' Emma rose tiredly to her feet. 'I'd best get this lot cleared up.'

'We'll do it,' Luke said.

Susan pulled a face, her voice a whine. 'Bella can help him. I've got a tummy ache.'

'That excuse is wearing a bit thin,' Dick told her. 'If you all muck in it'll be done in no time.'

Dick's voice was firm, and sulkily Susan began to help the others. Emma knew they did their best when they came home from school, but there were still jobs they were unable to tackle. The washing and ironing for starters, and if truth be known, with only the evenings to do these chores, Emma felt worn out trying to keep up with it all. Not only that, the school summer holidays would be starting soon and she dreaded leaving the children alone all day.

'Why the long face, Emma?' Dick asked.

'I'm worried about the kids when they break up from school.'

'They aren't babies, they'll be all right. Mind you, it wouldn't hurt to have a word with them,' Dick said. He called Luke and Susan to his side. 'Whilst Emma and I are at work during the holidays, Luke will be in charge.'

'But—'

'No buts, Susan. Luke is the eldest, and he'll be leaving school next year, which makes him almost a man.'

'He ain't a man. He's a cissy.'

'I ain't a cissy!'

'That's enough!' Dick's voice was loud. 'Luke will be in charge and, as before, Emma will have a word with Alice. You can go to her if you have any problems, but I don't want you running to her to sort out your silly spats. Now is that clear?'

They both nodded. Dick turned his attention to Bella and Ann. He went over the same things with them, only adding, 'I'm not far away at the market if you need me, but woe betide any of you if you get into trouble.'

Emma hadn't interrupted while Dick laid down the law. She knew that her brother was right, and Luke was old enough to be left in charge, but she couldn't entirely dismiss her worries.

The evening passed with the occasional squabble, but they were all in bed when Emma heard her father staggering up the ladder.

His head cleared the top, his voice loud. 'Emma, where's my bloody dinner?'

'I kept it hot for as long as possible. You'll find a few slices of Spam on a plate, but the potatoes will be cold.'

He muttered something, his head disappearing again, and Emma sighed with relief. She felt Susan stir beside her, but thankfully she didn't wake up, and as Emma closed her eyes against the sound of her father crashing about downstairs, her thoughts focused instead on Mr Bell's lovely house.

When Emma was leaving for work the next morning, Liz Dunston was waiting for her on the ground floor. With the largest flat and a small back garden, she thought herself a cut above the rest of them. Her husband was a milkman, up at the crack of dawn, and she had one son, who, at fifteen years old was a butcher's apprentice.

The tall, statuesque woman folded her arms across her chest, her voice high with indignation. 'Emma, the racket your father made when he came home last night woke my husband again. I've tried talking to him, but he ignores me, and when I came out to complain he swore at me.'

'I'm sorry, Mrs Dunston.'

Her face softened a little. 'I'm not blaming you, girl, but this can't go on. If it doesn't stop I'll be forced to complain to the landlord.'

'Oh, please, don't do that.'

'He's on his last chance, Emma. Have a word with him, will you?'

Emma murmured yes, but knew her father wouldn't take any notice of her. God, she'd be mortified if Mrs Dunston complained to Mr Bell. She wouldn't be able to look him in the face – and what if he gave her the sack?

Emma was still worrying when she reached Clapham Common. Letting herself into the house, she was surprised to see her employer in the hall.

'Hello, Emma,' he said, smiling pleasantly. 'Why the long face?'

'It's nothing, sir.'

'Now then, how many times have I told you not to call me sir? I'll be off in a minute or two, but I noticed that you cleaned my study yesterday. Did you move any papers from my desk?'

'Oh, no, Mr Bell, I didn't touch your desk.'

'Blast, I can't find them and need them urgently. I'll have another look.' He turned on his heels, heading for his study.

Emma went to get cleaning materials. As was her routine, she started with the drawing room. It looked lovely as she walked in, a ray of sun shining through the bay window and alighting on a crystal decanter. The cut glass sparkled in a rainbow of colours, and for a moment she stood mesmerised, but then, giving herself a mental shake, she started work. Alongside the sofa there was a small side table, and on it some papers. Emma glanced at the top sheet, saw it was a letter from a firm of solicitors, and picking them up, took them across to the study.

'Are these the papers you're looking for, Mr Bell?'

He came to her side, his eyes lighting up. 'Well done, Emma,' he cried and, putting an arm around her shoulder, he briefly hugged her.

Emma immediately stiffened, pulling away as she said, 'They . . . they were in the drawing room.'

'Of course, I was reading through them last night and forgot to return them to the study. Well done for finding them, my dear. Now I must get a move on or I'll be late for my appointment and as I may not be back today, I'll leave it to you to lock up as usual.'

Emma nodded, confused by Mr Bell's familiarity. He had hugged her, called her 'my dear', and she wondered what had come over him. Perhaps he was just pleased about the papers, but she left the study relieved that he was going to be out for the rest of the day.

Horace Bell was smiling as he headed for his solicitor's office. Tom Chambers was playing into his hands, just as he had hoped, the rent unpaid as usual. The more he saw of Emma, the more he desired her, and was growing impatient. Nevertheless, he would have to let the arrears accrue for another few weeks before putting his plan into action.

He passed St Barnabas' Church, his thoughts still on Emma. It would work, he was sure of it. As before, he was determined that things would be different this time, and in Emma he had found the perfect choice. She was young, meek, innocent, and could be easily moulded.

Horace was on time for his appointment, and after going over the finer points of the deal with his solicitor, he signed the documents, passing over the cheque. Another three houses were now in his hands, and they were in good condition. He'd divide them into flats as usual, and as they were in a better part of Battersea, they'd command more rent.

The next stop was the bank, and after that he'd go round to see Joyce. It had been nearly a week since he'd last seen her, and his loins stirred. Yet he knew when he made love to his mistress, in his imagination, the woman beneath him would be Emma Chambers.

7

Horace walked down the dimly lit road on a Saturday night, determination in his stride. He knew that Tom Chambers had been trying to avoid him, and when he reached the man's local, he flung open the door. The dark and gloomy public bar was crowded, men in caps standing at the counter, others sitting at rickety tables, ashtrays overflowing in front of them.

Smoke tainted the air, and as heads turned conversation ceased when Horace walked towards the bar. He knew that in his dark suit, collar and tie, he stood out like a sore thumb, but many of these men were his tenants and he ignored them.

'Hello, Tom,' he said as the buzz of conversation started up again.

Tom swung round, immediately defensive. 'If you're looking for your rent, I'll pay you next Friday.'

'Yes, you said that last week, and the week

before. In fact you're now a further six weeks in arrears.'

Tom hunched over the bar, his voice a hiss: 'I got laid off again, but I've got a job on another site, starting on Monday.'

'That's not good enough.'

'Look, you've got Emma working for you and can keep more of her wages.'

'The rent isn't Emma's responsibility, it's yours, and I'm not prepared to let the arrears mount any further. Either you pay up, or you'll be evicted.'

'Don't say that, Mr Bell. Surely you can give me a bit more time?'

'No, your time is up.'

'You can't put us on the streets. What about the kids?'

He looked at Tom's pint of ale, unable to hide his disgust. 'You seem to have money for drink.'

'I'm only having one. Surely you don't begrudge me that?'

'When you owe me a substantial amount of money, I do.'

Tom glanced along the bar, obviously embarrassed that other customers could hear their conversation. He pointed to an empty table in the corner. 'Can we sit down?'

'I suppose so.'

'What can I get you, sir?' the landlord asked Horace.

'Just give me a glass of port.'

'What about you, Tom?' the publican asked.

Horace ignored Tom's glance in his direction. If the man wanted another, he could pay for it himself.

'Not for me,' Tom said, picking up his half-empty glass. They walked to the table, taking opposite seats.

With a furtive look around, Tom's voice was little more than a whisper: 'Please, give me a bit more time. I'll give you a few bob now and surely we can come to some arrangement about the rest?'

'We already had an arrangement, one you have failed to keep.' Horace's tone hardened. 'You and I both know that you won't pay the outstanding rent, and I'm not prepared to give you any further leeway.'

'Mr Bell, have a heart. I know that things have gone to pot since my wife died, but I'm finding my feet again now. Can't we work something out?'

This was the opening Horace needed, and, now softening his voice, he said sadly, 'As you know, I too lost my wife. It's been nearly three years now.'

'Then you know what it's like,' Tom said eagerly.

'I still managed to keep my affairs in order,' Horace snapped. He then sighed heavily. 'However, I do know how it feels to lose one's partner in life. In fact, I've been considering taking another wife.'

89

'I don't blame you, mate. I've got my eye on a nice little widow too.'

'Have you?' Horace said, interested despite himself.

'Yeah, but it's only been eight months since my wife died and tongues round here would wag something rotten if I took her out.'

'Rubbish! You're still a young man and entitled to some comfort.'

'That's true, but it ain't just me. The kids could do with a new mum too. They're running wild these days and need taking in hand.'

'Well then, ignore the wagging tongues. Mind you, I have a problem with my choice too. You see, she's very young.'

'Blimey, what's wrong with that?'

'I'd be a lot older than her.'

'Leave it out, Mr Bell. You're still in your prime.'

As he had hoped, Horace had been able to lead the conversation to this point and now he plunged in, 'I'm glad to hear you say that. You see, I'm interested in Emma.'

'Emma! What, my Emma?'

Horace ignored the shock on the man's face. 'Yes, your daughter, and in fact, if you could persuade her to marry me, well—'

'Marry you?' Tom's voice was high as he broke in. 'Bloody hell, man, she's only seventeen! Have you talked to her about this?'

'No, you see I thought I should discuss it with you first. Anyway, you didn't seem to think that age was a problem a few moments ago.'

'Yeah, well, that was before I knew we were talking about Emma.'

'I'd be good to her, Tom, and if you can persuade her to marry me you need never worry about the rent again. In fact, you could live rent free for the rest of your life.'

Tom's face darkened. 'So, you'd be letting me off the hook in exchange for my daughter?'

'I don't see it that way. Think about it. With Emma as my wife, I could hardly take money from her father for renting one of my flats.'

Horace lifted his glass, taking a sip of port, and then leaned back in his chair. Tom needed to mull it over, to see the sense of his proposal, and, saying nothing more, he left him to do just that.

Tom glanced at Horace Bell. Then, taking out his tobacco pouch, he rolled a thin cigarette. He fished in his pocket and pulled out a box of matches, all the time avoiding the man's eyes as his thoughts raced. With his cigarette alight he sucked on it, coughing as the nicotine hit his throat, and then sat back in his chair, eyes narrowed as his mind turned.

Emma was only seventeen. Horace Bell might think himself a young man, but he must be in his mid-forties. Christ, the bloke was older than him, old enough to be her father. It didn't seem right and, anyway, he doubted Emma would agree.

Yet what about the rent? How the hell was he going to pay it? A small voice began to whisper persuasively at the back of Tom's mind. Horace Bell was a rich man. If Emma married him he'd be a part of their family. He'd already offered the flat rent free – what else might come their way? Enough, he hoped, to persuade Polly Letworth into his bed . . .

Tom took another drag on his cigarette and through the smoke shot Horace Bell a glance. All right, the man might be a bit old for Emma, but she would want for nothing and surely a mature man would be better than a young tyke without prospects?

The small voice continued to whisper persuasively. The man's money, the rent-free flat . . . Moments later it won the day. Tom picked up his glass, took a swig of beer and, wiping the back of his hand across his mouth, he said, 'All right, Mr Bell, you're on. I'll speak to Emma.'

Bell smiled, and then rose to his feet. 'Good man, Tom. Please put my proposal to Emma tomorrow. I'll call round in the afternoon for her answer.'

'Blimey, that soon? Can't you give me a bit of time to work on her first?'

Horace Bell's friendly demeanour disappeared. 'I'm not a patient man, Tom, and can see no good reason to wait. I want my answer tomorrow and hope you won't let me down. After all, you know what will happen if you do.'

Tom paled. Seeing Horace Bell's expression, he didn't doubt that the man would carry out his threat. 'All right, you needn't worry. Emma will do as she's told.'

8

It was Sunday morning and Dick was out working again. Emma was at the sink, peeling potatoes, the kids playing and giggling. She turned as her father shouted, ordering them outside to play, and gritted her teeth. They weren't being naughty, just a bit loud, but Emma knew it would be useless to protest. One by one they scrambled to their feet, running out, the door slamming behind them.

Her father gestured. 'Emma, come here. I want to talk to you.'

'Talk to me? What about?'

'Just get over here, girl.'

She dried her hands on a piece of rag, heaving a sigh as he indicated that she sit down. As he hurriedly spoke, she was unable to believe her ears and stared at him in horror.

When she managed to find her voice, her reply was a squeal. 'Me! Mr Bell wants to marry me?'

'That's what I said.'

Bewildered, her mind unable to take it in, Emma shook her head. 'But why me? He . . . he's a gentleman and I'm hardly in his class.'

'For Gawd's sake, don't you know how pretty you are? You're just like your mother and she was a knockout. As for class, well, Horace Bell obviously thinks you're good enough.'

'But I don't want to marry him,' Emma cried, sickened by the thought. 'He . . . he's an old man.'

'Don't be daft, he's in his prime. Anyway, you'll do as you're bloody well told.'

Emma jumped to her feet. 'I won't! I won't, and you . . . you can't make me.'

'Now you listen to me, my girl. If you turn him down, we're all out. Do you want to see your brothers and sisters on the street?'

Emma's eyes were wide, her mind reeling. 'But . . . but I'm working for Mr Bell to pay off the arrears. Why would he chuck us out?'

''Cos I ain't been paying the rent and the few bob he takes out of your wage is just a drop in the ocean.'

'You haven't paid! But why?'

'I got laid off again.'

Emma gawked at her father. He'd been taking her wages, and Dick's, but instead of keeping up with the rent, he'd been pouring drink down his throat. Frantic, she cried, 'But, Dad, you can get another job. In the meantime I'll work for nothing and Mr Bell can keep all of my wages.'

'I suggested that, but he won't stand for it. We owe too much. The only way out is for you to marry the man. When you do, he said he'll wipe out the arrears, and not only that,' he added eagerly, 'we can have this place rent free.'

'And if I refuse, he'll chuck us out? My God, it sounds like blackmail!'

Her father's tone changed, his voice becoming soft and persuasive. 'It ain't like that, Em. The man wants you, and as he said, he can hardly take money from me once you're his wife.'

'I don't care what he said! I *won't* marry him and you can't force me.'

'Who said anything about forcing you? Think about it, Em. You'd be living in that big house that you're so fond of, and us lot would never have to worry about eviction again.'

Emma's stomach was churning. She may have fantasised about living in Mr Bell's lovely house, of being rich, but she'd *never* dreamed of being his wife. Her eyes burned as she faced her father.

'It isn't *my* fault that we're facing eviction, it's yours. You've got us in this fix, and I'm supposed to marry an old man to get you out of it. What did you do, Dad?' she taunted. 'Did you offer me for sale to the highest bidder?'

Red faced and sounding indignant, Tom stammered, 'Of course I didn't, you silly cow! The man approached me. Anyway, I don't know what you're so upset about. All right, he may be a bit older than you, but he's rich, and instead of jumping at the chance of a lifetime, you're acting as though I'm sending you to the gallows.'

'You might as well be. I'd rather be dead than marry him!'

'Christ, your mother would turn in her grave if she knew what a selfish bitch you've turned into. You haven't given a thought to the kids. Let me tell you, we'll be out on the streets if you turn the man down.'

Emma's throat tightened, constricted with emotion. Her mouth opened in protest, but no words came. She turned on her heels, fleeing the room, taking the stairs two at a time and dashing out onto the street. She wasn't being selfish – she wasn't, it was just that the thought of being Mr Bell's wife made her blood run cold. She flung open the street door, running without thought of where she was going until, out of breath, she bent double, gasping for air.

When her breathing steadied, Emma began to walk, her mind twisting and turning, going over and over the same things. How could her father say she was selfish? She was working for Mr Bell to pay off the arrears. Surely that was enough?

But no, her father hadn't been paying the rent again, the money going over the bar at the King's Arms instead. It was *he* who was selfish, not her – his fault that they were going to be chucked out.

Emma continued to walk, her eyes fixed ahead yet seeing nothing around her, her thoughts always coming back to the knowledge that if she didn't marry Mr Bell, they'd be evicted. Yet she couldn't do it, she just couldn't! She'd have to sleep with the man, share his bed! There had to be another way. Maybe they could borrow money from somewhere? Who could she ask? Alice Moon, yes maybe Alice could help them.

With a little hope in her heart now, Emma turned for home, where she knocked on Alice's door.

'Hello, love. I'm afraid the boys aren't here. Cyril's taken them to the park.'

'Can I talk to you, Alice?'

'Of course you can. By the look on your face I can see something's wrong. Come on in.'

Alice led her through to the sitting room and indicated that she should sit down.

After refusing a cup of tea, Emma blurted it all out, ending with, 'So you see, if we pay the rent, I won't have to marry Mr Bell. I . . . I was wondering if you could lend it to us. I'll pay you back, honest I will.'

'Oh, love, I wish I could help, but I'm skint.

You see, I went a bit mad buying for the kids, and it's cleaned me out. You could try a money lender, but they charge a mint in interest and if you miss a payment they get nasty. Jack Marsh, who lives round the corner, got every finger in his hand broken, and when he still couldn't pay, the loan shark broke his leg. It ain't worth the risk, love. I've heard of other people who've been paying off loans for years, and with the exorbitant interest rates they never get close to clearing the debt.'

'It's my only hope, Alice.'

'Think about it, Emma. Your father isn't paying the rent, and even if he gets a loan to pay off the arrears, they'll soon mount up again. Then it's another loan, and another . . .'

Emma hung her head. Alice was right, and her last hope was dashed.

When Alice spoke again, her voice was gentle. 'I know you think Mr Bell is old, but he isn't, not really. If you marry him you'd want for nothing. You'd have that fine house and you'd be out of this dump.'

'Alice, you're pointing out the same things as my father, but I can't marry Mr Bell. I'd . . . I'd have to sleep with him, in his bed, and the thought of that makes me feel sick.'

'It ain't so bad, love, and if Mr Bell is anything like my Cyril, it's soon over.'

Emma's face flamed. Sex had been a taboo subject with her mother, and though she'd heard the goings-on often enough, she had no idea what actually happened. 'Does . . . does it hurt, Alice?'

'The first time can be a little painful, but after that, it's fine. In fact, it can be very enjoyable.'

The colour in Emma's face deepened and she lowered her eyes. There were so many questions, so much she wanted to ask Alice, but was too embarrassed. 'I still don't think I can marry the man. I . . . I don't love him.'

'Do you like him?'

'Well, yes, I suppose so, but I hardly know him.'

'Liking someone is a good enough start.' Leaning forward, she patted Emma's knee. 'There ain't many girls who get a chance to marry well and get away from these stinking streets. If you ask me, you should grab the chance.'

Emma shook her head against the advice as she rose to her feet. 'I'd best get back, Alice.'

'All right, love, but think about what I've said. Think very carefully.'

Slowly Emma climbed upstairs, her shoulders bent. She went into the attic room, tensing as her father jumped to his feet, his voice frantic.

'Where the bloody hell have you been?'

'For a walk.'

101

'And have you changed your mind?'

'No.'

'Please, Emma, see sense. Mr Bell will be here soon for his answer.'

'I don't care. I won't marry him.'

'Emma, for God's sake! Think what your mother would say. Surely she'd have encouraged you to get out of this dump – to have a better life.'

Emma looked at her father with disgust. He was using emotional blackmail again and, sickened, she slumped onto a stool. But his words had touched her, her thoughts turning to her mother. *Oh, Mum, what should I do?*

She looked around the room, at the damp, peeling wallpaper, and tears filled her eyes. For the last few years of her life, all her mother had known was this hovel, her life one of drudgery, giving birth to one child after another with barely enough money to feed them all. Why? Why did she put up with it? Though she wanted to deny it, Emma knew the answer: love. Her parents had known each other since childhood, falling in love whilst still at school. Huh, and look where love had got Mum. A life of grinding poverty and an early grave.

'Think of us, girl. If you don't marry Mr Bell, we'll be out on our ears.' As her father said these words there was a knock on the door. 'Bugger, he's here. For the love of God, Emma, don't turn him down.'

Emma's eyes darkened with hate as she glared at her father. 'It's you who should have thought of the kids.' There was another knock, louder this time, and she sighed heavily before saying, 'You'd better let him in.'

'Hello, Tom . . . Emma,' Horace Bell said as he stepped into the room.

She lowered her head, only returning his greeting with a murmur. Within seconds the door opened again, Dick coming home from his stint on the Sunday market. His eyes flicked to Mr Bell and, sensing the charged atmosphere, he asked, 'What's going on?'

'It's none of your business,' Tom snapped. 'We need to talk in private, so get lost for a while.'

Dick ignored his father, instead addressing Mr Bell. 'Are you here about the rent? Don't tell me it hasn't been paid again?'

Horace Bell just raised an eyebrow.

Dick persisted, 'If you want to talk to my father in private, how come Emma's here?'

'Because what we have to discuss concerns Emma.'

'Oh, yeah? In what way?'

Emma looked at her brother, seeing the lines of fatigue etched on his face. Poor Dick, up at the crack of dawn, working seven days a week, and passing most of his earnings over to their father. Yet despite that, the rent still hadn't been paid. Even if they were all out working, nothing would change and, as Alice had said, if they borrowed money, they'd never have the means to pay it back. She looked at her father, wondering how her mother could have loved this man.

Her eyes flicked to Mr Bell and in that instant Emma came to a decision. She didn't love him, could never love him, but she *did* like him. If she married the man, at least she'd be away from her father, and if Mr Bell was as well off as he appeared, she'd be able to do more for her brothers and sisters. She'd be able to buy them clothes, food ... But she was then struck by another thought. Without her, who'd look after them? Their father didn't give a damn, only wanting them out of his sight. Dick was at work, and though Luke was as good as gold, he wasn't capable of cooking, or doing the washing and ironing.

Emma chewed worriedly on her lower lip, hardly listening as Dick continued to quiz their father without success. At last her eyes met Mr Bell's and he smiled kindly. It was then that a light seemed to switch on in her mind, illuminating the obvious. What was she worrying about? Mr Bell's house was huge, with enough room for all of them! She doubted her father would object if she moved them all in, and as far as she was concerned he could stay in the flat and stew in his own juices.

With a smile, Emma rose to her feet, moving to touch Dick on the arm. 'It's all right, love. Mr Bell just needs to have a few words with me but it's nothing to worry about. Pop out for five minutes and I'll tell you all about it when you come back.'

'Are you sure, sis?'

'Yes, I'm sure.'

Emma waited until Dick had reluctantly left the room. Then, her tone abrupt she said, 'All right, Mr Bell, I'll marry you.'

9

Horace Bell was elated. When Emma's eldest brother had returned, there'd been some resistance from him, a heated argument before the young man stormed out again, but now the room was calm. He could see that Emma was upset, and glancing at Tom Chambers, he saw the man's face was still dark with fury. He had thought at one point that Tom was going to strike his son, but Emma had intervened, telling Dick firmly that she'd made up her mind and wouldn't change it.

As though sensing his thoughts, Tom growled, 'That young tyke is getting too big for his boots.'

'Don't worry. I'm sure he'll come round to the idea,' Horace said, wrinkling his nose. This awful room reeked of damp but before he could leave, there was still much to discuss. He wanted to persuade Emma to marry him sooner rather than later, and he might need her father's support.

Horace turned to Emma now and, composing

his face, smiled, his voice deliberately gentle. 'Emma, we haven't had a chance to talk, and I haven't thanked you yet for agreeing to be my wife. I'm sure we'll be very happy, my dear, and with this in mind I'd like to set a date for the wedding.'

'When are you thinking of?' Tom asked.

'I'd like it to be as soon as possible, perhaps next month. Also, if Emma doesn't mind, I'd prefer a civil ceremony.'

'Well, it's all the same to me, but I don't know about Emma. What do you think, girl?'

Both men now looked to Emma for her response. When it came her voice sounded dull, but resigned. 'Whatever you say.'

Horace breathed a sigh of relief. Unlike a church wedding, a civil marriage would be quick and easy to arrange, and he'd get on to it first thing in the morning. Emma rose to her feet and he watched her as she went to the sink, filling a mug with water before gulping it down. She looked pale, yet despite this, when she returned to her stool he was once again struck by her beauty. Yes, he had chosen well. She came from a poor background, but unlike his first wife, Emma would be undemanding. Of course her clothes were appalling and he'd have to buy new ones that were more suited to her position. For a moment, the thought of spending money made his lips tighten, but then he brightened. After the initial expense there would be no dress allowance, no unnecessary expenditure. Yes, things would be different this time, and he'd make sure the purse strings remained firmly in his hands.

'If I'm to make the arrangements tomorrow, I'll need Emma's birth certificate, and of course, your permission, Tom.'

'Yeah, right,' Tom said, finding the certificate in an old biscuit tin and handing it over.

There was a racket outside, the door flying back as three girls rushed into the room, followed by a young lad. They were filthy ragamuffins, and Horace moved hastily out of their path. As his eyes met those of the young lad, Horace paused, seeing that under the grime he was an exceptionally handsome boy. Their gazes locked, and Horace shivered, finding himself uncomfortable under the lad's intense scrutiny. There was something in his eyes, something deep and unfathomable, almost as if the boy could see into his soul.

'This is Luke, my second son,' Tom said, 'and the girls are Susan, Bella and Ann.'

'Emma, what's for dinner?' one of the girls cried.

Horace dragged his eyes away from the boy. He would have liked some time alone with Emma, but it was obvious that she had her hands full.

'I'll leave you to it,' he told her, 'but I'll see you in the morning and we'll talk again.'

Her brow creased. 'You . . . you want me to come to work?'

Horace could have kicked himself. Until Emma was his wife, he'd have to tread carefully. 'Goodness, what am I thinking of? I can't expect you to do the cleaning now. I'll find someone else to look after the house, but I doubt they'll keep it as lovely as you.'

'No, it's all right,' Emma said hurriedly. 'With so many lovely ornaments, I wouldn't want anyone cleaning them without supervision. We can find someone to replace me after we're married, but until then I'd rather look after them myself.'

'Married!' a voice squeaked.

Horace turned to see that the exclamation came from a snotty-nosed girl and shuddered.

Emma's smile seemed forced as she answered the child firmly. 'Susan, we'll talk later.'

Emma had been brought up in this area, and Horace knew that her diction needed work, but he'd soon sort that out. Little did she know that he had no intention of employing another cleaner, but that was something she'd find out after their marriage. Nevertheless, he was gratified that she showed such concern for his valued pieces of porcelain. 'Thank you, Emma. You're right; many of the ornaments are delicate and your concern is commendable. I'll see you in the morning, my dear.' Moving towards the door, he nodded briefly at Tom, about to leave when the man spoke.

'Hang on, I'll come with you. We should have a drink to celebrate.'

Horace hid a scowl as Tom joined him. He wanted nothing to do with the rest of Emma's family and the sooner Tom Chambers found that out, the better. He waited until they were outside before making his feelings plain.

'Now that Emma has agreed to marry me, you can continue to live in your flat rent free as agreed. However, when Emma is my wife, I won't stand for any interference. You and the rest of your family will not be welcome at my house, and this is the last of the free handouts.'

'Now then, there's no need for that,' Tom wheedled. 'Who said anything about free handouts? Come on, man, you seem to be forgetting that I'm soon to be your father-in-law. I only suggested a celebratory drink.'

'You're buying, are you?' Horace said sarcastically.

'Well, I must admit I'm a bit short at the moment . . .'

'Yes, I thought so. All right, Tom, I'll buy you a drink, but it'll be the last one you ever get out of me.'

* * *

111

Emma was relieved to see her father leave with Mr Bell. The children clamoured around her, Luke the most affected by the news.

'But why are you going to marry him, Emma?'

'Because he's got a lovely house, lots of money, and once we're married you can all come to live there.'

'Will I get a room all to myself?' Susan asked eagerly.

'I should think so.'

'And me?' Bella piped up.

It was Luke who burst the bubble. 'Has he said we can move in, Emma?'

'Well, no, but I'm sure he'll agree.'

Luke's face was grave. 'I don't think he will.'

'What makes you say that?' Emma asked, her voice sharp.

'I dunno. It's just a feeling.'

Emma paled. Luke didn't do this often, but as on other occasions, when he had a feeling about something it usually turned out to be true, like the time he had somehow foreseen that Susan would fall down the stairs, his prompt action averting a nasty accident.

Emma hid her concern, hoping she sounded more assured than she felt. 'Look, don't worry. I'll speak to Mr Bell about it in the morning and I'm sure it'll be all right.'

With her eyes veiled, Emma's thoughts raced.

If Horace refused to let the children move in, what would happen to them? If he said no, how could she leave them to fend for themselves? Unexpectedly, the responsibility of the children weighed heavily on her and she felt a surge of resentment. At first she'd been horrified at the idea of marriage, but then the thought of living permanently in that lovely house had swayed her. She had fantasised about it being hers, and now her fantasy was coming true. Of course, talking to Alice had helped, especially when the woman assured her that the sexual side of marriage wasn't as bad as she had feared.

Emma rose to her feet, ushering the girls from her side as she began to prepare their dinner. It all rested on what Mr Bell had to say about the children in the morning, and now she found herself wishing the hours away.

10

Tom scowled as Horace Bell left the pub. Bloody skinflint! He had been tempted to tell the uppity sod that he could forget marrying Emma, but common sense prevailed. He needed someone to take the kids on – the sods were driving him bloody mad – and if things went well with Polly, he might be able to tempt her with a rent-free flat. She might balk at the idea of taking on five kids, but Dick would be one less, old enough now to find a place of his own. Mind you, he'd miss the lad's money, but once Emma was married to Horace Bell, she was sure to tip him a few bob.

He licked his lips as he pictured Polly. Unlike Myra, who had been a smasher when he married her, Polly's face wasn't much to look at, but her figure was enough to tempt any man. She wasn't very tall, but nicely rounded, and as time was called in the pub, he decided to pop round to see her.

She lived in the next street, and another plus was that she didn't have any nippers of her own. As he knocked on the door, Tom was a little nervous. It had been a long time since he'd done this courting lark, and though Polly always stopped to have a word when she saw him, her smile warm and holding a coy invitation, he hadn't asked her out yet.

Her eyes rounded when she saw him on the step, but she soon regained her equilibrium.

'Tom, what a nice surprise! What can I do for you, love?'

'Er . . . I was wondering if I could have a word.'

'Of course you can.'

'Can I come in?'

Polly frowned and leaned forward, her eyes flicking up and down the street. 'Yeah, all right.'

Tom following the woman along a long narrow passage and into a small back kitchen. He glanced around. It wasn't much, but spotless, and that was another point in Polly's favour. 'Do you fancy a drink, Tom?'

'I wouldn't say no.'

'I've only got a bottle of gin but you're welcome to a snifter. Take a seat, love.'

Tom watched as Polly found two cups. Having opened the bottle she poured them each a good measure, her smile rueful.

'I hate Sundays, Tom. It's a family day and rotten

on your own. I ain't much of a drinker, but on Sundays this is my special treat and it gets me through. Anyway, what did you want to talk to me about?'

Tom took a swig of gin and grimaced. He wasn't fond of the stuff, but it gave him a bit of Dutch courage. 'Well, girl, I was wondering if I could take you out one night.'

'Me! You want to take me out?'

Tom chuckled at the expression on her face. 'Well, there ain't anyone else here and I wasn't talking to the wall.'

She didn't respond, only taking another sip of gin, but then their eyes met and she smiled. 'Blimey, this has come as a bit of a shock.'

'Leave it out, Polly. You must have twigged that I fancy you.'

'No, not really. I know we've had a chat now and then, but I thought with you losing your wife less than a year ago . . . well—'

Tom broke in, 'I'm just asking you out for a drink, that's all. There'd be no strings attached, and as for Myra, I know she wouldn't want me to sit at home moping.'

'No, of course she wouldn't. Your wife was a lovely woman. It's awful that she died so young.' Polly paused for a moment, then said, 'All right, Tom, you're on.'

'Smashing. How about tonight? We could walk

over to Chelsea and have a drink in a pub by the river.'

Polly shook her head. 'If it's all the same to you, Tom, I'd rather stick to our local. Some pubs still frown on women and I'd feel a bit uncomfortable. The landlord in the King's Arms doesn't turn a hair as long as I use the saloon bar.'

'Leave it out, love. Times are changing. Still, if you'd feel more comfortable in our local, it suits me. How about I pick you up at eight?'

'Yes, that's fine. Now would you like another drink?'

'Yeah, why not? I've nothing to rush home for.'

'Oh, well, how about staying for a bite to eat then?'

'I'd like that,' Tom said, relaxed now and leaning back in his chair.

He watched as she began to bustle around, a small smile on his face. Polly was a bit of all right, no oil painting, but a man could drown in those tits. Christ, he needed a woman and he wondered how long it would be before he could get her into bed . . .

Polly too was thinking hard as she prepared a cold meal. Christ, fancy Tom Chambers asking her out! They had both grown up in this area, and she'd seen him turn from a gawky schoolboy into a smashing-looking bloke. He'd had his pick of the girls, and it had been no surprise when he had chosen Myra. She had been a beauty, tall and leggy with natural blonde hair, but Polly had to admit that she'd gone down over the years. Mind you, with having that brood of kids it wasn't surprising.

She glanced surreptitiously at Tom, still unable to believe that he was sitting at her table. She had always fancied him, but he'd hardly looked her way until now. Polly sighed heavily. She craved men's arms around her, liking a bit of slap and tickle, but lately was growing fearful of her reputation. Gossip was spreading, keeping her indoors more than usual, and if anyone else had asked her out at the moment, she'd have said no.

As Polly turned to carry the plates to the table, their eyes met and Tom winked, his smile warm. Her hands shook. God, he was gorgeous.

'It's only a bit of Spam, tomatoes, bread and pickle.'

'That'll do me, love.'

They sat facing each other. With her throat constricted with nerves, Polly was hardly able to swallow her food, but what did it matter? It wasn't food she wanted, it was Tom Chambers. She wanted to drown in his arms, to feel his lips on hers, and then the thought of what might follow had her fidgeting with desire in her chair. Christ, she didn't want to ruin her chances, didn't want Tom to think her brazen. She would have to go carefully.

'You're only picking at your food, Polly. Are you feeling all right?'

'Yes, I'm fine. I'm not very hungry, that's all.'

As their eyes locked it was as if some sort of unspoken signal passed between them.

Tom stood up, holding out his hand. He said, 'Shall we go upstairs?'

Despite her desires, Polly hesitated. As much as she wanted Tom, if she slept with him now he'd think her a tart and that was the last thing she wanted. There were those around here who already thought it was true, and if gossip reached his ears he'd believe it.

'Tom, we can't.'

'Of course we can. I can see by the look in your eyes that your need is as great as mine.'

'It . . . it wouldn't be right. Anyway, I . . . I'm not that sort of woman.'

'Of course you're not, but what harm would it do? We're both free, both lonely, and I wouldn't think any less of you. Mind you, there's only one thing.'

'Oh, and what's that?'

'Promise you'll be gentle with me.'

Polly laughed as she took his hand and led him to her bed.

11

Horace was hovering in the hall when Emma arrived on Monday morning. He stepped up to greet her, leaning forward to plant a kiss on her cheek.

'Good morning, my dear.'

Emma moved hastily to one side. 'Good morning, Mr Bell.'

'Now then, Emma, we're engaged now. Surely you can call me Horace?'

He noted the blush that stained her pretty cheeks. She was a beauty all right, and, he was sure, totally innocent. So much so that he would have to be very gentle. After all, he didn't want to scare her off. 'Talking of engagement, come into the drawing room. I have something for you.'

She meekly followed him, which gratified Horace. Yes, she would be obedient. He was also pleased that he didn't have to buy a ring. His first wife's would suffice, though it might need altering to fit her slender finger. He drew her to the sofa, sitting a little apart as he took the ring from his pocket.

'I hope you like this, my dear. I chose it for the colour of your eyes.'

Emma's eyes rounded as he slipped the diamond and sapphire cluster onto her finger. Her voice was barely a whisper. 'It . . . it's lovely.'

'Oh dear, I'm afraid it's a little large. Never mind, I'll drop into the jeweller's today and have it altered. I'll also go to the registry office to arrange the ceremony. How do you feel about the last week in September?'

'That soon!'

'Well, yes, my dear. When I suggested yesterday that we marry next month, you didn't object.'

Emma sat quietly for a moment, but then nodded. 'All right then.'

She removed the ring, passing it to him, and he saw that her hands were shaking. So skittish and shy, he thought, wanting to pull her into his arms right there and then.

He resisted the urge, instead breaking the tension by saying, 'Why don't you go and make us both a cup of tea before I leave?'

She jumped to her feet, almost running from the room, and Horace settled back to await her return. Emma was a virgin, he was sure of it, and his excitement mounted. His first wife had been married before, but it had been her inheritance that attracted him. He had courted her, married her, expecting to gain control of her money, but Isabelle had been clever, thwarting his attempts at every turn. His thoughts turned to Joyce, his mistress, another woman of experience. He'd be rid of her soon, along with the expense of keeping her exclusively to himself. Instead he'd have Emma, and this time he'd be the first man to lay a hand on her body. He hardened, having to cover himself hastily when Emma came into the room.

She laid the tray on a side table. 'Err ... Mr Bell, sorry ... I mean Horace. How many bedrooms are there in this house?'

'Well, let me see, there are five on the first floor, and two more in the attic. Mind you, with just the two of us, I don't see much point in opening them up. One bedroom will be sufficient for our needs.'

He saw her eyes widen with dismay and wondered why. Was it his bedroom, the one she thought he'd shared with his wife? Huh, little did Emma know that Isabelle had demanded separate rooms. Still, maybe she would feel more comfortable if they slept somewhere else.

He took a set of keys out of his pocket, handing them to her. 'Perhaps you'd like to select another bedroom for us to share.'

Emma poured the tea, her cup rattling in the

saucer as she took a seat a little distance away from him. 'If I marry you, I can't leave my brothers and sisters to fend for themselves. With seven bedrooms . . . I . . . I was hoping you'd let them come here to live.'

Horace was fit to explode, to tell her in no uncertain terms that he wouldn't stand for that bloody horde of brats in his house, but then one word struck him. Emma had said *if* she married him – not *when*. He placed his teacup on the table, abruptly standing and striding to the window as his mind churned. He needed to talk to Tom Chambers, to nip this suggestion in the bud. In the meantime he'd have to stall Emma.

Fixing a smile, he said, 'Well, my dear, I don't think your father would agree to that.'

'He won't care. He hasn't any time for the kids, and I know they'd be happier with us. Please, Horace, they need someone to look after them, and I can't abandon them . . . I just can't.'

'Leave it with me, Emma. I'll have a word with your father to see what he has to say about it and then we'll talk again.' And to avoid any further discussion on the subject he glanced at the clock, adding hastily, 'Goodness, look at the time! I must be off now, but I'll try to return before you leave.'

Once again he gave her a kiss on the cheek, gratified when this time she didn't move hastily away. Instead she smiled shyly at him before

124

following him into the hall, giving him a little wave as he left.

Horace made his way to Clapham North underground station. With Emma's request on his mind, he would have preferred to see Tom Chambers before he started his day's business, but knew it would have to wait until that evening when he could waylay the man in his local pub again. Christ, five kids, albeit the eldest boy working. Emma must be mad to think he'd take them on. He shuddered. He couldn't stand children, and on the rare occasions that he'd been allowed in Isabelle's bed, he'd made quite sure she didn't become pregnant. He liked his life ordered, his home a haven, and anyway, children cost a bloody fortune in upkeep.

At the underground station Horace paid for a return fare to Balham. The agent had told him that the property he was going to see was a bargain and Horace hoped he wasn't being misled. According to the details it was a three-storey house with a basement, and once converted would yield an income from four flats. Balham was new territory for him, all of his other properties being in Battersea or Clapham, and though he wasn't actively looking for another house, this one sounded too good to miss. A small smile played around his thin lips. After this bit of business he'd go to the registry office ... He frowned. Maybe he should put if off until he'd spoken to Tom Chambers. He wanted desperately to marry Emma, but not if she expected him to take on her bloody brothers and sisters.

Emma was relieved when Mr Bell left. She then rebuked herself. Horace – she had to think of him as Horace now. When he'd suggested September for their wedding, she'd been tempted to ask for more time, but knowing that she still had to speak to him about moving the children in, she'd decided to go along with his plans. After all, she didn't want him upset. She smiled happily. He had agreed – well, almost. It was just a matter of talking to her father. For once Luke's prediction was wrong, his doubts unfounded. She held out her arms and on tiptoes spun around and around in the wide hall, her heart light as she imagined the kids' reactions to living in this house. Like her, they would love it, and they'd even have a garden to play in. Oh, she loved them all, but it had been the thought of leaving Luke that had been the hardest to bear.

Dizzy now, Emma came to a standstill, swaying slightly. She was also dizzy with the speed with which her life was changing. So much had happened in such a short time. Her mother, her beautiful mother, had died. James and Archie had gone to live with Alice, and now she was going to marry Mr Bell.

Emma shook her head, and as she regained her balance her eyes alighted on the staircase. She'd leave the dusting for now and instead would select the children's rooms. Other than Horace's bedroom and the bathroom, all the others had been locked, but now with the keys she hurried up to the first-floor landing.

Horace's room was at the front of the house. She passed it, heading for the four others on this floor. The key was stiff in the lock on the first one, but she eventually mastered it, stepping into another double bedroom. There were two oak wardrobes and a dressing table, the room decorated with pink flowered wallpaper. Emma smiled. This was a much brighter room, one she preferred, and Horace's current room would be ideal for Dick.

She moved over to one of the wardrobes, opened it and gasped. It was full of evening gowns, the scent of mothballs making her nostrils twitch. Inadvertently, her hand reached out to touch them, her fingers stroking silks, satins and velvets. Emma knew they must have belonged to Horace's first wife, and must have cost the earth. She closed the door and then opened the second wardrobe, finding this one full of day clothes. My God, she had thought that Alice had lovely clothes, but they were tawdry compared to these. She flicked along the rails, finding that all the garments were large. Mrs Bell must have been a big woman. Her curiosity was piqued. Mr Bell was generous, and he must have loved his wife very much to provide her with all these wonderful things.

Emma held a gown up in front of her. Would Horace buy her lovely gowns too? Would he buy her beautiful jewellery? The mirror was full length, and as she took in her appearance, a frown creased her forehead. Even dressed in such finery she would never be a lady. The way she spoke let her down, and her manners. If she wanted to wear clothes like these, she would have to learn – learn to speak correctly, learn to behave like a lady. Emma stiffened her resolve, determined to do just that.

She moved to the wardrobe again, placing the dress back on the rail. It was time these clothes were cleared, but perhaps Horace had hung on to them for sentimental value; perhaps it was too painful to let these reminders of his wife go?

Emma closed the wardrobe door and then moved on to the end bedroom. Again the lock was stiff, but this time it squeaked open to reveal a single room. It was small, but nice, the furniture not as solid as the other one, but the walls were pale blue and ideal for Luke.

The rooms at the back of the house were on

each side of the bathroom, but Emma was pleased to find another double and single, mentally assigning them to Susan and Bella. There was a small staircase leading to another floor, but she was disappointed to find it damp and musty. Horace had said there were seven bedrooms, and though they were furnished, the décor was old, the wallpaper peeling. Oh, well, it didn't matter. There was only a bedroom for Ann to find, and she was sure her sister would be happy to share the first-floor double with Bella . . .

Happily, Emma went back to the ground floor. Other than the attic rooms it was all so wonderful, so luxurious. She would keep everything perfect, pristine . . . With a little skip she started her routine. She no longer had to fantasise. This lovely house would be hers soon, ringing with the sound of children playing. Maybe Horace would put a swing in the garden? The girls would so love that.

Later that afternoon, Emma finished her tasks, disappointed that Horace hadn't returned. She knew he couldn't have talked to her father yet, but wasn't worried about that. Knowing her father, she was sure he'd agree to the children moving in, but with the wedding only a month away she was anxious to get the house in order.

There were his late wife's clothes to discuss, and

she hoped that clearing them wouldn't upset him too much. Along with this she wanted to talk about the top-floor rooms. Surely it would be better to get the damp sorted and the rooms decorated rather than leave them in such poor condition to deteriorate further?

Her mind had raced all day, leaving her with a slight headache, but it had kept her from thinking about the one thing that still concerned her. She had to sleep with Horace and she still found the thought sickening. Oh, he was a nice man, there was no denying that, but when making his bed her flesh crawled. She would have to lie next to him – have to let him touch her!

With one last look around the hall, Emma closed the door behind her and hurried home, trying to dismiss her fears as she again focused on how lovely it would be to live in such luxury.

Emma's heart sank when she arrived home to find Liz Dunston hovering in the hall, the woman's face pinched with anger.

'Listen to that racket, Emma, and it's been going on for hours. You may live on the top floor, but the noise still travels down and it's been driving me mad. Not only that, the kids have been running in and out all day long, thumping up and down the stairs with no thought for others.'

Emma didn't have to cock her ears to hear the shouting and screaming from their top-floor flat.

She frowned. 'Have you been up to see if there's anything wrong?'

'No I bloody well haven't. It ain't my place to keep your family in order. And, young lady, let me tell you that I am definitely going to have a word with Mr Bell when he calls for the rent on Friday.'

There were footsteps on the stairs and Emma looked round to see Susan running down them two at a time. 'Emma, Emma, tell Bella! She won't do as Luke says and it's upsetting Ann.'

'See what I mean?' Liz Dunston snapped. 'They're out of control and if you ask me, they shouldn't be left on their own. That's something else I'll report to the landlord.'

Emma's head was pounding now and something snapped. She glared at Liz Dunston, her tone haughty as the words came out of her mouth without thought. 'Well, Mrs Dunston, I'm sure my fiancé will be interested to hear your complaints. However, you need not concern yourself. When Mr Bell and I marry in a month's time, the children will be coming to live with us.'

'What! You're going to marry Horace Bell?'

'Yes, that's right. Now, come on, Susan, let's go and sort this out.'

On that note Emma marched upstairs, and despite her splitting headache she was unable to resist a grin at the expression on Liz Dunston's face. Her face then sobered. She had let the cat out of the bag now. The woman was a huge gossip and word would soon spread. Oh, what did it matter? She'd be leaving here soon, they'd all be leaving. Their lives were going to be so different and she couldn't wait to see the kids' faces when they saw their rooms. No more sleeping on mattresses on the floor. But at that thought Emma shivered. She'd rather share a mattress with her sisters any night of the week than sleep next to Horace Bell.

12

Tom looked round in surprise when Horace Bell joined him at the bar. The man didn't look too happy and Tom tensed. Had something gone wrong? Had Emma changed her mind?

'I need to talk to you,' Horace said. Ordering a port for himself, he waited until it was poured before indicating a table near the door.

Tom scowled. The man had kept his word and hadn't offered him a beer, but he picked up his almost empty pint glass and went to sit alongside him. Without preamble, Horace began to speak, and Tom's eyes rounded.

'Are you sure you heard right?'

'Of course I'm sure. I stalled Emma, told her I'd talk to you, but let me make this clear. I have no intentions of housing your bloody horde.'

Tom stiffened. 'I don't expect you to.'

'Huh, according to Emma you've no time for your kids, and she won't leave them to fend for themselves. I'm sure she won't marry me unless she knows they'll be cared for.'

Tom picked up his drink, gulping down the last of his beer whilst his mind turned over. 'Look, that widow woman I told you about is mad for me, but it's a bit too soon to talk about marriage. If you delay your wedding for a couple of months it'd give me a bit more time.'

'If she's mad for you, surely that isn't necessary?'

'Leave it out. I've only taken her out once and don't forget I'll be asking her to take the kids on. Not only that, my flat ain't exactly Buckingham Palace and she may not be too keen about sharing the attic with my lot.'

'Can't you move in with her?'

'With only one small bedroom there ain't room. Mind you, it ain't a bad little place compared to mine and I can't see her wanting to leave it.'

Horace was quiet for a moment. Then he said, 'Would it help if you could offer an incentive?'

'Like what?'

'I've been to see a house in Balham today, and it's a fine building. At the moment it's divided into two flats, both with three bedrooms, a bathroom and spacious kitchen. I had intended to convert it. However, if this woman will agree to marry you right away, you can have the ground floor. It's far superior to the flat you have now, and surely enough to tempt her.'

Tom licked his lips. 'Will it be rent free?'

Horace Bell's face suffused with colour and for a moment Tom thought he was going to burst a blood vessel, but then the man sighed heavily. 'Yes, it will be rent free, but in return I'll expect you to act as caretaker for the house.'

'What does that involve?'

'I'll put tenants in the other flat, and if anything goes wrong with the plumbing, electric or anything else, it will be up to you to put it right.'

'That's fine with me. I can turn my hand to most things so it won't be a problem. Right, you're on. I'll have a word with my widow woman later.'

'Make sure you do. Oh, and don't mention this conversation to Emma. I don't want her to think I had a hand in this. I'll call in to see you at around the same time tomorrow, and if you have good news for me, I'll go ahead and book the registry office.'

'Don't worry, I'll get it sorted. And you never know,' Tom added with a grin, 'we may be able to book a double wedding.'

'I don't think so,' Horace said, his face stiff.

Tom watched him leave. Pompous git! But fancy Emma expecting the man to let her move the kids

135

in. Daft cow. Still, it had worked in his favour and more good things were coming his way. The flat in Balham sounded just the ticket. He hadn't intended to ask Polly to marry him yet, but if last night was anything to go by, surely she'd agree. The sex had been amazing, and, unlike Myra, the woman had been wanton. With the thought of more of the same, he decided that there was no need to go home. Emma would be there to sort the kids out and now was as good a time as any to go round to Polly's. He'd wait until she was satisfied and cuddled in his arms, the perfect time to pop the question, and with this in mind, Tom hurriedly left the pub.

'Do what? Marry you! Blimey, Tom, have you lost your marbles? We've only been out together once.'

'No, of course I ain't lost me marbles. What does it matter that we've only had one date? I've known you for years, Polly, since we were nippers, and you've got to admit we're good together.'

Polly hid her dismay as she snuggled closer to Tom. The bed was a shambles, blankets in disarray, but after the sex they had just enjoyed, it wasn't surprising. Her first marriage had been a disaster, her husband violent and brutal, and she hadn't been sad when he'd copped it in Burma. She'd vowed never to marry again, never to let another man rule her, and local gossip had it that Tom's mind had been badly affected by the war. Mind you, she had never heard that he was violent, but she felt unwilling to take the risk.

With a small shake of her head and stroking his chest, she said, 'Can't we just leave things as they are? I mean, why get married?'

'Is it my kids? Is that what's putting you off?'

'Crumbs, I hadn't even considered the kids, but now you come to mention it, the thought is a bit daunting. I've never had nippers of my own and I'm not sure how to handle them. Emma wouldn't be any trouble, or Dick come to that, but the younger ones, well, I'm not sure, Tom.'

'Leave it out, Polly. You're a dinner lady at the school.'

'I just serve the food, that's all. It doesn't make me good with kids. Christ, Tom, you've got eight!'

'I know, but you must have heard that James and Archie are living with Alice Moon and I've agreed to her adopting them. It wasn't any easy decision,' Tom lied, 'but in the end I felt they'd be better off with her. At the time I had no idea that I'd be thinking of marriage again and it's too late to change my mind now.'

'So that leaves six?'

'No, love. You see Dick is old enough to find his own place, and Luke leaves school next year, so he'll soon follow. When he goes, that'll leave just Susan, Bella and Ann.'

'You're forgetting Emma, and I'm not so sure she'd take kindly to the idea. Come to that, your flat must be bursting at the seams.'

Tom took a deep breath. Now was the time to lay his trump card. 'Emma is getting married shortly.'

'Married! Your Emma! But she's only seventeen.'

'I know, but she had an offer she couldn't refuse.'

'Oh, yeah? What sort of offer?'

'She's going to marry Horace Bell.'

'Never!'

'Yes, in a month's time too. Bell was so chuffed that he's offered me a smashing flat in Balham. It's got three bedrooms, a bathroom, and a lovely big kitchen. Not only that, it'll be rent free.'

'Well, stone the crows.'

'Think about it, Polly. If you agree to marry me, with no rent to pay we'd be sitting pretty.'

She moved slightly away from him, her thoughts racing. Bloody hell, a rent-free flat, and with Emma marrying a rich man, what else might come their way? Married to Tom she wouldn't have to be a flaming school dinner lady, a job that sometimes drove her mad. Not only that, in Balham she could leave her growing reputation behind. For a moment Polly chewed on her lower lip. It might be nice to be respectable again, a married lady, and Tom seemed as keen on a bit of slap and tickle as she was. Then struck by another idea, she sat up.

'Hang on, Tom. With Emma leaving, are you sure you're not just looking for a replacement to look after the kids?'

'Leave it out, love. Why would I want a wife for that? Emma's been at work all day recently, and the kids have been on holiday from school. They ain't babies and they've managed fine with Luke to keep an eye on them.'

'So why do you want to marry me?'

Tom gathered her into his arms, his kiss passionate. He then drew back, smiling down at her. 'Do you need to ask?' Hoping his face didn't reflect the lie, he added, 'I think the world of you, Polly, and don't want to leave you here while I go to live in my posh flat in Balham. Please, girl, say you'll marry me.'

There was a moment's silence, Polly's lashes now veiling her eyes, whilst Tom held his breath. Had he done enough to convince her?

'When are you moving, Tom?'

'As soon as I get the keys.'

'And . . . and if I agree, when would you want to get married?'

'I don't want to wait. I'd like us to move to

Balham together. This flat can be a fresh start for both of us.'

For a moment she still hesitated, but then her head nodded slowly. 'All right, Tom Chambers, you're on.'

13

Tom went home at half-past ten with a spring in his step. Marriage hadn't been in his plans for a while yet, but needs must, and anyway, it made sense. Despite her reservations he was sure that Polly would be fine with the kids, and she would warm his bed nicely. In fact, more than nicely. Mind you, he hoped her willingness didn't wane. Things had been fine with Myra at first, but as the years passed she became more and more reluctant until it had become a nightly battle, with her lying like a bloody stone beneath him. Gawd, he hoped it wouldn't be the same with Polly. Tom brightened. Myra had never been like Polly. She had always been a little reluctant, whereas Polly was like a tigress and he had the scratches to prove it. He grinned, and the grin was still on his face when he walked into the flat.

'Your dinner's gone cold,' Emma said as he made for his chair.

'I'm not hungry. Are the kids in bed?'

'Yes, Dick and Luke too. I waited up to talk to you. Have you seen Mr Bell?'

Tom almost said yes, but then remembered that the man wanted their chat kept quiet. 'No, and why should I?'

'He said he'd talk to you.'

'What about?'

Emma lowered her head, her hands fidgeting in her lap. 'I asked him if the kids could move in with us and he said he'd discuss it with you.'

'Do what?' Tom cried, acting surprised.

'Dad, they'd be better off living with us. It's a lovely house with seven bedrooms and ... well ... when I marry Mr Bell, they can't be left to fend for themselves. I know Luke has tried, but they're running wild. Mrs Dunston collared me when I came home, doing her nut about the racket they're making. She said she's going to report us to the landlord.'

Tom's laugh was loud. 'I'd like to be there if she does. I reckon my new son-in-law to be would put her in her place.'

'Dad, please, I'm serious. If you agree, I'm sure Horace will too.'

Tom feigned anger. 'Now you listen to me, my girl. It's up to me where the kids live, not you, *or* Horace Bell.'

'I know that, Dad, but who'll look after them when I'm gone?'

'I've got that sorted.'

Emma frowned. 'How?'

Tom decided that he might as well tell her, but he'd have to keep the news of the flat in Balham quiet for now. 'If you must know, I'm getting married again.'

'Married! But Mum's only been dead for eight months. You . . . you can't.'

'I can do what I bloody well like!' Tom softened his tone. 'It's for the best, girl. You said yourself the kids are running wild. They need taking in hand, looking after, and Polly Letworth is just the woman to do it.'

'Polly Letworth? You're going to marry *her*!'

'Yes, that's right.'

'I didn't know you were seeing her.'

'I don't have to report my movements to you. Anyway, it's sorted and if you ask me, it'll be the best for all of us.'

Emma said no more as she rose to her feet, then disappeared up the ladder. Tom sat back in his chair. Well, he'd told her now, and no doubt she'd pass the news on to the kids.

Undressing, Emma lowered herself onto the mattress, gently nudging Susan to one side. She still had little room but, with her mind racing, hardly noticed. Her father's news had shocked her and she still couldn't take it in. Her dream of them all living in that lovely house was shattered. For a moment she wondered if this meant that she wouldn't have to marry Mr Bell, but then found herself unhappy with that thought too. With Polly Letworth living here, she'd have to listen to her father's nightly battles again, this time with Polly protesting as her mother had. At that image she blanched. God, married to Horace Bell she'd face the same nightly battle with him!

Emma's mind continued to race, keeping her awake as she went over the pros and cons, but always Mr Bell's lovely house won – that and memories of the life her mother had led. Polly Letworth might be happy to live here in poverty but she wasn't. She *wanted* Mr Bell's house, wanted a life of luxury. The only problem being that she *didn't* want the man! Could she do it? Could she share his bed?

The question continued to plague Emma, until at last she knew the answer. Anything would be better than living like this, and as she finally drifted off to sleep, she at last knew, without a shadow of doubt, that her marriage to Mr Bell would go ahead.

The morning brought more problems for Emma when her father left for work without a word. She fed the children, putting the moment off, but knew they would have to be told. Gossip soon spread, and she didn't want them to hear the news from anyone else. She wanted to break it gently, to take her time. Surely it wouldn't hurt to be a little late for work? Horace was a kind man and would understand. Dick had already left, but she'd pop to the market on her way to Clapham Common. Goodness knew how he'd react to the news, but in the meantime, she had to tell the others.

Emma sat down and they looked at her in surprise when she told them to do the same.

Luke paled, still on his feet when he said, 'You've got something important to tell us, ain't you?'

'Yes, love, I have.' Emma fought for words, a way to make it easier for them to accept. 'You see, when I get married, I won't be here to look after you and it's been worrying Dad.'

'Why? He never bothered about us before, and anyway, you said we can come to live with you.' Luke sat down, his mouth grim. 'I told you it wouldn't happen. Did Bell say no?'

'Horace agreed. It's just that Dad has sorted something else out.'

Susan's voice was high. 'Harry Warton was put in a home when his mum died. Dad ain't gonna do that to us is he, Emma?'

'No, of course not,' Emma said hastily. 'Harry's

father was killed in the war and when his mum died there was no one to look after him. That's not going to happen to you, because, well, you see Dad is getting married again and . . . and you'll have a new mum.'

There was a shocked silence.

'But I don't want a new mum,' Susan, the first one to react, cried.

'Me neither,' Bella said.

It was Luke who asked the question: 'Who's he going to marry?'

'You all know her, and she's nice. It's Polly Letworth.'

'Polly, our school dinner lady?' Bella said, her eyes rounding. 'She's nice, and one day when I had some money for a school dinner, she gave me lots of custard on my pudding.'

'I like her too,' Susan said, tears drying on her cheeks.

'There, I told you so. I know it's come as a bit of a shock, but when you get used to the idea and she comes here to live, I'm sure it'll be lovely.'

Ann ran to Emma's side. 'Will she give me lots of custard too?'

'I'm sure she will,' Emma told her, relieved that it had gone better than she'd expected. 'Polly is a lovely woman, but listen, I've got to go now. We can talk again later.'

'Does Dick know?' Luke asked.

146

'Not yet, but I'll tell him on my way to work, and please, kids, keep the noise down. I don't want Mrs Dunston doing her nut again.'

Emma walked through the market, seeing familiar faces, some stall-holders greeting her with waves as usual. Her life would be so different when she married Horace. She would have to find new shops, discover new neighbours, but she doubted they'd be as friendly as these locals. Emma shivered, wondering what sort of reception she'd receive from Horace's friends, sure they would find her unworldly, gauche, and she'd be tongue-tied in their company. She would have to change, learn to be a lady, and had better start soon.

Charlie Roper's stall was ahead and, dismissing her worries, she planted a smile on her face.

'Hello, Charlie.'

'Hello, Emma love, how are you doing?' he asked. Picking up an apple, he polished it before slapping it into her hand. 'Here you are, girl. That'll put a bit of colour in your cheeks.'

'Oh, thank you, Charlie. Is it all right if I have a word with Dick?'

'Of course it is. Oi, Dick, your lovely sister is here to see you.'

'Give us a minute, Em,' Dick called as he poured potatoes from the scales into an old woman's shopping bag. 'What else can I get you, Mrs

Moore? How about a nice head of cauliflower, fresh from Covent Garden this morning?'

'Oh, go on then, but make sure it's a nice white one.'

Charlie winked at Emma, his voice a whisper. 'All the old girls love Dick, and he can usually persuade them to buy a bit extra.'

Emma smiled, and as Dick came over, Charlie took over on the stall. She kept her voice low, telling him about their father's marriage, seeing her brother's face pale with shock.

He shook his head, bewildered, but then his eyes narrowed. 'Hold on, Em, it's all a bit strange, if you ask me. I haven't heard any gossip that Dad's been seeing Polly Letworth and news doesn't take long to spread around here. Now all of a sudden, just as you're getting married, he is too. I'd like to know what his game is.'

'He told me that he's been seeing her for a while.'

'If he has, he must have been keeping her well under wraps.'

'Perhaps he knew there'd be gossip.'

'Yeah, maybe. How do you feel about it, Em?'

'I was shocked at first and disappointed too. I had hoped to have you all living with me. Horace agreed and said he'd discuss it with Dad.'

Dick's eyes narrowed again. 'Huh, I can't believe that Horace Bell would want to take us lot on. If you ask me there's more to this than meets the eye. I'd like to have been a fly on the wall when they had their little chat.'

'But Horace hasn't seen Dad yet.'

'Are you sure?'

'Yes, of course I am. I asked Dad if he'd seen Horace when he came home last night and he said no.'

'I still think there's something fishy going on.'

'No, I don't think so. Dad's marriage is just a coincidence, that's all.'

'Dick, lad, we've got customers,' Charlie called as a small queue formed in front of the stall.

'Yeah, sorry, Charlie.'

Emma said goodbye to her brother, hurrying away, but if she had looked back she'd have seen that Dick's eyes were still narrowed in doubt.

14

When Emma told him of her father's forthcoming marriage, Horace composed his face to one of sadness.

'Oh, well, never mind. It would have been nice to have your brothers and sisters here, but with your father getting married again I suppose there's no need.'

Inwardly Horace was elated. He'd planned to see Tom Chambers again that evening, but thanks to Emma he already had the news he'd been waiting for. He wasn't too happy at the loss of revenue from the Balham property, although he was cheered by the thought that the house would still go up in value.

There was nothing now to keep him from the registry office, but before that he might as well use this opportunity to show his largesse to Emma. It would make her happy, exceedingly grateful, and also quell any suspicions that might arise.

'I'm pleased for your father, my dear, and do

you know I think I'd like to do something to help him, though I'm not sure what. Have you any ideas, my love?'

'No, not really. You've already agreed to let him live in our flat rent free.'

'Yes, and I hope that makes things a great deal easier for him, but there must be something else I can do.'

Emma was quiet for a moment, but then said, 'If it wouldn't be too much trouble, perhaps you could have the roof repaired. It . . . it leaks into the attic on my father's side.'

'Does it? How awful, and I had no idea,' he lied. 'Why didn't he report it?'

'I think he did.'

'Oh dear, I am sorry. I've been so busy and it must have slipped my mind.' Horace rubbed a hand around his chin, his eyes widening as though struck by a thought. 'Yes, I could get the roof fixed, but I have a better idea. I have a lovely three-bedroom property in Balham, and I think I'll offer it to your father.'

'Really! Oh, that would be wonderful.' And to Horace's gratification Emma threw herself into his arms.

He was only able to hold her momentarily before she stepped away, her face flushed, but it was enough to arouse him. God, he couldn't wait to get her into his bed.

With this in mind he said, 'I must go now. You were rather late this morning, but I wanted to see you before I left. It's time I went to the registry office to book our wedding.'

'Sorry. I wanted to tell the children about our father's marriage before they heard it from anyone else, and I'm afraid it held me up.'

'Emma, you have no need to apologise. I know you're still doing the cleaning, and I'm grateful, but you are my fiancée now, not my employee. In fact, you don't have to keep to regular hours. You can come and go as you please.'

Emma's head lowered. As though it took great courage to speak she heaved in a deep breath, saying on a rush, 'It's very kind of you, but you see, until we're married, I . . . I need my wages.'

'Oh, Emma, Emma, how thoughtless of me! We need to talk, my dear, but I'm afraid it will have to keep until I return. Will you wait for me?'

She nodded, her expression still one of embarrassment. Swiftly kissing her cheek, Horace hurried out.

Things had happened so quickly that he hadn't had time to think of everything but now the financial ramifications of his marriage had to be worked out. Once Emma was his wife he would give her a small housekeeping allowance, but make sure she knew nothing of their financial situation. In fact, with a little ruse planned, he was sure she'd agree to do without a cleaner. After all, he told himself, she managed perfectly adequately now, and it would be an unnecessary expenditure. Until then he would have to continue with her wages, but there was still the question of her clothes. She was to be his wife and he didn't want her turning up at the registry office dressed like a ragamuffin. My God, there was her family too! He shook his head. Well, he wasn't prepared to buy outfits for that lot, and somehow he had to ensure that they didn't attend the service.

Horace continued on his journey, planning and scheming, pleased when he finally found a way around the problem.

Dick was still suspicious about his father and Polly Letworth. When his day's work was finished, he helped Charlie to clear the stall, storing the fruit and vegetables in the old man's lockup.

'What's up, lad? You ain't been the same since your sister came to see you. Did she bring you bad news?'

Dick hesitated but, feeling the need to unburden, he shrugged. 'It depends on how you look at it. Apparently my father is going to marry Polly Letworth.'

'Blimey, it seems a bit quick.'

'Yeah, it is, and I didn't even know he was seeing the woman.'

Charlie was quiet for a while as they stacked the crates. Then: 'I've heard rumours that the woman's a bit of a goer. How do you feel about the marriage, lad?'

'I'm none too happy, even more so if there's any truth in the rumours.'

'You know what folks are like round here – it's probably just gossip. Maybe if your dad remarries it won't be such a bad thing, and it'd keep him out of the boozer.'

'Huh, that'll be the day.'

'Well, Dick, I'm sorry to say it's your father's decision and you'll just have to accept it.'

'Yeah, maybe . . .' Dick stacked the last crate and heaved a sigh. 'Right, that's done. I'll see you in the morning, Charlie.'

'Yeah, see you, lad.'

Dick didn't go straight home, instead he headed for the King's Arms, unsurprised to see his father propping up the bar.

With effort he forced a smile on his face, saying as he joined him, 'Hello, Dad, I hear congratulations are in order.'

'Yesh, that's right,' Tom slurred, already three sheets to the wind. 'Me mates here have heard the news too and we're having a bit of a shelebration.'

'I may be breaking a habit of many years,' the landlord said, 'but this time have a pint on me, Tom, and everyone in here will be like the three wise monkeys when I pour one for your son too. After all, from what I've heard, none of you will be around these parts for much longer.'

'Who told you that?'

'Come on, man, my missus heard it from the horse's mouth when she bumped into Polly this morning.'

'What's this, Dad?'

'Mind your own fucking business,' he snapped, but then shook his head. 'Oh, well, what does it matter? With the mouths around here you'd have heard about it soon enough. Once me and Polly get hitched, we're moving to Balham.'

'Balham? But that's miles from here. How am I supposed to get to work by six in the morning?'

'It ain't my problem, son, but if you want my advice, I suggest you find a place of your own.'

'Just like that!'

'You're old enough to fend for yourself and it'll be easier for Polly with one less to worry about.'

'Hang on, Dad. This is all a bit sudden. When Emma told me this morning that you're getting married, she never mentioned anything about Balham. How did this move come about?'

The landlord placed an overflowing pint of beer in front of him and Tom picked it up, downing almost half before putting it back on the bar. He grinned inanely. 'Never you mind. Let's just say it's one of the perks of Emma's marriage.

According to Bell, it's a lovely place, with three bedrooms too.'

Dick frowned. 'When did Bell offer this place to you?'

He saw his father stiffen, and instantly he seemed to sober.

'What's with all these questions? Now you listen to me. Keep your nose out, and you'd better not try to scupper Emma's marriage or you'll have me to deal with. I suggest you button your lip, and no matter what you think, or hear, keep it to yourself. Now finish your drink and clear off out.'

Dick didn't need telling twice, and thanking the landlord for his untouched drink, he marched out of the pub. He was still confused, still unable to piece it all together, determined to talk it over with Emma when he arrived home.

All this changed when Dick walked into the flat. Emma ran excitedly up to him, her face alight with happiness.

'Oh, Dick, where have you been? I've got some wonderful news and can't wait to tell you,' she babbled on, her hand gripping his arm. 'I must admit I didn't really want to marry Horace at first, but I'm glad I changed my mind. He's so kind, Dick, and so chuffed that Dad's getting married that he's going to give him a lovely flat in Balham.'

Dick was about to blurt out that he already

knew, but then Emma let go of his arm, her eyes shining. It had been a long time since he had seen his sister so happy and for a moment he said nothing, but there were still lingering doubts.

'I'm not so sure about Horace Bell.'

Her brow creased. 'What do you mean?'

'Oh, I dunno, Em. It just feels that the man's been manipulating everything. Your marriage . . . Dad's marriage . . .'

'Don't be daft,' she interrupted. 'How could Horace manipulate Dad's marriage? I'm sure you're imagining things. It's just a coincidence, that's all.'

'Maybe, but are you sure you want to marry him? It's not too late to back out.'

Emma smiled softly. 'Yes, I'm sure. Of course I'm a little disappointed that you won't be coming to live with us, but Horace has been so generous with his offer of a new flat for Dad. We'll all be out of this dump, the kids will be fine with Polly, and Balham isn't that far away so we'll still see lots of each other. Oh, Dick, it's going to be wonderful. A fresh start for all of us.'

Dick slumped into his father's chair. Emma looked chuffed, and maybe he shouldn't try to spoil things for her. He'd keep his mouth shut from now on, but his father had also made it obvious that he wasn't welcome in Balham. Christ, bit by bit the family was breaking up. James and

Archie were with Alice Moon; Emma was leaving to marry Horace Bell, and the rest of them, without him, moving out of the borough. From now on he was on his own. At that thought he stiffened his shoulders. Well, sod his father, he'd cope, but at the same time he'd keep a quiet watch on them. There was still more to this than met the eye, and he had a sudden feeling that there would come a time when Emma would need him. Need him badly.

15

It was the day before her wedding, and at ten in the morning Emma was hurrying to Clapham Common. Horace had been wonderful, having arranged a small reception for friends and family to be held at the house after the service. He had also ordered flowers to decorate the hall and drawing room but, worried that they'd wilt, Emma had agreed to be there today for the delivery. She didn't mind. It would give her a chance to arrange them prettily and to give the rooms a final lick and polish, ready for tomorrow's reception.

Emma smiled softly. Horace had bought her a lovely outfit to wear, and he'd been so thoughtful too, suggesting that she get ready at the house, whilst he went to a friend's for his own preparations. Of course she had jumped at the chance. She'd be able to have a bath, and to dress in peace, away from the cramped conditions at home. At first she'd been worried about the children, but

Dick, along with her father, had the day off and would be there to ensure they were washed and spruced up. When everyone was ready, they'd all meet up at the registry office.

She turned into the drive now, fumbling in her bag for the key, but as she let herself in, her face stretched in surprise. 'Horace! I thought you'd be at work.'

'Don't be silly, darling. I'd hardly go to work today. In fact I was just about to go to my friend's house. I'd better get a move on. I'll pick you up at twelve and I've arranged a taxi to take us to the registry office.'

'But . . . but, Horace. The wedding isn't until tomorrow.'

'Emma, what on earth are you talking about? Of course it isn't tomorrow. We're getting married today.'

'No, oh, no. You said the twenty-seventh.'

He walked over to the hall table, picking up a document. 'Here, look at this. What does that say?'

She shook her head frantically, refusing to see the date before her eyes. 'This doesn't make sense. How can it be today? Nothing is ready. The . . . the flowers. The reception.'

'Of course everything is ready, you silly goose. Look, haven't you noticed the flowers? I must admit I was surprised when you didn't turn up yesterday, but not to worry, they're fine and I hope you like your bouquet.'

'Bouquet?'

'Yes, it's in the kitchen. Now come on, come with me.' And, taking her arm, Horace led her to the dining room. 'Look, it's all prepared and the woman I employed was here before eight. She left about twenty minutes ago.'

There was a beautiful buffet laid out on the table and Emma stared at it in dismay. 'But it *can't* be today, Horace. It just can't,' she cried.

'Look, Emma, I don't know how this mix-up came about, but I can assure you our wedding service is in less than two hours' time. Now, it's getting late and I suggest you get ready. As I said, I'll call back for you at twelve o'clock.'

'But, Horace,' Emma wailed, 'what about my family? My father and Dick are at work and the children at school. They can't possibly be there for twelve.'

Horace sighed heavily. 'I'm sorry, my dear, but if that's the case they'll just have to miss the service. Oh, please, don't cry. It isn't the end of the world, and we can make it up to them by holding the reception this evening instead of this afternoon. In fact, I'll order some champagne and we can celebrate with them in style.'

Emma shook her head, still bewildered. She was sure that Horace had said the twenty-seventh of

September, yet the documents said differently. Maybe she *had* made a mistake. Oh, it was awful. How was she going to explain it to her family? 'Oh, Horace, I dread to think what my family are going to say.'

'Leave them to me, darling. They'll be fine, you'll see. Now, please, will you get ready?'

She saw the appeal in his eyes, and slowly nodded. 'Yes, all right.'

'Thank goodness for that. I would have hated to waste all this wonderful food, let alone the cost of the flowers. Right, I'm off to get ready and I'll pick you up later as arranged. 'Bye, darling,' he added, dropping a swift kiss onto the tip of her nose.

Emma watched him leave and then, sighing heavily, her shoulders slumped, she went upstairs to prepare for her wedding.

They arrived only just in time, and as Horace had told Emma, the service was short. She looked well, he thought, but he'd cringed at her diction when she spoke her vows. It was something he would have to sort out, and soon. He'd invited only three men – business acquaintances, all single – and when hearing of the supposed mix-up, two had stepped forward to act as witnesses.

Horace took Emma's arm, moving her towards the group. There was an assistant bank manager, a lawyer's clerk, and an estate agent, all men he met occasionally in his dealings and ones he knew coveted his business to further their careers. As expected, they had accepted his invitation, but now to move his plans forward, he had to get rid of these three buffoons.

'Thank you so much for coming, and I'm sorry about the mix-up. I had intended to invite you to our reception, but without my wife's family present, I'm afraid it's been cancelled.'

Obviously deciding to act as spokesperson for the group, it was the estate agent who said, 'Please, there's no need to apologise. We understand completely,' and then reaching out his hand he added, 'Let me be the first to congratulate you on your marriage.'

'Thank you,' Horace said, shaking the man's hand, and doing the same to the others.

The estate agent then turned to Emma and, obviously not sure what to do, he reached out his hand before dropping it back to his side. 'Congratulations, Mrs Bell. May I kiss the bride?'

Horace noted with pleasure that her eyes flew to him. 'Yes, you may,' he said, and after the man dropped a quick kiss on Emma's cheek, the others did the same.

For a moment there was an awkward silence and, anxious to be away, Horace said brusquely, 'Well, goodbye, and thank you once again for coming.'

He waited until Emma had said goodbye, this time shaking their hands, and then he led her away. Unfortunately for the estate agent, Horace had excellent hearing, and before they were out of earshot he heard the man say, 'The tight bastard could at least have bought us a drink.'

Horace narrowed his eyes, making a mental note not to deal with the man again as he grimly calculated what the day had already cost him. There was Emma's outfit, the caterer, the flowers, let alone the added amount of having to buy a couple of bottles of champagne. Still, he thought, heaving a sigh, at least he hadn't been lumbered with Emma's bloody family at the registry office, and arranging a small buffet at home had been a vast saving on using a hotel. He'd already bought gifts to placate them, but of course Emma didn't know that, and now there was only this evening to get through. After that, as far he was concerned, it would be the last time Emma's lot would be invited to his home. Despite the cost, he smiled now. Once the rest of his plan was in place, it would ensure that in future there would be a tight rein on the purse strings.

He glanced at Emma. She was so quiet, hardly saying a word, and noting how wan she looked, asked, 'Are you all right, my dear?'

'Yes, but it was over so quickly and until one of your friends called me Mrs Bell, it didn't seem real.' Her brow furrowed. 'I don't understand why you didn't invite them to the reception this evening. Instead you told them it's been cancelled.'

Horace had to think quickly. 'They're busy men and expected the reception to follow the service. I know they had other plans for this evening and didn't want to put them in a spot. Now look, there's a taxi.' He hailed it and opened the door for Emma, relieved that he'd managed to explain it away so easily, but he didn't want any more questions. As they settled in their seats, he took Emma's hand. 'When we get home, we'll have a small celebratory drink, and later I'll pop round to see your father. Now then, don't worry, I'm sure he'll understand, and I'll bring your whole family back with me for the reception.'

'As the mix-up was my fault, perhaps it would be better coming from me?'

'No, my dear, I'll talk to him.' Unable to resist any longer he pulled Emma into his arms, kissing her passionately. Her slim body trembled like a bird and there was no answering pressure from her lips, but Horace didn't mind. This was what he wanted. A meek wife, a biddable wife, and in Emma he had found just that.

At eight that evening, Emma was hovering at the window. Horace had gone to break the news to her family and, despite his reassurances, she was nervous about their reaction.

For her, the day had been fraught, her nerves jangling when she had met Horace's business acquaintances. Though she was dressed well, she had been scared to open her mouth to such well-spoken men. The afternoon hadn't been any better, Horace constantly showering her with kisses, and at one time she'd been terrified that he wanted to take it further. She had frantically pulled herself out of his arms and at first he'd looked a little annoyed, but then he had smiled, saying that in light of the reception, perhaps it would be better to wait until their wedding night. His remark had worried her, was still worrying her. She dreaded it and shuddered as she remembered her mother's nightly cries.

Her family were here. Trying to push her fears to one side, Emma hurried to the door. She threw it open, her father first into the hall, grinning as he said, 'You silly mare, fancy getting the dates mixed up! Still, never mind, and I must say that Horace has made up for it.'

'Has he?'

'Yeah, he gave me a bottle of whisky, but won't tell me how he managed to get hold of it. Ain't that right, Horace? Mind you, I ain't one to look a gift horse in the mouth.'

'Let's just say that I have my sources,' Horace replied.

Polly's look was flirtatious as she moved

forward, touching Horace on the arm. 'Gin's my tipple, and thanks for thinking of me too.'

Emma frowned, thinking that Polly seemed a bit brazen, but then stood back as the rest of her family came in, all smiling happily except for Dick.

'Look, Emma,' Ann cried, holding up a doll. 'Ain't she lovely? I've called her Ruby to match her dress.'

It was a pleasure to see Ann's joy. This was her first real doll, any others home-made from pegs or wool. Emma then watched as the rest of her family displayed their presents. Bella had a doll too; identical to Ann's except for the colour of her outfit. Emma looked at Luke, saw that his face was wan, and forced a smile.

'I see you've got a board game. What is it?'

'Monopoly.' He then moved forward, his voice a whisper. 'Em, now that you're married, we'll hardly see you.'

'Don't be silly, of course you will.'

'No, Em, things are going to change. I can feel it.'

'You'll never lose me, Luke, never,' Emma said emphatically, ignoring the shiver of apprehension that ran up her spine. Dick moved to their side and she forced a smile, asking, 'Did you get a present too?'

'Yeah, he dropped me a couple of bob.'

Emma frowned. Despite this, Dick looked

unhappy too, and linking arms with them she said, 'I'm so sorry that you missed the service. It was my fault, but I'm glad that Horace has tried to make it up to you.'

Only moments latter, Horace ushered them into the drawing room and from then on everyone seemed to relax as champagne corks popped, with Horace even pouring a small glass for each of the children. There was a toast, giggles and grimaces as the bubbles went up their noses, and shortly after they were all led to the dining room where they piled their plates with food from the buffet.

Emma felt her father at her side, his arm sweeping the room. 'Well, girl, you've certainly done all right for yourself.'

Yes, Emma thought, this place was a palace in comparison to her old home. She glanced at her brothers again, saw that Dick still looked unhappy, but it was after ten before she was able to talk to him away from the others.

'I'm sorry, Dick. I don't know how I managed to mix up the dates.'

'Leave it out. I know you, Em, and I don't think you've anything to apologise for. I've been keeping an eye out until I could prove something, and I now know the bastard's been leading you round by the nose. It ain't the first time either.'

'If you're talking about Horace, I don't know what you mean.'

'I'm talking about him all right. I've had my suspicions from the start, especially about Dad's new flat, and now there's this supposed mix-up with the wedding date. I ain't blind and reckon I've worked it out.'

'Worked what out?'

'Look, I know it's your wedding day and all that, but surely you're a bit suspicious?'

Emma frowned, shaking her head. 'About what?'

'Well, according to Horace, you mixed up the dates and thought the wedding was planned for tomorrow.'

'Yes, that's right.'

'I don't believe it, Em. You ain't that stupid, especially about something as important as your wedding day.'

'Horace booked the registry office, and he showed me the documents. It had to be my fault.'

'Oh yeah, and when did he show you these documents?'

'This morning.'

'Right, so before that he just told you the date – a date you're supposed to have got wrong?'

'Yes, that's right.'

'Now tell me this, after you got hitched, did Horace go off anywhere or did you come straight back here?'

'We came here.'

'So until he called round to our place this evening, he hasn't been out?'

'Well . . . no.'

'Huh, I thought so. He had this all planned from the start and you fell for it.'

'Dick, you're not making any sense.'

'All right, explain this then. Horace turned up with all these presents, telling us they were his way of saying sorry that we missed the service. Now tell me, Em. If he hasn't been out, how did he conjure them up?'

'I . . . I don't know. Maybe he found a shop open.'

'Oh, yeah, and what time did he leave for our place?'

'At six thirty.'

'And he arrived by seven, hardly time to stop off at shops and anyway, they'd have been shut. That means he already had the presents – that he planned the whole thing.'

Emma frowned. 'Yes, I see what you mean, but I don't understand why.'

'I've been trying to work that out, and the only thing I can come up with is that he didn't want us lot at the service.'

'No, that can't be right. Why wouldn't he want you there?'

'I dunno, perhaps we ain't good enough to mix

with his fancy friends. I mean, look at us, Em, we ain't exactly toffs, are we?'

'But he only had three friends ...' Emma paused, trying to make sense of it, but then jumped out of her skin when a voice spoke from behind.

'Hello, what are you two whispering about?'

Emma turned quickly, her face reddening. 'Oh, Horace, you made me jump. We ... we weren't whispering. We were just having a little chat.'

'I see. Well, my dear, I'm sorry to break up the party, but I'm afraid your youngest sister has fallen asleep on the sofa. Not only that, your father has had a little too much to drink, and before he passes out I think it would be best if everyone leaves now.'

Emma's mind was still churning but, distracted now, she didn't have time to think. It was Polly who took over, waking Ann and ushering the family together, ready to leave.

With a wide smile, Polly said, 'I'm surprised that Horace hasn't chucked us out earlier. After all, it's your wedding night, Emma, and the best bit's to come.'

Emma flushed, but as they all trooped out, Dick leaned forward to whisper in her ear, 'If you need me, Em, you know where I am.'

She nodded, but as the door closed behind them she was hardly able to draw breath before Horace took her elbow. 'Come, my dear, the clearing up can wait until the morning. I think it's time for bed.'

With a sinking heart, Emma let Horace lead her upstairs, and then the horror began. She was red with embarrassment as Horace watched her undressing, miserably trying to hide her body, but as she went to put on her nightdress, he ripped it from her hands.

'I don't think that's necessary, my dear,' he murmured huskily.

The expression in his eyes made her shiver with fear and then she was on her back, half across the bed, his hands feverish on her body.

'No, no, don't,' she protested, trying to cover her nakedness, trying to squirm away.

'Oh, Emma, Emma, you are so beautiful, so innocent . . .'

His hands gripped her arms, his legs forcing hers apart, his body on top of her now, and then . . . oh, the pain, more pain than she could ever have imagined.

She cried out, tried to move, tried to get out that awful thing that he had forced inside her. With Horace's weight upon her it was impossible, and as he grew more frantic, she beat his back with her fists, her screams rising. Horace ignored them and to Emma he was like a wild beast, his teeth sinking into her neck. *Oh God, please make him stop!*

At last his voice became a frantic cry, 'Yes, Emma! Yes!' and, slumping on top of her, he was left panting for breath.

Hands flailing, she pushed him off, scrambling to the far side of the bed, but it didn't help as only moments later Horace moved closer. He was sweating, his brow wet, but he was smiling as he fought her resistance and pulled her into his arms.

'I'm sorry if that hurt, darling, but it'll be better next time, I promise.'

Next time! Emma was as stiff as a board as she tried to resist his embrace. 'Oh no, Horace!' she begged. 'Please don't do it again.'

He chuckled. 'Well, I need a little time to recover, so not right this minute. Come on, relax, my dear, and let's have a little doze.'

Emma lay stiffly beside him, listening to his breathing and praying he would go to sleep, but only half an hour later felt his hands moving over her body.

With her eyes squeezed shut, she pretended to be asleep, but nothing stopped him and once again she was fighting.

'Now then, Emma, lovemaking is a part of married life and if you could just learn to relax, I'm sure you'll enjoy it.'

Lovemaking! He called this lovemaking! Emma

was sore, bruised and to her it was more like torture. At last, unable to fight any longer, she lay beneath him, hating the feel of his wet lips, his skin, her arms splayed out on each side, clutching the blankets in her fists.

He groaned and her bile rose. It was the same sound she had heard her father make, the same sound she had heard year in, year out in the close proximity of the attic. God, how had her mother put up with it? Would she too suffer the same fate each night? No, oh, please God. No!

16

Emma had been married for a week and now moved around the house like a shadow, dreading the times when Horace's eyes would darken when he looked at her, dreading the times she was in his arms. During the day when he was out, she coped by burying herself in dreams – that she was now a lady, the house hers, yet the dream was marred when she went to her scant wardrobe. She saw little of their neighbours, but those she had seen were well dressed, the women immaculate in suits, hats and gloves. What would happen when they began to socialise? When Horace introduced her to his friends?

Horace had given her a little housekeeping money, but it was gone now and she needed to buy new clothes, needed something to distract her mind from the dread of his lovemaking. Last night had been awful again, but oh, she didn't want to think about it. Instead she took a deep breath to

177

calm her nerves as they sat opposite each other at the breakfast table. 'Er . . . Horace, I need to buy a few things. Do you think I could have some money, please?'

'Money! But I gave you your housekeeping allowance on Monday.'

'I . . . I know, but I need to buy some clothes.'

'Emma, I am not a rich man and you must learn to be frugal. There is an excellent dressmaker nearby and I am sure she will be able to alter my late wife's clothes to fit you.'

'But I thought . . . I mean, all your property . . .'

'What property? I only have this house, Emma, and I inherited it from my wife.'

'But . . . but . . .'

'Emma, you seem to be under some sort of misapprehension. I have never claimed that I own property. I am merely an agent, managing property on behalf of my employer.'

Emma stared at Horace, feeling sick with disappointment. She had married him, thinking him rich, had put up with his sexual demands, and, other than ensuring that her family wouldn't be evicted, it had all been for nothing. She had sold herself, allowed herself to be sold, and now felt a wave of shame. God, what had she done?

Horace spoke again, his voice curt. 'There is no need to look so horrified, Emma. We have this house, and my earnings are sufficient to ensure a pleasant quality of life. One that will be far superior to the one you have left behind.'

Emma looked around the lovely drawing room, a room that in comparison to the attic in Battersea was filled with every luxury. It was a far cry from what she had come from, but the dream of beautiful clothes and lovely jewellery had died, leaving her frozen in shock. 'But . . . but your late wife's clothes are far too big for me and old-fashioned now.'

'With alteration they can be brought up to date.' Horace then pulled Emma from her chair and wrapping his arms around her, added, 'I must go now or I'll be late. I'll be back some time this afternoon.'

Emma was stiff as Horace's wet lips devoured hers. She remained ramrod straight, glad when at last he left.

Her mind was still reeling, her voice a whisper, as she sat down again. 'Oh, Mum, what have I done? Why didn't I refuse to marry him?'

Yet deep down, Emma knew the answer. Yes, she had wanted to keep her family from eviction, but the thought of riches, of fine things, had been a large factor in her decision. She had thought money would buy her happiness, a life away from the slums, but instead . . . *Oh, Mum.*

The minutes ticked by, Emma slumped over in despair, but then it was as if a voice whispered in her ear. She raised her head and looked around the room, at the beautiful ornaments, paintings and books that she had come to love. All right, they may not be rich, but she still had so much to be thankful for. Oh, she could be happy, she could, if only Horace would stop demanding sex. Once again she slumped forward, knowing it was a forlorn hope.

By the time another two weeks had passed, Emma was at the end of her tether. With Horace's revelation about their financial situation had come another, the realisation that Dick had been right. Horace had manipulated her, and though he may not have said he owned property, the inference had been there.

She thought back on the last few weeks, starting with her father's marriage to Polly. It too had been a quick affair. Her father didn't want any fuss, leaving the children at school, but there had been a booze-up at the local pub in the evening. Emma hadn't been allowed to go, of course. Horace told her that he didn't want his wife to be seen in a public house.

Now her family were in their lovely new flat in Balham and when Emma had first seen it, her heart had ached for her mother. How she would have loved it: the space, the high ceilings, but most of all, their own bathroom.

The clock chimed and she shuddered, praying

that Horace wouldn't come home today. It was bad enough at night, but lately nights weren't enough for him. He could turn up at any time during the day, demanding his so-called rights. He was like an animal, devouring her, and he didn't care where. Across the kitchen table, on a sofa in the drawing room, in fact anywhere she happened to be when he walked in the door.

She had tried protesting, but he held the upper hand, holding her father's flat over her like a gun to her head. He'd threaten to turn them out, to leave them homeless if she wasn't a compliant wife. The man she had thought so kind and generous was just an illusion.

God, she needed to talk to someone, to find out if Horace's sexual demands were normal. Surely it shouldn't be like this? Alice Moon had told her that it only hurt the first time, and after that it could be enjoyable. Enjoyable! The woman must be mad!

If Alice liked it, Emma couldn't complain to her, and that left only one person. She glanced nervously at the clock. If she went to Balham now she could be back before Horace's most usual return time. Hurriedly getting ready, she almost ran out of the house.

Polly looked at Emma's pink cheeks and knew she would have to choose her words carefully. If the girl tried to leave Horace Bell it would put the cat amongst the pigeons and they'd almost certainly lose this flat. All right, the man might be insatiable, but what was so bad about that? From what Emma described, he wasn't perverted, she wasn't being slapped around, so what did she have to complain about? Polly scratched her head, sure that it was Emma who had a problem.

Bloody hell, talking about sex was making her wet and she squirmed in her chair. Unlike Emma, she couldn't get enough of it. She was enjoying her marriage, the respectability of being a married woman again, and it was only the girls who occasionally marred her happiness. Still, she was beginning to sort them out. They'd been little sods at first, and Tom no help at all, but then she'd found that a little slap on their legs did the trick. Spare the rod, spoil the child, her father had said, and he'd turned out to be right. Unlike the girls, Luke was no trouble, and fast becoming her favourite. He was such a handsome lad, his young body developing into that of a man, and she loved giving him a cuddle.

She'd stuck to her determination that her marriage would be different this time, that she wouldn't be ruled, and despite her initial reservations Tom had turned out to be a good husband. He was a bit work shy, but she'd soon sorted that out, getting him out of bed with a pack of sandwiches and a flask to see him on his way. He wasn't generous with the housekeeping money, but she'd put her foot down there too, telling him in no uncertain terms that there'd be no fun in bed if he kept her short.

After wimpy Myra, it must have been a shock for Tom at first, but surprisingly there'd been little resistance. She kept him happy in bed, loving their sexual antics too. She kept the flat spotless, and made sure they were all well fed. Yes, things were going along nicely, and nowadays Tom seemed more than contented. When he went out for a drink a few nights a week, she didn't complain. In fact, on Saturday nights, with Luke in charge of the kids, she joined him at their new local.

With a start, Polly saw that Emma had stopped talking and was looking at her expectantly. She smiled sadly. 'Well love, if you ask me, I think it's you that has the problem. Horace is only doing what's natural and after all, you *are* his wife.'

Emma's head was low, her voice a murmur. 'So . . . so I should just let him do those things?'

'Christ, love, he isn't doing anything wrong. Of course you should. Look, you just need to relax and I'm sure you'll enjoy it.'

'Enjoy it! How can I enjoy it?'

'It ain't that bad, but then again, maybe you're frigid. Perhaps you could try a little drink, a drop of gin or something. It might loosen you up and do the trick.'

'But he makes me do it all the time,' Emma cried.

Polly chuckled. 'There's nothing unusual about that. Like me, you're newly married and the novelty ain't worn off for Horace yet.'

'Does . . . does that mean that he'll stop soon?'

'Well, I doubt he'll ever do without, but he might cut it down a bit.'

Emma sighed heavily. 'At least that would be something.' She then rose to her feet, her voice resigned. 'Maybe you're right, maybe it is me, especially as Alice Moon told me it could be enjoyable too.'

'There you are then.'

'I must go, Polly. I would have liked to stay longer, to see the children when they come home from school, but Horace doesn't like it if I'm not in when he comes home. He sometimes pops in during the day to see if I'm there and if I'm not, it causes such a row.'

'It sounds like his only fault is jealousy, and I suppose that's because you're a lot younger than him and he's frightened of losing you. You needn't worry about the kids, they're fine, and anyway, your place is with your husband.'

'I miss them, Polly, but Horace won't allow me to invite you to our place.'

Once again Polly chose her words carefully. 'Listen, Emma, you've got to realise that you have a different station in life now. You live in that big, posh house and we just wouldn't fit in. Blimey, love, if we came round we'd only be fit to use the tradesmen's entrance!'

'That's nonsense, Polly. We might live in a big house, but we aren't rich. Horace lied, only telling me after our marriage that other than our place, he doesn't own any property. He just acts as an agent, collecting the rents and so forth for his employer.'

'Oh, yeah, who does he work for then?'

'I don't know. Horace said the man likes to keep his business private.'

'To keep that big house running, he must earn a good few bob, though.'

'No, you're wrong. When his first wife died, he had to make severe cut-backs to avoid selling the house. That's why he got rid of the staff and closed so many rooms.'

'It all sounds a bit odd, if you ask me. If he's only an agent, how did he manage to buy that house in the first place?'

'He didn't. It belonged to his first wife. She was a spendthrift and it was only after her death that he found out they were almost penniless.'

Polly's eyes narrowed. 'So that's why you still do the cleaning?'

185

'Yes, but listen, Polly,' Emma added urgently, 'please don't tell my father or anyone else about this. I shouldn't have said anything. If Horace finds out he'll go mad. He likes people to think he owns all the property otherwise they'd run rings around him with their rent.'

'Well, he certainly fooled us. I mean, look at you, dressed up like a dog's dinner and talking like you've got a plum in your mouth.'

Emma's smile was grim. 'I'm wearing his late wife's clothes. To save on money, Horace paid a woman to alter them. As for my "diction", it still isn't good enough for him. He instructs me every evening and hates it if I don't speak correctly. I've lost count of the times I've had to say, "*How now brown cow.*"'

Polly chuckled. 'Well, love, with the front he's putting on, I suppose you can't blame him for that. Blimey, and there was us thinking you're living in clover.'

'In comparison to Battersea, I suppose I am. I get regular housekeeping money; I have lovely clothes, albeit second-hand, but oh, how I wish I could turn the clock back.'

'Leave it out, love. You may not be rich, but you're a darn sight better off now. If you ask me, you should count yourself lucky.'

'Lucky! You think I'm lucky? Oh, Polly, I wish I felt the same. Instead I feel like a prisoner, with Horace my gaoler.'

'Rubbish! You're a married woman now, and once spliced you can't expect the same freedom.' Polly knew she sounded harsh, but despite the shock of finding out that Horace wasn't a rich man, she still didn't think Emma had much to moan about. 'Come on now, get yourself home, and if you want my advice, stop complaining and count your blessings.'

Emma stared at her for a moment, but then said a curt goodbye, turning on her heel and marching out of the flat. Polly stood looking at the closed door for a moment, but then she sat down, thinking deeply.

So Horace Bell didn't own this house after all ... but if that was the case, how come they were living here rent free? It was all a bit odd, and she wondered what Tom would make of it. As for Emma's complaints about the sexual side of her marriage, Polly was sure the girl was exaggerating. Maybe in her innocence Emma had expected sex to be all romance and roses. Well, she had put her straight and hoped that was the last she'd hear of it. Bloody hell, she had enough on her plate with four kids. As far as she was concerned, Emma was old enough to look after herself.

Emma hurried home. With any luck Horace wouldn't discover she'd been to Balham, but just in case he'd popped home, she needed a cover story. She passed the grocer's, flying inside to purchase a few things, hoping that shopping would suffice as an excuse.

She walked into the house now, gratified to find it empty, and going through to the pantry she placed her shopping on the shelf. Polly's words were still churning in her mind. The last thing she'd expected was to be told that the problem was her fault – that she was frigid. Polly had said that Horace's demands were normal, but to her they were monstrous, and she still dreaded hearing his key in the door.

Emma tidied the house, then picked up a book, burying herself in the story. She read avidly now, loving the luxury of having so many authors to choose from. At the moment she was reading *Jane Eyre*. The Brontë sisters were fast becoming favourites. Reading was her solace, a way of drowning out the world and her unhappiness. Horace still hadn't introduced her to any of his friends, and they never socialised, leaving her feeling that he was ashamed of her. She felt lonely, isolated, and having found a book on household management on the shelves, along with one on etiquette, she had read them from cover to cover. Maybe if she became more of a lady, they'd have a social life. If they weren't always alone, if Horace had other distractions, his sexual demands might diminish – at least she hoped so.

At last Emma rose to prepare dinner, and when Horace came home at seven that evening, he greeted her as usual with a passionate kiss. Emma bore it, hating the way his tongue snaked into her mouth, but then the groping began and she became rigid.

'Dinner will be ruined,' she protested. 'Why don't you have a nice bath and it'll be ready by the time you come down?'

He huffed, but released her. 'I suppose I do need to freshen up, and we can continue this later.'

With that he went upstairs and, feeling sick inside, Emma returned to the cooker. When Horace returned she served dinner in the dining room and, hoping to keep him at bay, she forced a smile. 'I'll just clear the table and then I expect you'll want to give me another lesson on my diction.'

'Yes, it still needs work. When you've finished the dishes, join me in the drawing room.'

Emma took her time with the washing up, her legs feeling leaden as she carried a tray of coffee to the drawing room. The lesson began, one she usually enjoyed, but she couldn't concentrate, her eyes continually flicking to the clock. She wanted to delay Horace, to put off the inevitable. On that thought, Emma picked up a book saying, 'I saw a word I was unsure of in this novel. What does "irrevocable" mean?'

'Well, my dear, essentially it means inevitable, something incapable of being avoided. Why didn't you look it up in the dictionary?'

'I intended to, but I knew you'd be familiar with the word,' she said, hoping flattery would keep him in his chair. 'There was another one too, it's—'

As though aware of her ploy, Horace interrupted, his smile sickening. 'I think that's enough for this evening, and anyway, I would prefer that you find the meaning of words for yourself. It's the only way to learn. Nevertheless, I'm pleased with your progress.' He rose to his feet. 'Come now, I think it's time for bed.'

She couldn't do it again! She just couldn't. Oh, if only Horace would just go to sleep, to keep his hands off her body.

Drink! Polly had suggested a drink might help, and with this in mind Emma spluttered, 'I . . . I'll just rinse these cups and then I'll join you.'

'Very well, but don't be long.'

As soon as Horace left the room, Emma went to the drinks cabinet. She had never tasted whisky or brandy. Pouring half a glass, she sniffed it, her nose wrinkling with distaste. God, it smelled awful, but by now she was ready to try anything, so she gulped it down. She was left gasping, her throat on fire. It was dreadful, but maybe the brandy would be nicer. Again she poured a good measure, finding it equally bad, but Polly had said it would help, so another one might be in order.

By the time Emma had drunk three huge measures, she was swaying on her feet, giggling. Goodness, she did feel strange. Reeling across the room, she made it to the hall, holding on to the banister as she went upstairs. Her smile was inane as she stumbled into the bedroom, sure that the floor was tilting under her feet.

'Emma, what on earth's the matter?' Horace said, and she was aware of him hurrying to her side.

She blinked, unable to focus, and the last words she heard before passing out were, 'My God, woman. You're drunk!'

17

Tom listened to Polly, and like his wife, couldn't make sense of it. 'Hang on, love, are you sure you've got it right? I mean, Horace must own this place or he couldn't let us have it for nothing.'

'Maybe he's paying the rent.'

'No, that doesn't make sense either. If they're as hard up as Emma is making out, he wouldn't be able to afford it. If you ask me, I reckon Emma's got the wrong end of the stick.'

'I don't think so, Tom. If Horace had money they'd open up the house, employ a cleaner, and she certainly wouldn't be wearing his dead wife's clothes.'

'Huh, what does that prove? The man's known as a skinflint and hates putting his hand in his pocket.'

'He ain't rich, Tom. He's only an agent.'

'I don't believe it. He's too posh, too up his own arse to be a rent collector. If you ask me, I reckon he's been telling Emma porky pies and my daughter is daft enough to believe him.'

'But why would he do that?'

''Cos he doesn't want her spending his precious money.'

'But, Tom, that's awful!'

'Yeah, well, we can soon put her straight.'

Polly reared up in her seat. 'No, we can't say anything. He'd go mad if he found out that Emma has told us, and if we upset him he could chuck us out of this place.'

'All right, calm down.' Tom considered for a moment. 'You're right, and we'll say nothing, but it's a shame really. I'd love to show Horace up as a liar and wipe that supercilious look off his face.'

'Blimey, love, that's a bit of a mouthful! Where did that word come from?'

'Oh, I dunno, I must have heard it from somewhere.'

'You're beginning to sound like Emma. She talks as though she's swallowed a dictionary lately.'

'She's swallowed Horace's tosh too. Still, it ain't that bad. He may be hiding his bank balance, but she's still doing all right.'

'My thoughts exactly, love. Now do you fancy a cup of Ovaltine before we go to bed?'

'Yeah, I wouldn't say no,' Tom said, slumping back into his chair as his eyes roamed the room. Thanks to Emma's marriage, there'd been a change in his fortunes and he wasn't going to rock the boat. Nowadays he was a happy man. He still found his thoughts drifting to Myra at times, but had to admit that he'd made a good choice in Polly. She was marvellous with the kids and made sure the youngest were in bed by eight. Susan went half an hour later, and Luke, at fourteen, was allowed up until half-past nine. Nowadays Tom no longer dreaded coming home. His life was comfortable, ordered, his kids scrubbed and clean, and this place a far cry from that dump in Battersea. Instead he looked forward to the smashing meals that Polly dished up and, not only that, she didn't mind him going out for a drink in the evening.

Polly leaned forward to place a cup beside him, her breasts spilling out of her blouse.

Tom grinned. 'Come here, woman.'

She smiled back, and he gasped as she kneeled between his legs, her hands slowly unbuttoning his flies. Myra would never have done anything like this, and as Polly's mouth went down, he groaned with bliss, his thoughts now only on the feelings that ripped through his body.

In Battersea, Dick turned over in bed. Though the mattress was lumpy, it wasn't what was keeping him awake. He was content with his room in Charlie's house, the two of them mucking in well

195

together, and he was enjoying his independence. Well, that was until recently. He went to see the kids at his father's new flat once a week and was pleased to see them looking so well. Polly was a real mother hen and he'd been a bit envious. They seemed a proper family and he the odd one out. It didn't seem possible that the family had fragmented in such a short time. James and Archie were with Alice Moon, happy lads and blossoming. Emma was a married woman now, but Dick knew he was unwelcome in Horace Bell's house, the man showing his displeasure if he dared to call. Truth be told, he was missing them all but he'd have to get used to it. Dick fidgeted, thumping the pillow with impatience. He had to be up at the crack of dawn and needed to sleep. He tried to settle, but then, minutes later, with a groan he sat up and crawled out of bed. Maybe a hot drink would settle him down. With this in mind he tiptoed to the kitchen.

'Blimey, what are you doing up?' he asked, surprised to see Charlie slumped in a chair.

'My stomach is giving me gyp again.'

'You've been complaining about your stomach for months now. Why don't you see a doctor? He might be able to give you something to settle it down.'

'I've seen a doctor.' With a sigh Charlie added, 'Look, sit down, lad, I've got something to tell you, and as we're both up it might as well be now.'

There was something in Charlie's tone that made Dick stiffen and, taking a chair opposite him at the table, he looked at the old man worriedly.

For a moment Charlie said nothing, but then rheumy eyes met Dick's. 'It ain't good news, lad. You see, I ain't got long left.'

'What do you mean?'

'Fuck it. There ain't an easy way to put this, so I'll just spit it out. I'm dying.'

Dick shook his head in disbelief. 'Don't be daft! Of course you ain't.'

'I am. According to the doctor, I've only got a few months left.'

'No, he must be wrong! Can't he do something?'

'I'm afraid not, but don't worry, lad, I'm sort of resigned to it now.'

'How long have you known?'

'Oh, for a while. The doc gave me something for the pain, but lately it ain't doing much good. I've done me best, but I won't be able to run the stall for much longer, and I've been sitting here working out what to do.' Charlie grimaced, his hand involuntarily clutching his stomach, but when Dick reared to his feet, he said, 'Sit down, lad, it'll pass.'

'Where's this stuff the doctor gave you?'

'I can't have any more just yet, and anyway, it fogs me mind and I want to tell you what I've decided about the stall.'

Dick slumped down again.

Charlie said, 'I ain't got any family left, lad, and so I've decided to let you have the stall.'

'Me! You're giving it to me?'

'Yeah, and enough to keep you going for a while to buy stock. The stall ain't made me a rich man, but it's given me a fair living, and if you keep up the good work, you'll do all right.'

'But I know nothing about buying stock.'

'Then you'll learn. I'll give you a few pointers, but you'll have to keep your wits about you or you'll get palmed off with rubbish.' Charlie paused to gasp, his face creased with pain, but then he rallied again. 'There's this place too, but it's only rented. I could have a word with the landlord to see if he'll let you take it on, but to be honest, you're a bit young and I can't see him agreeing to it. You can have the furniture, such as it is, and you never know, if I tell the landlord about the stall, it might just swing it.'

Dick's mind was reeling. He couldn't take it in . . . Then seeing Charlie almost doubled up in agony he rushed to his side. 'Come on, forget about this now. Let's get you to bed and whether you like it or not, you're going to have a dose of that pain-killing stuff.'

'All right, I won't argue,' Charlie said as Dick heaved him to his feet.

Clinging like limpets, they struggled through to his bedroom. Dick helped the old man to undress, but after he'd swallowed a dose of medicine, Charlie urged Dick to leave him.

'You need to be up in the morning, lad. Go on, get some sleep yourself. I'll be fine now.'

Dick stared at him for a while, struggling to hold back his emotions. He managed, just, but when he got to his own bedroom, he broke down. He had worked for Charlie only since leaving school, but the man had become like a father to him – well, perhaps a grandfather, something he had missed out on when his own had died when he was just a nipper. Now Charlie was dying too and in dreadful pain. Dick knew he needed looking after, but how could he do that and run the stall? Bloody hell – a stall that was to become his? Well, sod the business for now, he'd worry about that later. At the moment he was more concerned about Charlie's care.

Dick climbed into bed, feeling that, at nearly sixteen, he had the weight of the world on his shoulders.

18

When Emma woke up in the morning her head was swimming and she had a foul taste in her mouth. Just the thought of brandy made her feel nauseous, but one good thing had come out of it. If Horace had made love to her, she wasn't aware of it. Her hands moved under the blankets. Oh, no, she was naked, and that meant Horace must have undressed her! He was already up and she dreaded facing him, but she was already late getting his breakfast.

She climbed out of bed, her head thumping and, once dressed, made her way to the kitchen.

'So, you're up,' Horace said.

'Why didn't you wake me?'

'Considering the condition you were in last night, I thought it would be a waste of time.'

'I . . . I'm sorry.'

'I left you to tidy up before coming to bed, but instead you decided to drink almost half a decanter of brandy. What on earth possessed you?'

Emma hung her head. 'I . . . I don't know.'

'You don't know! What sort of excuse is that? My first wife enjoyed a glass of sherry, which is acceptable, but she never disgraced herself by becoming drunk.'

'I'm sorry,' Emma said again.

He ignored her mumbled apology. 'I don't want to ever see you in that state again and . . .'

On and on he went, and Emma bore his tirade, but by the time he finally stalked out, saying he wouldn't be back until that evening, her headache had worsened to the extent that as soon as the door closed behind him, she went back to bed.

Emma awoke two hours later to the sound of someone banging on the front door. She groaned, but threw a dressing gown on to hurry downstairs. Gingerly she opened the front door to find Dick hovering anxiously outside.

'Emma, thank God you're in. I've been knocking for ages.' Dick paused. 'You look rough. Have you only just got up?'

Emma pulled him hastily inside. 'I've got a bad headache, that's all. Anyway, what are you doing here at this time of day?'

'I had to speak to you and found someone to mind the stall, but I ain't got long.'

'Someone to mind the stall. Why? Where's Charlie?'

'That's what I want to talk to you about.'

The taste in Emma's mouth made her grimace, and she was desperate for a cup of tea.

'Come through to the kitchen,' she urged. 'You can talk to me while I make a drink.'

Emma listened to Dick and when the tea was made she poured them each a cup. She tried to take in what he was saying, but her head was still thumping and now she felt sick too. Swallowing her nausea, she took a gulp of tea, and then, closing her eyes, she sat back in her chair.

'Sorry. What?'

'I said, what am I gonna do, Em? I can't look after Charlie *and* run the stall.'

'The word is "going", not "gonna".'

'Huh, I didn't come here for you to pick me up on my speech. Blimey, I can't believe how much you've changed in such a short time. Now you sound like Lady Muck. This big house has certainly gone to your head.'

'Oh, I'm sorry, Dick, it's just that I'm trying to improve myself and Horace corrects me every time I open my mouth. I didn't mean to sound like him and I'll try not to do it again. Anyway, back to Charlie. He needs a woman to look after him, or maybe he'd be better off in hospital.'

'I was wondering if you'd look after him, Em.'

Emma shook her head. 'I wish I could help, but I'm afraid Horace wouldn't stand for it.'

'Why not?'

She lowered her eyes, choosing her words carefully. 'He likes me to be here in case he comes home during the day, and if I'm not he can be very difficult.'

'Difficult! What do you mean?' Dick said, then his voice rose sharply. 'Here, he doesn't hit you, does he?'

'No, of course not.'

'That's all right then. Mind you, I still don't see why you have to sit here all day just in case he comes home.'

Emma felt the colour flooding her cheeks, and when Dick saw it the penny obviously dropped. He looked away and, embarrassed, she hurriedly changed the subject. 'Poor Charlie, but I'm sure you can persuade him to go into hospital.'

'I hope so,' Dick said as he looked up again, 'and it's good of him to give me the stall.'

'Yes ... yes it is.' But then something struck Emma. 'Are you sure he can pass it on to you? I mean, are you old enough?'

'I don't think the stall matters. It's more the pitch and I don't know where I stand with that.'

'Charlie must know what he's doing. I'm really sorry I can't be of more help. Is he in a lot of pain?'

'Yeah, he's really rough, but don't worry about

it, Em. I'm sure I'll be able to sort something out.' He swallowed the last of his drink. 'I'd best get back.'

Emma walked her brother to the door before returning to the kitchen. She flopped into a chair, her head still thumping, her shame at not being able to help Charlie, who had been so good to her brother, combining with her headache. It was a long time before she moved again.

Dick decided to check on Charlie before taking over the stall. When he went into the small terraced house, he found the old man still in bed, his face grey with pain.

'Charlie, you can't go on like this. I think you need to go into hospital.'

'No, lad, I want to die in my own bed.'

'You can't be left on your own all day. You need someone to look after you, but I can't do that and run the stall.'

The old man nodded. 'Yeah, I suppose you're right. Come to that, who's on the stall now?'

'One of the costermongers lent me his lad.'

'You're not much more than a lad yourself and I need a bit more time to get you up to scratch. Hospital can wait for a few more days – we'll have another chat about buying stock this evening.'

'All right, but in the meantime can you think of anyone I could ask to keep an eye on you?'

'No, lad, and anyway, I never could stand being made a fuss of. If you get some busybody of a woman in here I'd never get a minute's peace. Why do you think I never married? My mother was a battleaxe, ruling both my father and me. She was always fussing, always cleaning, always nagging and I was glad to leave home.'

Dick scratched his chin. 'Maybe it wouldn't hurt to leave the stall in the lockup for a few days.'

'Tell Johnny and Sid to pop in to see me. I want to talk to them about the pitch, and they might be willing to set up the stall too, running it between them.'

'Yeah, all right, but what's this about the pitch?'

'You need someone to take it on for a while, and then sign it over to you when you're older. I'd trust Johnny or Sid with my life and I reckon one of them would do it.'

It seemed the old man had thought of everything and Dick felt a surge of gratitude. 'I'll make you a drink before I go and I'll try to pop in later. While I'm at it, do you fancy something to eat?'

'No, I'm not hungry, but thanks anyway.'

Dick hurried to the scullery, and made Charlie a mug of tea.

Charlie managed a small wave goodbye before Dick hurried to the market, still unhappy about leaving him on his own. Well, sod the stall, he decided. If Sid and Johnny wouldn't run it, it could bloody well stay in the lockup.

By three in the afternoon, Emma was feeling better. She went to the drawing room, plumped up the cushions, and then flicked a duster around, thankful there wasn't much to do. The drinks cabinet was open, the lid off one of the decanters and, grimacing, she replaced it. Would she get another telling-off when Horace came home? Yes, probably, but she could stand that. It was the other thing she dreaded. Oh, if only drinking the brandy hadn't made her feel so awful. Not only that, she had passed out! Emma knew she had drunk too much, and maybe a smaller amount might help, but the thought of the smell and taste of the alcohol made her stomach turn again.

It was then that she noticed another bottle tucked away at the back of the cabinet and, drawing it forward, saw it was labelled 'Sherry'. Horace had said his wife had drunk this. Curious, Emma took the top off, lifting the bottle to sniff the contents. The smell was nice, sweet, and after swiftly looking over her shoulder like a naughty child that doesn't want to be caught, she took a sip straight from the bottle. Goodness, it was nice. Sweet, yes, but smooth too, with none of the harshness of brandy.

When Horace arrived home for dinner at seven

o'clock, Emma was pleasantly mellow. She had learned her lesson, only drinking enough sherry to ease her nerves.

'I see you're looking better,' he said.

'Yes, I'm fine, thank you.'

His expression changed to one she knew well, and grabbing her arm, he drew her onto the sofa. She hated it, hated the way that without preamble he pushed up her skirt. He fumbled with his trousers, thrusting into her, and she lay compliant beneath him. There was no enjoyment – she still hated it – but with the aid of sherry she was able to bear it until at last it was over.

Horace slumped on her for a moment, but then stood up, adjusting his clothes. 'Thank you, my dear,' he said, his voice tinged with sarcasm, 'but it was obvious as usual that you found it distasteful.'

As Horace left the room, Emma pulled down her skirt. Yes, sherry had helped, and as long as she was sensible, Horace need never know.

19

Polly was fidgeting in her chair. She wasn't happy that after just three months of marriage Tom's interest in sex had diminished. Oh, she had tried everything, but other than the occasional Sunday night, he fell asleep as soon as his head hit the pillow. It was his new job, and she regretted that he'd found a job as a hod carrier. The money was good, better than labouring, but, unused to the repetitive lifting, Tom's back was playing up and he came home exhausted every day.

Polly knew she was unnatural, knew that other women didn't crave sex as she did, and felt sick at what she was tempted to do. But, oh, she couldn't do without, she just couldn't.

The clatter of spoons in bowls interrupted her thought, the kids finishing their breakfast and soon off to school. She'd made a bit of a fuss at Christmas, buying a tree and putting presents under for the kids. Oh, it had been a joy to see their faces, to get so many cuddles. The last thing she had expected when she had married Tom was to grow fond of his children. The girls were beginning to feel like her own daughters.

Luke picked up the dishes, taking them to the sink, and Polly's eyes watched his every movement. Unlike the girls, she was unable to see him as her child. He was so beautiful, his young body lithe, and as Polly stood up to join him, she couldn't resist making sure that her ample breasts brushed against him. 'Are you all right, love?'

He coloured to the roots of his hair, avoiding her eyes as he mumbled, 'Yes, I'm fine.'

'Not long now and you'll be leaving school. You'll be a man, earning your own wage,' she said, running a hand along the fine hairs on his arm.

'He ain't a man,' Susan protested.

Polly jumped, moving swiftly away from Luke and saying brusquely, 'Come on now, get your coats on or you'll be late.'

They did as she asked, and only five minutes later left the house, Luke behind them like a shepherd with his flock, throwing a shy smile at her over his shoulder before closing the door.

Polly washed the breakfast dishes, hoping that when Tom came home that evening he'd go out for a drink. It would give her the opportunity she needed, the thought making her squirm in delicious anticipation.

For Emma, married only a little longer than Polly, sherry had become like a magical elixir, changing her life. She would be eighteen in a month, but still felt a prisoner, and though she still didn't like sex, and doubted she ever would, at least now it was bearable.

She was still the obedient wife, always there when Horace came home, no matter what time of the day, but her resentment was rising. She saw little of her family and was missing them. Not her father – she didn't miss him – but she longed to see more of her brothers and sisters. Christmas had been awful, just the two of them, though Horace had begrudgingly let her take presents to Balham for the children. Her eyes saddened. She had dreamed of riches, of being able to buy them wonderful presents, but instead had only managed to get them one small gift each from the little she'd saved from the housekeeping. Her own present from Horace had been a disappointment too, just a pair of leather gloves, with hers to him a scarf.

Emma took a sip of sherry and then picked up her book, but for once was unable to bury herself in the story. Horace had taken her reading in hand now, choosing books for her, and though she found most far too heavy-going, there were others that enthralled her.

At the moment she was reading Daniel Defoe, enjoying *Robinson Crusoe*, but as she once again tried to concentrate, her thoughts went back to Horace.

Emma's expression saddened. Despite trying to console herself, she couldn't shift her resentment. She took another sip of sherry, glad that as the alcohol took effect it fogged her mind, making her loneliness easier to bear. A loneliness that was emphasised when Dick had called to see her that morning. Worried that Horace would come home, she hadn't allowed him to stay long.

Poor Dick. Her heart had gone out to him. Charlie had died and her brother was devastated. It was good that the other costermongers were looking out for him, even running the stall whilst he arranged the old man's funeral, which was to be held on Monday. Emma frowned, determined now that no matter what Horace said, she wasn't going to leave her brother to face it on his own.

When Horace came home at two o'clock, despite the sherry, Emma was still ill prepared to talk to him. He seemed mellow and it gave her courage, so taking a deep breath, she carefully broached the subject of Charlie's funeral, ending with, 'So you see, I may be out for some time on Monday.'

He raised his brow, saying dismissively, 'No, Emma, I don't think your attendance is necessary.'

Horace's tone was intimidating, but Emma persisted. 'I feel that Dick needs my support.'

'For goodness' sake, he's not a child.'

'He's hardly a man.'

'Emma, I don't like your tone. You are my wife now and I don't think it's appropriate that you attend this . . . this costermonger's funeral. All the riffraff of the market will be there and it's hardly a fitting place for you to be seen.'

If she had been asking for anything on her own behalf, Emma would have meekly backed down, but this wasn't for her, it was for Dick, and she found herself rearing to her feet angrily. 'I don't care about being seen. I know most of the people who'll be there, and I want to support my brother.'

'I have a position to maintain and I have said no. Now please sit down and let us finish our lunch in peace.'

'A . . . a position to maintain. What position?' Now that she had started, Emma found that all her buried emotions rose to the surface and, hands on hips, she glared at her husband. 'You seem to forget that you lied to me, Horace, and not only to me, but to my father too. You gave us to understand that you owned property – that you were our landlord – but after our marriage revealed that you're just an agent. Everything you told us was a ruse, a ruse to get me to marry you.'

'Emma, that's enough!'

'Oh, no, it isn't nearly enough. You seem to think that I'm a fool, but I'm not. I know you're ashamed of my family, so much so that you didn't want them at our wedding. You even made me think that I was to blame for the mix-up with the dates, but instead it was something you planned all along.'

Horace gulped in air as though to compose himself, then said in a measured manner, 'That's rubbish, and I refuse to talk to you whilst you're acting like a fishwife. When you're prepared to act with the decorum my first wife had, we will discuss this again.'

His sanctimonious attitude was the final straw for Emma. She had been trying, striving to improve herself, and thought she was succeeding, but now it was as if the scales had been lifted from her eyes and she was seeing Horace for the lying snob that he was. She had been intimidated by him, and in truth, in awe of him, allowing him to dictate when she went out and who she saw. He wanted to change her, to mould her into a carbon copy of his first wife, but she would no longer be manipulated.

Maybe it was the sherry she'd drunk earlier that gave her the courage – she didn't know or care –

but her voice rose. 'Just who do you think you are? You're just an agent, that's all, and I refuse to be changed into the same type of woman as your first wife.'

'Turn you into Isabelle! God, you must be joking. She even hated taking my name, hated being Mrs Isabelle Bell.'

'No, I'm not joking. You're always throwing her in my face, yet I don't enjoy her privileges. After all, she was pampered, spoiled, and even had her own room.'

'What are you talking about?'

'I'm not blind. It didn't take me long to work out that you slept separately, something you categorically won't allow now.'

'My first wife was a lady, and a separate room was expected.'

'Oh, I see. She was a lady whereas I'm hardly more than a servant and can expect nothing better. I clean, I cook, I do the laundry, yet I wear her clothes to do these chores. I have to learn to talk like her, to act with her decorum, but also share your bed at night. Have I got it right, Horace?'

'Emma, you are going too far. Stop this now or I will be so angry that I'll throw your father out of his flat.'

'Do it then!' Emma screamed. 'I'm sick of you holding that over my head. All right, throw him out. My father is working regularly now and it won't be the end of the world. They'll find somewhere else to live, and in fact I think I'll encourage them to do just that. What will you be able to hold over me then? Nothing!'

Instead of anger, Emma was surprised when Horace sighed heavily, his face showing dismay. 'Please, Emma, stop this. I won't throw your father out, and as for my first wife, I'm not trying to turn you into Isabelle. I don't know what brought this on, but nothing could be further from the truth. Look, if all this came about because I said you can't attend a funeral, then I can only apologise. If it means so much to you, by all means go.'

'Really?'

'Yes, really. Now please, get that ferocious scowl off your face and let's finish this meal in peace.'

Her anger drained, Emma flopped onto a chair. She had done it. She had stood her ground and was still amazed that Horace had backed down. He smiled hesitantly across at her, but she kept her face straight, finding at the same time that all fear of the man had left her. She had one small victory under her belt now, but as far as she was concerned it would be the first of many.

Horace was in shock and struggling to hide his feelings. He'd made a terrible mistake in marrying

Emma, something he had found out almost from the start. He'd craved a virgin, expecting her to be perfect for his needs, but what a joke that had turned out to be. Sexually, Emma was a nightmare. She was cold, unresponsive, and she lay like a stone just waiting for it to be over. At first he hadn't been worried. After all, as a virgin she was inexperienced, but as the months had gone by, nothing had changed. He had been incensed with anger, making love to her both day and night in an attempt to arouse some passion, but to no avail.

There had been some compensation in her obedient behaviour. She'd been compliant in his attempts to correct her diction, and he'd made sure that she kept visits to her family down to a minimum. In fact she'd obeyed his every word. Until now! God, she had raged at him like a madwoman, and that was something he couldn't cope with.

Horace rubbed a hand across his face, hating his weakness. He was fine when dealing with men, ensuring that many of his tenants feared him. Their wives were a different matter. As long as they stayed soft, pleading for more time to pay the rent, it was all right. However, if one ever harangued him he would walk away, making sure that in future he dealt only with the husband.

He knew that when it came to women he was

easily intimidated but, raised by two aunts, he was haunted by his childhood. A childhood of harsh discipline, and frequent beatings, a childhood home he had run away from as soon as he could. Horace's shoulders straightened. He'd done well for himself. It hadn't been easy, but he'd fought his way up, wheeling and conniving until he'd hit the jackpot. His marriage to Isabelle had ensured his future . . . Now he frowned. By God he had suffered for it. She had been a demanding woman, a spiteful woman, controlling their finances and refusing him access to her bank account.

Horace glanced up, looked at Emma and shuddered. How was it possible that overnight she had changed from a meek and biddable wife to one who screamed at him like a banshee?

He'd been a complete and utter fool. Emma had been so beautiful, so innocent, that he'd become obsessed with the idea of marrying her. Huh, and look what it had got him. He should have been content with a mistress. At least they did as they were told, and as long as he paid them, were happy to be whatever he wanted them to be.

Horace pushed his plate away and abruptly stood up. He had to get out of here, to breathe fresh air and clear his head.

'Emma, I'm going out again and won't be back until this evening.'

He saw the relief on her face, and at one time

would have punished her by taking her body, but not now. Now all he wanted was to be away from her.

''Bye, Horace,' she said, adding with firmness in her voice, 'It's just as well that you'll be out for the rest of the day. I'm going to Balham to see Polly and the children.'

He just nodded, afraid now to argue. Without a backward glance, he hurried out of the house.

20

As Horace left the house, Emma felt a surge of relief. She had done it. She had stood up to him and from now on, things were going to change.

There was something else that was lying heavily on her mind, something she had been trying to deny and she urgently needed to see Polly. She had been trying to ignore the signs in her body and, fearing the worst, had diverted her mind by concentrating on Dick. But it could no longer be ignored and maybe Polly would be able to help.

It didn't take Emma long to get ready. Feeling a new sense of freedom, she was soon on her way to Balham. She wanted to see Polly alone, before the kids came home from school. As it was a long walk, she decided to take the train, making her way to the underground station.

Emma's strides were lengthy, the January day freezing and, glancing across at the Common, she saw that the grass was white with frost. She shivered, stuffing her hands into her pockets and cursing the fact that she had left the house without her gloves.

Paying for her ticket, she almost ran down the escalator, relieved to find a train pulling into the platform. The journey was short, and only a little while later she was walking along Polly's tree-lined road, a far cry from the mean street where they had lived in Battersea.

'My goodness, Emma, what a surprise. Is something wrong?' Polly cried when she opened the door.

'No, I just need to talk to you.'

'Talk to me. What about?'

Emma's brow creased. Polly looked nervous, tense. 'Well, if you'll let me over the doorstep I'll tell you.'

'Yes, yes, of course. Come on in.' Polly hurriedly filled the kettle. 'Get that coat off, Emma, and sit down.'

Emma sat close to the fire, appreciating its warmth, wondering why Polly was acting so skittishly. For a moment she gazed at the dancing flames, pushing her question to one side whilst forming her words. She waited until Polly had given her a cup of tea, and as the woman sat opposite, Emma blurted, 'Polly, can I ask you something?'

Polly's cup rattled in the saucer. 'Yeah, I suppose so.'

'Er . . . do you know if there's any way to get rid of a baby?'

Polly seemed to slump with relief. 'So that's why you've come to see me. Don't tell me you're pregnant?'

'No such luck,' Emma quickly lied. 'I . . . I'm asking for a friend. Are you all right, Polly? You seem a bit tense.'

'I'm fine, it's just a headache. Anyway, back to your problem, but as I've never had any kids of my own, I doubt I can help.'

'Polly, please, my friend is desperate. There must be something she can do.'

'Why? Ain't she married?'

Emma grasped the lie. 'No, and her father will kill her if he finds out.'

'Poor girl, but to be honest all I've heard about getting rid of babies is gossip. If she ain't too far gone, some say you can sit in a hot bath and drink a bottle of gin, but if you ask me it sounds like an old wives' tale.'

'She's less than three months pregnant.'

'Oh, really?' Polly said, her eyes narrowing with suspicion. 'Well, if the gin doesn't work, I know there are some who've had backstreet abortions. Mind you, I wouldn't recommend that. One I heard of used a knitting needle on a woman and she died.'

Emma shuddered, but what Polly said made sense. If her own mother could have easily got rid of babies, surely she wouldn't have had eight, the ninth one dying with her at birth? 'So you don't think there's anything my friend can do?'

'Not that I know of. Can't she get the father to marry her?'

'No, he . . . he's already married.'

'The soppy cow. She'll have to own up then, but I wouldn't like to be in her shoes when she tells her father.'

'Me neither,' Emma said, and then, wanting to change the subject, added, 'I'm going to Charlie's funeral on Monday.'

'Are you, love? That's nice,' Polly said, all trace of her early nervousness gone. 'Dick popped round to see us last night, and the poor lad looked ever so upset. Still, he's done all right for himself. He's got Charlie's stall, and one of the traders is taking on the pitch for him. Not bad for a lad of not yet sixteen.'

'Yes, I know, and he's even managed to rent Charlie's little house. I just hope he can cope financially.'

'He'll be fine. That stall's a goldmine. You're dad's right envious too.'

Emma's lip curled. 'Yes, I'm sure he is, but the stall belongs to Dick and I hope Dad doesn't try to muscle in.'

'He told Dick that he'd be willing to give him a hand, and I don't see what's wrong with that. You're too down on your dad and I don't understand why. He's a good man and a hard worker. If you ask me Dick should accept his offer. It ain't much fun working on building sites, and your dad's back is playing him up. He'd be better off working the stall.'

Emma was in no mood to argue with Polly. The woman was still wearing rose-tinted glasses, but she was determined to have a word with Dick. If her father got involved with the stall, he'd take all the profits, and she wasn't going to stand for that. She stood up, and with her own problem weighing on her mind, she put on her coat, forcing a smile.

'I'll be down to see the kids another day, but I must go now.'

'Well, that was a quick visit, but it was nice to see you.'

Emma said goodbye, but as she made for the underground station again, her heart was heavy. She doubted gin would work and couldn't face some old hag with a knitting needle. She would have to tell Horace but, God, she didn't want a baby. Or rather *his* baby.

Emma sat on the train, oblivious of other passengers as her thoughts continued to turn. Maybe being pregnant could have some benefits.

Perhaps it would give her an excuse to keep Horace out of her bed.

With a heavy sigh she knew it was unlikely. It hadn't stopped her father, the man still demanding his rights when her mother was nearly due to have each baby. Horace would be the same, but then Emma's lips tightened. No! She'd had enough and wouldn't stand for it any more. She'd tell him she was ill, pretend it was a difficult pregnancy, anything to keep him away from her.

With a good excuse worked out, Emma relaxed. Horace would probably be over the moon when she told him he was to be a father, but she'd wait until after dinner before breaking the news. In the meantime, when she arrived home, she'd prepare a separate bedroom, presenting it to him as a *fait accompli*.

When Horace returned home that evening, he hoped to find Emma in a better mood.

'Hello, my dear,' he said.

'Hello, Horace. Dinner is nearly ready.'

At one time he would have dragged her into his arms, kissed her, but now he hesitated. 'Oh, good, I'll just pop upstairs to freshen up.'

She smiled, nodded.

Horace headed for the stairs. He hated this, hated feeling nervous around his wife, in his own home, and wanted to get back to their old footing.

After sluicing his hands and face he returned downstairs to find Emma laying his dinner on the dining-room table. There was something about her manner, something about the small smile on her face that worried him, but as he took a seat opposite her, he couldn't have been prepared for the force of the shock that hit him when she spoke.

'You . . . you're what?'

'I said I'm pregnant, Horace. I'm having a baby.'

Horace's mind reeled. A baby! How the hell could she be pregnant? He'd been careful, he knew he had, wearing protection against such a thing happening. Had one been faulty? Was that the reason? Yes, it must have been . . . Then he became aware of Emma looking at him worriedly.

'Are you all right, Horace? You've gone awfully pale.'

Horace fought for composure. 'Yes, I'm fine. It was just a shock, that's all.'

'You don't look very happy. I thought you'd be pleased.'

'Oh, I am,' he lied, when in fact he felt as if his world had caved in. A child – he didn't want a bloody child! If Emma had been the wife he had dreamed of, he might, just might, have been able to stand it. He would have seen that she kept the child out of his way and, when old enough, it could have been sent away to school. Yet he couldn't even do that, he realised. Sending a child

227

to boarding school cost money, money that Emma had no idea they had. She thought they were hard up, that they only had this house, and he wanted to keep it that way.

He stood up, throwing his napkin down and heading for the drawing room. He opened the drinks cabinet, poured a large whisky and downed it in one gulp. He had to think, to work things out, but in the meantime he had to keep Emma sweet. He didn't want her throwing any more tantrums; after all, one had been enough to drive him out of the house. She came into the room and as she spoke he turned, fixing a smile on his face.

'I'm afraid I've been feeling unwell, Horace, but isn't this National Health Service wonderful? I went to see a doctor and he said that I need plenty of rest. I hope you don't mind, but with this in mind I've moved my things to another bedroom.'

Horace didn't care. In fact he was relieved. The thought of making love to a woman with a baby in her womb appalled him. God, her stomach would become grotesque and he didn't want to see it, didn't want to have to look at her. He poured another whisky, again gulping it down. Was he unnatural? Maybe, but he didn't care. He had never wanted a child, and didn't want one now.

The one thing Horace had learned from his first marriage was how to act, and this ability now came to the fore. His face showed concern as he spoke. 'Of course you need your rest. In fact, I would have insisted that you have a separate room.'

She smiled at him, but Horace was no fool and he saw it was a smile of triumph. Emma thought she had him where she wanted him, but she was wrong. He'd work something out, determined that one day soon he'd wipe that smile off her face.

21

Emma continued to use her pregnancy as an excuse to keep Horace out of her room and her bed. With a baby on the way she knew she had to take her drinking in hand and cut down on the sherry. She'd got used to drinking a glass every day, which had quickly become two glasses then three . . . It was hard at first, in fact harder than she'd expected, but now that she didn't have Horace's sexual demands to deal with, it wasn't necessary to dull her mind. Strangely enough, now that she no longer had to sleep with Horace, she was growing fond of him. If anything she saw him as a father figure, and even their kisses were chaste.

Though he continued to keep her short of money, Emma was happy nowadays, humming as she did the housework. Her new-found freedom had started when she went to Charlie's funeral and she kept it up, going to visit her family once a week. She also went to see Dick on the stall, pleased to see how well he was doing. He hadn't taken their father on, despite the pressure. Instead, now that Luke had left school, he'd given a job to him, and though she would have preferred Luke to learn a trade, she doubted either brother would listen to her, both thinking themselves too old to be given advice.

One beautiful day in spring, thinking of her brothers, she decided to go to see them, and now that the girls were on their Easter holiday from school, she'd pop round to Polly's too. Emma flicked a last glance around the drawing room before grabbing her handbag and heading for the market.

Dick smiled when he saw her, but he was busy with a customer. Luke had his back to her, piling cabbages onto the stall. Drawing close, Emma laid her hand on his arm. He jumped as though scalded, dropping a cabbage and snatching his arm away.

Puzzled, Emma asked, 'Goodness, what are you so jumpy about?'

Luke avoided her eyes. 'Nothing, you just startled me, that's all.'

Emma held her arms out. 'Well, are you going to give me a cuddle?'

He moved hesitantly forward, but was stiff as she held him, and after allowing a swift hug, pulled away. It was unlike him. Luke was usually demonstrative, happy to show affection, and she wondered what had brought about this change.

'Are you all right?' she asked.

'Yes, I just don't like to be touched.'

Emma's eyebrows rose. 'Since when?'

He ignored her, going back to his work whilst Emma watched him, shaking her head in bewilderment. Dick came to her side and wrapped an arm around her shoulder.

'How are you doing, love?'

'Fine. I'm on my way to see the girls. What's the matter with Luke? He seems a bit sullen.'

'I dunno. He's been acting a bit off for a while now. When I ask him what the problem is, he just clams up. Maybe he's fallen out with Dad or something. You could try asking Polly.'

'Yes, I'll do that. Oh, look, it's Alice, and she's got James and Archie with her.'

Alice was smiling as she approached, the boys rosy-cheeked and well-dressed. 'Hello, Emma, this is lovely! I've hardly set eyes on you since you got married. Come on, boys, say hello to your sister.'

Both James and Archie chorused a greeting, and then Dick threw them an apple each. Emma found herself filled with mixed emotions. It was lovely to see her youngest brothers looking so happy, but they already seemed distant. Maybe she should have tried to see more of them, but if they became unsettled it wouldn't be fair on Alice.

As if sensing her thoughts, Alice spoke gently. 'They're fine, Emma, and when your father agreed that we could officially adopt them, I was over the moon. And congratulations yourself, love,' she said, eyeing Emma's growing stomach. 'You wait, when you become a mother there's nothing like it in the world.'

'Mummy, can we go now?' James cried, pulling on Alice's skirt. 'You said we could go on the swings.'

Emma gulped, fighting to hide her emotions. 'Mummy' – James had called Alice '*Mummy*'. Oh, she had to stop thinking like this. They were fine, well adjusted, and it would be best if she didn't interfere in their lives.

'Sorry, Em, I've got to go. I won't get any peace until these two are at the playground.'

'Yes, of course. 'Bye, Alice. 'Bye, boys.'

Both Dick and Luke were busy, but raised their hands to wave as Alice moved away, the boys not looking back as they trotted along, one on each side of Alice and holding her hand.

Emma watched them go, then said goodbye to Dick and Luke and set off for Balham.

Emma sat on the bus, watching the passing scenery, finding her thoughts on her mother. Since her death the family had gone in all directions, their lives so different now. She missed her mother so much and there was hardly a day when she didn't think about her.

It wasn't far to Polly's and soon Emma was knocking on the door, forcing her unhappy thoughts away and glad to find that the girls were at home.

'Your belly's getting big,' Susan said as she hugged her.

'You must be six months gone now, Emma,' Polly said as she put the kettle on to boil. 'Sit yourself down, love.'

After giving all her sisters a hug, Emma sank gratefully onto a chair. Her eyes took in Polly's kitchen, and as usual it was sparkling clean. Her sisters looked lovely too, and Susan was blooming, all signs of the sickly child she had been gone.

In such a short time they had changed so much and were obviously fond of Polly, so much so that Emma doubted it would be much longer before they accepted her as their mother. She gulped, and as she had with James and Archie, she was unsure how she felt about it, how her mother would have felt about it. Yet surely it was what her mother would have wanted – to see her children happy, loved and well cared for?

At first she'd had concerns about Polly, finding the woman a bit brazen, but she had to admit her mistake, especially when Ann rushed up to Polly, giving her a hug.

'Can I have some lemonade?' Ann asked.

'Of course you can, darling,' Polly said, 'and what about you two?' she asked, her eyes going from Susan to Bella.

'Yes, please,' they chorused.

'When are you gonna have your baby, Emma?' Susan asked.

'When am I "going" to, not "gonna",' Emma automatically corrected. 'The baby will be born early July, and then you'll all be aunties.'

'You don't half talk posh, Emma,' Susan said, 'but Luke won't be an auntie. He'll be an uncle.'

'Yes, that's right. Dick too.' Emma felt the baby move and she beckoned Susan over. 'If you put your hand on my tummy, you might be able to feel the baby.'

'Me too,' cried Bella, rushing to get there first.

'Now then, not all at once,' Polly gently admonished. 'Here, Bella, come and get your lemonade.'

Bella pulled a face, but did as she was told, and when Susan failed to feel any movement, she moved for Bella to take a turn. With a hand on Emma's tummy and her head cocked to one side, she remained still for a moment, but then said, 'I can't feel nothing. I reckon you've just got fat, Emma.'

Both Emma and Polly roared with laughter, and as Polly poured them each a cup of tea, taking the chair opposite, Emma took a sip, then asked, 'How's Luke?'

She was surprised to see the woman looking disconcerted, her hand trembling slightly as she lifted the cup to her lips. 'He's all right. Why do you ask?'

Emma shrugged. 'He seems a bit strange, distant, as though something is worrying him.'

'He seems fine to me.' After a short pause, Polly blurted, 'Maybe it's your stomach. Some men find a woman's pregnancy embarrassing.'

Emma nodded slowly. 'Yes, perhaps that's it.'

'Your dad ain't too happy that Dick gave Luke the job on the stall.'

'It was his decision, and anyway, Dad's got a job.'

'Yeah, but as I said before, he was hoping to get away from the building game.'

'He'd have taken the stall over and that wouldn't have been fair on Dick.'

Polly bristled, but as the children once again vied for attention, she said no more, instead answering Susan, 'No, you can't go out to play. Emma's come to see you and the least you can do is to stay in until she leaves.'

She then reached down to pick up her knitting bag by the side of the chair and, pulling out a tiny garment, handed it to Emma. 'I made this for the baby, and I've just started another one.'

Emma took the little matinée coat and smiled with delight. 'Oh, Polly, it's lovely.'

'I'm glad you like it. I know it ain't much, and no doubt Horace is filling the place with the best that money can buy.' Polly then paled, saying quickly, 'What I mean is, he must be dead chuffed to be a father and is probably spending money that he can't afford.'

Emma fingered the lovely soft wool. 'You're wrong about Horace. He hasn't got anything for the baby, and when I bring up the subject he avoids it. As for the best that money can buy, I hardly think that's likely. He's always nagging me to not overspend, pointing out how much it costs to run the house.'

'Yeah, well, it must be a pretty penny and from what you've told me he's a careful man.'

Emma sighed heavily. 'Yes, he is, but he hardly mentions the baby. At times I've caught him looking at my tummy with an awful expression on his face. It's rather like he finds it disgusting.'

Polly pursed her lips. 'Maybe you're just feeling a bit sensitive. Mind you, I've never had kids of my own so I'm no expert.'

'You've got us, Polly,' Susan chimed in. Bella nodded.

'Yeah, I have, ain't I, and do you know what? I love you all to bits.'

Emma smiled as Ann ran up to Polly, clambering onto her lap. It was lovely to see the children getting so much affection, something she knew they had lacked since their mother died. She touched her tummy, looking up as Polly spoke again.

'They're all good girls, and I'm lucky to have them, it . . . it's just that sometimes you can love too much, and in the wrong place.'

Emma frowned, puzzled by Polly's cryptic remark. 'What do you mean?'

'Oh, take no notice of me, it's nothing,' she blustered. 'How about another cup of tea, or I've got some Camp coffee?'

'If it isn't too much trouble, coffee would be lovely.'

'Right, off you get, darling,' she said to Ann, but not before giving her another hug.

Emma was still pondering Polly's cryptic remark, but then they started chatting again and another hour quickly passed. The children were starting to bicker, obviously fed up with playing ludo and, knowing that they were itching to go out, Emma rose to her feet.

'Right, I'm off now. 'Bye, girls, I'll see you next week. 'Bye, Polly. It was lovely to see you.'

'It was nice to see you too,' Polly said.

Emma gave a small wave, but as she made her way home, she found herself thinking of Polly's strange comment again. She had said you could love someone too much, which sort of made sense, but what did she mean by 'in the wrong place'?

Emma's eyes widened. Surely Polly wasn't having an affair? No, it was ridiculous, of course she wasn't, but what other explanation could there be?

Horace, too, was on his way home, his thoughts on Emma. What a disaster his marriage had turned out to be. He was just about sick of it. Sick of watching Emma's stomach growing, and sick at the thought of the baby she was carrying.

He still couldn't believe it had happened. He'd been careful, he was sure of it, but still Emma had fallen pregnant. His eyes narrowed, a suspicion forming, one that made his guts churn. Christ, was that the reason? Was that why Emma had never welcomed him sexually? No, it couldn't be true, but even as Horace dismissed the thought, a seed had been planted in his mind.

Now, as he strolled along by the Common, he was surprised to see Emma coming towards him in the distance. So, she'd been out again, but who had she been to see? The seed grew, the sickening thought, and suddenly Horace knew what he wanted to do. Just the thought brought an immediate sense of relief, but would it be possible? God, he didn't have much time, and he stood to lose a lot, but even that was better than the alternative.

As Emma drew closer, she waved, and Horace grimaced. My God, look at the state of her with that stomach sticking out and lifting her skirt at the front! How much longer did she have to go? Three months maybe. Hopefully that was enough time to put his new plans into action. In the meantime he would have to ensure that he didn't arouse Emma's suspicions. So planting a smile on his face as they turned into the drive from opposite directions, he said, 'Hello, my dear. Where have you been?'

'I went to see Polly and my sisters,' Emma said. 'I wasn't expecting you home so early.'

Hmm, Horace thought. She was lying, of course, but he'd continue the act. 'That's nice. How were they?'

'Fine, they're all fine,' and as Horace opened the door she swept inside.

With his eyes on her back, Horace felt a surge of disgust – disgust that he'd been made a fool of – but he'd make her pay. As she swung round to smile at him, her cheeks pink and her blue eyes bright, for a moment he felt a surge of doubt. God, she was beautiful, maybe too beautiful. His eyes travelled to her stomach again, and needing an excuse to feel as he did, to think as he did, he dismissed the doubt, focusing instead on his plans. He'd put them into action first thing in the morning, and just hoped to God everything went smoothly.

* * *

241

Later, when they were sitting down to dinner, Horace was deep in thought, still planning, still scheming, and when Emma spoke he hardly heard her.

'Sorry, what did you say?'

'I said that Polly has knitted a lovely matinée jacket for the baby. Speaking of that, we really do need to start thinking about the nursery. We need a cot, a pram, nappies and, of course, clothes.'

'There's no hurry. You have months to go yet. Tell me, how are you getting on with *A Tale of Two Cities*? Have you finished the book?'

'No, I haven't, but please, Horace, don't change the subject. Every time I mention our baby, you do this. I know it's going to cost money, but if you allow me a bit more housekeeping each week, I can buy things a little at a time.'

Horace hid his annoyance, forming a lie. 'Stop worrying, my dear. I've been putting money aside, and when there's sufficient we'll get everything the baby needs all at once.'

'Really! Oh, that's wonderful.'

Horace lowered his head, hiding his satisfaction. Yes, my dear, he thought, you look happy now, but one day in the near future that smile will be wiped off your face.

22

It was hot in July, and in the last month of her pregnancy Emma was so huge that she remained at home. The baby kicked and she cupped her stomach, a soft smile on her face. She hadn't wanted this baby, but from the first time she felt it move, a fierce love had been born and it sickened her to think that she had once considered an abortion.

Horace was still reluctant to buy the things they needed, but once he'd explained how he felt, she understood. He was superstitious, he said, preferring to wait until the baby was born before kitting out the nursery. Nevertheless, some things couldn't wait, and she intended to speak to him again that evening.

There was a knock on the front door and Emma waddled to answer it.

'Hello, Dick, what are you doing here?'

'Are you on your own?'

'Yes, but Horace should be home soon.'

Dick followed her inside, saying without preamble, 'I'm worried about Luke.'

'Why? Is he ill?'

'No, but his behaviour is odd and growing worse.'

'I was worried about him too for a while, but Polly said he was probably embarrassed by my tummy.'

'No, there's more to it than that. He seems a nervous wreck. Something is upsetting him, worrying him, and he hardly talks nowadays. Not only that, Em, he's taken to going to church.'

'Has he? Have you had a word with him?'

'I tried, but he just says everything's fine.'

Emma saw the concern in her brother's eyes, saying sadly as she pointed to her tummy, 'I expect you want me to have a word with him, but to be honest I'm not up to going out and about at the moment.'

'I should have thought of that,' Dick said, smiling at last as he looked at her huge girth. 'Look, don't worry about it. I'll have another go at talking to him myself.'

Emma felt a twinge of pain and her eyes rounded. Was it time? Was this the start of her labour?

The pain was short-lived, but Dick must have noticed, his voice registering concern. 'Are you all right, Em? You looked a bit funny for a moment.'

'Yes, I'm fine,' she said, her head turning at the sound of the front door opening.

Horace walked into the room, but when he saw Dick he didn't say a word. Instead he marched straight out, shoulders rigid, and went upstairs.

'I see I'm still not welcome here,' Dick said.

'Oh, take no notice of him. As far as I'm concerned you can call round to see me as often as you like.'

'If you say so, but it's obvious that Horace doesn't feel the same. Anyway, I'm off. When I call round again, let's hope he's out.'

Emma walked with her brother to the door. 'Try talking to Luke and let me know how you get on.'

'Will do. See yer, sis.'

''Bye, love.' Emma watched her brother for a moment, and then with a sigh closed the front door. She had wanted to talk to Horace about the nursery, but after seeing that Dick had paid her a visit, he'd be in a rotten mood all evening.

It was ten minutes later when Emma felt another spasm of pain and once again wondered if she was in labour. She would have to time the contractions, and if they continued, Horace would have to take her to hospital. For a moment she felt a tremor of fear, but then as the pain subsided again she felt a wave of excitement. Her baby was ready to be born. She wondered how Horace would react to being a father. It would change things, change their relationship, and for the baby's sake somehow they had to make this marriage work.

Horace was annoyed to see Dick in the house and slammed his bedroom door. But then he shook his head. What did it matter now? He was ready. Everything was set up. A new house, a new mistress, and to avoid the area in future, he had sold all his properties. He was determined to be out before the child was born, a child he had no intention of supporting, and with this in mind had even changed his name. After all, he told himself, he'd been careful so there was no possibility that the child was his. Emma had never welcomed him sexually, and he was sure she had another man.

Horace had convinced himself that this was the case, and it had righteously given him the excuse he needed to put his plans into action. There had been twenty houses to sell and the wait for buyers hellish, but then he'd struck lucky when a businessman saw the potential, buying a whole block.

Horace rubbed his hands together gleefully.

The houses had increased in value beyond his expectations. He was a very rich man, exceedingly rich, so much so that he wouldn't have to risk selling the Balham property. He thought about Tom Chambers and scowled. He'd have liked to throw the man out, but what did it matter really? With the money he had now, the rent he'd gain by putting in new tenants would seem like peanuts. Not only that, there would be the problem of collecting it. Anyway, Emma would only move the lot of them in here so there would be no suffering. But oh, how he wanted them all to suffer, to see Emma suffer.

He smirked, pleased with how clever he'd been. If Emma found out how well off he was she was sure to come looking for him, but by retaining the house in Balham, and using another name, there'd be no way to trace him. Of course it helped that her family were uneducated louts. They knew nothing of the law, of finding people who didn't want to be found.

There was only one thing that remained to anger him. He wouldn't be able to divorce Emma. She would remain his wife, but one that wouldn't get a penny out of him. He consoled himself with that thought. They'd been married for less than a year, a brief period out of his life, and he was still young enough to start again. It was better to get out now, the marriage short, far preferable to the length of time he'd been with Isabelle.

Horace looked around his bedroom. At one time he had loved this house, thinking it the culmination of his dreams. Now it held nothing but bad memories – memories of the humiliation he'd suffered at Isabelle's hands and had hoped to eradicate when he married Emma. This time he'd intended to be the man of the house, with a beautiful, innocent, and obedient wife. Instead, Emma had destroyed that dream and as far as he was concerned she could rot in this house, until one day, in the distant future, he would sell it from under her.

His eyes continued to roam and he frowned. Not only this room but the rest of the house was full of choice pieces of furniture, paintings and fine porcelain. He hated leaving it behind, but when he left it had to be clean, swift, with no time for Emma to rally any of her family.

Horace shrugged, consoling himself again. What did it matter? He was a wealthy man, and his new home far superior to this one. He was starting afresh now, and he'd learned his lesson. It may have taken two marriages to see the light, but he'd never make the same mistakes again. Women were all the same, and from now on he'd stick to mistresses.

He went to the window, saw Emma's brother leaving and stiffened his shoulders. It was time.

Time for the confrontation – and though he felt a little nervous, what could Emma do? Nothing.

Horace found Emma in the kitchen. He interrupted her as she made to speak and was gratified to see the look of horror on her face.

'You're leaving. What do you mean?'

'I see I need to repeat myself. I'm leaving you, Emma, and I won't be back.'

'But . . . but why?' she cried, leaning over, hands clutching her tummy.

'Why? You have the audacity to ask *why*? I took you from the gutter, married you, and instead of being grateful, within a few months you turned into a shrew, berating me, and no doubt laughing at me behind my back.'

Emma gasped, still clutching her stomach, but he didn't give her time to protest, holding up his hands as she tried to interrupt.

'Don't bother trying to deny it. You seem to forget that you came from a slum into *my* house, but made it obvious from the start that you couldn't stand me near you. Why is that, Emma? Were you getting your pleasure elsewhere?'

'I don't know what you're talking about.'

'Don't you?' Horace said, his eyes travelling pointedly to Emma's stomach.

'What? Surely you're not suggesting that the baby isn't yours?'

Emma's voice had risen, and Horace shifted uncomfortably. Time to go – to get this over with. 'That's exactly what I'm suggesting, and now I'm leaving.'

'But what about me? What will I do?'

Horace swung on his heels. 'As far as I'm concerned, you can rot in hell, but you should be grateful that you have this house in which to do it. Mind you, it'll never be yours, madam. You may be able to live in it, but don't get too cosy.'

He heard Emma screech but didn't look back as he hurried through the hall. He had a train to catch, one that would take him far away from Battersea. He was just glad it was over with, that he was free.

He had no idea that he'd left Emma doubled over in pain, falling to the floor as the door had slammed behind him.

23

Emma groaned as another wave of pain gripped her stomach. She knew she had to get up, to find help and, struggling to her feet, just managed to make it to the hall before bending double again. Something was wrong, very wrong, and when the pain subsided again, Emma moved forward, but as she stepped outside she fell, the house keys in her apron pocket digging agonisingly into her side.

Someone must have come to her aid, but what happened next remained a blur. Emma was aware that she was in hospital; the pain excruciating, wave upon wave that swelled into an unbearable agony. She could hear a doctor speaking, knew she was having a breech birth and, remembering what happened to her mother, she expected to die.

On and on it went. What were they doing to her? *Please, just let me die.* Oh God, it felt as though they were ripping her apart, but suddenly, miraculously, the pain ceased. Emma opened dazed eyes, bathed in perspiration, and then minutes later all the pain was forgotten as her daughter was placed in her arms.

A nurse spoke, but Emma was so engrossed in her baby's tiny face that she hardly heard her. 'Sorry, what did you say?'

'You had a hard time of it, pet, but she's fine.'

'Yes,' Emma sighed. 'She's beautiful.'

The nurse leaned forward to take the baby. 'She needs a little clean up, and no doubt your husband will be here to see her later.'

Emma's arms involuntarily tightened around her daughter. *Horace.* Yes, Horace. My God, he had left her! She saw that the nurse was looking at her strangely and managed to croak, 'My husband . . . he . . . he's away on business.'

'Oh dear, what a shame. Is there any way you can contact him?'

'Er . . . no,' Emma said, grasping on a lie. 'He's due back next week, but we didn't expect the baby to be born before then.'

'Well, never mind, his daughter will be a lovely surprise when he gets back.'

'Yes, she will, won't she,' Emma said, managing a smile.

'Well, pet, here's Nurse Jones to get you cleaned up too, and then you'll be taken to the ward.'

'What . . . what time is it?'

'It's six in the morning.'

Emma's head reeled. She must have been in labour all night. All she wanted now was to get out of this hospital – to go home. Her stomach lurched. Horace had left her, and what was she going to do? She may have the house to live in, but she had hardly any money, not even enough to buy a cot for the baby. Oh God, it was all too much. She felt a wave of utter tiredness. When the nurse took her daughter, Emma didn't protest, instead she meekly allowed them to give her a bed bath before her eyes closed and she escaped into the sanctuary of sleep.

When Emma awoke two hours later she was amazed to find herself in a ward. She dragged herself up into a sitting position, grimacing a little, but seeing a nurse she attracted her attention. 'Can I see my baby?'

'She's in the nursery, asleep. Breakfast will be here shortly, and then the babies will be brought in for a feed. You'll see her then.'

Emma wanted to protest, to say that she wanted to see her baby now, but found the stern-looking nurse intimidating. As the woman walked away, her starched uniform rustling, Emma looked down the ward. It was long, with beds on both sides all occupied by young women. A voice came from the next bed. Emma turned her head to see a blousy-looking woman.

'What did you have, dearie? A boy or a girl?'

'A girl,' Emma said.

'You're lucky. I had another bloody boy and that makes five.'

Emma forced a smile. She didn't want to talk to anyone, she just wanted to think. It was strange really. She'd given birth, but not one of her family knew, and Horace – my God, he didn't think the baby was his! How could he? How could he have accused her of sleeping with another man?

She slumped back on her pillow, closing her eyes to avert any further conversation. As soon as she could, she'd leave the hospital. They couldn't stop her, and anyway, just let them try. She had to sort things out, to raise money somehow, and she couldn't do that if she was stuck in here.

Emma left the hospital three days later, and it caused a furore. The doctor was annoyed, advising against it, but she didn't care. Nothing was going to stop her, not even the matron who marched into the ward like a ship in full sail.

Once outside, she looked up and down the street, and without money for the bus fare home she began to walk, cutting across the Common with the baby clutched to her chest. With no baby clothes, her daughter was dressed in a hospital

254

nightgown, and wrapped in a blanket that she'd promised to return.

It wasn't long before Emma felt her weakness, her legs rubbery underneath her. She had lost a lot of blood during the birth and knew she was acting foolishly, but hadn't been able to stand the sly innuendoes from some of the other women in the ward. When the doors were opened in the evening to admit a stream of visitors, none had come to her bed, and though she had told them that Horace was away on business, it was obvious they didn't believe her. They looked pointedly at her wedding ring as though it was made of brass, and she had borne their looks of disgust until she could stand it no more.

The baby stirred and Emma looked down at her daughter, her heart surging with love. She had racked her brains for a name, but now suddenly Patricia popped into her mind and there it remained. Yes, she would call her Patricia and, despite Horace's horrid accusation, she would be Patricia Bell on her birth certificate.

Emma was staggering by the time she arrived home, carefully laying the baby on the sofa in the drawing room and flopping down beside her. The house was silent, and after the noisy ward, soothing as she rested for a while.

Thirsty now, Emma checked that Patricia was still asleep before going to the kitchen. She made a pot of tea, waited for it to brew, and then poured a cup, adding a liberal teaspoon of condensed milk. Back in the drawing room she sat beside the baby, thoughts turning. Her most pressing problem was money. Patricia needed nappies, clothes, a pram, and of course somewhere to sleep, but Emma didn't have a penny to her name. Oh, she was too tired to think, and she was still so sore, worn out by the events of the day.

After resting for a while, Emma's hard upbringing came to the rescue. She had been used to make do and mend, resourceful as she cut up old towels for nappies. Pleased there was enough food in the larder for a few days, and after making herself something to eat, she lined a large drawer with soft linen to use as a cot.

It was enough for now. As the evening drew to a close she wearily climbed the stairs to bed. When Patricia woke up in the night, Emma tucked her beside her in the bed, holding her daughter as she suckled, her heart full of love, along with worry about their future.

24

Over the next two days, Emma was content to be alone with her baby. She knew she had to sort out her financial situation soon, but couldn't seem to arouse the energy. Instead she doted on Patricia, holding her constantly, with a fierce, protective love.

The larder stocks were getting low, but as long as she produced enough milk for the baby, Emma struggled to keep her worries at bay. She bathed Patricia in the kitchen sink, gently splashing warm water over her daughter, loving every tiny finger and toe, still unable to believe that she had ever considered an abortion.

On day four, Emma knew she had to face up to her problems, and not only that, she wanted to show off her baby, wanted her family to see Patricia. Oh, they would love her, she was sure of it, but how could she take the child out wrapped in only cut-down blankets? Patricia needed clothes, proper nappies, and as Emma kissed the top of the baby's soft, downy hair, worry began to eat at her stomach, making it clench in fear.

So much had happened that she had tried to block it from her mind, concentrating instead on her baby. But now it hit her. She was alone; she was penniless, left to bring up her daughter on her own.

Oh, Mum, Mum, she thought, I wish you were here. You have a granddaughter and she's beautiful. Oh, you'd have loved her, Mum, but what am I going to do? Unbidden tears came then, tears that Emma was unable to stop.

Gradually, Emma stemmed the flow, dashing her hand across her sodden face. Despondently, she rose to her feet, still holding Patricia as she wandered into the drawing room. Yes, she had this lovely house, but for how long? Horace had threatened to sell it, and anyway, she didn't have the money with which to run it. Her eyes took in the luxury that surrounded her, and it was then that she was struck by an idea that could solve her immediate problems.

Emma looked at a porcelain figurine, calculating, but then there was a knock on the door and she went to answer it. Dick was standing on the step and she felt a surge of relief.

'Oh, thank God you've come.'

His eyes widened when he saw Patricia in her

arms. 'Bloody hell, you've dropped the sprog. Are you all right, Em? You look a bit rough. Have you been crying?'

'Yes, but don't worry, I'm just tired, that's all. I lost a lot of blood during the birth and it's left me a bit weak.'

Dick looked doubtful, but followed her through to the kitchen.

'I can't tell you how pleased I am to see you,' Emma told him.

'She's a little cracker,' Dick said, his eyes soft as he gazed at Patricia. 'Bloody hell, I'm an uncle!'

'Would you like to hold her?'

'Yeah, all right.' Gingerly he took the baby, smiling down on her.

'I expect you've been worrying about Luke, and you were right to worry,' he began. 'Honestly, Em, you could have knocked me down with a feather when he told me—'

With more pressing concerns, Emma interrupted, 'You can tell me about Luke later, but for now I need you to take something to the pawnbroker for me. Don't pawn it, sell it, and get as much as you can.'

'What? Hang on, Em. What's all this about? I know Horace ain't a rich man, but surely you don't need to pawn stuff.'

'Horace has gone.'

'Gone! What do you mean, *gone*?'

Dick listened, jiggling the baby as his jaw dropped. When she had finished, he growled, 'The bastard. Did you tell him that he's wrong? That the baby's his?'

'He didn't give me a chance.'

'Surely he's still got to support you? Look, where's he gone? I'll round up a few of the blokes off the market and we'll soon sort him out.'

'I don't know where he is. He could be anywhere.'

'Bloody hell! Here, you'd better take the baby.' As Emma took Patricia from his arms, Dick urged, 'Don't worry. We'll find Horace.'

'I doubt that. He's a clever man and no doubt has covered his tracks. To be honest, I don't care if I never see him again. As long as I can raise some money, I'll be all right.'

'Instead of flogging bits and pieces, why don't you sell this place?'

'I can't. It isn't mine – it's in Horace's name, and you can be sure he'll have made sure I can't sell it.'

'The bastard!' Dick spat again. 'Here – what about Dad's flat?'

'I don't know, but I'm sure Dad would have been round here if he'd been given notice to quit.'

'Yeah, and I suppose if the worst came to the worst you've got plenty of room for them in this place. Though after what I've got to tell you I don't think you'll want Polly here.'

'Polly's all right, but I wouldn't take Dad in, not after he almost blackmailed me into marrying Horace.'

'He did what? Bloody hell, I always thought it was a bit odd that you married the man.'

'Dad was way behind with the rent and it was the only way to stop us being evicted. It's all right, don't get upset. I'm just as much to blame. I loved this house and wanted a better life, so much so that I virtually sold myself.'

'I reckon Dad's new flat was part of the deal,' Dick said bitterly.

'Maybe, but it doesn't matter now. My marriage is over, and despite the worry over money, I'm glad.'

Patricia stirred, and moments later began to cry. Dick turned away as Emma unbuttoned her top, and continued to keep his eyes averted whilst the baby suckled. Struck by a thought, Emma said, 'What about you and Luke? Would you both like to move in here?'

'No offence, Em, and I can't speak for Luke, but to be honest it's too far away from the market. Anyway, I rather like having my own place. After years of sleeping in that loft, it's heaven.'

Emma understood and hid her disappointment. 'All right, but I really do need to buy some things for the baby. Can you go to the pawnbroker now?'

'Yeah, all right. I suppose it won't hurt to leave the lad in charge of the stall for a bit longer. What do you want to sell?'

'Lad – what lad? Why isn't Luke on the stall?'

'He's having a bit of time off.'

Emma was distracted again when Patricia began to whimper. Wind, she thought, placing the baby against her chest and gently patting her back. That done, she decided a clean nappy could wait, and asked Dick to follow her into the drawing room.

'Here, would you like to hold her?' Emma asked, and as Dick took the baby, she considered the ornaments. There were so many that she loved and hated to part with, but with no other choice, she selected a fine porcelain figurine of a woman sitting on a panther.

'Horace made it clear when I came here as a cleaner that this is a valuable piece. It's Parian porcelain by Minton, so don't let the pawnbroker take you for a mug.'

'I'll do me best, Em,' Dick said. Passing the baby back again, he took the ornament. 'I shouldn't be long and we can talk about Luke when I come back.'

Emma walked with him to the door, her heart lighter now. The sale of the ornament would give her some much-needed money and time to make a longer-term plan.

*　　*　　*

It was over an hour later before Dick returned, handing her a few notes. 'This is the best I could do, Em.'

Emma stared at the money with dismay. 'But that ornament must have been worth more than this.'

'I didn't know enough about it to argue. He was a right old skinflint and, to be honest, I didn't have time to haggle. I've got to get back to the stall.'

'Oh, Dick, I'm so sorry. I should have realised that you wouldn't leave the stall unless it's important. You came to talk to me about Luke but I hardly gave you the chance.'

'It'll have to wait now. I'll pop back this evening.'

Emma nodded, laying a hand on Dick's arm. 'Thanks for going to the pawnshop for me. It was good of you, and though it isn't as much as I expected, this money will keep me going for a while. I bet Luke will be chuffed to hear I've had my baby. I can't wait to see his face this evening.'

Dick frowned. 'I won't bring Luke, not this evening. I need to speak to you alone first, Em.'

Emma saw the worry on her brother's face, but before she could question him further he turned to leave, insisting he had to get back to the stall and almost running from the house.

Emma was left chewing her bottom lip. She had been so wrapped up in the baby, in her own problems, that she had given little thought to what was worrying Dick. He was evidently concerned about Luke, agitated.

Wondering what the problem was, she now found herself waiting impatiently for his return.

It was seven o'clock before Dick knocked on the door, and Emma hurried to answer it. She led him through to the drawing room, and after a quick peep at Patricia, asleep in her drawer, he took a seat.

Emma saw that his face was still drawn with worry, but he sat, hanging his head, saying nothing. 'Come on, Dick, spit it out,' she urged.

He exhaled loudly. 'All right, but this ain't gonna be easy. Luke left home and he's staying at my place.'

'But why?'

'It took me ages to get it out of him, but apparently he came to his senses and when that happened, he couldn't stand the guilt.'

'Slow down, you're rambling and not making any sense.'

'Sorry, I'm doing my best. According to Luke, he's been keeping Polly happy.'

'Keeping her happy. What on earth do you mean?'

'Blimey, Em, do I have to spell it out?'

'Yes, because I don't understand what you're talking about.'

'Oh Christ, I don't know how to say this,' Dick

said, his face flushing. 'Polly has been . . . well . . . making Luke go with her.'

'Go with her! What do you mean?' The penny finally dropped and Emma stared at her brother in horror. 'No, surely not!' Emma continued to look at her brother in stunned dismay, but then a memory surfaced. Polly had once said something about loving too much, and in the wrong places. Luke! She had been talking about Luke!

'He's in a terrible state, Em, and spends more and more time at church. The guilt seems to be eating away at him.'

'What has Luke got to feel guilty about? My God, I can't believe this. What does Polly want with Luke? He's just a fifteen-year-old boy.'

'It started a few months after Dad married Polly. Luke feels bad because he enjoyed it. Well, he did at first, but then as I said, he came to his senses. I told him that he shouldn't feel guilty, that I enjoyed a bit of a feel too, and started with a girl behind the bike sheds at school.'

'But Polly isn't a schoolgirl. She . . . she's his stepmother! Have you told Dad?'

'No, not yet, but it was hard to keep my mouth shut. He came down to my place looking for Luke, but the lad became hysterical and begged me not to say anything.'

'So what excuse did you give him for Luke leaving home?'

'It was a bit sticky, but in the end I just said that he'd had a bit of a fall-out with Polly. I said that as I live nearer to the market, he might as well stay with me.'

Emma's mind was reeling. First Horace had left her, then she'd had the baby, and now this. She flopped back on the sofa. 'I don't know if I'm coming or going. I can't take this in.'

'Bloody hell, you've got enough on your plate and I should have kept my mouth shut. Come on, Luke's all right with me for now, and we can sort Polly out later.'

'But what about the girls? We can't leave them with that . . . that woman.'

'That's just it, Em. According to Luke, the girls are very fond of Polly, and she dotes on them. It would break their hearts if the family broke up; it would be like losing their mother all over again. The thought of putting them through that is tearing Luke apart and that's why he doesn't want us to say anything.'

Oh, poor Luke, Emma thought. Always the quiet and sensitive one, always so protective of the girls. Bile rose in her throat. 'But Polly isn't fit to be a mother. She must be sick in the head or something. My God, it . . . it's disgusting.'

Dick hung his head. Then, red-faced, he said, 'Look, some women are a bit mad for sex and I think Polly is one of them. Luke's a good-looking lad, and maybe she couldn't resist, but it doesn't mean that she's incapable of looking after the girls.'

'I can't believe you're saying that. Luke was a minor, under-aged. Surely it must be illegal.'

'Maybe, but if you get the police involved, it'll only make matters worse.'

'But we can't just do nothing, Dick, it wouldn't be right.'

'Yeah, I know, but so far Luke won't see it that way. Look, Em, it's obvious that you're not up to dealing with this now. I'll bring Luke down to see you on Sunday, and between the pair of us I'm sure we can persuade him to see sense.'

Emma wanted to argue, but in truth she needed time to think, to plan, to work out what they were going to do. 'Yes, all right.'

Dick rose to his feet. 'I know you're in a bit of a fix, Em, and I wish I could help you out a bit. I ain't got much in the way of money, but I can always supply you with fruit and vegetables.'

Emma stood up too, and went across to give her brother a cuddle. 'Thanks, love, but don't worry, I'll be fine. There are loads more ornaments to sell, along with a few other things.'

'Yeah, and I bet you can get more out of that old skinflint of a pawnbroker than I did. Anyway, I'd best be off. Take care and I'll see you on Sunday.'

It was only when Dick left that Emma's

emotions rose to the surface again, but she fought the tears. Crying solved nothing. Instead she was determined to help Luke. She felt a wave of disgust at what Polly had done, resolving not to let the woman get away with it. Not only that, now she could move Luke in here, and she was thrilled at the thought. It would be lovely to have her favourite brother close again, and she'd no longer be alone. In fact, the girls could move in too. There were still plenty of things to sell, and they'd be fine.

25

On Sunday afternoon, Emma opened the door to Dick and saw Luke hovering behind him. 'Come in,' she invited, but though Dick smiled, she saw that Luke kept his head lowered, and he continued to avoid her eyes as they went into the drawing room.

Patricia was asleep, but acted like a magnet to Luke, his expression brightening as he looked down on her. With just one finger he gently stroked her cheek.

'Hello, Tinker,' he whispered.

'Patricia,' Emma corrected.

'Yeah, Patricia, but I reckon she's gonna be a right little tinker.' He then smiled at last, adding, 'And with the surname of Bell, she'll be Tinker Bell.'

Emma chuckled. 'She's Patricia Myra Bell.'

'That's nice,' Dick said. 'Mum would've liked that.'

'Why is she sleeping in a drawer?' Luke asked.

'I haven't been well enough until now to get her a cot or anything else. I'm going shopping tomorrow, but without a pram it won't be easy.'

'I know a place that sells second-hand prams,' Dick said. 'Pop down to the market and I'll show you where it is.'

Emma would have loved a new pram for Patricia, but knowing that money was going to be tight, she nodded. 'Yes, I'll do that.'

'I'll give you a hand,' Luke said.

'Thanks, with so much to buy, it'll be welcome.'

They all fell silent, but then Dick blurted, 'Dad came down the market yesterday, and I told him you'd had the baby. Mind you, I didn't tell him that Horace has buggered off. If I did he'd be down here like a shot to see what he can get his hands on.'

'Yes, he would, and anyway, I don't want him here.'

Luke asked to use the bathroom, and as soon as he was out of sight, Dick said, 'Be gentle with him, Em.'

'Of course I will,' Emma said, and when Luke came back into the room she told him to sit down, perching beside him on the arm of the chair. 'Luke, I know you're upset, but we have to talk about what happened with Polly. For a start, Dad needs to know.'

'No!' Luke cried. 'You can't say anything to Dad or anyone else. It'll break up the marriage, and you can't do that to the girls.'

'Luke, can't you see that she isn't fit to look after them?'

'They think the world of her, Em, and it would break their hearts. Don't you understand – they see Polly as their mother now.' Luke stood up, pacing the room. 'Look, what we did was wrong and I shouldn't have gone along with it from the start, but I'm just as much to blame as Polly. Oh, Em, I hate myself for allowing it to happen.'

'Who instigated it, Luke?'

'Well, Polly did, but I should have said no.'

'Luke, you were only fourteen, a minor, and Polly knew that. She's the adult, the responsible one, and you're her stepson. What she did was terrible, sick, and we can't let her get away with it. In fact, I'm feeling much better and I think we should all go to Balham now. Dad's got to be told.'

'No! I'm not going anywhere near Dad. If you tell him, he . . . he'll kill me.'

'All right, calm down,' Dick placated, 'but you've got to see sense. Like us, Dad isn't going to blame you, so put that worry out of your mind. If you like, you can stay here. Emma and me will sort it out.'

'Emma and I,' she automatically corrected, and then flushed. From now on she could be herself, and if she used incorrect grammar, what did it matter? 'Sorry,' she murmured, 'force of habit, but Dick's right. You can stay here until we come back.'

'Please,' Luke begged, 'please don't go. It's over now, finished with, and I promise I'll never go near Polly again.'

'Oh, Luke, can't you see that what Polly did to you was tantamount to rape?'

Luke's face reddened. 'It *wasn't* rape!'

'All right, calm down,' Dick urged, and then obviously trying to break the tension he forced a laugh. 'Bloody hell, Em, what sort of word is "tantamount"?'

Emma went along with him. 'Oh, you have no idea how many new words I have in my vocabulary. Let me tell you, I could write a dictionary.'

'Listen, both of you,' Luke said, suddenly sounding older than his years. 'Don't you understand that if you bring this out into the open, it will be the girls who suffer? If Dad chucks Polly out, who'll look after them?'

'I'd already decided that they can come here – you too, Luke.'

'And what will you do for money, Em? From what Dick has told me, Horace has left you penniless.'

'I'll manage. I'll find a way.'

Luke's eyes took on a strange, unfocused look

that made Emma shiver. 'No, you won't, Em. In fact I have a feeling that things will become increasingly hard for you.'

Emma stared at Luke worriedly. He sounded so sure of himself. Patricia woke up squalling and she moved to pick her up.

Luke spoke again, his voice hard, and Emma hardly recognised her brother, the innocent boy gone. 'I'll tell you something else. If you tell Dad, if you tell anyone, I'll leave Battersea; in fact, I'll leave the bloody country.'

Emma shivered again. She knew that Luke meant every word. Oh, what had Polly done to her brother? She couldn't bear the thought of never seeing him again, she just couldn't.

Dick, too, looked horrified, but he shook his head in denial. 'Luke, leave it out. Don't say things like that.'

'What choice have you given me? Dad's going to go potty, and I can't, I *won't*, stay around here to see the girls hurt.'

Emma could see the hardness in Luke's eyes, the determination. 'He means it, Dick.' She paced up and down, her mind twisting and turning. 'All right, you win, we won't tell Dad. But even if I have to grin and bear it, having to sit in the same room as that bloody woman, I intend to keep an eye on her and the girls.'

Dick heaved a sigh. 'It still sticks in my craw,

but if it's the only way to stop you doing a runner, I'll go along with Emma.'

Luke seemed to fold, slumping onto a chair in obvious relief. Looking at him, Emma's back stiffened. All right, she may have to keep her mouth shut now, but one day the girls would grow up, leave home, and when that day came, by God she'd have her time with Polly.

26

Emma felt well enough to go shopping on Monday, but knowing it would be impossible to manage without a pram, she wrapped Patricia in a cut-down blanket, praying she wouldn't bump into anyone she knew as she went straight to the market.

Dick greeted her with a smile, but Luke still looked strained, though once again he brightened when he saw the baby. 'Hello, Tinker Bell.'

Resisting the urge to correct him, Emma said, 'Dick, where's this place that sells prams?'

'Come on, I'll show you. We aren't busy so Luke can manage the stall for a while. If you ask me, the nipper could do with some togs too.'

'I know that, but this is the first chance I've had to go shopping. After buying a pram I doubt I'll have any money left so I've brought another piece to take to the pawnbrokers. I've looked it up in one of Horace's catalogues, so this time I'll make sure I get a decent price.'

'Yeah, well, in that case you're bound to do better than me.'

They moved away from the stall, and were out of earshot before Dick spoke again. 'After leaving you yesterday, I sent Luke home and then went to Balham.'

'Did you say anything?'

'No, of course not, but if you ask me, Polly is worried sick. She must have asked me three times if Luke was all right.'

'What about the girls?'

'They're missing Luke, but he's right, they think the world of Polly. She also asked about you, about the baby, and when you'll be taking her to see them.'

Emma's mouth drooped. She wanted to see her sisters, to let them see Patricia, but dreaded being in Polly's company. With a sigh she said, 'All right, once I've got a pram and some decent clothes for Patricia, I'll go to Balham, but I'm not looking forward to it.'

'There's something else. If you ask me Polly is up to something. She was on about a letter she'd had from her sister and the possibility of a really good job for Dad.'

'Why does that mean she's up to something?'

"Cos the job is where her sister lives, and that's in Kent.'

Emma shook her head. 'There's no way Dad would move out of London, or give up a rent-free flat.'

'Now that Horace has gone, it may not stay rent free. Have you thought of that?'

The colour drained from Emma's face. God, she'd been too wrapped up in her own problems to give her father's flat a thought. She had no idea how Horace had wangled the rent, or if he was going to let it continue.

'I . . . I'll have to tell him that Horace has gone.'

'Yeah, I suppose so, but watch it, Em. You know what he's like and rather than pay rent, he might want to move in with you.'

'No! Never! I'd have the girls like a shot, but not him, or . . . or that woman.'

'Look, don't get in a state. If someone comes knocking for rent, you'll soon know about it. Dad will come marching down to see Horace, but until then, say nothing.'

Emma nodded, and when Dick indicated the shop, they went inside. She inspected the prams, a frown on her face. A lot of them were rusty, the insides dirty, but finally she found one that looked in a decent condition. It was large, well sprung, and opening the hood she couldn't see any sign of wear. 'I like this one,' she whispered to Dick.

'Leave the bargaining to me,' he hissed back,

and then Emma stood back to watch her brother's haggling skills.

They left with smiles on their faces, but Dick had to go back to the stall whilst Emma continued her shopping. Her first stop was the pawnbrokers. Handing him a small Royal Doulton figurine, she watched as the portly, almost bald man inspected it.

The bargaining began, the man trying to wear her down, but Emma wouldn't give in. She knew it was a valuable piece, and finally, when he offered her a price she felt was acceptable, they shook hands on the deal.

Her next stop was for bedding for the pram, which she immediately put into use, covering Patricia with a new pink, fluffy blanket. She then bought nappies and clothes, worried by how rapidly the money was going down, but then brightened. There were many ornaments left to sell, and if she continued to get good prices, there would be enough money to keep her going for a long time.

When Emma returned to the market, the pram piled high, Dick added to it, loading her with vegetables. 'But I can't take all this,' she protested.

'You can pay me back when you're on your feet,' Dick said dismissively. 'Are you still going to Balham today?'

'It's a fair old walk from my place, and to be honest, I'm worn out already. I'll go tomorrow.'

'All right. Let me know how you get on.'

Luke finished serving a customer, and joined them to hear the last part of this conversation, his expression anxious. 'You won't say anything, Em?'

'Don't worry, I won't,' she assured him and then gave both brothers impulsive hugs before moving away.

It was a long walk home, and by the time she got there, Emma was reeling with exhaustion. The birth had been hard, but surely she should have recovered by now? A wave of sadness washed over her. Her recovery might be slow, but if her mother had been in hospital, if she'd received the same medical attention, maybe she'd have survived a breech birth too. Oh, why was life so cruel?

Emma pulled the pram into the hall and, soothed by the movements, the baby remained asleep. She looked at her daughter's tiny, innocent face and felt a surge of love along with a fierce sense of protection. Yes, life was cruel, but she would do all in her power to make sure that Patricia was kept safe, wanting for nothing. Horace had abandoned them, but somehow she'd cope. Even when she had nothing else to sell, she'd find a way to make enough money to ensure that her daughter would never know poverty, but as Emma went through to the kitchen a small voice whispered, '*Yes, but how?*'

27

Polly had sent the girls out to play on Tuesday morning and was now alone in the kitchen. She'd be glad when the summer holidays were over and they were back at school. Yet it wasn't the girls who were upsetting her. She was worried sick and almost at the end of her tether. She couldn't stand it any more. She couldn't eat, couldn't sleep, the uncertainty agonising, and it had been like this every day since Luke had left home. She'd told Tom that the lad had been cheeky and had walked out when she had tried to discipline him, but then had stupidly overplayed the part of a concerned mother. Tom told her not to worry and had gone looking for Luke, whilst she sat at home shaking with nerves. If the lad opened his mouth, and his father believed him, she knew her marriage would be over.

When Tom returned he said that Luke was staying at Dick's and as they had fallen out, he wanted to remain there. Fallen out! God, she had almost fainted with relief.

What had possessed her? Why did she have these cravings? It was unnatural, she knew that, but they were so powerful that in frustration she had turned in desperation to Luke. Oh, he had protested at first, but gradually she knew he had come to love it as much as she did. It had been wonderful and she'd enjoyed initiating the lad, teaching him how to please her, but then he'd grown sullen, beginning to turn her down. God, why had she forced the issue? Why hadn't she stopped? But she hadn't, continuing to push him until one day he'd walked out without any explanation as to where he was going.

Polly rose to her feet, pacing the room. Her relief that Luke had said nothing was short-lived. When Dick had called round to see the girls he could hardly meet her eyes. She continued to pace, wringing her hands. Maybe she'd imagined it. Surely if Dick knew he'd have said something? Oh God, the uncertainty was driving her mad.

Polly's eyes flicked to the mantelpiece. Her sister's letter had been a godsend, a way out, but Tom still hadn't come to a decision. He had to agree, he just had to, and she'd try a little more persuasion when he came home from work. In the meantime she had to do something to occupy her mind or she'd go batty.

282

Polly set to work, giving the place a thorough clean, then tackled the ironing. By three in the afternoon she was worn out, but calmer, until there was a knock on the front door. God, who was that? Nervously, she opened it, forcing a smile when she saw Emma.

'Hello, love. Dick told us you'd had the baby. I can't wait to see her. We would have called round to see you, but well, we know how Horace feels about us coming to your place.'

'Yes, he can be difficult,' Emma said, her face set. 'Where shall I put the pram?'

'Bring it into the hall. I must say you look a bit pale. Surely you didn't walk all this way?'

'Yes, I did. I admit I feel a bit tired.'

'Leave the baby to me, love. Go and sit down.'

Emma didn't argue, but as Polly lifted the baby out of the pram, her heart was thumping in her ribs. Emma hadn't cracked a smile yet. Was it just that she was tired, or did she know? She looked at the baby, seeing a tiny face, a wisp of pale hair, and, carrying her through to the kitchen, she stood rocking her. 'She's lovely.'

Emma held out her arms, her face still straight. 'Thank you. I've called her Patricia Myra, after my mum.'

'That's nice,' Polly said as she laid the baby in Emma's arms. 'Now, would you like a cold drink or a cup of tea?'

283

'Something cold would be nice, thank you. Where are the girls?'

Emma was being so polite, so formal and as Polly poured her a glass of lemonade, her hands were shaking. 'They've gone out to play. Here, I expect you need this.' She handed over the glass. 'The girls will be chuffed to see the baby, she's a real little beauty.'

For the first time Emma smiled, though to Polly it looked forced. 'Yes, they're little aunties now.'

'Gawd, yeah, and Ann's only eight.'

The baby stared to cry and, frowning, Emma said, 'She seems to want a feed every couple of hours. Do you mind?' she added, opening her blouse.

'Of course not,' Polly said, and as she watched the baby suckling, the room grew silent for a minute or two.

'Oh, by the way, Polly. What's this Dick tells me about a job for Dad in Kent?'

'It's a good offer and more than a job,' Polly said eagerly. Perhaps Emma didn't know about Luke after all. 'But your dad hasn't made up his mind yet. You see, my sister and her husband, Alfie, have a little pub in Hythe, but she wrote to say that poor Alfie has passed away. She's devastated, and not only that, she's worrying about running the pub on her own. My sister is being more than generous, offering us an eventual partnership if we'll help her out.'

'Really!' Emma said, her eyes widening in surprise. 'And where would you live?'

'On the premises, above the pub.'

'And you say my dad hasn't made up his mind. I'm surprised that he hasn't jumped at the chance. Living above a pub would be his idea of heaven.'

'Oh, he was dead keen at first, but for some reason he went off the boil. I tried talking to him last night, but he just says he needs more time to make up his mind. If you ask me, he'd be mad to turn it down. After all, a partnership in a pub isn't something to be sniffed at. Maybe you could have a word with him, Emma?'

'Oh, I'd love to have a word with him,' Emma said, her eyes now hard, a chilly undertone in her voice, 'and about more than a job in a pub.'

She knew! God, she knew! Polly felt sick and, unbidden, the words blurted out. 'Don't tell him, Emma. Please, I beg you.'

'Don't tell him what?'

'Please, don't play games.' Polly rose to her feet, fear making her voice high. 'You have no idea how awful I feel. It was wrong of me, dreadful.'

'Couldn't help yourself! My God, what are you, sex mad or something?'

'I dunno, Em, it's just that when your dad lost interest, I couldn't help myself.'

'God, you make me sick!'

'Is . . . is Luke all right?'

'No he isn't,' Emma spat. 'He's eaten up with guilt. Not that *he* should be the one feeling guilty.'

'Emma, please, I'm so sorry, but I beg you, don't tell your father.'

'Luke also begged me not to, and I agreed, but I'm not happy about it.'

Emma was looking at her as if she was dirt under her feet and Polly hung her head. The girl was eighteen now, but she sounded so much older, her voice hard and her manner unforgiving.

'I can understand how you feel, but honestly, Emma, I hate being like this.'

'Then you should try to get some sort of help.'

'Do you think that's possible?'

Emma's expression was still hard. 'I hope so, but it's a shame you didn't think of getting help before you ruined my brother.'

Polly felt tears gathering in her eyes, but the sound of the girls coming in from outside carried in and she quickly dashed them away.

Ann was the first through the door, running straight to her and jumping onto her lap.

'My friend's dog has had puppies and we've been to see them. Can we have one, Mummy, can we?'

'You'll have to ask your dad, darling,' she said, hugging the child to her. Ann was a smashing kid, sweet and loving, and suddenly realising how close she was to losing her, to losing her marriage, a sob rose in her throat.

Thankfully, Ann jumped off her lap, running to Emma and too distracted by the baby to notice. Both Bella and Susan crowded round their sister, all cooing.

'Look at her little hands,' Bella cried. 'Can I hold her, Emma?'

'No, I want to hold her,' Susan demanded.

'Now then, don't argue,' Emma said. 'If she's jiggled about she'll be sick.'

Susan pulled a face, but then she turned away, running to Polly. 'I'm hungry. Can I have a piece of cake?'

Polly struggled to pull herself together. 'Yes, but a small slice or you'll spoil your dinner.'

Susan gave her a swift kiss on the cheek before hurrying to find the cake tin, and now Bella asked, 'Can I have a bit too, Mummy?'

'Of course you can, and give some to Ann.'

Emma spoke, her voice low but her tone still hard. 'I can see they're still fond of you, not that you deserve it.'

'Don't you think I know that?' Polly hissed. 'They're lovely kids and I . . . I think the world of them too.'

'At least you haven't ruined them like you've ruined Luke.'

'Oh, Emma, don't exaggerate. Given time he'll get over it.' Polly looked into Emma's eyes and felt a wave of fear. She was making matters worse, and if she didn't watch her tongue, Emma wouldn't keep her mouth shut. Suddenly she felt sick, her stomach churning and, holding a hand over her mouth, she dashed to the bathroom.

Despite seeing how loving the girls were towards Polly, Emma couldn't help feeling disgusted every time she looked at the woman.

While Bella and Ann were munching on their cake, Emma laid the baby on the sofa and they stared at her in fascination.

'She's gorgeous,' Susan said in awe. 'Look at her tiny fingers and toes!'

'Yeah, she's like a little doll,' Bella said.

'Hello,' Susan cooed. 'I'm your auntie.'

It was lovely to see and Emma smiled, but the smile quickly disappeared. If her father took the job in Kent, they would all be so far away. Emma had to try, had to see if she could keep them close. 'Do you know, I've got loads of room in my house. How would you all feel about moving in with me?'

'Cor, I'd like that, Em,' Susan said. 'We could see the baby every day then.'

'Yeah, me too,' Bella agreed. 'You've got a lovely big garden.'

Emma took a deep breath. 'Of course it would mean leaving Polly and Dad behind.'

'Leave our mum and dad! Oh, no, I don't want to do that,' Susan gasped.

'Why can't they come too?'

Emma was about to answer when Polly came back into the room, the girls immediately crowding around her. 'Mum, we don't want to live in Emma's house without you,' Susan cried.

'What's all this about, Emma?' Polly asked, ashen-faced.

'I thought that if you and my father move to Kent, the girls could stay with me.'

'No, Mummy, don't go, don't leave us,' Bella cried, clinging to Polly's skirt. 'Take us with you.'

'Of course we will. Me and your dad wouldn't go anywhere without you.'

Their cries had set Patricia off, Emma moving to pick her up. 'Look, it was just an idea, that's all.'

It took a while for Polly to calm the girls down. Finally she managed, but Emma could see the sullen look that remained on Susan's face. Ann refused to leave Polly's side and, watching the scene, Emma realised that as much as she didn't like it, Luke was right: it would break the girls' hearts if they lost Polly and she couldn't do that to them. They'd already suffered enough tragedy in their young lives. If they moved to Kent, she would have to let them go, but the thought saddened her so much that she found herself fighting back tears.

Emma rose brusquely to her feet. She had to

get out of there or she'd break down. 'I'd best be off.'

Usually there were protests when she left, but this time Ann was the only one who seemed unhappy to see her leave.

As Emma placed Patricia in her pram in the hall, Polly managed to extract herself from Ann and followed behind. 'Emma, please, I'm worried sick. You won't change your mind, will you? You won't tell your dad?'

'No, Polly, I won't say anything, but I think you need to get help.'

'Oh, I will, Emma, I promise.'

Emma knew she would have to be content with that.

On the way home she decided she would tell Dick what had happened, but would keep her confrontation with Polly from Luke. She didn't want him upset again, still nervous that he might carry out his threat to leave the area. It was bad enough that the girls might be leaving for Kent, without losing her brother too.

28

Tom leaned on the bar, staring down into his pint of beer. He might live in Balham now, but he still saw his mates and heard the rumours. He still couldn't take them in, but according to the latest gossip, Horace Bell had buggered off and there was to be a new agent in the area collecting rents. He shook his head. Surely it couldn't be true? Dick had told him that Emma had given birth, but had made no mention of Horace leaving the girl.

Tom frowned. Not only that, nowadays there was a strange atmosphere at home. Polly was skittish, a bundle of nerves, and he had no idea why. At first he'd thought it was because of the falling-out she'd had with Luke and the boy leaving home. Maybe she thought he'd do his nut about it. No, that couldn't be it. The lad had been cheeky and Tom had sided with Polly, telling her that as far as he was concerned Luke could stay away. He was old enough to live with Dick now.

His sons were working the stall and he was still smarting about that. When Charlie had left it to Dick, Tom had seen it as a way to get off the bloody building sites. Dick was too young to take over the pitch, so he planned to sign up for it, running the stall with the boy working for him.

Tom swallowed a mouthful of beer, a scowl on his face as he swiped a hand across his mouth. He'd been well scuppered. Someone else had signed up for the pitch, and the bloke had told him in no uncertain terms that Dick was working for him. It was a lie, of course, but he couldn't prove anything, and that bloody lot down the market must have been laughing at him behind his back.

His thoughts shifted again. When he went home, Polly would start again about the pub in Kent. At first he'd been keen – well, until he'd heard the latest rumour about Horace. If it *was* true, and the man had buggered off, had he left Emma that big house? Christ, it must be worth a fortune, and if he could persuade Emma to sell it, then sod a possible partnership of a pub in Kent! They could have a pub of their own.

He downed the last of his pint, slamming the glass on the bar. Well, there was only one way to find out, and so he set off to see Emma.

The evening was hot and muggy, but at last he

arrived at Emma's house, and she opened the door, obviously surprised to see him.

'Dad, what are you doing here?'

'I thought I'd pop down to see my new grand-child.'

With reluctance, she stepped to one side. 'All right, you'd better come in.'

Tom's eyes flicked around as they went into Emma's posh drawing room. 'Is Horace in?'

'Er . . . no. He . . . he's out on business.'

'But it's after eight o'clock.'

'He's often late.'

'So, the rumours ain't true then?'

'What rumours?'

'There's talk that Horace has left you.'

He saw the colour drain from Emma's face. She lowered her head, but then with an audible sigh she admitted, 'I should have known there'd be gossip. Yes, Horace has left me.'

'Blimey, girl, this must be the shortest marriage in history! Why did he leave?'

'I don't know,' she said, but then her tone hardened. 'Why are you here, Dad? You certainly haven't come to see the baby.'

'I came to see if you're all right.'

Cold eyes met his. 'Don't give me that. What are you after?'

'Well, that's nice, ain't it? I'm not after anything. It's like I said, I came to see if you're all right.'

293

'I'm fine. If you must know I'm glad that Horace has gone.'

'Really? Well, he must have left you sitting pretty then. You've got this place and no doubt a good few bob too.'

'No, Dad, he's left me with nothing. You seem to forget that Horace isn't the rich man he pretended to be.'

'Rubbish! I know he told you he was only an agent, but if you ask me you were daft to believe it. He's rich, all right, and you should make sure you get your fair share.'

'Look, even if what you say is true, which I doubt, how am I supposed to find Horace? He could be anywhere, and if he's as well off as you claim, he'll have made sure I can't get my hands on his money.'

'You could see a lawyer.'

'With what, Dad? A lawyer would cost money. Money I haven't got.'

'There's this place. You could sell it. In fact, I've been giving it some thought. You'd get a good price and we could buy a business, a pub for instance.'

'So that's it!' Emma cried. 'My God, you've got it all worked out, haven't you? But you can forget it. The house isn't mine, it's in Horace's name, and even if I could sell it, buying a pub is the last thing I'd do.'

'There's no need to shout. It was just a suggestion, that's all. Anyway, you must have some rights and I still think you should see a lawyer or something. Here, I've just had another thought. Did Horace say anything about my place?'

'No, he didn't, but if you have to start paying rent it wouldn't be the end of the world.'

'Leave it out! With a place like mine the rent wouldn't be peanuts.' Tom's eyes flicked around the huge room, taking in the plush furniture, the drinks cabinet, the luxurious rugs. He brightened. 'Sod the flat. You've got plenty of room; we can all move in here.'

'There's no way on earth I'd let you move in here!'

'Why not? I'm your father.'

'You dare to ask me why? You came here for one reason, one reason only, and that was because you thought I had money you could get your hands on.' Emma shook her head in disgust. 'Just get out, and don't come back.'

'Who do you think you're talking to? I'm your father, and you should show me some respect.'

'Respect! You forced me into this marriage, and . . . and, worse, if it wasn't for you my mother would still be alive.'

'Why you . . . you . . .' Tom growled. He moved forward, his hand raised to strike her.

Emma stepped back and snatched up the poker, which she brandished at him. 'I said get out!'

Tom froze. It was as if his late wife was standing before him. The same face, the golden hair, the vivid blue eyes. Of course it wasn't Myra, it was Emma, but the anger drained from his body. Unable to stand the vision and without another word, he turned on his heels, feeling sick to his stomach as he stomped from the house.

Tom walked home. He could have gone to the underground station and caught a train, but he was swamped with self-pity, his head low as he crossed Clapham Common. God, what was going on with his kids? First Dick had stolen the stall from under his feet, and now Emma had ruined any plans he had of running his own pub. All right, so she couldn't sell the house, but you'd think she'd want them to live with her. After all, it was like a bloody palace!

Anger flared to replace self-pity. Well, sod them. Sod Dick, Luke and Emma. They would stew in their own bloody juices from now on. He'd cut them out of his life, and they'd be no loss. Tight-lipped, he thought about Horace Bell. The bastard! He'd promised a rent-free flat, but now an agent would be calling, demanding rent that he wasn't prepared to pay. Well, sod him too.

By the time Tom arrived home, his mind was made up. Throwing open the door, he yelled, 'Polly! Where are you?'

'Blimey, Tom,' she said, scuttling from the

kitchen. 'Where have you been? Your dinner's ruined.'

'Never mind that. First thing in the morning, start packing. We're going to Kent.'

As the door slammed behind her father, Emma slumped, the poker falling from her hand and landing with a thump on the floor. Tears came then, tears that she was unable to control since giving birth to Patricia. She knew she was an emotional wreck, but was powerless to do anything about it. She had to pull herself together, but one awful event seemed to follow another and she just couldn't cope. She wanted to shut herself away from all of them, to be left in peace. Patricia needed her, needed a mother who wasn't falling apart at the seams, and until she regained her self-control, she'd have to stay away from her family.

The decision made, Emma felt a surge of relief. She fed Patricia, changed her, and then cradled the baby in her arms as she went upstairs. She wanted only to go to bed, to sleep, and to shut out the world.

29

It was five days later, and Emma hadn't left the house. Depression overwhelmed her. She went through the motions, feeding and caring for Patricia, but cared nothing for her own appearance. Her nightclothes remained on all day, the curtains drawn against the outside world.

Someone had called, but she ignored the rapping on the door. It would be one of her family, wanting something from her that she just couldn't give. Emotionally she was drained. Her hair was lank, her body unwashed, but she didn't care, didn't notice, and most of the day when the baby was asleep, she would doze too.

It was now seven in the evening and someone was knocking on the door again. Emma didn't move, just wanting whoever it was to go away. At last the rapping stopped, quiet once again descending, but shortly after she heard another sound. Someone was coming in, footsteps crossing the hall, and she sat up on the sofa, staring fearfully at the door.

'Emma, thank Christ! We've been worried sick.'

Luke and Dick stood there, both looking anxious, but she felt only despondency. Why couldn't they just leave her alone? 'How . . . how did you get in?'

'We used the side door, and it's a bit dodgy that you left it unlocked,' Dick said, moving further into the room. 'You look terrible. Are you all right?'

'I've got a headache, that's all.'

'No, Em, there's more to this than a headache. Christ, look at you! When was the last time you had a wash or combed your hair?'

Emma said nothing.

Luke moved forward now, his eyes dark with worry, but unlike Dick, he didn't comment on her appearance, saying only, 'Dad's gone, Emma. He took that offer in Kent and they've all gone. We wouldn't have known if Dick hadn't called round to see the girls. Would you believe that Dad was going to leave without telling us?'

Emma tried to rally herself, attempted to take an interest, but instead, and unbidden, she found tears spurting from her eyes. She felt the seat dip beside her, an arm wrapping itself around her shoulder and Luke saying, 'Don't take on so, Em. I know you'll miss the girls, but Dick said they were really excited about moving to the country.'

She felt strange, her head buzzing, and as darkness descended, the last thing she heard before passing out, was Luke's frightened cry.

When Emma came to she found herself laid out on the sofa, her brothers looking down at her worriedly.

Dick perched himself beside her. 'Emma, you fainted. Are you feeling all right?'

'Yes,' she said, but as she tried to sit up, her head was still swimming.

'Luke, make Emma a cup of tea, and see that it's strong.'

As soon as he left the room, Dick said, 'Do you want me to find a doctor to have a look at you?'

'No, no, I'm all right.'

'Em, we've called before, but when you didn't come to the door, we thought you were out. I ain't being funny, love, but you stink to high heaven.'

'I . . . I just wanted a bit of peace, that's all.'

'Leave it out, this ain't like you. What's going on?'

'Please, Dick, I don't feel like talking.'

He was quiet for a moment, chewing on his bottom lip, but then as Patricia stirred, he said, 'Hold on, when I come to think about it, I can remember Mum acting like this once, just after she had Archie. I was about twelve at the time and if I remember rightly Alice Moon took over. She told us not to worry, that some women get like it after having a baby.'

Yes, Emma remembered as well. Her mother had cried a lot too, slept a lot, her mood low. Maybe she was suffering with the same problem, but the thought didn't comfort her. She closed her eyes, wanting only to sleep.

'Come on, buck up,' Dick said, but she ignored him.

She heard Luke returning to the room, the rattle of a cup in the saucer, and then whispered voices. Dick touched her arm and she opened her eyes. 'When was the last time you had anything to eat, Em?'

'I don't know, this morning maybe,' she said tiredly.

'Listen, love, Luke's gonna stay with you for a while, just until you get on your feet.'

There was a time when Emma would have welcomed Luke with open arms but not now. All she wanted now was to go back to sleep. 'No, please, there's no need.'

'There's no point in arguing, Em. He's staying, and that's that.'

Emma wanted to protest again, but found her eyelids drooping. She closed her eyes instead, sinking back into the darkness.

* * *

It took a few weeks, but at last Emma took an interest in life again. Luke had been marvellous, trying to arouse her interest with snippets of information, the latest being that Princess Elizabeth had given birth to her second baby, this time a girl called Anne. With something in common with her favourite princess, she managed a smile.

Emma had to admit that Luke was marvellous with Patricia. Of course he insisted on calling her Tinker – Dick too – and somehow the name had stuck. Until now she hadn't thought about the stall, or how Dick was coping, but when he called round one evening in late October, she asked him anxiously.

'Oh, don't worry. I took on a lad to help me out and he's doing all right.'

'I'm fine now so there's no reason why Luke can't return to work.'

A glance passed between her brothers, and she saw Dick shake his head.

'What's going on?' she asked. 'Is there something you're not telling me?'

'It's nothing for you to worry about,' Dick said.

'Stop treating me like a child! I told you, I'm fine now.'

'She'll have to be told, Dick. It can't wait much longer.'

'All right, tell her, but I just hope it doesn't set her off again.'

Luke swallowed deeply. 'I'm not going back to work on the stall, Em.'

'You aren't, but why?'

'It just isn't my cup of tea. Oh, don't get me wrong, it was great of Dick to take me on, and to let me live with him, but it's made me realise that it isn't what I want to do with my life.'

'There's nothing wrong with that. Are you going to learn a trade?'

'Well, yes, in a way. You see I'm going to Ireland, to a sort of school, then college, and . . . and eventually I hope to become a priest.'

'What! But you aren't even a Catholic; we don't belong to any Church.'

'I've been going to church for years, Em.'

She stared at her brother in amazement. 'You have? But I thought it was only recently.'

'I used to sneak off to St Margaret's every chance I got. I didn't say anything, because, let's face it, Em, you'd all have laughed at me, especially Dad.'

'No, Luke, I for one wouldn't have laughed. But hold on . . . surely you're too young for this? Surely you need Dad's permission?'

'He gave it, Em, though he treated it as a joke. What we haven't told you is that before Dad left for Kent, Father O'Malley went to see him.'

Emma swallowed deeply. Was Luke serious or, like her, was he trying to run away from life? He must still be racked with guilt over Polly, and thought this was the only way to make amends. 'Luke, are you doing this to clear your conscience? Because if you are there's no need. The fault lies with Polly – you didn't do anything wrong.'

'Em, this has nothing to do with Polly. Yes, I've been tearing myself apart over it, but I've been to confession and made my penance. I've also been praying, and have found peace now.'

'You're . . . you're not running away then?'

'No, of course not. I don't know how to explain this, Emma, but you see, when I'm at church I feel a sort of calling. I resisted it at first, but once I allowed my heart to open to God, I felt such a sense of relief, as if my whole life had led me to this point.'

'But, Luke, you're so young and . . . and Ireland! We'll never see you.'

'Believe me, this isn't something I've taken lightly and it hasn't been easy to arrange.'

Once again Emma stared at Luke. Now that she had got over the shock, she wasn't all that surprised. He had always been different, somehow spiritual, but he'd be so far away! Unbidden, tears welled again.

'Oh, Em, please don't cry.'

'Everyone has gone,' she sobbed. 'First the girls to Kent, and I didn't get a chance to say goodbye. Now you're going away too.'

'We'll keep in touch, Em. I promise,' Luke said.

'I ain't going anywhere,' Dick said. Trying to lighten the atmosphere, he added, 'Come on, Em. You've still got me, and little Tinker.'

Luke looked so anxious and, seeing this, Emma managed to smile through her tears. She took his hand. 'As long as you're happy, that's all that matters, but I'm going to miss you so much.'

'I'll miss you too, but I have to do this, Em.'

'When are you leaving?'

'On Monday.'

'What! So soon?'

'Yes, it's all arranged, but I must admit I've been getting a bit worried. You've been rough for weeks and I couldn't have left you in that state.'

'Well, I'm fine now,' she said lightly, adding, 'and no doubt you've been praying for my recovery.'

'Yes, and it seems my prayers have been answered. You're like your old self again, and as Dick said, you've still got him.'

Emma didn't voice her thoughts. Yes, she still had Dick and she loved her brother, but he wasn't Luke. *Oh Mum, I wonder how you would have felt about this? Your son is going to be a priest.*

'Emma, I know that Horace has left you in a fix, but you won't do anything silly, will you?' Luke asked.

'Silly? What do you mean?'

'I don't know. But if things ever become desperate, go to Dick. He'll help you out.'

'Yeah, I can still chuck a few vegetables your way,' Dick said.

'I'll be fine, Luke. I've still got loads of stuff to sell, enough to keep me going for ages.'

He nodded, his face clearing of concern. 'Yes, of course you have.'

Emma smiled. Just hark at the pair of them, acting as though she was a child that needed babysitting. Mind you, she must have given them both a bit of a scare. Still, she was all right now, and from now on she'd sort her own life out, stand on her own two feet. Yes, she'd miss Luke, miss him badly, but she had Dick, and best of all, she had her lovely daughter. It was time for a fresh start.

30

By the time almost another year had passed, instead of growing closer, Emma and Dick had drifted apart. Dick was courting now, spending most evenings with Mandy, a local girl from a large family who had taken Dick under their wing. The whole family were Salvationists, and though Dick hadn't joined the Sally Army yet, Emma had a feeling that it was only a matter of time. She had met Mandy, a buxom, homely girl who obviously thought the world of Dick, but their visits were rare nowadays, and likewise, she stayed away from Dick's stall, embarrassed by the way he always loaded her up with vegetables. But oh, how she could do with some now.

It was odd really. If anyone had predicted that both Luke and Dick would become tied up in religion, she'd have laughed, thinking it ridiculous. Well, maybe not with Luke, as he'd always been different and she had recognised his spirituality, but it was the last thing she expected of Dick. As a child he had been a bit of a rogue, stealing to keep the family going.

She heard from Luke occasionally, intent on his studies in Ireland. It seemed so long since she had seen him. He had his own life now, his ever-deepening beliefs and goals, and the distance between them seemed to grow wider.

There wasn't much left to sell now, and Emma was growing desperate. The ornaments had been depleted a long time ago, and then she had started on the paintings and furniture. The dining room was empty, the lovely inlaid mahogany chairs, along with the table, fetching a good price from an antique dealer. The once plush drawing room looked almost empty too, with only one sofa and a side table that was too scratched to sell. With Patricia to look after, a job was impossible, and it would be years yet before she started school.

The winter had been awful, fuel Emma's main concern, but now it was a hot July evening and as she stood looking out of the window, her stomach rumbled with hunger. The woman was there again, standing at the edge of the Common and hanging around for a pick-up as usual. She'd been there every night for a week now and Emma's lips once again tightened. A prostitute. A woman who sold her body for money. How could she do that? How could she stand sex with so many different men?

Emma shuddered. She had thought it bad enough with Horace, and he'd been her husband. There had been no word from him, no sightings, and no rumours about where he might be. Sometimes she wondered if her father had been right, that Horace was a rich man. As he hadn't carried out his threat to sell this house from under her, maybe it was true. Oh, what did it matter? She'd never be able to find him and, if truth be known, desperate as she was, she didn't want to. She was still his wife, this was still his house, and the thought of his return only filled her with dread.

Emma's eyes remained on the woman as her thoughts continued to turn. She had written to her sisters and Polly, only to get a reply from her father saying that he and they wanted nothing to do with her. Emma didn't believe him, sure that they hadn't been given the letters. One day, when she could afford it, and despite what her father said, she was determined to travel to Kent to see her sisters.

She missed her family, missed the closeness they had once shared. In truth, she was lonely. Yet she had become reclusive, keeping away from her neighbours because she was ashamed at the thought of them calling round and seeing the inside of her house. There were no comforts now, and with the sale of so much, the large rooms looked desolate. She had no friends – her marriage to Horace had seen to that – and, other than going out to sell things or to the shops, she spent all of her time alone with just Patricia for company.

Emma's eyes widened. A man had approached the woman, his arms waving in obvious anger. The prostitute backed away, but not far enough and he floored her with one blow. She was still on the ground when he started to kick her, the woman curling into a ball. Emma continued to watch, horrified as he lashed out, his heavy boots driving again and again into her defenceless body.

Frozen to the spot, Emma was unable to think coherently, but then instinct took over. She had to do something – anything – and without thought she flew outside.

'Hey!' she yelled from the end of the drive. 'Stop or I'll call the police!'

The man heard her. He delivered one last kick before running off across the Common. Emma remained where she was, but when she saw no movement from the woman, she ran across the road, flinging herself down onto the grass by her side. 'Are you all right?'

There a groan and, as she turned her head, Emma saw that the woman's nose was streaming with blood. 'Gawd,' she gasped. 'Has he gone?'

'Yes, he ran off,' Emma said, hurriedly pulling

312

a handkerchief from her sleeve and handing to the woman. 'Why did he attack you like that?'

'I dunno. I've never seen him before in me life.'

She tried to move, but gasped in pain, and Emma floundered. What should she do? She couldn't leave the woman in this state.

'If you think you can make it, I only live across the road. Come on, let me help you up,' she said impulsively.

It took a while, each movement obviously agony for the woman, but at last, leaning heavily on Emma, she staggered up the drive and through to the kitchen.

As soon as the woman was sitting down, Emma rushed to the sink, wetted a tea towel and handed it to her. 'Here, put that to your nose to stem the blood.'

She then set the kettle on to boil, but with only a tiny amount of tea left she had to leave it to brew for a while before pouring it. Even so, it was weak, but the woman didn't seem to notice as she gulped it down.

'Thanks, ducks,' she gasped. 'Christ, every breath feels like agony.'

'You may have broken ribs or something. I think you should see a doctor.'

'No, I'll be all right. I've had worse.'

'What! Have you been beaten up before?'

'Yeah, a few times. It's a risk of the game.'

Emma at last took a seat, unable to resist asking, 'Why do you do it?'

'Look, love, I appreciate your help, but don't go all high and mighty on me. All right, I'm on the game, but why I do it is my business. I'm fine now and I'll get out of your hair.' She tried to stand, but cried out, collapsing back onto the chair.

'You can't leave in that state,' Emma told her.

'I can't stay here.'

'Until you're feeling better, you'll have to,' Emma said firmly. 'Now come on, I think you'd better lie down. Can you manage to walk to the drawing room?'

'If you insist, I'll give it a go.'

Emma returned her smile. Strangely enough, she found herself liking the woman. A woman she had looked down on with disgust. There was something about her, something honest and straightforward, and Emma was happy to have some company at long last.

Three days passed, and Doris Hewlett slowly recovered. Without her thick make-up she was attractive, about thirty, with shoulder-length brunette hair and warm brown eyes. When she was up to it, the two women talked, their conversations stilted at first, but gradually an unlikely friendship began to form. Emma found that she could talk to Doris as she had never spoken to anyone before. She talked about her childhood, her mother's death, her family, the marriage to Horace, and Doris listened without censure.

When she realised Emma's financial situation she dug into her pocket, handing over five shillings. 'Here,' she urged. 'Go and get some grub in. Tasty as it is, I'm sick to death of that vegetable stew that you live on.'

'No, I can't take your money.'

'Why not? Ain't it good enough for you? Do you think it's tainted?'

'Oh, Doris, of course I don't. To do what you've been doing, you must be desperate for money, and well, taking it from you wouldn't be right.'

Doris heaved herself up, the effort obviously painful. 'You've told me all about yourself, and now it's my turn. I just wish I could get off this sofa and go home. My poor mum must be worried sick. No doubt the old girl next door is keeping an eye on her, but even so, I need to get back.'

'Your mother!'

'Don't look so shocked, love. Of course I've got a mother, but she's all I've got.'

'What happened to your father?'

'I've never had one of those. Christ, you're looking shocked again. Bloody hell, you're a married woman, you've had a baby, but you still seem so innocent. Look, my mother was left pregnant when the bloke ran off. She brought me up on her own, and I can tell you she had a hard time of it. Now, though, she's ill, confined to her bed, and it's my turn to look after her.'

'Is that why you became a ... a ...'

'A tart,' Doris supplied. 'You can use the word, I don't care. Yeah, it was how I got started, and anyway, doing this is the only way I can earn enough to support us.'

'I still don't understand why you get beaten up.'

'Neither do I, but it happens. Maybe some men get a kick out of giving prostitutes a hiding, maybe they can't do the act and it's a way of getting rid of their frustration.' She shrugged. 'I've been on the game since the war, and nothing about men surprises me any more.'

'You haven't always done it then?'

'No, love, I had a legitimate job once, but when my mum got so ill that she couldn't get out of bed, I had to give it up.'

'She must have been ill for a long time.'

'Yes, she has, and she's steadily getting worse. Still, as I said, the old girl next door is as good as gold and sits with her every evening while I'm working, but I can't expect her to do it all day too.'

'Does ... does your mother know what you do?'

'I don't think so. Mind you, she may have her suspicions. I pay the rent, buy her medicine, feed us, and she must wonder how I manage to do it when I only go out to work in the evenings. Still, she's never asked, not even when I go home with the occasional black eye, and I ain't about to tell her.'

'And . . . and you don't mind doing it?'

'Well, I can't say I enjoy it, but I shut my mind until it's over.'

'When my husband wanted me, I could only relax with the aid of sherry.'

'Blimey, I can't see you as a drinker! Now, me, I got started when the Yanks came over and one of them took me up an alley for a bit of a slap and tickle. Things got out of hand, and, well, it happened. What I didn't expect was the pound note he shoved in my hand afterwards. Bloody hell, a pound, and all for a bit of loving.'

'A pound! As much as that?'

'Yeah, but I never struck that lucky again. Still, with lots of lonely soldiers about who were willing to pay, it seemed so easy. Nowadays I don't make that much money, but more than I'd get working behind a bar or something. Mind you, I'd earn decent money if I could rent a room and it ain't much fun doing it up an alley or against a tree.'

'Why don't you rent a room?'

'I can't stay in one place for long. If I don't

keep moving about a flaming pimp will get hold of me.'

'What's a pimp?'

'A bastard, a leech who says he'll look after you, but then takes almost every penny you earn. Once they get hold of you, it's impossible to get away, and if you think I've had a beating, you should see what they do to their girls if they don't do as they're told.' She sank back, her eyes drooping. 'Gawd, I feel rough.'

Emma knew that Doris still tired easily, but she refused to see a doctor. 'Just rest and I'll go to see if my daughter's awake.'

Quietly leaving the room, Emma went upstairs, Patricia stirring as she went into the room. She was a beautiful child, blonde and blue-eyed like her mother, and though she couldn't walk yet, she could get around by crawling.

'Come on, Tinker,' Emma said, lifting her out of her cot. 'Let's get you changed and smartened up.'

The toddler grinned, touching Emma's cheek. It was strange really. She always smiled when called Tinker, her given name not having the same effect. It didn't take Emma long to get her bathed, Tinker loving the water, splashing and soaking them both as usual. When she took her downstairs, Doris was dozing, but she opened her eyes as they walked into the room.

'She's a doll,' she said. 'I wish I could hold her, but it's too painful.'

Emma put Tinker onto the floor, and though she was unused to strangers, it surprised Emma how quickly she had taken to Doris. She immediately went on all fours, crawling across to the sofa, holding onto the edge to pull herself up on sturdy little legs.

'Hello, darling,' Doris said, gently touching her face. 'I reckon you'll be walking soon.'

Tinker chuckled as though she understood every word.

Doris said, 'Please, Emma, take this five bob to buy some grub, and would you do me a favour? If I tell you where I live, will you pop down to my place and let my mum know that I'm all right? Make up some story; tell her I had a little accident or something, but that I'll be able to come home soon.'

'Yes, of course I will, and all right, I'll take the money. I'll buy some tea, but it'll only be three ounces a head as usual. It's about time this rationing ended, but with any luck I'll be able to get a bit of meat, maybe a belly of pork.'

'That sounds lovely, and if my mum needs anything, here's another few bob.'

'Where do you live?'

'In Emerson Street. Go down Mysore Road and on the other side of Lavender Hill, you'll see

Lavender Hill Road. Go to the bottom and cross over, taking the third street on the right . . .'

Emma struggled to take in the directions. It was a long walk and in an area she was unfamiliar with. 'But why did you come all this way to . . . to work?'

'I told you,' she said tiredly. 'I have to keep moving around.'

Emma sighed. 'Well, I'd best get a move on then.'

'Thanks, love.'

Emma picked Tinker up, put her into the pram and heaved it outside. She decided to go to Emerson Street first, but it was a hot, sultry day and by the time she was walking down Lavender Hill Road, she was wet with perspiration. Her thoughts roamed. Who'd have thought she'd become friends with a prostitute? But now that she was getting to know Doris, her preconceptions had changed. She had looked down on her type in the past, thinking them disgusting, but Doris had changed all that. She liked the woman, although she would never like her occupation, one that not only appalled her, but seemed fraught with danger.

Emma at last turned into Doris's street, seeing a row of terraced houses with front doors leading straight onto the narrow pavement. Doris's house looked run down, dilapidated, but when she tentatively knocked on the door it was opened by a statuesque, elderly lady.

'Can I have a word with Mrs Hewlett?' Emma asked. 'I have news of her daughter.'

'Well, thank the Lord for that. Is she all right? Gertie's been going out of her mind with worry.' Before Emma could summon a reply she added, 'Do you want to bring that pram inside?'

Emma nodded, manoeuvring the pram into the small room, the woman still not giving her time to speak. 'I'll just pop up to tell Gertie you're here.'

She was soon back and, nodding at Tinker, she said, 'Go on up. I'll keep an eye on the nipper.'

Surprisingly, Tinker was smiling at the old lady, obviously liking what she saw. 'Thank you,' Emma said.

She climbed the stairs, her face stretching when she saw the old, wizened lady in the bed. This couldn't be Doris's mother – she looked more as if she would be her gran. 'Mrs Hewlett?'

'Speak up, love, I can't hear you. Are you here about my Doris?'

Emma approached the bed with her rehearsed story. 'She's been in an accident and is in hospital, but don't worry, it's nothing serious. She'll be home in a few days.'

'Accident! What sort of accident?'

'She . . . she fell when the bus she was on braked

321

sharply. Most of her injuries are minor, a bruised nose, but she also cracked a few ribs.'

'Blimey, the poor girl. But it ain't the first time. I reckon she's a bit accident prone. She's always bumping into things and bruising her face. I think she might need glasses, but she won't hear of it. Too vain.'

'Yes, you could be right,' Emma said, hiding a smile. So that's why the old lady didn't question Doris's occasional black eye.

'How do you know my daughter? Do you work at the hospital as a nurse or something?'

Mrs Hewlett's gaze was intense and Emma felt colour flooding her cheeks. 'Er . . . yes, that's right, but I must go now. Is there anything you need?'

'No, I'm all right, ducks, but will you give my love to Doris? Tell her that Mrs Knox is taking care of me and she has no need to worry.'

'Yes, I will. Goodbye, Mrs Hewlett.'

'Bye, and thanks again for letting me know.'

Before Emma left she thrust a few shillings into Mrs Knox's hand. 'That's to get Mrs Hewlett anything she needs. Doris will be back in a few days.'

'I hope so, love. I'm fair worn out with going up and down those stairs.'

'Yes, I am sure you are,' Emma said, adding a hurried goodbye. Yet as she walked home, she couldn't help thinking about Doris's home. She knew what it was to live in poverty, and poor

Mrs Hewlett was stuck in that drab room day in and day out. Oh, she could see that Doris had tried to improve it for her mother, with a pretty spread on the bed, but a musty damp smell pervaded the air. It didn't seem fair. Doris had told her that her mother had spent years doing early morning cleaning to earn enough money to raise her, and now she was ending her life stuck in that awful place.

By the time Emma had finished her shopping, her hair damp and clinging to her head in the heat, she was glad to get home. Tinker was asleep in her pram and so she left her in the hall, going straight through to the drawing room.

'Gawd, love, you look a wreck,' Doris said. 'Was my mum all right?'

'Yes, she's fine, and said to tell you not to worry about her.'

'Thanks for going – it's put my mind at rest.'

Emma chuckled, 'No wonder she doesn't question you about the occasional black eye. She thinks you bump into things because you need glasses.'

'Bless her, but it's a good cover.'

'Now that I've been shopping, I'll make us a cup of tea.'

'Luverly.'

It wasn't long before Emma was carrying a tray through to the drawing room, checking to see that

Tinker was still asleep as she passed. Doris greeted her with a smile.

'I've been thinking while you were out and I might have come up with a solution to your problems.'

'Well, as long as you're not suggesting I go on the game, I'm all ears.'

'Huh, very funny. From what you've told me you're so frigid that you'd turn the poor punters to ice.'

'I can't help it, Doris,' Emma said seriously.

'I know you can't, love, but it's a shame that you're missing out on something that can be wonderful. Oh, not when you're on the game, but if you love a man, well, it's smashing.' She heaved a sigh. 'All right, I can see you don't believe me, but back to my idea. I ain't been up to looking around, but I know this house is a fair old size. How many rooms have you got?'

Emma counted them off on her fingers. 'This drawing room, the dining room, study, kitchen, laundry room, scullery and toilet. Upstairs there are seven bedrooms and a bathroom.'

'Blimey, and there's just you and Tinker. Well then, why don't you take in lodgers?'

Emma paused in the act of pouring the tea, her eyes rounding. My God, why hadn't she thought of that? She'd been selling her lovely things, when all the time the answer to her problem was right

324

under her nose. 'Doris, I can't believe I didn't think of it myself. Yes, lodgers! How much do you think I could charge?'

Doris pursed her lips. 'If you offer to cook meals too, I reckon a couple of quid a week.'

Emma did a rapid calculation, realising that that if she found enough lodgers, her money worries would be over in an instant. 'I'll start getting the rooms ready in the morning. I won't be rich, but at least I'll be able to make ends meet.'

'If you want riches, you'd have to turn this place into a brothel.'

'You must be joking. A brothel! Never!'

'Now then, don't go all high and mighty on me again. All right, I know it's a daft idea, but though you've turned your nose up, let me tell you that there's a lot of money to be made from a brothel. With a place this size it could be a little goldmine. You'd make a small fortune.'

'I don't care. I wouldn't even consider it.'

Doris shrugged. 'If you ever change your mind, let me know. For a fair share in the profits, I'd help you to run it.'

'I won't be changing my mind,' Emma said firmly.

'Please yourself, but the offer's there.'

Emma finished pouring the tea, her mind already making plans. Yes, she'd sort out the bedrooms in the morning, and then she'd have to write out a card to put in the newsagent's window. As she passed a cup to Doris, her smile was warm. The future looked brighter now, and it was all thanks to her new friend.

31

Emma was missing Doris. She had insisted on going home as soon as she could stand up and, though bent in pain, nothing could stop her. They promised to stay in touch, but now over a week had passed and the advertisement in the newsagent's window hadn't borne fruit. Emma was growing increasingly worried. If someone didn't come soon, she'd have to find something else to sell. But what?

It was half-past eight, Tinker was asleep and, dispirited, Emma was gazing out of the window when she saw Dick and Mandy turning into the drive. Smiling, she ran to open the door.

'Hello, you two, it's lovely to see you.'

'We can't stop long, Em, but as you haven't been to see me on the stall for a while, I thought we should pop round to see how you're doing.'

Emma led them through to the drawing room. Not wanting to worry Dick, she said brightly, 'Oh,

I'm fine, and things are looking up. I'm going to take in lodgers.'

Dick's eyes widened. 'Blimey, that's a good idea and I don't know why we didn't think of it before.'

'Language, Dick,' Mandy said, her face stern.

'Yeah, sorry, love,' he said contritely, then turning to Emma again: 'And how's my niece?'

'She's fine, but asleep, I'm afraid.'

Dick looked around the room, frowning, 'It looks even worse than the last time I saw it. You haven't got anything else to sell, so I'm glad you'll be taking in lodgers.'

There was another knock on the door and, surprised, Emma hurried to answer it. Was it someone replying to the advert? God, she hoped so.

'Can I help you?' she asked, studying the man. He was well dressed in a grey, double-breasted suit, and she noticed that he was carrying a brief-case. His eyes were grey too, and crinkled at the corners when he smiled. A nice smile and a nice face, Emma decided.

When he lifted his trilby hat, Emma saw brown, well-groomed hair and his voice was well modulated when he spoke. 'I saw your card in the newsagent's window. Do you still have vacancies?'

'Oh yes, please, come in,' Emma welcomed.

'Thank you.' He stepped inside and scanned the hall. He then held out his hand.

'My name is Maurice Derivale. Pleased to meet you.'

Emma flushed as she shook his hand. 'Mrs Emma Bell,' she said, wondering what to do next. 'Er . . . would you like to see the available rooms?'

'Yes, please, and I understand that you offer breakfast and evening meals too?'

'That's right,' Emma said. 'If you'll just excuse me for a moment . . .'

Sticking her head around the drawing-room door, she hissed, 'Someone is here to see about a room.'

'Oh, right, we'll leave you to it then,' Dick said, eyeing the man as he came into the hall.

'Good evening,' Maurice Derivale said.

'Evening,' Dick said shortly. 'We're just off.'

'Oh, you needn't leave,' Emma appealed.

'We've got a church meeting to go to,' Mandy insisted.

Emma was disappointed, but walked them to the door, her brother hissing, 'Are you sure about this, Em? I mean, you'll be in the house alone with the bloke.'

'He won't be my only lodger, Dick. I'll be fine.'

'Yeah, of course you will, and at least your money worries will be over. I'm chuffed for you, Em.'

She smiled her thanks and said goodbye, lifting her hand in a small wave before closing the door behind them. Then, turning to Maurice Derivale, she said, 'If you'd like to follow me upstairs, I'll show you the rooms.'

Emma showed him the nicest double room and then two singles, her fingers crossed behind her back as he looked around.

'I think this single would suit me just fine. How much is it?'

'With meals included, I was hoping for two pounds a week.'

'Is linen included?'

Emma swallowed. Linen, goodness, she hadn't thought of that, but surely it was expected that clean sheets were provided? 'Yes, of course,' she said, trying to sound more assured than she felt, 'and the bathroom is just along the landing.'

'How many lodgers do you have?'

'Er . . . none at the moment, the advert is new.'

'I'd like to take the room, with meals. Is it all right if I move in now?'

'Well . . .' Emma hesitated. Dick was right, she knew nothing about this man, yet he'd be living under her roof.

As if sensing her hesitation, he broke in, 'I've only just arrived in the area and at this hour I don't want to spend more time looking for accommodation. I work for an insurance company and have a reference if you'd like to see it.'

'Yes, please,' Emma said.

He withdrew a letter from the inside pocket of

his suit and she took it. The headed paper was that of an insurance company, the details stating that Mr Derivale had been with the company for five years, along with a testimony to his good character. Emma handed it back. It would take time to verify the reference, but if she refused to let Mr Derivale move in now, he'd find somewhere else to stay and she'd continue to be penniless.

She met his eyes, found them honest, direct, and came to a swift decision. 'Thank you, Mr Derivale, that's fine, and yes, you can move in now, though I must insist on a week's rent in advance.'

He took out a brown leather wallet and extracted two pound notes.

'I know this is a bit of a cheek and it's too late for dinner, but I've had a long journey and could do with something to eat. Is there any chance of a sandwich?'

'Er . . . well, yes, I suppose so. In fact, I know it isn't much, but I could heat up a bowl of vegetable stew, if you like?'

'That sounds wonderful,' he said, his smile charming.

Emma stood awkwardly, and as he threw his suitcase onto the bed she said, 'I'll leave you to settle in.'

She rushed back downstairs, clutching the two pound notes, a smile on her face. Things were looking up – a lodger at last, and maybe there'd be more to follow. As Emma heated up the stew she was humming, but nearly jumped out of her skin when a voice spoke from behind her.

'Is it all right if I come in?' Mr Derivale asked.

She spun round. 'Yes, of course, and if you don't mind eating in the kitchen, please sit down.'

'The kitchen is fine,' he said, pulling out a chair from under the table.

Emma had made a pot of tea, and she poured it, her hands shaking slightly. It felt strange to have a man in the house, and this was only one lodger. One to make breakfast and dinner for, but when all the rooms were let she'd have another four or five. Emma pursed her lips. She'd have to be organised. Arrange set times for meals, and also lay down some rules. For one, she wanted a room to herself that was out of bounds to her lodgers. Maybe she could turn the study into a sort of communal living and dining area, keeping the drawing room private.

Maurice Derivale sipped his tea, his eyes roaming around the kitchen. 'This is a lovely house.'

'Thank you.'

'Is this the first time you've taken in lodgers?'

'Yes, is it that obvious?'

He smiled. 'I've moved around the country quite a lot and must admit that you aren't a typical

332

landlady. This house is a cut above others too. It's rather grand. I'm curious. Are you a widow? Is that why you've decided to take in lodgers?'

Emma wasn't sure that she liked this man's questions, or how she should answer them. Her tone was clipped in response. 'No, Mr Derivale, I'm not a widow.'

'Oh dear, I can see I've upset you. Please forgive my assumptions. I let my curiosity get the better of me and had no right to probe your private life.'

He looked so contrite that Emma had to smile. 'It's all right, you haven't upset me.' She moved to the stove, pouring a good helping of the stew into a bowl, and placed it and a chunk of bread in front of him.

'Thank you, it looks wonderful.'

Emma saw her lodger tuck in with appreciation, but when he had finished he rose immediately to his feet. 'That was delicious, and again, thank you. It's been a long day and I think I'll turn in. Good night, Mrs Bell.'

'What time would you like breakfast in the morning?' Emma's hand flew to her mouth. 'Oh dear, I'm afraid I wasn't expecting anyone to move in this evening and I haven't much to offer you.'

'Don't worry, something simple will do, and perhaps at half-past seven. Will I meet your husband in the morning?'

'No, I'm afraid not,' Emma said, desperately

searching for an excuse and gratefully stumbling upon an old one. 'I'm afraid he's away on business.'

'Oh well, maybe when he returns then . . .'

'Good night, Mr Derivale,' Emma said dismissively, unwilling to compound the lie.

One eyebrow lifted but then, with a charming smile followed by a small salute, he left.

Emma washed the dishes whilst wondering what she could offer Mr Derivale for breakfast. She had a little porridge, plus a quarter loaf of bread if he'd like toast, but no preserves. It would have to do until she went shopping, but she'd need to start planning the meals.

It was an hour later before Emma went to bed, and as she reached the landing, her eyes went to Mr Derivale's door. Although it felt odd having someone in the house, and she disliked his questions, Emma decided she liked her first lodger well enough.

When Mr Derivale came down to breakfast the next morning, Emma was holding Tinker in her arms.

'Good morning,' she said. 'This is my daughter, Patricia, but she goes by the nickname of Tinker.'

'What a lovely little girl,' he said, 'and just like her mother.'

Tinker buried her head in Emma's neck, and bashful at the compliment, Emma was glad of the distraction. 'I'm afraid I can only offer you porridge or toast.'

'Porridge, please,' he said.

As she had no high chair, Emma had pulled the pram into the kitchen, placing Tinker in it with a cushion behind her back, and strapping her in. She then poured her lodger a cup of tea before going on to prepare his breakfast. Usually a contented child, Emma was surprised when Tinker squalled, and turned to see Mr Derivale approaching the pram.

'I'm sorry,' she said hastily, 'I'm afraid my daughter isn't used to strangers.'

He backed away, but Tinker continued to cry, her arms out in appeal to Emma. 'In a minute, darling,' she placated, relieved when the porridge thickened. Maurice Derivale had sat down again. Quickly dishing up his breakfast, Emma placed it on the table before taking Tinker out of the pram.

'I'm sorry, Mr Derivale,' she said loudly over Tinker's cries, 'I have to see to my daughter.'

He nodded, his smile charming, and as Emma left the kitchen she said as an afterthought, 'Please help yourself to more tea.'

Tinker's cries had almost stopped by the time Emma reached the drawing room. She laid the child on the sofa to change her nappy, tickling her toes, her daughter starting to chuckle and her sturdy little legs kicking wildly.

'Well, that's better,' Emma told her, 'but as we might have more lodgers soon, you'd better get used to strangers.'

When the nappy was in place, Tinker struggled to get off the sofa. Emma lifted her to the floor, amazed when instead of going on all fours her daughter took a few tentative steps before crumbling. 'Oh my God! Tinker, you walked!'

Emma jumped to her feet, sweeping the child up, hugging her with delight, but then without warning, the door opened, Mr Derivale poking his head into the room.

'I'm off now, Mrs Bell. I'll see you this evening.'

Emma was annoyed that the man hadn't knocked, and seeing him, Tinker started to squall again. Emma decided she'd have to have a word with the man, tell him to respect her privacy, but not wanting to lose her first lodger, she'd need to do it gently. With Tinker squirming in her arms, she knew it would have to wait until this evening so, forcing a smile, Emma said, 'Goodbye, Mr Derivale.'

With a small wave he was gone, and as the door closed behind him, Emma decided to put her plans for privacy in place before he returned. She'd rearrange the study, move a few more chairs in there, and she'd put some sort of sign on the drawing-room door.

32

Mr Derivale's eyebrows had risen when he saw the 'Private' sign on the drawing-room door, but had been appreciative of the study. There were already two rather worn leather wing chairs, placed each side of the hearth, and Emma had dragged an old table out of the scullery. She covered the scratched surface with a chenille table-cloth, tucking a few rather old but serviceable chairs underneath.

Emma was pleased that Mr Derivale now largely kept out of her way, and as nearly a week passed, she became more relaxed in his company. Tinker remained a problem, though, crying every time she saw him, and to overcome this Emma had insisted that he eat his meals in the study.

At eight o'clock that evening, when Emma had settled Tinker for the night, she went to the study to clear the table, finding Mr Derivale sitting in one of the wing chairs.

'Thank you, Mrs Bell, dinner was very nice.'

'I'm glad you enjoyed it.'

'When are you expecting your husband to return from his business trip?'

'Er . . . I . . . I'm not sure,' Emma spluttered.

'Sorry, I didn't mean to embarrass you. I was just trying to make conversation.'

Wanting to divert the topic, Emma picked up his plate. 'Is there anything else I can get you?'

'If it isn't too much trouble, I'd love a cup of tea.'

'It's no trouble,' Emma assured him, worried about her dwindling supply, but glad to leave the room. She was sure that Maurice Derivale was only being friendly, but she wasn't ready to admit that Horace had left her.

When the drink was made she carried it through to the study.

'Thank you,' he said, then, lifting his book, added, 'Have you read this?'

Emma saw it was by someone called Leslie Charteris and called, *Saint Errant*. 'No, I'm not familiar with the author. I'm afraid I don't have any modern books, only classics.'

'Charteris is now an American citizen and writes mystery fiction. He's best known for his creation of a character called Simon Templar, alias, the Saint. This one's very good. I'm on the last chapter. If you like, I'll pass it on to you when I've finished.'

'Oh, yes, please,' Emma replied. She had been so busy of late that she hadn't picked up a book in weeks, but had gone through nearly all those in Horace's collection.

'Who do you like to read?'

Emma perched on the edge of a chair, naming some of her favourite books. Mr Derivale was well read and they went on to discuss one author after another, Emma loving the lively debate. She also found herself enjoying his company, maybe too much. During a lull she rose to her feet. 'Goodness, look at the time and I haven't washed the dishes yet.'

'I'll give you a hand.'

'Please, there's no need.'

He waved her protest away, following her into the kitchen, and as Emma washed up, he dried, the two of them chatting the whole time. Oh, he was nice, Emma decided, glad that she had found such a pleasant lodger. She hoped she'd have more soon and that they too would be as nice as Mr Derivale.

There were no enquiries for rooms over the next few days, but Emma hadn't grown despondent, sure that if Mr Derivale had seen her advertisement, others would too. She would have to be patient, but it wouldn't hurt to check that the card was still in place in the newsagent's window.

A routine had developed and each evening, after

settling Tinker for the night, Emma would make a pot of tea, joining her lodger in the study. Mr Derivale was always polite, and, unlike Horace, treated her as an intellectual equal. Emma's wide knowledge, gained from reading on a range of subjects, now came to the fore. They spoke of the acclaimed author George Orwell's death the previous year, going on to exchange political views. Emma expressed how pleased she was that Clement Attlee returned Labour to power, albeit by a small minority, and instead of belittling her political views, Mr Derivale enjoyed the lively debate.

She was laughing at something Mr Derivale said one evening when there was a knock on the street door, and excusing herself, Emma hurried to answer it, hoping it was another enquiry for a room.

'Hello, love,' Doris said as Emma opened the door, 'I thought I'd pop in to see how you are.'

Emma grinned widely. 'It's lovely to see you. Come on in.'

Doris stepped into the hall, her face caked in make-up, skirt tight and blouse low. At the same time Maurice walked out of the study and her brow lifted.

'Well, well, and who's this then?'

Emma quickly made the introduction. 'This is Mr Derivale, my first lodger.'

With a cheeky wink, Doris said, 'Watcha, ducks.'

He didn't return the greeting, his look disdainful, and as his eyes flicked to Emma he said curtly, 'I'm going to my room.'

They watched him climb the stairs, Doris saying when he was out of earshot, 'Bit stuck up, ain't he?'

Emma frowned. Mr Derivale had turned his nose up, obviously taking Doris for what she was. She took her friend's arm, dragging her into the drawing room. 'Oh, take no notice of him. Now tell me, how are you feeling?'

'To be honest, I'm still a bit rough, but money's a bit tight so I've gone back to work.'

'I hate to think of you out on the streets again.'

'Don't worry, I'll be fine.'

Emma indicated a chair, praying Doris was right, unable to forget how she had looked when she found her that day. 'I bet your mother was pleased to see you.'

'Yes, she was, but she ain't too good and, to be honest, I didn't want to leave her. Mrs Knox is keeping an eye on her and that eases my mind.' Doris's smile seemed forced then as she added, 'Now enough about me. I want to hear all about Mr Derivale, even if he is a stuck-up git. And how's Tinker?'

'She's walking now, and into everything.'

'Is she? Blimey! Still, things must be looking up now you've got a lodger.'

'Yes, but one isn't enough.'

'You'll get more, and hopefully they'll be a darn sight friendlier than him.'

'He's all right, Doris. He's very polite. He works for an insurance company, but I know little else about the man.'

'He ain't bad-looking, I'll say that, but is it enough to melt the ice queen? Oh, don't look at me like that, love. I'm sorry, it's just that with your looks I can't believe the bloke hasn't tried it on.'

'Well, he hasn't and he'd better not. Now if you don't mind, can we change the subject?'

'Yeah, all right, but I can't stay long. I didn't want to hang about near your house, so I've moved on from this area. I'm working Clapham Junction now and it's a bit of a walk from here. Never mind, I'll pop round to see you again, or if you fancy coming to my place, you'd be welcome.'

'I'd like that,' Emma said, and after chatting for another five minutes she showed her friend out. Poor Doris, what an awful way to earn money. She couldn't help worrying about the dangers her friend faced. At least, Emma thought, she had this house, and as time passed she was growing less and less concerned about Horace and his threat of selling it. After all, she was still his wife and must have some rights.

Mr Derivale didn't come downstairs again and at eleven o'clock Emma tidied up before going to bed. Tinker was sleeping soundly, a pudgy fist tucked under her chin, and for a moment Emma stood gazing down at her daughter. She seemed to be growing daily, and clothes were a problem, but unless she filled all of the rooms with lodgers, shopping for new ones was impossible. Oh, she had wanted to give her daughter so much, to dress her like a princess, but instead it was a daily struggle just to pay the bills and feed them.

Sighing heavily, Emma undressed and climbed into bed, turning off her bedside lamp. It was hot, humid, and an hour later, finding the heat oppressive, she was still awake. It was then that her bedroom door was flung open, and she saw a man silhouetted in the doorway. Hastily clutching the sheet to her chest she cried out, 'Who ... who's there?'

As the figure advanced into the room, Emma's hand fumbled for the light in terror. At last she was able to switch it on, illuminating the man at the foot of her bed.

'Mr Derivale! What are you doing in my room?'

'I should think it's obvious.'

Emma tensed, her voice high. 'Not to me it isn't. You have no right to come in here. Please ... go away.'

'Come on,' he drawled, 'I've got you pegged so you can drop the innocent act.'

'Act! What act? I don't know what you're talking about.'

'Oh, you know all right. You might think you can take me for a mug, but seeing your so-called *friend* earlier, the puzzle fell into place. I couldn't work out how you manage to maintain this huge place, especially as I'm the only lodger. What am I? A front? A token lodger to cover up what's *really* going on?'

'Going on? There's nothing going on!'

He moved swiftly to the side of the bed, and heart thumping with fear, Emma scrambled out the other side as he spat, 'You fooled me for a while with your ladylike ways, but you're no lady, are you, Mrs Bell? You're a madam!'

'A . . . a what?'

'I said, drop the act. This is a brothel and a very clever one too. I never heard a thing and that means you must have a separate entrance, another part of this house for your girls and their punters.'

'You're mad!' Emma cried, eyes wild as she stared at the man across the width of the bed.

Maurice Derivale smirked and before she could react he lunged across the bed, grabbing her, his grip tight on her arms.

'Let me go!' Emma shouted.

'Oh, I don't think so.'

There was a tiny cry, and her eyes flew to the cot. Tinker was beginning to stir and Emma's voice was a hiss. 'Please, my daughter is waking up. Listen, you're wrong, totally wrong. Doris is just a friend, that's all, and I'm certainly not running a brothel.'

'I said don't take me for a mug,' the man repeated, pulling her down until she was prone on the bed, his fingers digging into her flesh.

Emma was unable to help a yelp of pain and terror, but hearing another whimper her eyes again flew to the cot and she fought to get away, her hands tearing at the edge of the mattress. 'Please ... please ... my daughter.'

'Stop struggling or I'll make *sure* she wakes up,' Maurice Derivale threatened, his voice a low growl.

Emma went limp then, her thoughts only for her child as the fight went out of her. He turned her over, forced her legs apart, and as the assault began, Emma's cries were inside her head. *Oh God, help me, please, make him stop!* He entered her and she stifled another yelp of pain, lying broken and unmoving beneath him as he thrust into her again and again. She felt helpless, her eyes squeezed shut, and inside her tortured mind Emma begged for only one thing. *Oh, please, let it be over!*

At last, with a loud cry of triumph, Maurice Derivale came to a frenzied climax and Emma's eyes flew open as Tinker stirred. The child struggled to sit up, her cries animating Emma as she frantically shoved the man away. She scrambled from the bed, snatching Tinker from her cot, holding her daughter protectively to her chest.

With Tinker in her arms, sobbing now, Emma's eyes burned with hate as she faced Mr Derivale. 'You *raped* me and I'll see that the police hunt you down.'

'Who are you kidding? You won't tell the police anything. After all, you've got too much to hide.'

'I've *nothing* to hide. My house is *not* a brothel!'

At last she saw fear in his eyes, and without a word he hurried from the room, whilst Emma remained rooted to the spot until at last she heard his footsteps running downstairs. As the street door slammed behind him, the rigidity left her body and, knees collapsing, she sank onto the side of the bed.

She had thought the man charming, polite, but instead she had housed a monster. Clutching Tinker to her, Emma rocked back and forth, tears blinding her eyes and sobs racking her body. He could have killed her or worse, hurt Tinker! How could she have been so blind?

Maurice Derivale hurried along the road. Christ, had he got it wrong? No, of course he hadn't. As soon as he'd seen that tart it had all clicked into place, but just in case Emma Bell carried out her threat to call the police, he needed to get out of the area. And fast.

He headed for the train station, calm by the time he arrived. It had been a cushy little job, the money good, and now he smiled. There had been a nice little perk at the end, but he wouldn't include that in his report. In fact, without proof, it might be better to leave his suspicions out too. He'd say that he'd checked up on the woman, that she was taking in lodgers, and leave it at that. His hand unconsciously rubbed his crotch. She was a beautiful woman, a right tasty piece, and he'd easily fooled her with his act. Insurance agent. Huh, what a laugh.

Maurice had no idea why the client had paid him to check up on Emma Bell, but now wondered who the man was, and what he wanted. He had never set eyes on him, the deal made by telephone and the money paid straight into his account as agreed. Now all he had to do was to return to his office, wait for the phone call, give his report and that was another job done. He smiled again. It had been more enjoyable than most, and as his train drew in he climbed into a carriage, preparing to face the long journey home.

Emma had no idea how long she remained on the side of her bed, but at last her tears subsided as she took deep juddering breaths. Amazingly, Tinker had fallen asleep in her arms, and now Emma laid her gently in the cot. She crept from the room then, wanting only to scrub her body until all traces of Maurice Derivale had been removed.

She felt dirty, degraded, but something fundamental had shifted within her. All traces of innocence had been stripped away as hardness and hatred filled her heart. Never again would a man touch her. She was determined to make Mr Derivale pay for what he had done – to make *all* men pay. As Emma continued to scrub her body, a plan was forming, one for which the seed had been planted not long ago, but that she would never have considered until now.

33

Emma wasted no time, still icy and determined the next morning as she placed Tinker in her pram, setting out for Doris's house. It was a long walk and by the time she arrived, Tinker, soothed by the movement of the pram, had fallen asleep.

When she knocked on the door, Mrs Knox opened it, whey-faced as she beckoned Emma inside.

Doris was slumped at the kitchen table, her eyes red and wild when she looked up at Emma. 'I shouldn't have left her, Em. I should have been here.'

'What is it? What's happened?'

Doris shook her head, unable to answer, and it was Mrs Knox who said with a sob, 'It's Gertie. She passed away last night.'

'Oh no! Oh, Doris, I'm so sorry.'

'I . . . I didn't even get a chance to say goodbye. Oh . . . oh, Mum . . .' Doris wailed.

'I didn't know how to get hold of you, Doris,' Mrs Knox cried. 'I flew next door and asked young Eric to go to the pub you said you worked in, but the landlord said he'd never heard of you.'

'I . . . I changed jobs. Oh, what does it matter now? Mum's gone and it's all my fault. I knew she was rough, but I didn't realise she was that bad.'

'You heard the doctor – he said it was her heart. It just gave out, and even if you'd been here, you couldn't have done anything.'

'I could have been with her!' Doris cried.

Emma didn't know what to do, how to find words to comfort Doris, all thoughts of her own troubles pushed to one side as she stood ineffectually patting her friend's shoulder. She heard Tinker waking up and went to lift her daughter from the pram. For a moment Emma floundered, wondering what to do. She didn't want to leave Doris in such a state, but wasn't sure how Tinker would react to the sorrow inside. Hoping that Tinker would be all right, she tentatively walked back into the kitchen, and seeing the child, Doris's arms lifted.

Tinker went to Doris without protest, snuggling to her chest, seemingly unfazed as the woman's tears fell. For a moment they were all silent, but then, drawing in a huge breath, Doris fought to pull herself together. She looked drained, her face wan, free of the heavy make-up she usually wore.

'I'm so tired, I can't seem to think straight. There's so much to do and I don't know where to start.'

'You've been up all night so it's hardly surprising,' Mrs Knox commented. 'I know you've got arrangements to make, but there's no panic. You should get some sleep first.'

'Is there anything I can do?' Emma asked.

Doris shook her head, her eyes desolate as they met Emma's. 'No, but thanks for the offer. Oh God, I can't believe she's gone . . . oh . . .' and once again tears began to fall.

This time, Tinker reacted, looking frightened as she stared up at Doris, and seeing that her daughter was about to cry too, Emma took her, holding her close.

'I . . . I think Mrs Knox is right, Doris. Why don't you try to get some sleep, and if it's all right with you, I'll come back later, or maybe tomorrow?'

Doris nodded, rising tiredly to her feet. 'Yes, all right, I . . . I'd like that.'

Impulsively, Emma kissed Doris on the cheek and, still feeling helpless, she whispered goodbye, her heart heavy as she made her way home.

Emma did all she could to support Doris, but every time she went to her house, she was appalled by the woman's living conditions. The house hadn't been up to much to start with, but now Doris had let the place go, uninterested in house-work, her grief inconsolable.

The funeral was a sad affair, with only a few in attendance. Afterwards, when Mrs Knox had gone home, Emma and Doris sat in the small kitchen, Tinker asleep in her pram. Doris looked a shadow of her former self.

'She was all I had, Em, and I couldn't even give her the send-off she deserved,' Doris said.

Emma reached out to take her hand, murmuring softly, 'I only met your mother once but found her a lovely lady. She'd understand, love.'

'I . . . I'm sort of lost, Em. I don't know what to do with myself now.'

Emma wondered if this was the time to broach her plans to Doris. It might be just what she needed, something else to think about, but was it too soon? Her voice was hesitant when she spoke. 'Are you going back on the . . . the game?'

Doris shook her head emphatically. 'No. I'm finished with that. I'll get a job of some sort but it'll have to pay enough to keep this roof over my head.' She managed a parody of a smile, adding, 'Not that this place is up to much, but the land-lord said I can take over the tenancy.'

Emma wanted to put her plan forward, but without Doris's help she felt it would be impos-sible. Could she persuade her to change her mind?

'Now if I had a place like yours,' Doris continued, 'I could get a lodger, but nobody would want to live in a dump like this.' Her hand flew to her mouth. 'Blimey, Em, I've been so wrapped up in myself I haven't even asked you how you're getting on. Have you rented any more rooms out?'

Emma returned to her chair and, taking a deep breath, she told Doris what had happened, hesitantly at first, but then her voice gained in strength. 'He . . . he raped me, Doris. My lodger raped me.'

'The bastard! Did you get the law on him?'

'No, I was too ashamed.'

'But why, you daft mare? You ain't got nothing to be ashamed of.'

'I just couldn't face it, Doris. I haven't told anyone, not even my brother. Dick would kill Maurice Derivale if he knew, and I wouldn't want that on my conscience. Instead, I've come up with another idea.'

'Oh yeah. What are you gonna do then? Cut his balls off? It'd be no more than he deserves.'

'I wish I could,' Emma said, pausing as she chose her words carefully. 'I don't want to risk taking in lodgers now, but . . . well . . . I think I might take up your suggestion.'

'My suggestion? What do you mean?'

'Doris, I know you said you're giving up the

game, and you probably don't want to get involved, but what I want to do is this . . .'

When Emma had finished speaking, Doris replied in astonishment and her voice was high. 'What? You want me to come to live with you and to help turn your house into a brothel?'

'Why are you so shocked? It was you who gave me the idea.'

'Yeah, but I never expected you to take it seriously. Blimey, Emma, have you got any idea what you're letting yourself in for?'

'No, not really, but I've got a few plans. I think we could live on the ground floor, turning the dining room into a bedroom for Tinker and me. You could have the study. It isn't huge, but will take a single bed and a wardrobe. That will leave the whole of the upstairs free for the business.'

'Yeah, that makes sense, but I still don't think you've thought it through. Christ, Emma, you just ain't the type to be a madam!'

'I know that, and that's why I'm asking you to come in with me.' Then seeing the expression on Doris's face, she added hastily, 'You won't have to sleep with . . . with the clients. You see, I thought that maybe I could see to the practical side of things – looking after the rooms, the cleaning, along with the finances – whilst you take over the rest. You could recruit the girls and when we're up and running, you could act as a sort of hostess.'

'I dunno, Em. Like I said, I want to get out of the game. After all these years, I want a fresh start, to live a normal life.'

Emma played her last card, her expression earnest. 'I understand, but if you change your mind, well, I'll give you a good share of the profits. You won't have any rent to pay, or keep, and will be able to build up a nice little nest egg. One day you might even save enough to buy a place of your own.'

Doris was silent for a moment, her eyes shadowed, but then she said, 'It's tempting, I'll admit that, but I'll have to think about it. But even if I agree to come in with you, are you really sure you know what you're doing? There'll be risks involved, and one of them would be the police. If they get wind of the place, we could both end up in the nick.'

'Yes, I've thought about that, but I think the risk is minimal. My house is in an ideal spot. It faces the Common, we aren't overlooked, and you've got to admit that it's a quiet area at night.'

'Yeah, but all that would change when punters start knocking at the door.'

'The drive is sheltered by shrubbery, and surely they won't all turn up at once? We could think of some sort of front, put up a plaque or something to explain the callers. Maybe say it's a dance academy or something like that?'

'Blimey, Em, you really are a dark horse. I had no idea you had such a devious mind.'

'I'm not devious, Doris, just desperate. I need to make money, enough to ensure my daughter's future. Not only that, I want to be my own woman, a woman who is never dependent on a man again.'

Once again Doris was quiet whilst Emma sat facing her, holding her breath, thinking, Oh, let her agree. Please let her agree.

Finally Doris looked up and their eyes met. 'All right, Em, I've thought about it. With all my earnings on the game going into paying the rent and looking after Mum, I've no savings. I haven't any skills and if I get a job of some sort, it won't pay much and may not even be enough to scrape by. I'd certainly never be in a position to buy a place of my own.'

'Does . . . does that mean . . . ?'

For the first time since her mother's death, Doris chuckled. 'Yeah, I'm in. When do we start?'

'As soon as you've packed your bags.'

'Well, love, there's no time like the present,' Doris said, rising to her feet.

34

In less than three months, the business was up and running. Doris had recruited the girls, all of whom were glad to give up working the streets. Emma was relieved that Doris was dealing with that side of the business, finding herself unable to relate to these women who sold their bodies for money.

At first Emma had tried, greeting the girls when they turned up for work; but her attitude obviously rubbed them up the wrong way and she knew they had taken to calling her Lady Muck, a name that Dick had once used.

The girls Doris had recruited seemed harder, blowsier than Doris herself, and though they may have had good reasons for turning to prostitution, Emma didn't want to know, preferring to keep things on a business footing. A deal had been cut, one that gave Emma a percentage of the girls' earnings that Doris had assured her was fair.

Nowadays, Emma kept out of the way, concentrating instead of keeping their girls' rooms sparkling clean and dealing with the accounts. When the men called, she kept out of sight, leaving Doris to take them upstairs to make their selection.

Emma frowned, unable to help shuddering when she thought about what went on above her head, but with money now rolling in, she closed her mind to it.

One evening, at about eight o'clock, there was a knock on the door. Assuming it was a client, Emma left Doris to answer it. When the drawing-room door swung open, Emma stiffened.

'Goodness! Hello stranger,' she said, rising to her feet.

'What's going on, Em?' Dick snapped.

'Going on? What do you mean?'

'There's word on the grapevine that you're running a knocking shop. Tell me it ain't true.'

Emma reddened and, lowering her eyes, she nodded. 'It's true.'

'You must be fucking joking.'

'Please don't swear, Dick.'

His laugh was derisive. 'Don't swear! You're a fucking madam, but you've got the cheek to tell me not to swear! Well, let me tell you, I don't use bad language nowadays because Mandy wouldn't like it, but you're enough to make a bleedin' saint swear!' He lifted a hand, fingers raking through his hair. 'Christ, I can't believe this. My sister, running a knocking shop! Have you gone out of your mind?'

'No, Dick, I'm doing this because I haven't any choice.'

'No choice! What the hell are you talking about? Has someone forced you into this, because if they have I'll take their bloody head off.'

'No, it isn't like that. Look, I was desperate for money. You know I tried taking in lodgers, but it didn't work. This seemed the only answer.'

'The only answer?' Dick yelled. 'Of course it ain't the only answer. If you needed money you should have come to me.'

'Don't be silly. The costs of running this house are exorbitant, and that's without buying food. You couldn't have helped me.'

'Hark at yourself! I see you're still spouting your big words. Huh, exorbitant indeed. You're just making excuses, Em. You don't have to stay in this place. You could find something smaller; in fact, do anything rather than running a bloody brothel.'

'Leave and go where? I can't sell this place, Horace saw to that, and if I left here to go some-where else I'd have rent to pay.'

'Decent women don't run brothels. Blimey, my Mandy would rather live in a hovel and take on cleaning jobs than do this.'

'Well, bully for her, but I've lived in a hovel, Dick, we both have, and there is no way I intend to go back to that. I want a better life for my daughter, one in which she wants for nothing, and this is the way to achieve that.'

'What! Having a mother who's a madam? You're out of your mind.' His voice softened suddenly, becoming a plea. 'Please, Em, see sense. You got to close this place down.'

'No, Dick, I haven't *got* to do anything.'

'Christ,' he cried, fingers once again raking his hair in agitation, 'when I was told what you're up to, I nearly died of shame. God knows what Luke will say when he hears about it. Please, Em, please see sense.'

'For the first time in ages I *am* seeing sense. For once, I have plenty of food in the cupboard and my daughter has decent clothes on her back.'

Dick's face darkened. 'Either you pack this game in or you'll never see me again. You'll be no sister of mine.'

Emma hid her feelings, concealed her sadness in a show of bravado. 'If that's how you want it, that's fine with me.'

For a moment, Dick stood glaring at her, but then he yelled, 'Right, sod you, I'm off and you won't see me again. Luke either, when I write to tell him what you're up to.'

With that, Dick swung on his heels and the

door slammed shut behind him. Emma slumped. She had acted with bravado, but now the ramifications of her actions hit her. She knew that Dick meant every word he had said, that she was losing her brother, but oh, she was just starting to make money. After struggling for so long, after trying to take in lodgers, only to be raped, she now had a good income, one that she couldn't – and wouldn't – give up.

There was a small cry. Their angry voices had disturbed Tinker and, forcing herself to overcome her tears, Emma went to the bedroom, quietening her daughter down. All the time her mind churned. She and her brothers had grown distant, all leading their own lives, but even so, the thought of never seeing Luke or Dick again was hard for Emma to bear. What should she do? Should she close down? And if she did, how was she going to survive?

Emma's head began to thump, the pain a band around her forehead. She felt drained, torn in two, but finally, irrevocably, unable to think of any other way, she knew she had to carry on – had to run the brothel to secure her financial security. She fought to push her brothers from her mind, her survival instincts kicking in as she hardened her heart once more, putting up emotional barriers. Frozen-faced, she left her daughter's side to return to the drawing room.

*   *   *

'Well, that's another night over with,' Doris said as she closed the door at the end of business. 'We didn't do bad, but Jenny's leaving.'

'Leaving! Why?'

''Cos she's up the spout.'

'What! You're telling me that one of the punters got her pregnant?'

'No, you daft cow. It's her old man's, and her third kid. You could have knocked me down with a feather when she told me she's four months gone. I didn't see any sign of it.'

'My God, I had no idea that Jenny's married, and has a family.'

'She ain't the only one that's married. Eva is too.'

'Do their husbands know that they're ... they're ...'

'Prostitutes,' Doris finished for her. 'Blimey, Em, the word still sticks in your craw, doesn't it?'

'I'm sorry.'

'They ain't a bad bunch. All right, they're on the game, but they ain't robbers or murderers. And to answer your question, yes, sometimes the husbands know. Oh, don't look so shocked. A lot of prostitutes are married women. They like the money, the means to buy what their husband's wages can't provide. I know one girl whose old man knows what's going on, but he doesn't seem to mind. In fact, I think he enjoys the extra cash too.'

Emma shook her head, unable to comprehend how a man could let his wife sell her body. What sort of men were they? She scowled, shaking her head. She shouldn't be surprised – nothing men did should surprise her any more. She took the money Doris proffered, counted it, and handed the woman her cut.

'You'll have to scout around for a replacement for Jenny.'

'Yeah, I'll get on to it first thing tomorrow. But what's up, Em? You're a bit down in the mouth.'

'Oh, it's my brother. He went mad about the brothel.'

'Well, that ain't surprising really. He'll get over it.'

'No, I don't think so. He's changed so much, courting a girl in the Sally Army, and unless I close down I won't see him again.'

'What are you gonna do?'

'I'm not shutting shop, that's for sure.' Emma sighed heavily. 'Maybe he'll come round eventually, but I won't count on it.'

Doris offered more words of sympathy, but then said she was bone tired and was going to turn in.

'Yes, me too,' Emma said. She still found herself having to push thoughts of Dick away, concentrating instead on the cleaning she would have to undertake in the morning. She hated going

363

upstairs, hated changing the sheets on the beds, holding them away from her as if contaminated. Every room seemed to smell of sex and cheap perfume, but cleaning them was preferable to taking on Doris's role, something she could never do.

Emma went to her room, where standing by the cot, she gazed down at Tinker. The night's takings were still clutched in her hand, and though she hated what she was doing, what the house had become, the money would ensure her daughter's future. Yes, she had lost Dick, and Luke, but not for Tinker the poverty they had known. An icy coldness encased her heart. As long as there were men willing to pay for their so-called pleasure, she would let them, and the cash would continue to roll in.

Horace Bell steepled his fingers under his chin. Several months had passed since he'd arranged to have Emma checked on. He'd left, expecting to let the past go, but the thought of Emma profiting from the house – *his house* – had played on his mind. He'd been told that she was struggling, trying to take in lodgers, and if Maurice Derivale's report was accurate, so hard up that the house would probably fall around her ears from lack of maintenance. Huh, lodgers! Even if she filled every room, she'd never be a rich woman. Horace smiled in satisfaction at the thought.

So be it, he decided, all emotional feelings for the property now dead – as dead as his marriage. He wouldn't check up on Emma again and his only remaining regret was that, legally, she was still his wife. For a moment Horace frowned, annoyed that the man's report on Emma had included mention of the child. A girl. Thankfully he had got out before he'd been lumbered with the brat. A brat he was convinced wasn't his.

Horace leaned back in his chair, lifting a glass to his lips and savouring the taste of fine brandy. They could both rot in hell, both Emma and her bastard, whilst he went on to make even more money.

'Felicity,' he shouted, pleased to see how his latest mistress sashayed into the room. This one was a bit different, a high-class filly, and if she played her cards right she could stay longer than the others. 'Get me another drink,' he ordered.

'Is that all you'd like?' she asked huskily.

'It'll do to start with,' he said, all thoughts of Emma and the past fading as Felicity moved towards him.

35

Emma was smiling as she counted the takings.
Another year had passed, but she'd been so busy
that many of the earlier events of 1952 had gone
unnoticed by her. Of course she'd been saddened
when King George died in February, but after
suffering a lung condition, at least he had died
peacefully in his sleep.

If thoughts of her family invaded her mind,
Emma would push them away, and in order to
survive emotionally a hard shell had grown
around her heart that she was determined
nobody would be able to crack. Luke was the
only one she still heard from, his letters infrequent but reading like sermons as he continued
to beg her to give up the brothel. She didn't
answer them these days, but now she put her
takings aside and picked up his last one to read
again.

Dear Emma,

Dick has written to tell me that despite my prayers, you are still running a house of sin. Emma, please, can't you see that it's an abomination in God's eyes? Our Saviour is loving and forgiving, and it is not too late to turn to Him . . .

Emma could read no more and, scrunching the letter into a ball, she tossed it into the bin, forcing Luke's sanctimonious words from her mind as Doris entered the room.

'We've done well, but there's still not enough profit to buy the empty house next door,' Emma told her.

'Blimey, love, that's a bit ambitious.'

'I know, but after what happened last night, I'd like the business entirely separate from the house.'

'But it's already separate. We live down here and the rest goes on upstairs.'

'I know that,' Emma said impatiently, 'but we all use the same entrance, and clients have to cross the hall to go upstairs. When that one turned nasty last night, it could have woken Tinker and I don't want that happening again.'

'All right, I know it was a bit hairy, but I dealt with it and it doesn't happen very often. Most punters leave without a murmur. It's just that the bloke couldn't perform and blamed Rose, wanting his money back.'

Emma sighed. Yes, Doris had dealt with it, but it could have been worse. What if the punter had forced his way into their private rooms? Oh, if only the clients didn't have to infringe on their private quarters, albeit by using only the front door and hall.

An idea suddenly formed, one that could solve the problem, and Emma's eyes lit up. 'If we had a separate staircase, a way to turn the top floor into a self-contained flat, it would make all the difference.'

'I suppose it could be done, but it won't be easy. You've told me that the house isn't in your name so are you sure you can alter it?'

'I haven't heard from my husband since he left me,' Emma said dismissively, 'and I doubt a builder would want to see the deeds to the house.'

'You hope,' Doris said.

Emma shrugged off Doris's concern, asking instead, 'How is Rose? Will she be able to work tonight?'

'With a split lip, I doubt it.'

Emma huffed, annoyed that they were likely to be a girl short. 'I hope she recovers soon or there'll be a drop in profits.'

'You and your profits. Honestly, Emma, I can't get over how much you've changed. When I met you just over a year ago you were so innocent, so high and mighty, and horrified at the idea of running a brothel, but now look at you, willing to work girls even if they aren't really up to it.'

'I wasn't just an innocent, I was a fool.'

'No, love, not a fool. You just had a bit of bad luck.'

'Bad luck? I was raped, Doris!'

'Christ, when are you gonna let it go? You've become bitter, twisted and hard as nails. All right, that bastard Derivale raped you, but it was a long time ago now.'

'To you, maybe, but I can't forget it, and never will.'

'Oh, I see, so you're saying that because I was a prostitute, rape wouldn't have affected me?'

'No, I'm not saying that, but you have to admit that for you, it wouldn't have been as bad.'

Doris's face hardened and she reared to her feet. 'I've got a lot to thank you for, Emma, and you've been good to me, but sometimes you go too far. Despite running a brothel, you still think yourself a cut above the rest of us and I'm just about sick of it.'

Doris stormed from the room, slamming the door behind her, whilst Emma's lips thinned. Who the bloody hell did Doris think she was? Yes, it was true, she'd grown hard, but after what she had been through it was hardly surprising.

She had lost her family and, all right, she was running a brothel, but it was just a means to an end. A way of making money, lots of money. She wanted to be rich, to never let a man, any man, have control over her again – not her father, not her husband, not another Maurice Derivale. They were all pigs and she would use them – use their weaknesses – to make her fortune.

Emma eventually calmed down, and with this came the realisation that Doris was right. She *had* said that rape wouldn't have been as bad for her. Now she lowered her eyes in shame. She owed Doris an apology and, rising to her feet, Emma made for the kitchen, but as she passed the street door, someone rattled the letterbox.

'Dick!' she exclaimed, surprised when she saw her brother on the step. Had he changed his mind? Had he decided not to cast her out? 'Would you like to come in?' she asked eagerly.

Dick's expression showed his distaste. 'Is this still a knocking shop?'

'If that's what you want to call it.'

'In that case, I won't come in.'

Emma's expression hardened. 'What do you want, Dick? After all this time, have you come to give me another lecture?'

'Would it do any good?'

'No, so don't waste your breath.'

'All right, I won't, but I was hoping that you'd have come to your senses. Anyway, just so you know, I've got my call-up papers and I'm off to do my national service.'

'What about your stall?'

'Mandy's brother is going to run it for me, and when I've finished my stint in the army, I'm gonna become a Salvationist and me and Mandy are going to get married.'

'I'm pleased for you.'

'Don't give me that, Em. You don't give a sod about me, or anyone else in the family.'

'That isn't true.'

'Yes it is. When was the last time you went to see Archie and James?'

Emma lowered her eyes guiltily. It was true, she hadn't been to see James and Archie, convincing herself that it was for their own good, yet in truth she was ashamed and feared the inevitable questions from Alice about how she made her money. Hiding her feelings she said brusquely, 'Oh, and you go to visit them regularly, do you?'

'Well, no, but if Alice has them with her when she comes to the market, we always have a little chat.'

'Well, that's all right then,' Emma said sarcastically.

'You don't care about the girls either.'

'For God's sake, come off it, Dick! You know I

372

tried to write to them, but Dad returned my letters.'

'So you just gave up.'

'Eventually, yes, but what about you? Have you been in touch with them?'

'Well, no, but—'

'So who are you to stand in judgement of me?'

'What about Luke? I know he's been writing to you.'

'Oh yes, he writes, but his letters read like sermons.'

'You're running a knocking shop so what do you expect? Like me, he's ashamed of you.'

Emma bristled. 'Just why have you come to see me, Dick? I can't believe it's just to tell me that you're off to do your national service.'

'If you must know, it was Mandy's idea. She said everyone can be saved and I should give it another go.'

'I don't need saving, thank you. I'm fine.'

'No you're not, Em, you're a tart and our mum must be turning in her grave.'

Emma blanched but fought to hide her feelings, forcing her voice to drip with sarcasm instead. 'Hark at you, Mr Perfect all of a sudden. Just go away, Dick. Go and do your national service and maybe it'll make you grow up. At least I hope so.'

'I'm going, and it'll be the last you'll see of me.

As I said before, you're no sister of mine, and I'm glad that Mum ain't alive to see what you've become.'

Emma slammed the door, marching to the kitchen with her back stiff. How dare he throw their mother in her face!

She walked to the window, gazing out on the garden, her arms folded defensively across her chest.

'I'm sorry, Emma. I shouldn't have spoken to you like that before.'

She spun round to see Doris in the doorway. 'No, it's me who should apologise. You're right, I have been acting like Lady Muck and I'm not surprised at my nickname, but it won't happen again.'

Doris smiled. 'No, Emma, if truth be known you *are* a bit different from the rest of us. You run this place, but you don't sleep with the punters.'

'Nor do you, Doris, not any more, and I couldn't manage without you.' Emma didn't want to think about Dick, about the things he had said, and now pulled out a chair. She needed distraction. 'Come on, let's sit down and see if we can plan some alterations to the house.'

'Who was that at the door?'

'It was my brother, but we won't be seeing him again.'

Doris sat down, her hand reaching out to cover Emma's. 'Did he have a go at you?'

'Yes, but it doesn't matter. It would take a lot

374

more than Dick to upset me these days.' She forced a smile, willing it to be true, and grabbed a notepad and pencil. 'Let's forget my brother. As I said, I'd like to turn the house into two self-contained flats. If we can somehow have a staircase installed, do you think the clients would mind using the side entrance?'

'Leave it out, love. Most of the punters skulk up the front stairs, and though they're pretty shielded by shrubs, I'm sure they'd prefer to scuttle around to the side of the house.'

'Good, that's one problem solved. But we'll need to have a bathroom put in down here.'

'Yeah, and a kitchen upstairs.'

Emma's eyebrows lifted. 'I don't think the girls will need a kitchen. After all, they're not here to cook meals.'

Doris chuckled. 'Yeah, you're right. As long as they've got somewhere to make a drink between punters, they'll be happy.'

Emma drew a rough sketch, but was flummoxed by how to fit in a separate staircase. 'It's no good, Doris. I need someone to give me advice, a builder.'

'I know just the bloke. He's a bit of a rough diamond, and won't ask any questions. If you give him the job he'll do it on the cheap for cash.'

'That's fine with me,' Emma said, relieved she wouldn't have to worry about the deeds, 'but when can you get hold of him?'

'I could pop down to see him now, if you like.'

'Yes, do that. If he can find a way to install a staircase and gives me a good price, the job's his.'

'Right, you're on.' As she stood, Doris added, 'You may get a bit of a shock when you see Terry Green. He's a big bloke and looks intimidating, but he's a bit of a softie really.'

'As long as he can get the job done, I don't care what he looks like.'

Doris giggled as she left the room, saying over her shoulder, 'I still can't wait to see your face when you meet him. See you later, love.'

As soon as Doris left, Emma went back to her plans. She wanted as little disruption to the business as possible, and somehow the girls would have to carry on working. She frowned, tapping the pencil on her teeth. The building work was going to be noisy but, once completed, maybe they could extend their hours, the girls seeing punters during the day. It would increase profits, but to see if it was feasible, she'd have to speak to Doris.

She heard a cry and rose to her feet. Tinker was waking from her afternoon nap. At the moment Emma was able to keep the business activities away from her daughter, more so when they were self-contained, but when Tinker was older a separate house would be imperative. She *had* to make more money.

36

'Emma, this is Terry Green,' Doris said later that day.

Oh my God, Emma thought, her neck craning as she looked up at the man. He was at least six feet three, with massive shoulders, but as he looked down on her she saw that his smile was gentle. 'Er . . . how do you do, Mr Green?'

'Terry, call me Terry, Mrs Bell. Doris tells me that you want some work done on the house?'

'Yes, that's right,' she said, but then saw Doris doing a fair imitation of a gorilla behind Terry's back. Choking back laughter and holding a hand over her mouth, she spluttered, 'Please, would you excuse me for a moment,' and was only just able to make it to the hall before doubling over with mirth.

'Well, that's nice, ain't it?' Doris said as she joined her. 'It's good to see you having a laugh for a change, but fancy scooting out like that. I've told Terry to sit down and I'm off to make him a cup of tea. I just hope he didn't hear you laughing your socks off.'

'But it's your fault! You were prancing about like a gorilla. If you ask me, it's lucky he didn't see you.'

'Oh, don't worry about Terry. I told you, he's a lovely bloke, but when you talk to him you're in for a treat.'

'What do you mean?'

Doris grinned. 'I think I'll leave you to find out for yourself.'

'God, I've left Tinker in there. He isn't a sandwich short of a picnic, is he?'

'Oh, no, Terry's bright enough, but I'm not saying anything else. Anyway, you'd best get back in.'

Fearing for her daughter, Emma rushed to the drawing room, but then halted on the threshold. Terry was holding Tinker in the air, bouncing her up and down in massive hands, and what was more, Tinker was giggling, obviously loving it.

'Funny man, Mummy,' she said and then, looking down on Terry's smiling face, demanded, 'Do it again.'

'Bit of a bossy boots, ain't you?' Terry said, 'and you're starting a bit young.'

'Yes, she's only two and already a bit of a chatterbox,' Emma said, smiling indulgently.

Terry lowered Tinker to the floor, and as he sat

down, Emma was amazed to see Tinker clambering onto his lap. His massive arms enfolded her, and her daughter happily settled down, leaning her head against his chest.

For a moment, Emma was dumbstruck, but then with a small shake of her head she took a seat opposite him. 'I see my daughter has taken to you.'

'Yeah, I'm good with kids. My sister's got six and she calls me the Paid Piper of Hamlet.'

'Sorry? The who?'

'The Paid Piper of Hamlet. Haven't you heard of him?'

'Yes, but I call him the *Pied* Piper of Hamelin.'

'You don't say,' Terry said, grinning widely. 'There must be two of them.'

God, I'll kill Doris, Emma thought, her face straining not to laugh. 'Anyway, down to business. I'd like to convert this house into two flats, the upstairs one using the side entrance. The problem is there isn't a staircase and I wonder if it's possible to install one.'

'I'll have a look, but as long as there's space, it shouldn't be a problem.'

'Have you done this sort of work before?'

'Yes, I've been a builder all my life and you'll find I'm an unconscious worker. Mind you, since damaging my back I don't do any of the heavy stuff. I'll get a Labrador to do that.'

It was too much for Emma and she once again

fled the room, spluttering excuses over her shoulder. Doris was in the kitchen, laying a tray. Almost falling onto a chair, Emma howled with laughter, finally able to gasp, 'He . . . he said he's an "unconscious" worker instead of "conscientious", and he called a "labourer" a "Labrador".'

'Yeah, Terry's fond of getting his words mixed up, but don't worry, he's used to people laughing at him. Most act like you and run. Mind you, seeing his size, it ain't surprising. Don't let it put you off, Emma. He really is a smashing bloke, and he'll give you a fair price for the job.'

'I'll trust you on this one, and anyway, Tinker is sticking to him like glue. After the way she responded to Mr Derivale, for me that's as good as a reference. Better in fact,' she said, thinking of the sheet of paper Derivale had brandished, testifying to his character.

'I've told you, it's time you stopped dwelling on that bastard.'

'I know, but Tinker didn't like him from the start and it should have warned me.'

'She's only a baby, love.'

'Yes, but even so she seems to have good instincts. Anyway, back to Terry Green. Does he know what sort of business we run?'

'Yeah, he knows, and it doesn't bother him. I told you, Terry's a rough diamond – when he was younger he was mixed up with a few local villains.'

'Villains! I'm not sure I like the sound of that.'

'He's been straight for a long time so you've nothing to worry about.'

'He isn't violent, is he?'

'No, of course not. Now come on, stop worrying and let's take this tea through.'

Emma followed Doris back to the drawing room to see that Tinker hadn't moved from Terry's lap. He was quite a nice-looking man, she decided, with dark hair, brown eyes and a kind smile.

'He cuddly bear, Mummy,' Tinker said, reaching out to stroke the thick, dark hairs on Terry's arm.

Emma stiffened, expecting Terry to be offended, but instead he grinned at Tinker. 'Yes, that's me. A big cuddly bear. Now why don't you go to your mummy and I'll have a look around the house?'

'No, I stay with you,' Tinker said.

'All right, little 'un, if you insist.'

'Not 'un. I'm Tinker.'

He caught on straightaway. 'Tinker Bell – well, ain't that nice.'

'Her name is Patricia, but she prefers to be called Tinker.' As Emma reached for the pot she added, 'Have a cup of tea before you look around.'

'Thanks, Mrs Bell, I won't say no.'

Emma poured the tea, sure now that she was going to employ this giant of a man. 'Would you like a biscuit?' she asked, holding out a plate.

'Yes, please. Digressives are my favourite.'

Emma spluttered again, her eyes flying to Doris. Her friend laughed, saying, 'No, Terry, not digressives. They're digestives.'

'Well, you know me, Doris, but I'm glad I've given you a laugh.' He winked then, adding, 'I'm getting good at it too.'

'Terry Green! Don't tell me you do it deliberately?'

'Well, that's for me to know and you to find out, Doris.'

Emma liked this man; one she felt sure was self-deprecating to make people laugh, and as he broke off a piece of biscuit to give to Tinker, she could see that her daughter was enamoured with him too.

Emma frowned. What was the matter with her? Terry Green was a man, and they were all the same. She had learned from running this brothel that no matter how old, whether married or single, the sexual act was all they cared about, so much that they were willing to pay for it. Her lips pursed. Well, that suited her fine. She was making them pay all right, and would continue to do so to ensure the lifestyle she wanted for her daughter.

She rose to her feet, her manner now brusque. 'If you've finished your tea, Mr Green, perhaps we can get back to business. If you'll come with me I'll show you the alterations I have in mind, and I'd like an estimate as soon as possible.'

His forehead creased, but he too stood up, Tinker's arms around his neck as she clung to him like a limpet. 'Yes, Mrs Bell, that won't be a problem.'

With that, Emma turned on her heels, both Terry Green and Doris following behind. She showed the man her rough sketches, and then he slowly walked around the house, the women in his wake.

They returned to the kitchen instead of the drawing room, Terry pulling out a chair and sitting down with Tinker on his lap again.

'Well, Mrs Bell, now that I've had a look around I can offer a few suggestions. Firstly, if you can do without the scullery, I could block it off, using the space for a staircase.'

'Oh yes, I can do without the scullery.'

'Good. And as for a bathroom down here, the only place I can see that might work is the laundry room. It'll be a bit small, but I reckon it'd take a bath and a hand basin.'

'I'm sure we'd manage,' Emma said, then frowned. 'My only concern is the present staircase that leads upstairs from the front hall. The reason for having the house converted is to keep my daughter away from our business activities. With it still in place anyone could come down here into our private accommodation.'

'I hope you ain't thinking about taking it out.

If you do that it will greatly decrease the value of the property. It would be easier to put a door at the top and make sure it's got a good, strong lock.'

Emma was quiet as she mulled it over, watching as Tinker pulled on Terry's sleeve to get his attention. 'All right, we'll leave the existing staircase, and your suggestion of adding a door sounds fine. Is it possible to give me a rough idea of what it will all cost?'

Terry pulled a pencil out of his pocket, and tongue sticking out in concentration, he wrote a few figures, then scribbled a price. 'This is only an estimate, but I don't think it'll be far out.'

As he handed it to her, Emma's face brightened. It was below what she had expected. 'This is fine. When could you start?'

'You're lucky. I've just finished a job so I'm available on Monday.'

'In that case, Mr Green, the job's yours.'

'Thanks very much, Mrs Bell. Me and my Labrador will be here bright and early on Monday morning.'

Emma kept her face straight this time, but Doris giggled. Terry ruffled Tinker's hair and put her on the floor, but as he made to leave, she wouldn't let go of his trousers. He crouched down, smiling as he said, 'Sorry, sweetheart, but I must go. I've got to see a man about a dog.'

'Dog! Doggie for me?'

'Oh blimey,' he said, 'now I've put my foot in it. Yes, all right, a doggie for you.'

'I don't want any pets, Mr Green,' Emma protested.

'Don't worry,' he whispered as he stood up, 'it won't be a real one.'

'Doggie, doggie, doggie,' Tinker cried excitedly as she jumped up and down.

'Yes, well, I just hope my daughter won't be too disappointed.'

'I'd better make sure the dog's a bit special then. 'Bye, Mrs Bell, 'bye, Doris. See you on Monday.'

Tinker became quiet as he left, her brow furrowed. 'Bear come back, Mummy?'

'Yes, darling, you'll see him soon,' Emma said, and though she was loath to admit it, she too was looking forward to Monday.

Emma wanted to talk to the girls before any punters arrived, so that evening as they turned up for work she called them into her drawing room. 'I'm having building work done on the house so there will be some disruption whilst it's carried out. Hopefully it won't take long, and when completed there will be a separate entrance to the upstairs rooms.'

Linda was chewing gum as usual, her eyes hard in a heavily made-up face. 'Where will this entrance be?'

'At the side of the house.'

'So we'll be in a sort of self-contained flat?'

'Yes, that's right.'

Linda shrugged. 'Fine.'

Emma's eyes flicked to Rose, frowning as she noticed her swollen lip. Both Linda and Rose had been with them from the start, but Emma still knew little about them. She was unable to feel any connection to them, to any of the girls, keeping out of their way as much as possible, but Doris's accusation was heavy on her mind. It was true. She did keep her distance, but she was unable to comprehend how they could entertain one man after another – how they could let complete strangers defile their bodies for money. God, she'd been a bitch, taking the profits with no interest in their welfare, content to leave all that side of things to Doris. Yet in truth Emma knew she was unable to change, unable to involve herself in the goings-on upstairs.

With a small tight smile she said, 'Your lip looks sore, Rose. Are you sure you're up to working this evening?'

'Yeah, I'll be all right. I can't afford not to be.'

Emma knew she should pursue this conversation, but with all the girls waiting to start work, she knew that now wasn't the time. She'd leave it for now, find out from Doris later why Rose was so short of money. With a start she realised that one of the girls was speaking, the others nodding in agreement.

'Sorry, Jessie, what did you say?'

'I said that after what happened last night with Rose, it proves we need a minder, someone to turf out any punters that turn nasty.'

'It's a rare occurrence and I hardly think employing a man for protection is necessary.'

'Huh, rare or not, if that punter had a weapon, a knife or something, Rose would have got more than a split lip. If you ain't prepared to see that we have proper protection, we'll find somewhere else to do business, won't we, girls?' Jessie said, her eyes sweeping the room.

Several nodded. Emma balked. If the girls left it would take time to replace them. There'd be no money coming in and she didn't want that. It would mean paying a man a wage, something she didn't want to do, but she had to admit that Jessie had a point. It could have been worse, and at the thought of a man running amok with a knife, she blanched.

'All right, leave it with me and I'll speak to Doris about finding a minder.'

'Thanks, Mrs Bell,' Jessie said. 'I knew you'd see sense.'

There was a knock on the front door. Doris came in to say that a punter had arrived. One by one the girls filed out, whilst Emma remained where she was. Jessie had only been with them for a few months, but it seemed she was the ring-leader, the spokesperson, and Emma wondered why Doris hadn't mentioned this before.

After locking up for the night, Doris walked into the drawing room, handing Emma the night's takings.

Emma waited until she had counted the notes before voicing her thoughts. 'You've told me that Rose is popular, so she must be earning well, yet she said she's hard up. Why is she so short of money?'

''Cos she passes most of what she earns over to her old man. I've told her to hold some back, but she won't listen.'

'These girls never cease to amaze me,' Emma said, shaking her head in disgust. 'Rose must be mad to put up with it.'

'Yeah, I know, but she's besotted with the bloke.'

'More fool her. Another thing I wanted to speak to you about is Jessie. She seems a troublemaker.'

'Jessie's all right. Like me, she had a bad beating once, one that left her hospitalised. It left her a nervous wreck and it's one of the reasons she was glad to come here. Anyway, Em, if you ask me, she's right. We do need a minder.'

'Yes, I know, and Jessie made me realise that.

388

Let's get this building work out of the way first, and then we'll take one on.'

'Fair enough. I'll pass the word on to the girls.'

Emma handed Doris her usual share of the takings, both women then deciding to turn in. Emma crawled into bed, finding that, behind closed lids, Terry Green's face appeared.

She turned over, fighting the image as she thumped her pillow. She didn't want to think about him, about any man. She was fine on her own and intended to stay that way.

37

Though pleased with how the building work was progressing, Emma avoided Terry Green as much as possible over the next few days. Doris, on the other hand, was obviously smitten with the man and chatted to him at every opportunity. God, talk about making herself obvious. Tinker was as bad but, worried by the dangers of building work in progress, Emma kept her out of the way, much to her daughter's obvious disgust. Tinker's sulks would last until Terry and his labourer came into the kitchen for their tea breaks.

True to his word, Terry had turned up the first morning with a dog, but one on wheels. It was a brown terrier with glass eyes, and Tinker fell in love with it at first sight, now pushing it everywhere.

'Here you are, Mrs B,' Terry said as they came into the kitchen on Friday morning for their first break of the day.

'Tewwy,' Tinker cried happily, and as he sat down she immediately climbed onto his lap, the dog, called TT, by their side. The name had been Terry's idea, a combination of the first letters of both their names.

Emma took the brown paper bag Terry proffered, her jaw dropping when she saw it was full of tea. 'My goodness, where on earth did you get this?'

Terry winked, his eyes twinkling. 'From a mate of mine.'

'But I can't take this much. It's still on ration.'

'Now then, don't look a gift horse in the mouth.'

'How on earth did your friend get hold of it?'

'It ain't nicked, if that's what you're thinking, and with the amount of tea me and Eric drink, I'm sure it'll come in handy.'

Doris reached up to rest her hand on his shoulder. 'It's good of you, Terry, and thanks.'

'Er . . . yes, thanks,' Emma said, turning to busy herself with filling the teapot.

When she placed it on the table, Terry's young labourer smiled shyly. Eric was a quiet lad. His face was covered in angry-looking spots, which obviously embarrassed him. He was always polite and beneath the spots he reminded Emma in some ways of Luke.

On that thought she frowned. There had been a letter from him that morning, his words, as before, almost fanatical. On and on he went about the sins of women, how she had to repent and, upset, she had crushed this letter into a ball too before throwing it into the bin. Luke seemed so distant now, so far away, so alien from the brother she had known.

Oh, she didn't want to think about Luke and instead busied herself with pouring the tea. Tinker was chatting to Terry as usual, demanding his attention, and Emma caught a frown on Doris's face. God, the woman was being ridiculous, acting as if she saw the two-year-old as a rival. If this didn't stop she'd have something to say to her friend. Not only that, she was fed up with Doris interrupting Terry's work.

For a while they were quiet as they drank their tea. Then Eric carried their cups to the sink, rinsing them out as usual. At first his actions had surprised Emma. Her father, Horace and most men seemed to consider anything to do with housework to be women's work. They wouldn't have dreamed of helping, so she found Eric's attitude refreshing. When gently questioned, he'd told her that his father had been killed during the war, and that his mother worked full time in a factory, a job that kept her on her feet all day. He had three brothers, and the lot of them mucked in, but now they were all working, they hoped to persuade their mother to give up work.

Tinker protested as Terry lifted her from his knee. 'Sorry, little 'un, but I've got to get back to work.'

'Bang, bang, bang,' Tinker said.

'Yeah, that's right, now play with TT and I'll see you later.'

Emma had to smile at her daughter's description. Yes, the building work was a constant racket and she'd be glad when it was over. Terry Green and his labourer would be gone, the house back to normal. Oh, and that reminded her, she still had to talk to Doris about extending their hours. When the men had left she made sure that Tinker was occupied before raising the subject.

'I don't know, love,' Doris said. 'I'm sure the girls won't fancy it, and it would be a bit risky to operate during the day.'

'The girls will earn a lot more money, so why would they complain?'

'Christ, Emma, they ain't machines. They've got lives of their own, you know. Take me, for instance. When I was on the game I had my mother to see to during the day and only worked at night. A couple of the girls have got kids, and I think Annie is in the same position as I was.'

Emma frowned, annoyed that Doris hadn't welcomed her suggestion. Yes, she could see that it might be difficult for some of the girls, but others might welcome extended hours. 'Put it to them and see what they say. I still want to open for business in the afternoon and if they don't like it, we'll find other girls for the shift.'

'We! More like me, you mean.'

'Are you complaining, Doris?'

'No, of course not, but I still think you haven't thought about the risks. We'll have men turning up at all hours and questions might be asked.'

'By who?'

'Well, the neighbours for one thing.'

'The house next door is still empty, and there's no sign of a "For Sale" board. We face the Common, so the comings and goings aren't that noticeable to anyone else. I think you're worrying about nothing.'

'If you say so, but if the rozzers get wind of this place we'll be in trouble.'

'Then we'll just have to hope the new plaque explains our callers.'

'You seem to have it all worked out so I don't know why you're bothering to ask for my opinion.'

Emma sighed. 'Because I value your input and, as I've said many times before, I couldn't have set this place up without you. Not only that, it'll mean you'll be working more hours too.'

'That doesn't worry me. After being on the game, this hostess lark is a doddle.'

'It's more than I could do,' Emma said, shuddering at the thought. 'The building work is going well, and we'll need to find a minder soon. Though how we're supposed to get one is beyond me. After all, we can hardly advertise.'

'Don't worry. I've got the perfect person in mind.'

'Really? Well, that's good. Have a word with him, but don't go mad on what you offer him in wages.'

'I won't, but he won't work for peanuts.'

'All right, I'll leave it to you. You didn't put me wrong with a builder, and I'm sure you have the perfect candidate in mind.'

By the time another week had passed, Emma could see light at the end of the tunnel. The new staircase was in place, leading on to the first-floor landing, and she hoped Terry would soon be ready to install the bathroom. She was still keeping him at arm's length, her tone businesslike when she spoke to him, but he remained friendly and informal.

Doris had spoken to the girls, but only two were interested in the extended hours. She was now on the hunt for a couple of others, without luck so far, but when Doris came back that afternoon she was smiling.

'Rose put me on to a couple of girls that were interested and I've taken them on. They're both married and prefer day work, so I've told them they can start as soon as the alterations are finished.'

'Good. You've been out for ages, though, and I expect you could do with a cup of tea?'

'Yes please, love. I'll just pop round to tell Terry that you're making a brew. His back is playing up something awful, and no doubt he'll need a break.'

'I didn't notice anything when they stopped for lunch, and he didn't complain.'

'You hardly look at the man and Terry ain't one to moan. I reckon he should pack up this building lark before he cripples himself. I know he doesn't take on big jobs nowadays but, despite having a labourer, he still gets stuck in. He ain't that interested in money and there are easier ways to earn a few bob. Anyway, you get the kettle boiling and I'll be back in a tick.'

On that note, Doris shot out, whilst Emma turned to her task. Tinker was having her afternoon nap, and Emma relished the peace. Her daughter was becoming a handful, a wilful streak showing in her nature, and though she was only two she was beginning to rule the roost. Of course, Emma chided herself, it didn't help that she spoiled the child, and as Doris returned with the men in tow, she realised that the only person her daughter listened to these days was Terry.

It was going to be hard for Tinker when the man left. Maybe she should do more to keep her out of his way, though how she was going to achieve this, she had no idea.

'Hello, Mrs B,' Terry said as he drew out a chair to sit down.

'Mrs Bell,' Emma corrected him.

'Sorry,' he said, but his smile wasn't in any way contrite.

'Emma, I've been talking to Terry and persuaded him to stop taking on building work.'

'Have you, Doris? Well, I hope he's going to finish this job first.'

'Of course he is. Ain't that right, Terry?'

'Yes, it'll be finished in another week. Doris is right, my back is getting worse and the building game isn't worth the risk of doing it permanent damage. Anyway, I rather fancy the new job you've offered me.'

'New job! What new job?'

He looked puzzled for a moment, his eyes darting to Doris, and it was she who answered. 'I've asked Terry to be our minder. And he's agreed.'

38

It didn't take Terry long to settle into his new job, but on his way to work at twelve o'clock that day, his thoughts were on Emma Bell. Christ, she was an uppity cow, but how a woman who ran a brothel could act like the Queen of Sheba was beyond him.

Doris had told him a little of Emma's past, and finding out that her background was working class had left him gobsmacked. She acted like a lady, spoke like a lady, and treated him like a bloody servant. Unlike Doris, Emma hadn't been on the game, but that still didn't give her cause to act like the lady of the manor. The trouble was he fancied her rotten, and had done since the first time he laid eyes on her. It was mad – she wouldn't give him the time of day and he knew that – but despite trying, he couldn't get her out of his head. He deliberately turned up early every day, hoping to see her, and nine times out of ten he did.

Of course Doris was on offer, making it obvious that she was available, but though she wasn't a bad-looking bird, she'd once been a tart. He didn't have anything against prostitutes, but taking one out was another matter. Christ, thinking of all the blokes who'd been there before him made his stomach turn.

'Hello, love,' Doris said when she answered the door. 'You're early as usual.'

He nodded in acknowledgement, following her through to the kitchen and hoping to see Emma. She was there, sitting at the table with Tinker propped on cushions by her side; the child's mouth opening like a hungry little bird as Emma spooned in food. 'Hello, Mrs B.'

There was a heavy sigh. 'Look, will you stop calling me Mrs B? It's Mrs Bell, but if that's too hard for you, perhaps you should call me Emma.'

His eyes widened. Was this a breakthrough? Was she going to drop the airs and graces? 'Right, Emma it is, and how's my Tinker Bell?'

'TT not well.'

'Oh dear, what's wrong with him?'

'He's got bad eye.'

'I'd better take a look at him then.' Bending down, Terry peered at the toy dog. One of the glass eyes was loose, but could be easily mended. Giving Tinker a reassuring smile he said, 'I'll have him fixed in two ticks.'

The child smiled at him with delight and Terry grinned back. She was a lovely little girl, with the same fair colouring as her mother, and he had already grown very fond of her. She could sometimes be a little madam, demanding attention, but his sister's kids at that age had been the same.

'Here's your tea, Terry,' Doris said. 'I was certainly glad you were here last night. It's unbelievable. We've been running for a year without any problems, but in the last month we've had two punters turning nasty.'

'He was half cut and soon sorted.'

'What half cut?' Tinker asked.

Emma reared to her feet angrily. 'Haven't you two got any sense? I *do not* want business discussed in front of my daughter.'

'Leave it out, Em, Tinker's only a nipper. She doesn't understand what we're talking about,' Doris placated.

'She picked up on Terry saying, "half cut", and who knows what else she takes in. When my daughter is in the room, I don't want any discussions about the business. Is that clear?'

God, she's gorgeous, Terry thought, anger heightening the colour in her cheeks, her vivid blue eyes flashing. She was right, of course; they shouldn't talk in front of Tinker, and he'd make sure it never happened again. 'Yes, it's clear and I'm sorry.'

'Yeah, me too, Em,' Doris said sulkily.

Emma nodded in acknowledgement, but her lips remained tight. The atmosphere was strained and, refusing to accept another mouthful of food, Tinker struggled to get down. Emma gave in, lifting her daughter to the floor where she immediately flew onto Terry's lap.

He hugged her to him, glad of the distraction, and trying to think of some way to turn the conversation. 'Did you hear about the disaster at the Farnborough Air Show?'

'No, what happened?' Doris asked.

'Well, from what I read in the paper, a jet fighter had just broken the sound barrier when it fell apart over speculators. They reckon that at least twenty-seven people were killed.'

'I think you mean "spectators", Terry,' Doris corrected, 'and now we know your game, why don't you drop the act?'

'Yeah, all right, but loads of people were injured too.'

'What's innered, Tewwy?' Tinker asked.

'See, and I used the right word this time. "Injured" means hurt, sweetheart.'

'Like my doggie?'

'Yes, that's right, but how about I fix him now?'

'I help,' Tinker said, scrambling from his lap.

'I couldn't do it without you, darling,' he said. Glancing at Emma, he was relieved to see that the tension had left her face.

When TT's eye was fixed, Tinker insisted that he needed a bandage, and it was Emma who found one. She joined them on the floor, tying the bandage over his eye and around his head. With a bow fastened on top, the toy dog looked comical and Emma laughed. Terry saw that her eyes were warm as they met his, and for a moment, he dared to hope.

Almost immediately, her expression hardened and, rising to her feet, Emma said brusquely, 'Right, Tinker, let's get you dressed and we'll go shopping.'

'No, Mummy. I stay with Terry.'

'He has work to do, and so does Auntie Doris.'

Tinker tried her usual trick, throwing herself to the floor in a tantrum, arms and legs kicking wildly in protest.

Terry spoke firmly. 'Now then, stop this. Be a good girl for me, and do as Mummy says.'

'You no go away, Tewwy?'

'No, darling, I won't go away and I'll pop down to see you later.' But as he said these words he looked at Emma, relieved to see her small nod.

Mollified, Tinker's tantrum ceased, and with a sigh of what sounded like annoyance, but could have been relief, Emma took the child's hand, leading her into the hall.

'You've got a way with kids,' Doris said as she watched them depart. 'I reckon you'd make a smashing dad – and I wouldn't mind being a mum one day,' she said hopefully.

Terry knew he had to nip this in the bud. Doris was making her feelings more and more obvious. 'Yeah, I might have a way with Tinker, but I'm getting nowhere with her mother.'

'Emma! Don't tell me you've got your eye on Emma.'

'Well, you've got to admit she's a smasher.'

'You haven't got a chance. Emma isn't interested in men.'

'Blimey . . . don't tell me she prefers women?'

'No, of course not, but she hates men. Not only that, Emma's frigid.'

Terry stared at Doris, sure that it wasn't true. It was just sour grapes, it had to be.

'Come on,' she now said, 'it's time for us to open up.'

Terry, his mind still on Emma, rose to his feet and followed Doris upstairs. Only ten minutes later the girls began to arrive, their banter at first going over his head. In the small sitting room they used to wait for punters, Lena put the kettle on, and the noise of cups rattling finally broke into his thoughts.

'Here, Terry, my old man is talking about buying a car,' Maureen chirped.

Terry smiled thinly, noting Maureen's blousy appearance. Her skirt was short, revealing pudgy knees, and her tight sweater low cut. 'Is he? New or second-hand?'

'He fancies a new one, but I'll have to increase my shifts to raise the money.'

Maureen's husband knew that she was on the game, and it never ceased to amaze Terry. 'How does your old man feel about that?'

'Oh, he won't mind. He's a funny sod and when we're at it, he loves me to describe how the punters perform.' She winked. 'It sort of titillates him, if you know what I mean.'

Lena, a slim thirty-year-old with bleached, platinum-blonde hair, paused with the teapot in her hand, lips pursed. 'It sounds a bit sick, if you ask me,' she commented. 'Blimey, if my old man found out what I was up to, he'd kill me.'

'My boyfriend knows, but never mentions it,' said Jane, the youngest of the group, her innocent face belying her trade. 'He's happy to take the money I earn and most of it goes down his throat in whisky.'

'You're mad to put up with it. I've told you before, you should tell him that what you earn is yours, and if he doesn't like it, he can bugger off,' Lena snapped.

'Yeah, you've told me, and if you remember, when I took your advice all I had to show for it was a black eye.'

'So leave him.'

'Oh, no, I couldn't do that,' Jane protested, raising a hand to flick long, dark hair away from her face. 'He might be a drinker, but he cares about me.'

'Cares about you? Are you mad, girl?' Maureen said. 'If my old man so much as raised a finger to me, I'd tear his head off and you should do the same.'

Their doorbell rang and Terry went down to answer it, returning with another of the girls.

'Watcha,' said Elsie, a redhead who tottered on high heels. Her eyes swept over them and, sensing the atmosphere, she added, 'What's up?'

'It's nothing,' Doris said, 'just a difference of opinion. Now, before any punters arrive, I want a word with you about the rooms. The girls on the evening shift have complained about the state they're left in and Mrs Bell isn't happy about it. She cleans the rooms every morning, and they're immaculate when you start work, but by the time you leave they're a tip. She doesn't mind changing the sheets, but that should be all that needs doing. You, for instance, Lena, left face powder all over the dressing table yesterday.'

'Oh, I do beg your pardon, I'm sure,' Lena said, her voice dripping with sarcasm as she folded pudgy arms defensively under her huge bust. 'Didn't Her Highness like clearing it up?'

'That's enough,' Doris snapped. 'This house is

Mrs Bell's and if it wasn't for her, you'd be plying your trade on the streets.'

'Yeah, maybe, but she does all right out of us, taking a good percentage of what we earn.'

'And you do all right too. You're well looked after, safe, but if you'd prefer a pimp, you're welcome to leave. That goes for all of you.'

'I ain't complaining,' Maureen protested, 'but I don't leave my room in a mess.'

'I know. But as for the rest of you, I've said my piece and we'll leave it at that.'

There were a few murmurs of dissent, but Doris ignored them, and as the doorbell rang again, the girls fussed with their appearances whilst Doris went downstairs to let in the first punter of the day.

Terry kept out of the way, knowing his presence could put a punter off, but he remained in hearing distance whilst the man made his selection. In his fifties he was a familiar face, a regular. As usual he chose Jane. The man had never caused any problems, paying up without complaint, and Terry relaxed.

Jane led the man to her room, and Terry closed his mind to what went on inside. He knew that within half an hour, Jane would be available again, and as she was a popular girl, more men would follow. He grimaced. He was a minder, for Gawd's sake, but couldn't help his prudish attitude. He looked after the girls, liked them, but there wasn't one he would touch with a barge pole. His mind drifted back to Emma, still unable to believe what Doris had said. Once again he was sure that it was sour grapes, Doris only saying that because he refused to show any interest in her.

39

A month later, Emma was walking towards the grocer's when she saw the young man walking towards her, and halted in her tracks. He drew closer, his face set and unsmiling, whereas Emma's lips turned upwards.

'My goodness, Luke, it's been so long since I've seen you! You never mentioned that you were coming over.'

'I had to get permission to leave my studies, but I just had to come.' His eyes went to the pushchair. 'She's beautiful,' he murmured. 'So pretty . . . so innocent.'

Emma saw that Tinker was frowning as she looked up at Luke and was saddened. This was her uncle yet, like the rest of her family, he was a stranger to her.

'I suppose you've heard that Dick is doing his national service. Have you been to see anyone else?'

'No, Emma. I travelled from Ireland for one specific purpose, and that is to see you. You've ignored my letters but I have to make you see the error of your ways.'

Luke's voice was pompous, older-sounding than his years, and Emma protested, 'Oh no, not another sermon.'

'Emma, can't you see that what you are doing is an abomination? Before I left for Ireland I feared for you. I warned you there would be a time when you became desperate and told you to go to Dick. Yet even I didn't foresee this. When Dick first wrote to tell me what you were up to, I was shocked to the core, but felt sure you would come to your senses. It seems I was wrong. I have prayed for you, constantly, but you're still running a house of sin.'

Emma's back was rigid. Luke had been her favourite brother, but the young man standing before her now a stranger. 'Well, Luke, I'm sorry that you've had to be dragged away from your studies, but I'm doing what I have to do in order to survive.'

'There are other ways, Emma. You must stop. You must find a decent way to make a living. If you turn to God, pray for redemption, He will help you.'

'God! Don't make me laugh. Where was God when I was half starving? Where was God when I tried to earn a so-called decent living? Where was God when I was raped by my first lodger?'

Luke blanched, but then recovered his equilibrium. 'Oh, Emma, I am so sorry to hear that you have suffered, but you have a daughter, a beautiful innocent child. How can you bring her up in a brothel? How can you taint her with your sinful ways?'

Emma's eyes were rounded with shock as she listened to her brother. Sinful, he thought her sinful, yet in truth she felt more sinned against. Without any understanding of what she had been through, he was judging her, and her voice now echoed her anger.

'How dare you? I don't sleep with the clients and never will. As for my daughter, she will *not* be tainted and I'll see to that. Now I suggest you go back to Ireland and in future keep your nose out of my business.'

'No, Emma, I'm not going anywhere until you've come to your senses.'

'I didn't invite you here, Luke, and I certainly don't have to listen to you.'

'Please, Emma, please . . . for the sake of your child . . .'

Tinker was crying now, obviously upset by the argument.

Swinging the pushchair round, Emma spat, 'Just go away, Luke. Save your lectures and sermons for those that want to hear them.'

Emma didn't look back as she marched home,

her shopping forgotten as anger coursed through her veins.

It took a while to comfort Tinker, and Emma stayed with her, holding her hand until she fell asleep. She then crept from the room, the encounter with Luke and his harsh words consuming her mind. Now that her anger had abated, she felt a wave of sadness. Why did her brothers have to be so judgemental? She wasn't like the girls, she didn't sleep with the punters, and if they weren't using her house, they would only ply their trade elsewhere, perhaps facing the dangers of the streets.

For a while Emma just sat, reliving her childhood and the relationship she had once shared with her brothers – a relationship that because she wouldn't do as they asked had become well and truly severed. Luke, like Dick, wanted her to close the business, but she had no intention of doing that, no intention of ever returning to a life of poverty. On that thought, Emma rose to her feet and, grabbing her cleaning materials, decided to tackle some housework, vigorously polishing her furniture whilst her heart grew even harder as she forced her brother from her mind.

An hour later she peeped in on Tinker, finding her daughter awake.

'Hello, darling.'

'Where's Tewwy?'

'He's busy, darling.'

'Want Tewwy!'

Emma could see that a tantrum was imminent, and felt a wave of annoyance. Terry was the only one who seemed to have any control over her daughter. She had hoped to keep the child away from the man, but it seemed impossible. From the start, she should have kept to her resolution that these private quarters remained private and off limits to Terry.

Of course it didn't help that Doris welcomed the man in every time he knocked on the door, and now she couldn't think of a good excuse to keep him out.

'You'll see Terry soon,' she promised, taking Tinker through to the kitchen where she poured her a glass of juice.

The child began to play with her numerous toys, and as Emma watched her, she couldn't help thinking of her sisters and how little they had had in comparison. Peg or rag dolls had been their playthings, but things had improved when her father married Polly. At that thought, Luke entered her mind again, but she forced him away, forced them all away. She couldn't, wouldn't, think about her family.

Her idea of opening in the afternoon had paid dividends and the money was rolling in. She had already almost replenished the money laid out on the alterations, and soon she'd be able to replace more of the furniture that she'd been forced to sell. She just hoped that Doris had spoken to the girls, ensuring that they kept the rooms up to scratch.

Half an hour later there was a knock on the front door. Emma picked Tinker up, and went to answer it. Surely it wasn't Luke? Surely he hadn't come back to give her another lecture? Frowning, she opened the door to see a middle-aged man sporting a trilby hat.

'Yes, can I help you?'

He looked furtively over his shoulder and, seeing this action she snapped, 'Use the side entrance.'

His brow rose, and for a moment Emma thought she saw a hint of amusement in his eyes, but then after briefly raising his hat, he said, 'Yes, ma'am,' before walking back down the front steps and heading around the corner of the house.

Emma sharply closed the door, annoyed. It didn't happen often that clients knocked on the front door, but any intrusion from the business side of the house into her private quarters annoyed her. Maybe they should make the sign larger, the small plaque at the bottom of the drive only saying 'French Lessons' with an arrow pointing to the side entrance. French lessons – what a joke – but it mostly did the trick.

With a sigh, Emma decided to talk to Terry about making the directions more obvious, and then settling Tinker with her toys again, she began to clean the cooker. Doris said she was obsessed with cleaning, but Emma didn't care. She wanted everything perfect, every room sparkling clean, and anyway, she didn't want Tinker picking up any germs.

It was ten o'clock at night when Emma heard the door at the top of the stairs opening and footsteps hurrying down the stairs. It was unusual for Doris to take a break at this time, and she felt a shiver of apprehension when she saw the expression on her friend's face as she burst into the room.

'What is it? What's wrong?'

'We've got a problem, Em, and a big one.'

'I didn't hear anything. Is someone causing trouble again?'

'Yeah, but not in the way you think.' Doris flopped down beside Emma, exhaling loudly. 'There's someone upstairs who wants a back-hander and I don't think we've got a lot of choice.'

'Doris, for God's sake, what are you talking about?'

'It's a copper, from CID, and if you want to keep this place open we'll have to keep him sweet.'

'No! I can't believe it. Surely you've got it wrong! Plain clothes or not, he's still a policeman.'

'Gawd, wake up, girl. All right, most coppers are straight, and those in uniform are the best, but even so, there are a few bent ones.'

'How much does he want?'

'I dunno. He insists on talking to you.'

'No, no, I don't want to. Can't you do it?'

'I tried, but he ain't having it. For once, girl, you're going to have to get your hands dirty.'

Doris had warned her that this might happen, but she hadn't believed her. Emma wanted to run, to hide, but knew she had to see this man. 'All right, bring him down.'

When the man walked into the room, Emma's jaw dropped.

'Good evening, ma'am,' he said, and though this time he wasn't wearing his hat, Emma immediately recognised him.

'You . . . you were here earlier.'

'Yes, that's right, and I came back to check my facts before speaking to you.'

Emma hated the way he was looking at her, a mixture of amusement again in his eyes, along with calculation. 'I've been told that you're with the CID, but I'd like to see some sort of identification.'

He nodded, showing her his ID and then without invitation, took a seat. 'From what I've seen, you've got a nice little earner going on upstairs, and if you want to stay open, I want a percentage of the takings.'

'You're disgusting,' Emma snapped. 'You're supposed to enforce the law, not use it to make money.'

His eyes hardened. 'Fine, if that's your attitude, then I'll arrest you for running a brothel.'

'And I'll tell your senior officer that you were trying to blackmail me.'

He laughed derisively. 'Oh, yeah? And who do you think he'd believe? Me, or a madam, even one who speaks with a plum in her mouth. Think about it. One call from me and this place will be swarming with police, and you'll be in a cell.'

Emma felt the colour drain from her face. My God, prison! She could go to prison! He smiled, a sickening leer, and she knew there was no choice. 'All right, how much do you want?'

He named a price and Emma balked. 'But that's ridiculous.'

'For what you'll get in return, it's a small price to pay.'

'Just what will I be getting?'

'You can leave it to me to make sure that these premises don't come into question again. Oh yes, and I'll take my first payment now.'

With a sigh Emma rose to her feet. Going through to her bedroom, she cast a quick glance over her shoulder before taking the tin cash box from its hiding place. It made her stomach churn to take out the money, but, teeth grinding, she returned to the living room and handed it to the officer.

'Right, good girl. I'll see you again next week.'

'That won't be necessary,' Emma said hurriedly. 'I'll leave the money upstairs with my assistant.'

'Assistant! Considering she's a tom, that's a good one.' His eyes then roamed over her body. 'I think I'd rather deal with you.'

'No,' Emma said, fumbling for a lie. 'I'm not always here.'

For a moment his eyes narrowed, but she held his gaze, relieved when he said, 'All right, I'll pick it up from your so-called assistant, but in case you're thinking of changing your mind, remember that I can have this place shut down any time I like.'

'You'll get your money,' and though quaking inside, she added, 'I'd like you to leave now.'

He looked momentarily annoyed at the order, but then shrugged. 'Fair enough, but no doubt we'll see each other again. Soon.'

When Emma had closed the street door behind him, she slumped with relief.

'Are you all right, Emma?'

She spun round. 'Yes, I'm fine, Terry, but how did you get down here so quickly?'

'I've been here all the time, keeping out of sight but within earshot. Do you want me to take care of that bastard?'

'If you're suggesting what I think you are, then no. I don't want any violence, Terry, and anyway, what good would it do? He'd only shut us down, and I don't want that.'

'All right, if you say so, but are you sure you wouldn't rather pack this game in? There's more to life than money, you know, and easier ways to make a living.'

It was as though Luke's words had returned to haunt her. Annoyed, she snapped, 'I tried that, Terry, and it didn't work. Now you'd best get back upstairs.'

He shook his head, but said nothing further, and as he left, Emma slumped again. Yes, she'd tried a so-called easier way to make a living and, as she had told Luke, she'd been raped. Now another man was invading her life, this time raping her of money. Oh, she hated them. Hated them all.

40

Emma was a very rich woman by the time the 1950s drew to a close. She was now twenty-eight years old and all traces of the innocent girl she had once been had gone. She was a beautiful, statuesque woman who drew eyes, but one that none would dare to interfere with. She had seen too much, had grown so hard that her shell was impenetrable. Only one person saw softness, and that was her daughter, ten-year-old Tinker, spoiled, manipulative, and able to get her own way not only with her mother, but Terry Green too, the pair of them wrapped firmly around her finger.

Though Emma would never welcome Terry as a lover, over the years they had become friends, and he was one of the few men she was relaxed with. Doris had given up on him years ago, finally accepting that the man would never be interested in her. They had in some ways become a family, replacing the one that Emma had lost, and though Terry was a strong man, it was Emma who always held the dominant role.

There had been times when Emma thought about her family, but mostly she pushed the memories away, finding the only way to cope was to keep her barriers up. There had been a time, many years earlier, when she'd been determined to see her sisters, but as the years passed with all of her letters returned, she had finally let it go. They would be grown up now, and if they knew how she made her living, no doubt, like Dick and Luke, they would reject her.

And so to avoid hurt, Emma's veneer had thickened; her emotions firmly under lock and key. It was unfortunate that Tinker didn't know her uncles and aunties, but Doris still lived in the flat, becoming a surrogate auntie, and with Terry coming and going more or less as he pleased, Emma was sure the child didn't lack love or affection.

The flat was now a little palace. Emma was unable to resist buying every luxury that had been on offer when rationing ended. She had splashed out on deep red, plush, velvet curtains, a new sofa, piled with cushions, and a lovely mahogany display cabinet for her growing collection of Royal Crown Derby figurines. Yet few saw the beauty of her private quarters. Tinker rebelled, of course, wanting to invite her school friends round, but this was the one instance where her mother wouldn't be swayed.

'Tinker, get on with your homework,' Emma said when she saw her daughter daydreaming.

'Do I have to? I hate history. It's boring.'

'Hate it or not, it's got to be done. You'll be taking the eleven-plus examinations soon and I want you to pass.'

'I don't care if I don't.'

'Well, I do, darling. I want you to have a good education, to go to grammar school and then on to college.'

'Why?'

'We've been through this before. You know why. I've told you over and over again, education is important. It will open up so many opportunities for you, and if you gain qualifications you'll be able to get a good job instead of being stuck in a factory or shop.'

'I wouldn't mind working in a shop. Cor, especially a sweet shop.'

'Stop saying, "cor". It makes you sound common.'

'Terry says it, and so does Auntie Doris. Mummy, why are they upstairs every night?'

'Not this again. I've told you, they're working.'

'But how? They don't speak French.'

'Now that's enough. You're just asking questions

to get out of doing your homework, but it won't work.'

Tinker scowled, but returned to her books whilst Emma watched her, lost in thought. It was getting harder and harder to fob Tinker off. Though Emma was loath to spend money, it really was time to move the business premises. The house next door remained empty and would have been ideal, but structural damage had put off any buyers for all these years, her included. Of course there was always the possibility that she could rent somewhere suitable, leaving her considerable savings intact. One way or another she would have to sort out something very soon. The situation could only get worse and she had to protect her daughter.

The room was quiet, Tinker's pen scratching across the page, but then the child looked up.

'Is Terry my daddy?'

Emma stiffened. 'Of course not. What on earth makes you think that?'

'All my friends have daddies that live with them, and Terry is always here.'

'Well, I can assure you that he isn't your father. He works for me, darling, that's all.'

'Where's my daddy then?'

Emma had heard this question many times before and gave the same answer. 'I've told you, darling. Your daddy left us before you were born and I don't know where he is.'

'Can't you find him? My friends have got dads and I want one.'

'No, darling, I can't find him, but surely it's not the end of the world? You have me, your auntie Doris, and Terry.'

'I still want a dad.'

'I know, and I'm sorry. Now come on, be a good girl and get that homework finished.'

Tinker scowled, but she did as she was told, whilst Emma picked up a book, finding that the words swam before her eyes. She had lied to her daughter again, and knew that for a while the child would be satisfied, but what about when she grew older, into her teens, what then? Would she want to find her father? God, she hoped not. There would be nothing for her there but disappointment and heartbreak. Horace hadn't wanted her before she was born and he certainly wouldn't want her now. Briefly, she wondered where he was, but then dismissed him from her mind. She had more things to worry about than Horace, and uppermost was finding suitable premises to rent.

When Doris came down that evening she sat next to Emma on the sofa, picked up the evening paper and scanned the front page. 'Gawd blimey, I thought I recognised that geezer. Look,' she said, stabbing her finger at the picture she thrust under

Emma's nose, 'his wife looks a right smasher, but it didn't stop him coming here last night.'

'Never!' Emma cried as she took in the man's face. He was often featured in newspapers as he was prominent and popular in the music industry. 'You must be mistaken. Why on earth would he come here?'

'Blimey, Em, after all these years I don't think I need to answer that question. He came for the usual, well, sort of. He wanted a much younger girl, but in the end settled for Lucy. She can just about pass for sixteen if the lights are dim.'

'Lucy is only nineteen – surely that's young enough? Oh, don't tell me he's one of those disgusting types that turn up now and then?'

'I reckon he was. Some geezers actually come here demanding a virgin, the daft buggers, and maybe that's what he was looking for.'

'You should have given him to Bridget.'

Doris sniggered. 'Yeah, she'd have sorted him out. Men's preferences never cease to amaze me and, if you ask me, Bridget's got the cushiest job here. Huh, bondage! Who'd have thought some men just want a girl to inflict pain? All she has to do is whip them, hurt them, and they're happy. It's just as well she uses one of the attic rooms or you'd probably hear them begging for more.'

Emma's lips curled. 'As long as they pay for their so-called pleasure, it suits me, and as far as

I'm concerned Bridget can inflict as much pain as she likes.'

'Sometimes I think you envy Bridget,' Doris chuckled. 'Mind you, I wouldn't mind seeing you in her black leather bondage gear. That'd be a sight to behold.'

'I can think of quite a few men I wouldn't mind inflicting pain on, especially the latest one looking for a backhander.'

'Yeah, I know. When that last bloke from the CID retired, another one soon took his place, but at least this time he just wants the money. He doesn't expect one of the girls as an extra perk. The last one took his pick, usually going for a young one. Jane was his favourite and the girl said he liked it rough too, but at least he never marked her.'

Emma was sickened, closing her eyes momentarily. Then she said, 'Did Terry check all the rooms upstairs and then lock up?'

'You ask that every night and you get the same answer. Of course he did, and this flat is locked up like a bloody fortress. You worry too much.'

'Maybe, but it's better to be safe than sorry.'

'I still think it wouldn't hurt to let Terry live in.'

'No, we've been over this time and time again. I don't want a man in my house – even Terry. In fact, I think it's time to move the business.'

'You've been saying that for ages.'

'I mean it this time. Tinker isn't a baby any more. She's getting too inquisitive. I know we're careful, but I still have this horror that one day she'll find her way upstairs. I want her to have a normal home, one that she can invite her friends to and not one that houses a brothel.'

'Have you somewhere in mind?'

'No, but we can start scouting around. It'll have to be somewhere that's tucked away, detached, with good, private access.'

'It sounds like you want a mirror image of this place and that's gonna cost a pretty penny.'

'I'm talking about renting, not buying.'

'Oh yeah, and how are you gonna find a landlord that's prepared to let you turn his place into a brothel?'

Emma slapped her forehead with the palm of her hand. 'Oh God, I'm an idiot. I didn't think of that.' She bit hard on her bottom lip whilst doing a mental calculation. 'All right, I'll have to buy somewhere, but it'll be nothing like this place.'

'If you ask me, the answer's right under your nose. Keep this place for the business, and buy somewhere smaller for us and Tinker.'

Emma stared at her friend, unwilling to see the sense of her suggestion. She loved her home, her beautiful, plush flat, full of the antiques that had replaced the ones she'd been forced to sell so many years before. Yes, she could buy a smaller house, but it would have none of this grandeur, a grandeur that she was unwilling to give up. In the past she had worried that Horace might return to sell it from under her nose, but as the years went by, her concerns diminished. If Horace tried to get her out now, he'd have a fight on his hands. She was no longer an innocent. She was a businesswoman who wouldn't be intimidated by Horace, or any man.

'No, Doris, I don't want a smaller house. I love this place and no matter what, I'm keeping it.'

'Back to square one then,' Doris murmured, 'but the sort of place you want will be hard to find, well, unless you're prepared to pay a bloody fortune for it.'

Emma sat pondering, but then straightened up, her face animated. 'There was a time when I considered buying the house next door, but the structural damage put me off. It's been on the market for years now and would probably go for a song.'

'Yeah, maybe, but if it's that badly damaged, it won't be fit to live in.'

'I could get Terry to have a look at it. He'd know if it can be made habitable and what it would cost. It's worth a try.'

'All right, but for now if you don't mind I think I'll turn in. It was a busy night and I'm whacked.'

'Yes, I'm ready for bed too,' Emma said.

The two women left the room, and as was Emma's routine, she checked that the street door was firmly locked. She then waited until Doris was safely in her room before switching off the hall lights. In darkness she headed for the bedroom she still shared with her daughter, another reason for buying separate premises for the business. Emma paused on the threshold, feeling a shiver of apprehension. With ears pricked she stood motionless, holding her breath, but the house was still, with only the ticking of the grand-father clock breaking the silence. With a sigh of relief she stepped into her room, closing the door behind her. She didn't know why she was feeling jittery, why she felt she was being watched. Trying to dismiss her unease, Emma climbed into bed, but she found sleep elusive.

It was past midnight and Horace Bell was leaning forward over his desk, his eyes on the snapshot of Emma's daughter. Until now he had done his best to forget his wife and had almost been successful, but since getting the results of his tests, he couldn't get her daughter out of his mind.

When told that his disease was too far advanced to be cured, he had railed at fate, at the thought of dying. He had no belief in God, no belief in an afterlife, and for the first time realised that with his death his line would be gone for ever. There would be nothing to show for his existence, for all the years he had taken building his considerable fortune, a fortune that meant nothing now, the money unable to buy a medical cure.

Once again, he scanned the small photograph, looking for signs that this child might be his – his flesh and blood. There was no getting away from the fact that she was like her mother, but he was sure he could see something of himself in her features. His mind turned, remembering when Emma told him she was pregnant, and his horror at the thought. He hadn't wanted a child, choosing instead to believe that Emma had been unfaithful. It had given him further reason to desert her.

Now though, as he gazed at the photograph, he was facing the truth. Emma had been innocent when he married her, a virgin, and in reality he doubted that she'd had an affair so soon after their marriage. Horace finally accepted that the child was his and unexpected emotions rose to the surface. His fingers shook as he put down the photograph to pick up the report, scanning the contents. The man had been thorough, keeping a watch on Emma's movements for months, even managing to find out how well her daughter was doing at school. The child was bright, intelligent, and as Horace turned to the next page, he felt a surge of rage. A brothel, his house was being used as a brothel, and worse, his child was living on the premises!

He stood up, pacing the room in anger, at last calming down as he came to a decision. There was still time to do something, to put plans for the child in place, and first thing in the morning, he intended to do just that.

41

When Terry arrived the following morning he had the newspaper as usual. Emma made a pot of tea and then, sitting at the kitchen table, they tackled the crossword. It was a routine that had developed over the years, sharing a love of words.

'The only one we're stuck on now is seven across. I don't know much about herbs.'

Emma cocked her head to one side, frowning. The clue was eluding her too, but then suddenly she smiled. 'Lovage, it's a herb, but does it fit?'

'Yeah – but that's a new one on me. Well done, Emma.'

The crossword finished, Terry pushed it to one side. Emma refilled his cup, then said, 'I'd like to know what sort of condition the house next door is in. Would you come with me to take a look at it?'

'Yes, but why?'

'I'm thinking of buying it.' Eagerly Emma went on to tell him of her plans.

Terry swallowed the last of his tea before rising to his feet. 'All right, let's go.'

Emma eagerly followed him next door, but as Terry walked slowly around the perimeter of the property, his lips set in a grimace. 'It'll need a lot of work, Emma. To start with it needs underpinning, and that's a nasty crack in the wall.'

Emma looked to where Terry was pointing and had to admit the house looked almost derelict. 'What about the roof?'

'It wants replacing, and with the other things I've pointed out, that's just the start. Gawd knows what it's like on the inside.'

She held up the keys. 'I got them from the agent.'

'Where is he?'

'I think he's given up on trying to sell it, and when I said I wanted my builder to take a look at the place, he just handed them over.'

'Shouldn't that tell you something?'

'Well, yes, but come on,' she beckoned.

The street door was so warped that Terry had a job to push it open, but after putting his shoulder to it, they managed to get inside. Emma's face fell. The house stank of damp, the once beautiful central staircase, which should have been a mirror image of hers, so badly damaged that it looked beyond repair. She went into the drawing room, saw that the original cornices and fireplace remained, but could see daylight through a large crack in the wall.

'Oh, Terry,' she gasped, 'it's a wreck.'

'Yeah, I guessed as much.'

'But it's such a shame,' Emma said as they wandered back into the hall. 'It has the same beautiful proportions as my house, yet only looks fit for demolition.'

Terry puffed out his cheeks, saying nothing as they continued the tour. In the kitchen they found only a badly stained sink and battered cupboard, yet the original flag tiles underfoot appeared undamaged. Emma shook her head as they went from room to room, wishing now she hadn't built her hopes up.

'Come on, we might as well go.'

'Yeah, in a minute,' Terry said, continuing to inspect floors and walls.

When they finally stepped outside again, Terry paused on the top step, looking towards the Common. 'Look, I know you had your heart set on this place, and I must admit when I first saw it I thought you were mad. Now though, I'm not so sure. Like yours, this house is in a great position. It faces the Common and has good-size grounds. Yeah, it'll cost an arm and a leg to put right, but the potential is there, and you'll be building yourself a nice little nest egg.'

'Hold on, Terry. Are you saying I should buy it?'

'That depends on the price. As I said, it's gonna cost money, a lot of money, to put right, and I'm not sure how you're fixed.'

'How much are we talking about?'

'Depends on the builder, and it's been a while since I was in the game.'

'A rough idea would do.'

Terry pursed his lips, and when he named a price Emma's eyes widened. She wasn't prepared to tell Terry how much she was worth, but his estimate was double what she'd anticipated. Still, if she could bargain the price down, well down, it was still possible.

'Thanks, Terry. I'll take the keys back and have a word with the agent. If I do manage to buy it, can you recommend any builders?'

'Yeah, I know a good crew, but are you sure about this, Em?'

Once again her eyes roamed over the façade, seeing in her mind's eye the house restored to its former glory. 'Yes, I'd love to buy it, but it all rests on the price.'

Emma had been pleased with her bargaining skills and now, only two months later, work was progressing on the house next door. The renovation costs had been higher than Terry's rough estimate, but after scouring estate agents and seeing how much property of the same size fetched, it still seemed a good deal.

It was nearly one o'clock on a fine autumn afternoon as she sat at the kitchen table, turning over swatches of material for the perfect soft furnishings.

Doris pursed her lips. 'Ain't you jumping the gun, Em? It'll be ages before the place is fit to decorate.'

'I like to be prepared. What do you think of this duck-egg-blue satin, for the curtains?'

'Now don't go spending a fortune on décor, Em. I know you want the place to look nice, but at the end of the day it'll still be a knocking shop.'

Terry was absorbed in a crossword, some of the clues eluding both him and Emma. He looked up, his brows creased. 'Hang on. Surely you're not moving the business next door?'

'Well, yes, I thought you knew that.'

'No, I didn't, and if you ask me, it doesn't make sense.'

'Yes it does,' Emma snapped. 'I want my daughter away from the goings on upstairs.'

'I know that, but the business works fine from here. This is the last house on the row, and the nicely concealed side entrance is perfect.'

'But I love this house.'

'The one next door is the same, except it isn't converted into flats.'

'He's right, love,' Doris said, 'and if you think about it, it'll be one in the eye for Horace if he ever turns up.'

'After all this time, I don't think it's likely.'

'Yeah, but what if he did? He left you in the shit, saying this place is in his name and you can never sell it. Can't you just see it, Em? He'd turn up to find his precious house is now a knocking shop, and that you'd managed to buy an identical one next door on the proceeds. That'd be *your* house, Em, in *your* name.'

Emma realised Doris was right. She loved this house so much that it had become an obsession to keep it. Yet it still wasn't hers. It had never been hers. Her eyes sparkled up with excitement. 'Yes, I'll move next door into *my* house and, not only that, I'll do it up like a palace.'

'Looking at what you've done with this flat, I don't doubt it,' Doris commented. 'There's only one thing, Em. When you move, this flat will be empty. I'd really like my own place again, so is there any chance I could stay here?'

'Well . . . I suppose so,' Emma said, disliking the thought of living separately from her friend, 'but I'd miss you.'

'But I'd only be next door.'

Emma paused, thinking it over. Doris looked

so keen on the idea, her face bright with anticipation. With a sigh she said, 'All right, you can
have it, but what about furniture? I'll be taking
most of this stuff with me.'

'Oh, don't worry about that. I've got a nice few
bob saved so it won't be a problem.'

'That's a shame,' Terry commented, his expression sad.

'What's a shame?'

'Oh, it's nothing. It's just that I had my eye on
this place too.'

'Never mind, love,' Doris said, grinning
cheekily, 'you can always move in with me.'

Terry winked. 'Well, Doris, it's lucky for you
that I'm a gentleman or I might've taken you up
on the offer.'

'You don't have to be a gentleman with me,
Terry.'

'Really? Well, girl, I might just think about it.'

Emma surged to her feet. 'If you two have
finished flirting, it's about time you opened up
for business, and,' she added, 'I'm not sure about
you having the flat now, Doris. It would make
more sense to take on more girls, using the extra
rooms for business.'

Doris stood up. 'Emma Bell, if I didn't know
you better, I'd think you were jealous,' she
commented as she marched from the room.

Terry flung Emma a look before following

Doris, but Emma refused to meet his eyes. Jealous indeed! What did she care if Doris and Terry turned this place into a love nest? Emma sat down again, trying to dismiss the idea from her mind as she turned back to the swatches of material.

It was nearly teatime before Emma saw Doris again, the woman dour as she came into the sitting room. Emma raised her eyebrows as she asked, 'What on earth's the matter with you?'

'If you don't know, I ain't gonna tell you.'

'Don't be childish. If you've got something on your mind, then spit it out.'

'Not in front of the nipper,' Doris hissed.

'I'm not a nipper,' Tinker protested, her voice now pleading as she added, 'Mummy, can I watch television now?'

'You spend far too much time watching television and I'm beginning to regret buying it. Why don't you read a nice book?'

'But, Mummy, *Blue Peter* is on.'

'Oh, very well,' Emma conceded, 'but as soon as it's finished I want to see you doing your homework.'

Tinker nodded, and after switching on the set she sat crosslegged on the floor, her eyes glued to the screen.

Emma watched her for a while, saw she was

absorbed, and then turned to Doris, her voice low, 'Right, now tell me what's on your mind.'

'If you must know, I'm annoyed about this flat. You agreed I could have it, but as soon as I had a joke with Terry about him moving in with me, you changed your mind. It ain't fair, Em.'

'Oh, for goodness' sake, if it means so much to you, then have the flat. And as for Terry living with you, well, I couldn't care less.'

'Really? Well you could have fooled me. I reckon you think more of Terry than you're prepared to admit.'

Emma's eyes hardened. 'I see Terry as a friend, that's all, and if you think there's more to it than that, you're mad.'

Doris didn't look convinced but she shrugged. 'Yeah, if you say so. Anyway, about the flat. I've been thinking we can still use some of the rooms to expand the business. After all, I'll only be using one bedroom.'

'I'll leave that up to you, Doris. If you're happy to have punters down here, that's fine.'

'And if Terry really does want to move in with me?'

'Then let him.'

Doris grinned, 'Just testing, but you needn't worry. I've known for years that I don't stand a chance with Terry. There's only one woman he's got his eye on.'

Emma refused to accept the surge of pleasure that suffused her. She didn't believe that Terry had his eye on her, and even if he did she wasn't interested. She wasn't interested in any man.

42

Emma was smiling with pleasure as she went to wake her daughter for school, thrilled that Tinker had passed her exams. It wouldn't be long now before the work was completed next door, and though the renovation costs had depleted her hoard of money, business was still doing well and it would be replenished in time.

There was only the wallpaper to hang before they could move in. She had chosen the décor carefully. Not for her the garish fashions of this decade. Instead she had chosen tasteful wallpaper with soft furnishings that would complement her antiques. The house was *hers* – she had bought it, the deeds in *her* name – and Horace could never take it from her.

Tinker's long, wavy blonde hair was spread over her pillow. 'Come on, darling, it's time to get up or you'll be late for school.'

'I don't feel well, Mummy,' she said, her voice feeble.

'You tried that yesterday and it didn't work. You're a big girl now, at grammar school, and you can't keep having time off.'

'I'm hot, Mummy.'

Emma frowned as she laid a hand across Tinker's forehead. 'You do seem to have a fever. Does your throat hurt?'

Tinker shook her head, but even so, as Emma tucked the blankets around her daughter she knew that the child couldn't go to school. 'All right, you can stay home today. I'll be back in a minute.'

She hurried to the kitchen, saying to Doris, 'Tinker's got a bit of a fever. I think I'll give her half an aspirin.'

'Has she? I'll go and have a look at her.'

Whilst Doris scurried from the room, Emma grabbed the pills, breaking one in half before filling a glass with water.

'She does feel a bit hot,' Doris said as Emma returned to the bedroom and coaxed Tinker to swallow the pill.

'Maybe you should call the doctor,' Doris suggested.

'You know what he's like if you call him out for nothing. I'll see if the aspirin brings her temperature down first.'

'Yeah, you're probably right, he's a miserable old sod.'

'I'll stay with her for a while.'

Doris gazed down at Tinker. 'Have a bit of a kip, sweetheart.'

Tinker didn't answer, her eyes closing as the woman quietly left the room. Emma settled down beside her daughter, gently stroking her hair. It was only half an hour later when Doris stuck her head round the door. 'How's she doing?'

'She hasn't stirred.'

'I've made a fresh pot of tea if you want one.'

Anxious not to disturb Tinker, Emma stood up carefully and followed Doris to the kitchen. 'I thought she was just trying to get out of school again.'

'Yeah, well, she's fond of doing that so it ain't surprising.'

They spent the morning cleaning the kitchen, and took it in turns to check on Tinker. Then, at eleven o'clock, there was a ring on the doorbell.

'That's probably Terry,' Doris said. 'He's early as usual.'

She bustled out, returning with Terry in tow, his nose red from the cold and forehead creased with concern. 'What's this about Tinker?'

'I don't think it's anything to worry about.'

'I'll have a look at her,' he said, and he hurried to Tinker's bedroom. Emma and Doris followed him.

Tinker was still asleep, but her face looked

flushed and her hair was damp. 'Blimey,' Terry said, 'she looks rough.'

'She's got a temperature. I think it might be her tonsils again.'

'You should call the doctor.'

'I'm waiting to see if her fever comes down.'

Tinker stirred, but her eyes opened only briefly before she closed them again. 'Do you mind if I sit with her for a while?' Terry asked.

'Of course not, but don't disturb her.'

'I won't, but I still think you should call the doctor.'

'Look,' Emma said impatiently, 'the last time Tinker had a fever and I asked the doctor to make a house call, it turned out to be just a chill. He wasn't happy about being dragged out for nothing and inferred that I'm an over-protective mother.'

'Sod what he said! If you ask me it's better to be safe than sorry.'

'I didn't ask you. Now if you don't mind, I've got things to do.' Emma left the room, annoyed that Terry was questioning her decision. She grabbed her cleaning materials, determined to keep busy as she began to polish the hall table. It was cold, but working hard she soon warmed up. When the clock chimed twelve, Emma stopped, throwing down her duster to check on Tinker.

'She doesn't look any better,' Terry said as she

went into the room. 'I think you should call the doctor now.'

Emma felt Tinker's forehead. Terry was right; she was very hot, but soundly asleep. 'Though her fever hasn't gone down, she doesn't seem any worse. I think I'll give it another hour.'

'Why wait?'

'I've told you why.'

Terry frowned, his concern for Tinker clear to see. 'I'll stay with her for a while longer.'

Emma had always secretly been grateful that she'd had a man in her life, someone her daughter could look up to, especially as her brothers had deserted her. 'All right, but it really isn't necessary.'

He shrugged and, saying nothing more, Emma left the room.

Half an hour later, Terry was growing increasingly worried. Tinker stirred occasionally, but her eyes were glassy, unfocused. As Terry gazed at her, he was once again struck by Tinker's resemblance to her mother. Their eyes were the same beautiful blue, but unlike Emma's, Tinker's were soft. She might be a handful at times, but he loved this child and at the thought of anything happening to her, he gulped.

Once again Tinker stirred, groaned, and he reached out to smooth the damp hair from her forehead. It surprised him that Emma refused to call the doctor; it was so unlike her. Usually the child only had to sneeze and she went into a panic, so what was different this time? Maybe it was her fear of the man that held her back, but that was ridiculous. It was part of a doctor's job to make house calls and Emma knew that. Anyway she wasn't a woman to show fear, her façade icy and strong.

Doris had once told him that Emma was cold, frigid, and though he'd dismissed it at first, he sensed it was true. She always avoided close contact and the only time she relaxed around him was when they sat together doing a crossword. Yet he still loved her, would always love her, clinging on to the forlorn hope that one day she'd look his way. Christ, you're a daft sod, Terry told himself, shaking his head. It was a wasted cause, yet he couldn't leave. Emma held him, Tinker held him, and so he remained, watching over them, keeping them safe, and he'd do so for as long as they needed him.

Tinker whimpered again, and Terry rose to his feet. This time he'd insist that Emma called the surgery. He found her in the kitchen, and without preamble said, 'I don't care whether the doctor likes it or not. He's gonna have to come out.'

Emma marched off and he followed, watching whilst she felt Tinker's forehead. She then said, 'I still think it can wait a while longer.'

'Look, she's not getting any better and if you don't call him, I will.'

She spun round, her eyes blazing. 'How dare you issue me an ultimatum? You're overstepping the mark and it's only because of your concern for my daughter that I'm making allowances.'

'All right, I'm sorry, but just call him, will you?'

'Very well,' Emma said, 'but be it on *your* head if it isn't necessary.'

Terry's shoulders slumped with relief. God, she was a right madam, but at least it had done the trick. So, he'd overstepped the mark, had he? Well, sod her! Christ, this was another one of those times when he was tempted to walk out, to tell her to stick her bloody job. He was sick of it, sick of being treated like something she'd wiped off her feet.

As Terry sat beside Tinker again, he shook his head in bemusement. He couldn't make sense of Emma. Most of the time she was friendly, treating him as one of the family, but she could turn on a penny, reverting to the haughty woman she'd been when they first met.

When Emma returned from making the call, he saw the worry in her eyes. 'I left it too late – the doctor's out on his rounds. The receptionist said she'd pass on my message, but doubted he'd be here now until after the evening surgery.'

'See, I told you to call him earlier. If you hadn't

been so bloody worried about what the man might say, he'd have been here by now.'

'If you must know, I didn't want to waste the doctor's time, and I still don't. It was my decision to make. Tinker is *my* daughter, not yours, and I'll thank you to remember that.'

'Huh, if she *was* my daughter I wouldn't have hesitated to call the doctor.'

Emma glared at him. 'I don't want to disturb Tinker, so I suggest we carry on this conversation outside,' she hissed.

'Fine,' Terry growled as the two of them went into the hall.

Emma stood facing him, arms wrapped around her body for warmth, her blue eyes icy as they met his. 'You seem to forget that I'm your employer and before I say something I might regret, I suggest you go upstairs where you belong.'

Terry knew he should keep his mouth shut, but she had got his back up. 'Don't hold back, Mrs B. If you've got something to say, just spit it out.'

Her lips ground together. 'Don't push me, Terry.'

'Why not? Are you threatening to give me the sack? Is that it?'

'All right, fine, you're fired. Now get out of my sight!'

'God, you're an impossible woman. Do you think I don't know what's brought this on? It's

450

guilt, ain't it? Guilt that you didn't call the doctor earlier and now you're taking it out on me.'

'Here, what's this? What's going on?' Doris asked as she hurried to their side.

'Mrs B has just given me the sack.'

Doris shook her head and, acting the peacemaker, she touched Emma's arm, her voice cajoling. 'Look, you don't mean it, I know you don't. You're worried about Tinker, we all are, and it's making us edgy.'

Emma shrugged off Doris's hand. Terry expected sparks to fly, but instead Emma went into the kitchen, where she slumped onto a chair and buried her face in her hands. 'Terry's right, I should have called the doctor earlier.'

As though someone had doused him with water, Terry's anger died. He went to crouch by her side, saying softly, 'My car's outside – if you don't want to wait we can run her to casualty.'

Terry couldn't have been more surprised when Emma actually lifted her head to smile at him, saying softly, 'It's good of you, but maybe we should wait for another couple of hours. I still think it's the start of tonsillitis, and no doubt the doctor will say the same. Mind you, this time I think I'll insist that he refers her to hospital to have them removed.'

'All right, but if you change your mind, the offer's there.'

'Thanks, and I'm sorry for saying you're fired. You will stay, won't you?'

'Yeah, of course I will.'

She rose to her feet. 'Thanks, Terry.'

As he stood up, he met Doris's eyes, the woman looking as surprised as he was, but it was only when Emma left the room that she spoke. 'Bloody hell,' she said, 'I never thought I'd see the day when Emma apologised to anyone, let alone express her thanks.'

Me neither, Terry thought. He wondered if he dared feel a spark of hope. With a shake of his head he berated himself. If the day came when he held Emma Bell in his arms, hell would freeze over.

After finding no change in Tinker, Emma returned to the kitchen, insisting that Doris and Terry went upstairs to open for business. She was still angry with herself for not listening to Terry. She should have rung the surgery earlier, especially when Tinker's temperature didn't go down. Yet surely she wasn't ill enough to take to casualty?

Emma bit on her bottom lip. She shouldn't have acted like that, shouldn't have fired Terry, but his criticism only served to increase her guilt. As soon as the words had left her mouth she wanted to take them back. The thought of not having him around to look out for them was appalling. If he'd taken her at her word, no doubt they'd have found a replacement minder, but she would never be able to trust another man as she did Terry. She felt safe with him; sure he would never attempt to touch her, and in her own way she was fond of him. It was difficult not to be. He was kind, funny, and still reminded her of a gentle bear. Yes, he was a nice man, their relationship reminding her of the one she had once shared with her brothers. On that thought, Emma frowned.

It had been many, many years since she'd seen them, though Luke, now a priest, still posted her the occasional sermon, which she ignored. When Dick had finished his national service he had married Mandy, but she hadn't received an invitation. She'd sent them a present, but it had been returned, Dick making it clear that he despised where the money had come from to buy it.

She had closed her heart and her mind to them. Now Tinker was her only family and the most important person in her life. The time ticked by and now Emma remained by her daughter's side, with Terry and Doris taking it in turns to pop down every half an hour or so. She hated the dividing door at the top of the stairs opening so often, but couldn't find it in her heart to stop them.

'How's she doing?' Terry asked as he walked in.

'She's no better.'

'We could still shut shop and take her to casualty.'

'No, it's all right. She may not be any better, but I don't think she's any worse. Anyway, the doctor is sure to be here soon.'

'If he turns a bit funny with you, let me know and I'll soon sort him out.'

Emma had to smile. 'I don't think that will be necessary, but thanks anyway.'

He looked down on Tinker, his eyes dark with concern. 'I hope you're right and it is just her tonsils. I'd best get back upstairs now, but no doubt Doris will be down again soon.'

'Yes, I'm sure she will,' Emma said, then added, 'Mind you, if we're busy, I'd prefer the two of you to remain upstairs.'

'Yeah, we're busy, but it won't hurt to pop down now and then,' Terry insisted.

'Very well, but I don't want the girls left without protection. You stay upstairs and just let Doris come down.'

'All right, you're the boss,' Terry said.

He left then, and Emma turned to Tinker. When she groaned again she lifted her daughter's head to give her a sip of water, alarmed to feel that her whole body felt so hot. God, she was burning up.

* * *

454

The bell rang and Emma was relieved to see the doctor on the step. 'Well, what's the problem this time, Mrs Bell?'

'I'm sorry to call you out,' Emma said as she led him through to the bedroom, 'but I really am worried. My daughter's temperature won't go down and she's complaining of a bad headache.'

'Humph,' was his only comment as he bent to examine her. After he had returned his stethoscope and thermometer to his bag, he asked, 'How long has she been like this?'

'Since this morning.'

'Why didn't you call me earlier?'

Emma bit back the words that sprang to her lips. 'When I rang the surgery you had already left on your rounds.' Alerted by the doctor's concerned expression her voice rose. 'What is it? What's wrong with her?'

He pursed his lips. 'I've ruled out measles but I'm not happy with her symptoms. I think she should be admitted to hospital for further investigation.'

'Hospital?'

'Yes, and as soon as possible. I'll use your telephone to ring for an ambulance.'

'Oh, no! Do you think it's something serious?'

'I can't be sure, but I suspect meningitis.'

Emma felt her knees almost give way, but she managed to stay on her feet. She showed the doctor where the telephone was, praying that he was wrong. It couldn't be meningitis, it just couldn't. She'd never forgive herself if it was!

The wait for the ambulance seemed interminable. Doris appeared just as it arrived. 'We'll close down. I'll come with you,' she cried as Emma climbed in with her daughter.

The doors swung shut, cutting off Emma's reply and then they sped off, all Emma's focus now on Tinker.

Emma unconsciously wrung her hands. She felt so helpless, useless . . . Tears filled her eyes. *Please, please, let her be all right* – the chant filled her mind as they drove to hospital.

Tinker was wheeled into casualty at speed, Emma almost running alongside the trolley.

They were put into a cubicle and Emma stood by the bed, frantic to see that Tinker was barely conscious now. In seconds a doctor arrived.

Tinker groaned as he examined her, and then he turned to question Emma. 'Has she complained of a stiff neck?'

'No.'

'When did you first notice that she's sensitive to light?'

'I . . . I didn't notice.'

Tinker suddenly heaved, and Emma spun away from the doctor just in time to see a nurse supporting her daughter's head as she was sick into a metal dish.

'Until we carry out further tests, I'm afraid your daughter will have to be put in isolation, Mrs Bell.'

'Isolation! But why?'

'There are two strains of meningitis, viral and bacterial. Viral meningitis is contagious and therefore caution is necessary until we get the test results.'

'Can I stay with her?' Emma begged.

'No, I'm afraid not.'

'Oh God!'

He turned, brusquely ordering the nurse to arrange for Tinker to be taken to the ICU isolation area. When he had gone, Emma stood frozen for a moment, unable to command coherent thought. 'You might as well go home, Mrs Bell,' the nurse advised.

'Home! No . . . I can't leave her.'

'She'll be in good hands.'

'Can I at least wait until she's settled?'

'If you go up to ICU, you can wait there, but you'll only be able to see her through a glass partition.'

'But I'm her mother.'

'I'm sorry, but as the doctor told you, viral meningitis is highly contagious.'

'But it might not be viral.'

'I know, and if it isn't, you'll have your daughter home again in a few days.'

Emma tried to hold on to this as Tinker was wheeled away, and though she hurried to ICU, it was half an hour later before she was led to a small window. As she looked through the glass, tears blurred her eyes. She wanted to be in there with Tinker, to hold her, comfort her. Oh God, why hadn't she called the doctor earlier? Curtains were pulled across the glass, obscuring her view.

A nurse came to her side. 'I'm sorry, Mrs Bell, but your daughter is having tests so you should leave now.'

'No . . . no . . . I can't leave!'

'There's nothing you can do. After the tests Patricia will be settled for the night and you'll be able to see her again in the morning.'

'She . . . she likes to be called Tinker.'

The nurse smiled. 'Oh, isn't that a pretty name?'

Emma felt a gentle touch on her shoulder and swung round. 'Oh, Terry,' she cried, falling into his arms. Tinker couldn't leave her; she just couldn't.

In the back seat of the car, Emma was barely aware of the drive home. Doris held her hand, all three of them silent with shock. As they turned into the drive Emma saw a man hovering by the steps. As soon as they stopped, Terry was the first out of the car. He spoke to the man and then, shaking his head with what looked like annoyance, the

458

man walked away. Terry returned to open the car door, and as Emma climbed out he solicitously held her arm.

'Who . . . who was that?' she asked.

'It was just a punter. Now come on, let's get you inside.'

'He won't be the only one to turn up this evening. I . . . I'll be all right. You and Doris can open for business.'

'What?'

Terry looked astounded, but Emma ignored it. She wanted to be alone, to scream out her anguish, to release the emotions she was barely holding in check. 'You heard me,' she managed to grind out through clenched teeth. Then, shrugging off Terry's hand, she fumbled for her keys, opened the door and dashed inside, slamming it behind her.

It was Tinker's bed she headed for and, alone at last, she flung herself across it, hugging her daughter's pillow as tears flowed. *Oh, please don't let her die – please, please, God.*

Once she had started crying, Emma was unable to stop, and it was some time later when she felt the bed dip beside her. She looked up, her face awash with tears, expecting to see Doris, but it was Terry.

'Come on, come here,' he urged and, pulling her into his arms, he held her close.

Emma clung to Terry, wanting to draw strength from him, to drown out her fears, to forget everything for a while. Her head was on his chest, his fingers stroking her hair, but then there was a subtle change as Terry began to move his hands over her.

She found herself responding, finding comfort in his touch, and raised her face. Terry's lips dipped to meet hers, his kiss arousing feelings unfelt before. She groaned softly, losing herself in the moment, and then they were laying together, Terry gently removing her clothes.

His tongue moved down her body, and as he reached that special place, her back arched. 'Ohhh,' she gasped, unable to believe the waves of pleasure that rippled through her body. 'Oh, please . . .' she groaned, and as Terry at last entered her, she welcomed him.

Emma came to her senses only when it was over, appalled by what had happened. She had let Terry make love to her and, refusing to accept that she'd enjoyed it, flung herself off the bed. 'How . . . how could you? Get out! Get out now!'

Terry looked puzzled, a frown creasing his brow. 'What's wrong, Emma?'

'Wrong! You dare to ask me what's wrong? I was in an awful state and . . . and you took advantage of that – of me.'

'No, it wasn't like that,' Terry protested. 'I came down to see if you were all right and found you in an awful state. I was only trying to comfort you, that's all.'

'Sex! You call sex comforting me?'

'Well, no, but it just sort of happened.'

Emma's eyes blazed with anger. Underlying this was self-disgust. How could she? How could she do something so disgusting whilst Tinker was ill, dangerously ill?

'I told you to get out, Terry, and I meant it. I never want to see you again. You're ... you're fired!'

His expression changed, hardened. 'Right, that suits me, but just for the record, you enjoyed it as much as I did.'

'I did not!' Emma screamed.

Terry was flinging on his clothes, and suddenly, realising she was naked, Emma snatched a blanket from the bed, holding it up in front of her. He didn't look at her, didn't say another word as he marched from the room, and Emma didn't move until she heard the street door closing behind him.

She then hurriedly dressed, her mind sickened. Despite his protests she knew that Terry *had* taken advantage of her. If she hadn't been upset, hadn't been out of her mind with worry, she would never have allowed it to happen. *You could have said no,* a small voice whispered at the back of her mind, but Emma quickly dismissed it. Terry had just confirmed everything she had ever thought about men. They were all the same – all just wanting one thing!

'Where's Terry? He's needed upstairs.' Doris said when she came downstairs half an hour later.

'He's gone.'

'Gone! What do you mean?'

'I fired him.'

'Again? But why?'

'That's my business,' Emma snapped.

'Leave it out, Emma. I know Terry and can't think of any reason to sack him.'

Her emotions were all over the place and this was the last straw for Emma. She rose to her feet, glaring at Doris. 'I had good reason, and if you're not careful, you won't be far behind him.'

She expected Doris to react with anger too, but instead she walked to her side, saying softly, 'Come on, Emma, sit down. I don't know what brought this on, but I suspect it's worry over Tinker.'

Emma slumped, tears filling her eyes again as she blurted out, 'Oh, Doris, if it's viral meningitis she could die!'

'Don't say that, Em. It might not be, and you should hold on to that.'

'But you saw her. You saw how awful she looks.

It's my fault, Doris. I should have listened to Terry. I should have called the doctor earlier!'

'Emma, stop blaming yourself! You couldn't have known that it was meningitis, and, let's face it, she's had a fever before. Now come on, tell me why you sacked Terry.'

'I . . . I can't.'

'If you ask him to, he'll come back.'

'No! I never want to see him again.'

Doris shook her head, then said worriedly, 'Look, I'd best get back. One of the punters is being a bit funny and I can't leave the girls on their own. We'll talk about this later.'

Emma didn't reply. Doris could talk all she liked, but she wasn't going to change her mind.

She sat wringing her hands, but only five minutes later jumped to her feet to ring the hospital. The wait seemed interminable, but at last she was put through to ICU, the ward sister telling her that Tinker had settled down well for the night and they were awaiting the test results.

Desolately, Emma replaced the receiver and then returned to the drawing room, wishing the hours away – wishing for the morning so she could return to the hospital, wishing only to be near her daughter.

43

It was a fraught few days, Emma almost going out of her mind with worry. She couldn't eat, couldn't sleep, and though not allowed into the room, spent many hours looking through the window at Tinker, willing her to get better.

Doris stayed by her side, handing over much of the running of the business to Rose, one of the girls who had been with them from the start.

When at last her daughter was diagnosed, Emma almost collapsed with relief. Tinker had bacterial meningitis, not viral and, smiling, the doctor told her that she could take her home at the end of the week. She'd been allowed in to see Tinker, the child clinging to her like a limpet, her fever down and her grip strong around Emma's neck.

'I saw you through the glass, Mummy,' she said, 'but the nurse said you couldn't come in.'

'I'm here now, darling,' Emma said, almost

choking on her emotions. If anything had happened to Tinker, her life would have been meaningless. The thought of being without her child was unbearable.

'Well, Patricia,' the nurse said, 'I'm sure you're pleased to hear you'll be going home soon, but in the meantime, we're taking you to a ward where there'll be other children for company.'

Automatically, Emma said, 'Tinker. She likes to be called Tinker.'

'No, Mummy, I'm not a baby now and I want to be called Patricia or Pat.'

Emma gazed at her daughter, seeing a subtle change. She was only eleven years old, yet there was a maturity in her eyes that she hadn't seen before.

'All right, darling, but it's going to be hard to remember at first.'

'Where's Terry?'

'Er . . . er . . .' Emma stammered, 'he . . . he's busy, darling, but you'll see him soon.'

'And Doris?'

'I'm here,' Doris said, poking her head around the door. 'I thought I'd leave you alone with Mummy for a minute, but can I come in now?'

'Yes, of course,' Emma said, thankful that her friend was there to divert attention from Terry's absence.

'Blimey, Tinker, you gave us all a fright for a while,' Doris said, hugging the child fiercely.

466

'Call me Pat, or Patricia.'

'Yeah, I heard, love, but you've been Tinker since you were a baby, and you've got to admit it's a cute name.'

'I'm not a baby now.'

'Oh, so you're all grown up, are you?'

'Well, I am eleven, you know.'

Doris roared with laughter. 'Yeah, and by the sound of it, going on twenty-one.'

Then the porters arrived to take Tinker to the ward. Emma and Doris followed behind, waited until she was settled. After sitting with her for another half-hour, they were asked by the ward sister to leave. 'I'm afraid visiting time is over,' she said, 'but you can see her again between four and six this afternoon.'

Emma was loath to go, but happy to see her daughter taking an interest in her surroundings again. She hugged and kissed her, pleased to see that her eyes were bright. 'We'll be back later, darling.'

Doris kissed Tinker too, and then they were almost at the end of the ward when the doors swung open, Terry appearing. He halted when he saw them, but his lips were tight with determination. 'I've come to see Tinker.'

'Visiting time is over,' Emma snapped.

It was too late; Tinker had seen him, her voice ringing down the ward: 'Terry! Terry!'

Emma swung round to see the child waving frantically, but then the ward sister was again at their side. 'If you have come to visit Patricia I'm afraid visiting time is over.'

'Have a heart, love,' Terry protested. 'Look at her, she's waving, and surely it wouldn't hurt if I just pop along to say hello?'

'Oh, very well.'

Emma wanted to object, wanted to tell the nurse that she didn't want this man near her daughter, but seeing the excitement on Tinker's face, she just couldn't do it. She managed to force a smile towards her daughter before marching out of the ward.

'Come on, Doris,' Emma demanded.

'Can't we wait for Terry? He'll be able to give us a lift home.'

'No, we are *not* waiting. We'll get the bus.'

'Look, this is bloody daft. You've been in a state so I've kept my mouth shut, but now we know that Tinker's gonna be all right I reckon you can tell me why you sacked Terry.'

'I've got nothing to say.'

'Christ, you're a stubborn cow. All right, don't tell me, but knowing the two of you it was probably just a flash in the pan. Tinker thinks the world of Terry and for her sake I reckon you should let bygones be bygones.'

'Patricia,' Emma snapped, 'she wants to be

called Patricia, and as for letting bygones be bygones, hell will freeze over before that happens. Now come on, there's a bus coming and if we get a move on we'll catch it.'

The two women began to run, both breathless as they sank onto a seat. Doris then returned to the subject. 'Look, one of you has got to make the first move. If you won't talk to Terry, I will.'

'No you won't. He's fired and that's that.'

Doris said nothing and the two women sat in silence for the rest of the journey home.

Terry kissed Tinker on the cheek, sad that he'd arrived too late to stay long. He waved as he left the ward, but on leaving the hospital he couldn't see any sign of Emma or Doris.

His initial anger had worn off to be replaced by shame. Emma was right. What had happened between them only came about because of her vulnerable state, but once they'd started he'd been unable to stop. When she'd responded to his touch, the years of loving her, wanting her, had drowned out reason. Christ, when it was over, she'd gone mad, and thinking about it now, he didn't blame her.

Terry sighed heavily as he got into his Ford Zephyr car. Many years ago he'd heard Emma's history from Doris. She'd had it rough, there was no denying that, but it had hardened her. Anyone who hurt Emma had been cut out of her life. First her father, then her brothers, and now, with a small, sad shake of his head, Terry knew he'd be joining that list. It was over. He'd watched over her, loved her, stuck around and hoped, but knew now that he had well and truly blown it.

Emma and Doris returned to the hospital at visiting time, but there was still tension between them. They put on a front for Patricia, both glad to see her looking so much better, but the excitement of the move to a children's ward had obviously worn her out and before six her eyes were already drooping.

'Why didn't Terry come to see me again?' she asked.

'He's busy, darling.'

Emma heard Doris's grunt, but ignored it. She held her daughter's hand, watching as she drifted off to sleep. 'Come on, Doris,' she whispered. 'We might as well go.'

They kissed Tinker on her cheek, leaving quietly, and soon were on the bus home.

It was Doris who broke the silence. 'I'm gonna pop down to see Terry before we open up for business.'

Emma's head turned swiftly, her eyes glaring. 'I've made my decision and I don't want you interfering.'

'Who said anything about interfering? Terry's a mate and I'm going to see him, that's all.'

'Fine, but don't bother trying to act the role of peacemaker. I said I wouldn't take him back and I mean it.'

When they got off at their stop, Doris said, 'Right, I'm off. Don't worry; I'll be back in time to open up.'

Emma said nothing, her back straight as she turned into the drive. Would Terry tell Doris what had happened between them? God, she hoped not, and once inside the house she paced up and down until Doris returned.

When at last Doris came home, Emma was unable to help blurting out, 'Well, what did he say?'

'Not much, just that you've fallen out. But you'll be moving next door soon and I don't fancy running the business without a man for protection.'

'Then find someone to replace him.'

'The girls feel safe with Terry, and all right, I can find someone else but it won't be the same. There's Tinker too. Have you thought about how much she's going to miss him?'

'Of course I've thought about it, but as you pointed out, we'll be moving next door. It'll be a fresh start and, though she'll miss Terry, she'll get over it.'

'I doubt that, Emma.'

'Tinker, I mean Patricia, will be able to bring her friends home. She'll have a normal life, one where she can do without Terry.'

'I don't see why you're being so bloody stubborn.'

'Doris, don't push me. I've made my decision and that's an end to it.'

'Well I've made up my mind too. Either you make it up with Terry, or you can run this place on your own.'

Emma was shocked, but her pride stepped in and she refused to show it. She surged to her feet, hands on hips. 'If you want to go, that's fine with me. I don't need you – or Terry!'

Doris marched from the room, but Emma wasn't worried. Doris was bluffing, she was sure of it. She sat by the hearth and held her hands towards the fire. Yes, the house next door was ready and after visiting Patricia in the morning she'd start packing, having everything in place for her daughter's return.

As she gazed at the flames, Terry's face formed in her mind, but she firmly pushed it away. She didn't want to think about him, didn't want to admit that she was missing him. He had dared to touch her body, something she could never forgive. She trembled, remembering how he had made her feel. How could she have enjoyed it?

But you did, that treacherous voice whispered again. I didn't. I didn't, she told herself, refusing to acknowledge the truth.

When she heard the front door slam, puzzled, Emma rose to her feet, hurrying to the window. Her stomach lurched. Doris hadn't been bluffing. She was leaving, a suitcase clutched in her hand.

Emma struggled to open the window, to call out, but the sash was stiff and by the time she managed, Doris was out of sight. 'Come back,' she cried. 'Doris, come back!'

Frantic, Emma rushed into the hall and out of the house, heedless that she wasn't wearing a coat as she ran along the road. Where was Doris? Had she turned down one of the side roads?

At last Emma gave up, bending over as she dragged air into her lungs. She saw one of the girls walking towards her, realising with a shock that it was time to open for business. Oh God, she'd have to ask Rose to take the job on, but there was something about the girl, something sly, and takings had been down since she had temporarily taken over Doris's role. Yet what choice did she have?

Rose reached her side, saying worriedly, 'Are you all right, Mrs Bell?'

'Yes, I'm fine, but we have a bit of a problem.'

'Gawd! Don't tell me we've been raided.'

'How can we have been raided when we've yet to open for business?'

'Yeah, of course, I didn't think.'

Emma felt the cold penetrating her clothes and began to hurry back to the house. When they reached the drive she turned to Rose. 'Doris has gone, leaving us without a hostess. You've stood in for her a few times whilst my daughter has been ill, but would you be prepared to take the job on permanently? It would mean working both the afternoon and evening shifts.'

'Cor, not 'arf, and I don't mind the extra hours.'

'Are you sure you can cope?'

'Of course I can. It ain't that hard. Like Doris, I just have to greet the punters, let them select a girl and then take their money.'

'Yes, but as Doris isn't here, at the close of business, bring the takings to me.'

'Righto.' Then, visibly straightening, Rose said, 'I want the same share of the profits as Doris.'

'How do you know about our arrangement?'

'When Doris recruited me, she made it clear from the start that she's no longer a tom. We all chat between clients and we asked her if she was making the same sort of money. She told us about your little deal, but not how much she was raking in, but I ain't daft and it didn't take much working out that she was on a nice little earner.'

'I see. Very well then, I'll give you the same percentage as Doris.'

'Right, I'd best get the ball rolling then.'

'You'll need the keys to get in.' After rushing inside to get them, Emma offered a word of warning as she held them out. '*Do not*, in *any* circumstances, open the dividing door to my flat.'

'What if I need you for something?'

'You can come round to my front door.'

'Seems daft, if you ask me.'

'I'm not asking you, Rose.'

They both heard a rustling sound and spun round, staring into the bushes. They remained frozen for a moment but, seeing nothing, Rose shrugged. 'It was probably a cat,' she said. 'Anyway, Mrs Bell, there's just one thing. I know Terry has gone too, but what about someone to replace him?'

'Oh, I don't know. Can you think of anyone suitable?'

'My brother might be interested,' Rose said eagerly. 'He's done a bit of boxing so knows how to look after himself.'

'All right, bring him to see me,' Emma said, anxious to get inside. She had left that side of the business to Doris and was still reeling with shock that she'd gone. Surely she'd come back? In the meantime she just hoped that Rose would be able to cope, and that her brother was suitable.

Emma closed the door behind her, determined that things would be different this time. She had let Terry become part of the family, allowed him to become too familiar, and look what that had led to! Never again, Emma thought.

To Emma the evening was interminable as she fought her emotions. She wanted to go to bed, to close her mind in sleep. She didn't want to think about Doris or Terry, but now that they had gone, she felt so very alone. They had become her family, replacing the one she had lost, and the hard shell she had cultivated over so many years began to crack.

There had been so many losses in the past: her mother's death, her youngest brothers going to Alice Moon, and then her sisters . . . oh, it had been so many years since she'd seen them. The memories flooded back, memories that, in order to survive, she had fought to repress. The attic, and yes, it had been awful, cold and desolate, but when their mother had been alive there had been happy times. She had tried to deny them; thinking only of bad times when her father returned from the war, but before that there had been laughter, games, giggles as they lay on the mattress vying for blankets. But most of all, there had been love.

Emma's eyes filled. Next came Luke, dear Luke, and in truth she had missed him the most, but he was now unforgiving in his anger that she was running a brothel, an anger that matched that of Dick, another brother lost to her.

Emma dashed a hand across her face. She didn't want to cry, wouldn't cry. Rising swiftly to her feet, she forced her mind to focus on something else. After all the anguish, the fear that she might lose her precious daughter, Tinker was coming home. Emma ran to prepare her things, folding clothes and putting them into a bag to take to the hospital, all the time fighting to strengthen her resolve, struggling to put the barriers up again.

She'd manage, she'd cope. She had done so before and would do so again. She would never take Terry back, and if there was no other choice, she'd do without Doris too. Emma's mouth was grim, set. She still had her daughter, the most important person in the world, and in the morning she'd have a word with the builders, pay them to move her furniture next door. Yes, Tinker would be home soon, and moving next door would be a fresh start. It would be all right, wouldn't it? Surely it would be all right . . .

The hours passed and, as Rose came to the door, Emma invited her in. She counted the takings, a frown on her face, finally saying, 'It must have been a quiet night.'

'Yeah, it was,' Rose said, her eyes flicking away

and roaming the room. 'I reckon the cold weather kept the punters away. Blimey, you ain't half got it nice in here.'

'There's a chance that my daughter will be allowed home tomorrow, so I'll be moving next door.'

'Will you? What's going to happen to this flat?'

'I had promised it to Doris.'

'Well if she ain't coming back, can I have it?'

'No, I don't think so.'

'Why not? I'm taking over her job and it would make things easier if I could live on the premises.'

Emma lowered her head, unwilling to accept that Doris wouldn't return. 'Give me time to think about it,' she stalled, 'and in the meantime, have you any idea where Doris might be?'

Rose shook her head. 'No, but didn't she used to live off of Lavender Hill? You could try there.'

'She gave her mother's house up when she moved in with me.'

Rose shrugged. 'Well, I can't think of anywhere else.'

Emma hid her feelings, handing Rose her share of the takings. 'Do you think any of the other girls might know where Doris is?'

Rose grabbed the notes avidly, quickly checking them. 'I don't think so, but you could ask them.'

'Yes, I'll do that.'

'I'll say good night then, Mrs Bell, and I'll have a word with my brother about the minder's job when I get home.'

She followed Rose to the door, locking it securely behind her, and then returned to the drawing room, banking down the fire. With a last glance around the room, she flicked off the light and went to her bedroom, shivering as she undressed. There was nobody to call good night to, the house empty, desolate, without Doris and Tinker. Emma scrambled into bed, lying in darkness, her ears pricking nervously at any sound.

Hours later Emma was still awake. She tried to console herself with thoughts of Tinker's homecoming, but it was the early hours of the morning before she finally drifted into an uneasy sleep.

The man was crouched out of view, unmoving until he saw the lights go out. He was freezing, his limbs screaming in pain as he straightened up. There had been a sticky moment earlier when he thought he'd been discovered, but he'd heard their exchange. Huh, a cat, they'd thought, but then again he'd have to be catlike to succeed.

It had meant another night of watching them, but it had paid dividends and he knew that the time was ripe to make his move. It would take a bit of careful planning and wouldn't be easy, but then nothing worthwhile ever was.

Moving stealthily, he left the drive, pausing for one last look at the façade of the house. Yes, he would make his move soon, but he would need to be certain that he left no trace of his identity.

44

The builders had been wonderful, moving Emma's furniture without complaint. She had added a little extra to their final payment, and then tipped each of the men before they left. Alone now, Emma looked around her new home. Everything was clean and new, the décor fitting, and though still aching to find Doris, she felt just a little brighter.

Emma went upstairs. The ward sister had told her that Patricia might be allowed home that afternoon, but this was dependent on the doctor's decision when he made his rounds. Emma flung open Patricia's bedroom door, hoping that her daughter would be pleased with the room. She had chosen Tinker's favourite colour, and to Emma's eyes the décor looked fit for a princess. Over the bed there was a white lace canopy, tied back with pink ribbons, and her dressing table was draped with the same lace. The wallpaper had a white background, patterned with tiny pink rosebuds, with matching curtains and a pink rug.

It was a room Emma would have loved as a child, one that was a far cry from the attic she had shared with her whole family. Oh, she didn't want to think about her family again, didn't want to think about the past. It was gone, they were gone, and she could only look forward now, but surely – oh, please – there had to be a chance that Doris would return.

Terry's face, his warm smile, invaded her mind but she pushed it away. As she went downstairs, the silence of the house seemed to close in around her. To fill the void, Emma switched on the radio, twiddling the knob until she found a station playing music. As the sound of a big band filled the room, playing 'Little Brown Jug', an old Glenn Miller number, she moved to the fire, poking it to life, the dancing flames and music lifting her spirits a little.

When she heard a knock on the front door Emma went eagerly to open it, praying it was Doris. Her face dropped when she saw Rose.

'Hello, Mrs Bell, I know I'm early, but I thought you'd want to see my brother.'

Emma's heart sank when she saw the young man, but reluctantly stood back to let them in. He looked hardly more than a teenager and, unlike Terry, he was slim, surely too slight to hold his own against a difficult punter. She led them through to the sitting room, already deciding that Rose's brother wasn't suitable for the job.

'Please, sit down,' she invited.

They sat on the sofa, Rose the first to speak. 'This is Tony and, as I said, he's done a bit of boxing.'

Emma saw the eagerness in both their eyes and swallowed. Then, focusing on Tony, she asked, 'Are you sure you could cope with this job? There are occasions when clients become difficult and it would be necessary for you to remove them from the premises.'

'Don't worry about me, missus. I can take of myself.'

'Yes, I'm sure you can, but we're not talking about a boxing match here. In fact, we don't want anyone hurt. It's more a matter of persuading them to leave without using violence.'

'Eh?'

'What I'm trying to explain is that Terry's size was enough to intimidate, and a quiet word in their ear, along with a firm hand in the direction of the door, was usually enough.'

'Oh, yeah, I get your meaning. Well, I'm sure I can handle that.'

'I can see you're a fit young man, but you hardly look intimidating.'

'Honestly, Mrs Bell, he can handle it,' Rose interjected. 'I've seen Tony in action and, believe me, the punters will leave if he tells them to.'

Unconvinced, Emma shook her head, but Rose wasn't ready to give up.

'I don't know anyone else, Mrs Bell, so for the time being, why don't you give Tony a try? I don't fancy another night without a man around, especially as we both thought we heard someone lurking in the bushes last night.'

'You said it was a cat.'

'Yeah, but what if it had been a geezer?'

Emma lowered her eyes. Rose was right, and maybe it wouldn't hurt to give this young man a try, at least until they found someone more suitable.

'Very well, you can have the job on a trial basis, Tony.'

'Cor, thanks, Mrs Bell, and don't worry, I won't let you down.'

'It's the girls you'll have to protect, Tony, not me. If you can start this afternoon, go with Rose and she'll show you the ropes.'

They both rose to their feet, smiling as they left, leaving Emma hoping she had made the right decision. She glanced at the clock, dismissing them from her mind for the time being as she prepared to go to the hospital.

Coat on, and clutching Patricia's bag of clothes

as she left the house, she prayed her daughter would be allowed home.

'I love it, Mummy,' Patricia cried as she bounced on her bed. 'It's so pretty.'

'I'm glad you like it, darling,' Emma said, joyful to have her daughter home. 'Now let's go downstairs and have our dinner.'

Patricia jumped down, running ahead of Emma. As they reached the kitchen she spun round. 'Where's Auntie Doris?'

Emma had dreaded this moment, but had prepared a story she hoped would hold until she could find Doris. 'She's having a little holiday, darling, but don't worry, she'll be back soon.'

'But people don't go on holiday in the winter.'

'Well, Auntie Doris has. Now come on, I've made your favourite dinner,' Emma said as she placed two sausages onto her daughter's plate.

'Where's Terry? Did he go with her?'

Emma grasped at this. 'Yes, that's right.'

'It's not fair. I want to go on holiday too. Why can't we go with them?'

'Because you haven't been well, darling. Now come on, eat up and then you can watch television for a while.'

Thankfully this was enough to mollify Patricia temporarily, but at bedtime things became difficult again.

'I don't want to sleep in here on my own,' she cried. 'I want to sleep in your room, Mummy.'

'Darling, when we lived next door we had to share a room, but you're a big girl now and I decorated this bedroom especially for you.'

With a little more persuasion, Patricia finally agreed, but insisted that the door was left open. Emma conceded, also leaving the landing light on.

It was almost ten o'clock, past the child's normal bedtime, but they had been snuggled together on the sofa all evening and Emma had been reluctant to put her daughter to bed. Now, though, she returned downstairs and flopped onto a chair beside the sitting-room hearth. She was missing Doris so much, and was desperate to find her friend, but had no idea where to start. She'd ask the girls tomorrow, see if they knew where she might be, and if she apologised, surely Doris would come back?

Emma kept her ears pricked, but her daughter didn't make a sound and she smiled with relief. It had been an eventful day and Emma was tired, but she had to wait for Rose to bring the takings round before she could go to bed.

At last the girl arrived, but having counted the money, Emma found takings were down by about twenty pounds. Too tired to worry about it now, she gave Rose her cut.

'How did it work out with Tony?'

'He was fine. One punter got a little funny, but Tony soon dealt with him.'

'Really? Funny in what way?'

'He didn't want to part with his money.'

'Oh, well, we can't have that. Right, Rose, thank you and I'll see you tomorrow.'

'Yeah, all right. Good night, Mrs Bell.'

Emma closed and locked the door, and then as usual she banked down the fire before going to bed. She looked in on Patricia, saw her daughter was fast asleep, pulled the blankets up to the child's chin, then went to her own room. The house still felt strange, the smell of fresh paint invasive, but her bed felt wonderfully familiar as she climbed into it. She snuggled down, and for the first time in ages, immediately fell asleep.

The man crept closer. He had watched, he had planned, and crouched in the bushes the night before, had heard the conversation between Emma and one of her tarts. It seemed fortuitous, his timing perfect. The child was home now, they were alone, and it was time to make his move.

It wasn't easy to get in, but he'd been practising on locks, and finally, when he opened the door, he made no sound. The narrow beam of his torch swept around the hall, and on soft-soled shoes he crept upstairs.

The landing light was on, her door open. Cautiously he moved to the side of the bed. For a moment in the small ray of light shining in from the landing, he studied her face. She looked so pretty, so innocent, and for a moment he balked at the task.

With a soft sigh he took a small, glass bottle from his pocket, unhappy about this stage of his plan, but there was no other way to get her soundlessly out of the house. It had to be done. Soaking a small cloth, he held it over the child's face. For a moment her eyes opened and she began to struggle, but it was too late to stop the effects of the anaesthetic. With infinite gentleness he lifted her limp body from the bed, her head lolling on his shoulder as he quietly left the room.

45

Emma slowly awoke and, reluctant to leave the warmth of the blankets, she remained snuggly tucked in for a few minutes. She then climbed gingerly out of bed, throwing on her dressing gown and shivering as she groped for her slippers. The windows were frosty, but before going downstairs to light the fire, she went into Patricia's room.

Emma's brow lifted to see the bed empty, the bathroom too, and, guessing that her daughter must have wanted to explore the new house, she ran downstairs, expecting to find Patricia there.

'Where are you, darling?' she called.

Silence.

'Come on, sweetheart, it's too early in the morning for games.'

Finding the kitchen empty, Emma tried the other rooms, her voice growing impatient. 'Patricia, for goodness' sake, where are you?'

Emma returned upstairs, but when she found all the bedrooms empty the first *frisson* of alarm clutched her stomach. 'Patricia! Tinker!' she cried. She ran downstairs again to check the rear garden.

There was no sign of the child, and the grass was white with untrodden frost. Turning, Emma hurried across the hall and threw open the front door. For a moment she stood on the top step, her eyes searching the street in both directions before alighting on the Common. No, Tinker knew better than to cross the road. As the cold wind penetrated her dressing gown, Emma wrapped her arms around her body, frantically considering her options. God, where was she?

Next door! Maybe she'd gone next door? No, the house was empty and, anyway, Tinker couldn't get in. Maybe a window had been left open? Emma dashed inside, grabbing a set of keys, uncaring of her appearance as she ran to the adjacent house.

Emma walked into the hall, shouting 'Tinker! Patricia!' but her voice echoed back in the empty silence. She checked every room, calling out again and again. Then, with nowhere else to look, she ran upstairs to open the door leading to the flat. The lock was heavy, her fingers numb with cold, but finally she managed it, only to find the flat empty, her nostrils twitching at the smell of cheap perfume that pervaded every room.

Oh, Tinker – Tinker, where are you? Emma scurried home, her heart now thumping in panic as she ran from room to room. 'Patricia,' she yelled. 'Please, darling, if you're hiding, please come out.'

She stood still for a moment, listening, but heard nothing. Her stomach churned with fear. She flung open the front door again, her eyes desperately scanning the Common, until finally, half an hour later, and almost out of her mind with distress, Emma rang the police.

Tired of the questions and only wanting the policeman now sitting on her sofa to do something to find her daughter, Emma's voice rose. 'No, of course she wouldn't run away. For goodness' sake, she's only eleven years old!'

'We've had runaways younger than that, Mrs Bell. Now tell me, was she upset about anything?'

'No, I've told you. She's been in hospital and it was her first night at home.'

'You said earlier that you're separated. Would she have gone to see her father?'

Emma surged impatiently to her feet. 'No, it's impossible. He left before she was born and, like me, Tinker has no idea where he is.'

'Tinker – I thought you said her name is Patricia.'

'Yes, sorry, it's her nickname. Oh, please, all these questions are a waste of time. My daughter wouldn't run away. Please, it's after ten and she's been missing for hours. Someone must have taken her.'

'We'll need your husband's full name.'

'His name is Horace Archibald Bell, but if you think he's involved, you're wrong.'

'What about other relatives? Friends?'

'My father lives in Kent, but Patricia doesn't have his address. One of my brothers has a stall in Belling Street Market, but we aren't in contact with him. My other brother is a priest, living in Ireland. As for friends, there are only those at Patricia's school.'

'I'll need all the addresses.'

Emma took her notebook from the bureau. 'My daughter is a happy child and even if she knew any of these addresses, she wouldn't go off without telling me.' She paused. 'Well, there's Terry, but she thinks he's away on holiday.'

'Terry? Who's he?'

'Until recently, he worked for me, and I must admit that my daughter is fond of him.'

'You'd best give me his details too, Mrs Bell. His full name and address.'

'Please, why won't you listen to me? I'm sure that someone broke in last night and took my daughter.'

'There's no sign of forced entry.'

'But I keep telling you. She wouldn't run away,

and if she'd gone to see Terry, he'd have brought her back.'

'We'll still need to check. His details, please?' the officer urged.

After writing all the addresses in his notebook, the police officer rose to his feet. 'Try not to worry, Mrs Bell. In ninety-nine per cent of cases, runaways turn up safe and sound in a couple of hours.'

She choked back her protest, watching as he tucked Patricia's last school photograph into his pocket alongside his notebook. Tinker wouldn't run away, she was sure of it.

Over two hours passed and Emma couldn't settle. She rang the police station again, but the desk sergeant told her there was no news. As she replaced the receiver there was a knock on the door. Emma flew across the hall to answer it, stepping back nervously when she saw Terry on the step, his face livid with anger as he stormed inside.

'What the hell's going on? I've had the police questioning me. I can't believe you told them that I might have taken Tinker.'

'But . . . but I didn't! They were asking me about friends, relatives, they're sure that she ran away. I just said that she's fond of you, that's all.'

'Well it didn't sound like that to me.'

Somewhere inside of Emma, she had clung to one last hope. That somehow Tinker hadn't believed that Terry was on holiday and had gone to find him. As she gazed at Terry this last vestige of hope died and her knees collapsed from under her. She felt arms around her, and half carrying her to the sitting room Terry urged her onto the sofa.

Emma buried her head in her hands, fear gripping her heart as she turned to God, silently and fervently praying, Oh God, please bring my baby back to me. I'll do anything, anything you ask. Just keep her safe and bring her home.

When Terry spoke she looked up at him, tears blurring her eyes.

'Look, I'm sorry for flying off the handle, Em, but this has knocked me for six. Why would Tinker run away?'

'But she hasn't! I'm sure she hasn't. I . . . I think someone took her.'

'What? When?'

'I put her to bed last night, but when I woke up this morning she was gone.' The last flicker of colour drained from Emma's face. 'Oh, Terry! Rose and I thought we heard someone lurking around the night before last. What if it was a punter, one of those funny ones that you've had to chuck out?'

'Did you see him?'

'No, we thought it was a cat.'

'That's probably all it was, but just in case, you'd best report it to the police.'

Emma blanched. If the police questioned the girls they would discover the brothel, but what did that matter if it helped to find Tinker? She had to tell them – had no choice – and as horrific images of what might have happened to her daughter filled her mind, her head began to buzz. The light became dim and she was barely aware of Terry hurrying from the room.

'Come on, girl, don't go fainting on me. Drink this.'

Emma took the glass from him, her hands shaking, but after taking a few sips of water her head began to clear.

'Oh Terry, if . . . if one of those monsters has taken Tinker, I'll never forgive myself. It'll be my fault – my fault for running a brothel and putting her in danger.'

'Don't jump the gun, Em. The police may be right. She may have taken it into her head to run away.'

'You know she wouldn't do that.'

'Kids can be funny buggers, but you shouldn't be on your own. Do you want me to fetch Doris?'

'You know where she is?'

'Yeah, she's at my place.'

So they had finally got together. But Emma couldn't think about it now. All she cared about was Tinker. 'Yes, but I doubt she'll come.'

'Don't be silly, of course she will. Now I'm off

to have a scout around, but is there anything I can get you before I go?'

'No, there's nothing.' Managing to stand up, Emma added, 'I'll call the police now, tell them about the other night.'

'Yeah, do that. Chin up, girl, and in no time you'll have Tinker back.'

Emma wanted to throw herself into Terry's arms, to draw comfort from this bear of a man, but resisted. He was with Doris now and she couldn't come between them. 'I feel I should be doing something, but the police said I should stay here in case she turns up.'

'They're right. Now if I leave, are you sure you'll be all right?'

Emma nodded, though in truth her stomach was clenched in fear at the nightmare images that invaded her mind. *God, don't let a monster touch my baby.* She held herself together until Terry left, and then, fighting back tears, she rang the police again.

When the sergeant came to the phone, Emma didn't hesitate. 'Hello, Sergeant. There's something I didn't tell you . . .'

46

At one thirty there was a knock on the door and eagerly Emma went to answer it. Had God answered her prayers? As she opened the door, Doris stood there and Emma flung herself into the woman's arms.

'Oh, Doris! I'm nearly going out of my mind.'

'They'll find her, love.'

'But what if one of those awful men who . . . who like children has got her? Oh, my baby!'

'Come on, Em, don't think the worst. The police may be right and she's run away.'

'Don't you think I want to believe that?'

Doris took her arm, leading her to the kitchen. 'Sit down and I'll make us both a drink.'

Emma sat, rubbing a hand across her forehead.

'Terry's in a right old state and is out looking for her,' Doris said.

'I'm grateful. I feel I should be searching too,

but I daren't leave the house in case Tinker comes back.'

'That's the ticket, love. Keep thinking like that. She'll come back soon, I'm sure of it.'

'I . . . I'm glad that you and Terry have got together.'

'We're just friends, Em.'

But Emma didn't hear her friend's reply. The images of Tinker in peril had returned, making her head buzz, and as Doris placed a cup of tea in front of her she grasped it, taking a gulp of hot liquid, uncaring as it seared her throat.

'It's my fault,' she cried, hand shaking as she returned the cup to its saucer. 'I shouldn't have put Tinker in danger.'

'No, love, you can't blame yourself.'

'The police will be here soon. I rang to tell them there might have been someone lurking in the bushes and they're coming round to talk to the girls.'

'You told them about the brothel?'

'Yes, but I had no choice,' Emma said. What did the business matter now? She would do anything – anything – to get Tinker back. If interviewing the girls helped, then so be it.

Only moments later the police arrived, along with a face Emma recognised from CID. She knew she had opened herself up to arrest, but for the first time she wondered if the back-handers she had given over the years might come in useful. She couldn't be arrested, couldn't be in a cell. She had to be there in case Tinker came home.

Forcing a hard, implacable manner that she no longer felt, Emma faced the man. 'I'd like to talk to you in private.'

One eyebrow lifted, but he nodded, and as Emma took him through to the drawing room she closed the door firmly behind them before saying, 'I don't care how you do it, but you've got to prevent any arrests. If you don't, then I have nothing to lose any more. If I go down, I'll see that you come with me.'

'I don't like threats.'

'I don't like making them, but you and your predecessor have done well out of me over the years. It's time for me to get something in return.'

They faced each other, eyes locked, Emma quaking inside but refusing to show it.

He was the first to break contact. 'I'll do what I can, but you'll have to close down.'

'Fine, that's fine with me.'

As the man left the room, Emma's shoulders slumped. She walked to the hall, saw him in conversation with uniformed officers, saw their eyes flick in her direction as she returned to the kitchen.

'What was all that about, Em?' Doris asked.

Emma repeated the conversation. Doris smiled. 'That was a good idea and it might work.'

'Mrs Bell, we need to go next door to question the girls,' the CID officer said as he walked into the room.

Emma nodded, but found no reassurance in the man's eyes as she and Doris escorted him and uniformed officers to the brothel.

Rose was interviewed first, her manner sullen, jaws working as she chewed on gum. 'I saw nothing,' she insisted. 'We heard a noise in the bushes, but I reckon it was only a cat.'

The other girls were unable to help, their interviews short. Emma didn't know how he achieved it, but the CID officer had managed to smooth the path, ensuring there were no arrests. When he came to speak to Emma, his face was grave.

'We'll be back this evening to talk to the other girls, and though I've managed a cover story, I won't be able to offer protection if you open for business again.'

'I understand, and thank you,' Emma told him.

Emma waited until the police had left, dreading what she had to do next. 'Doris, I'll have to tell the girls that I'm closing the brothel.'

'Leave it to me, Emma. You've got enough on your plate at the moment.'

'Are you sure you don't mind?'

'Of course I don't. Now go on, get yourself home.'

Emma was glad to leave the flat, but it was only half an hour later when Doris joined her. 'How did they take it?' she asked.

'I think they were just relieved to get off the premises without arrest. Rose was the only one who kicked up.'

'I didn't trust her, Doris. I'm sure she was dipping into the takings.' Emma ran a hand across her face. 'Oh what does it matter! What does money matter? All I care about is Tinker! Oh, where is she, Doris? Where is my little girl?'

'She'll turn up, love.'

Emma gripped her friend's hand. 'I don't know what I'd have done without your help, but I haven't even apologised for driving you away.'

'Look, forget it. All right, we fell out, but it's in the past, and the least of your worries at the moment.' Doris's fingers flew to her lips. 'Oh Christ, trust me to put my foot in my mouth.'

'Don't apologise, I know you mean well.'

Emma was so grateful that Doris was there, but now that the police had gone, nothing could still her mind.

'Doris, I should be out there, looking for Tinker. Oh God, I feel so helpless, so useless. Look at the time – it's after three and she's been missing for over seven hours!'

'They'll find her, love, you'll see.'

Emma could only hope that Doris was right, but a sense of dread consumed her mind.

At seven that evening, after telephoning the station at regular intervals, to be told there was no news, Emma and Doris went next door, waiting for the evening girls to arrive. They would have to break the news that the brothel had closed. Whilst waiting, Emma paced. Over eleven hours had passed now since Tinker went missing, and cold fear gripped her heart.

When at last the girls turned up it was Doris who broke the news, adding an assurance that they wouldn't be arrested. Then the police returned and Emma prayed one of the girls had seen something – anything that could help – but her hopes were dashed. After being interviewed by the police, they left one by one, some hurriedly, some cockily, all never to return.

Emma couldn't settle and self-loathing filled her mind. If anything happened to her precious daughter, she would never forgive herself.

Doris gripped her arm. 'Come on, love, they've all gone. Let's go next door. You look exhausted.'

Emma found herself being led outside and, once in her drawing room, she almost fell onto a chair. She'd never run a brothel again, but it was too late to save her daughter.

'I know it's only nine thirty, but why don't you get some sleep? I'll stay if you want me to,' Doris said.

Sleep! She wouldn't be able to sleep, but she needed to be alone. There were things she had to do, in private, and though loath to let Doris go, she forced the words from her mouth as she stood up. 'Thanks, but you needn't stay. I'll be all right. You get yourself home to Terry.'

'I'd hardly call it home. Mind you, I'm surprised that Terry hasn't been round to see you, but then again, he could still be out looking for Tinker. Anyway, if you're sure, and you really are going to bed, I'll be off, but don't worry, I'll be back in the morning.'

When they reached the hall they hugged, but as Emma closed the door behind her friend, she turned to slump against it. She was sure now that Tinker had been snatched, and she was bent like an old woman as she walked to her bedroom. Her hands were shaking as she grabbed her cash box, unlocking it to stare at the notes, her eyes dark with hatred. Why? Why had she let the accumulation of money become her god?

She'd been warned but refused to listen, only wanting more wealth, more money to fill her coffers, and now she was being punished. She deserved this – this pain and anguish.

Despite the cost of buying and renovating this house, there was still money – money she had to get rid of. Almost out of her mind now, Emma snatched the notes. She ran to the drawing room and flung the bundles into the fire, seeing them catch, flames rushing up the chimney as she begged forgiveness.

'Here, take it – take my money. You can punish me, do anything to me, but please, please, keep my daughter safe. Oh God, don't let her be hurt. I beg you, bring her back to me.'

47

A week passed and still there was no news. Emma left the house on the seventh day, wandering the streets and the Common, her hair lank, uncombed, and like her body, unwashed. With no income now, she had been to the pawnbroker, something she had never expected to do again. She had sold some of her Royal Crown Derby. Emma barely haggled, uncaring as long as she had enough money to get by on.

Her voice became a croak from her constantly calling her daughter's name. On her way home, her head bowed low with exhaustion, a man suddenly stepped in her path.

'Emma, it's me.'

She looked up and through blurred eyes, barely recognised the mature, good-looking man. It was Dick, and for a moment she dared to hope. 'Dick, have you seen her? Have you seen Tinker?'

'No, but Mandy's been nagging me for nearly a week to check if you're all right.'

'How did you know?'

'The police came round, but we couldn't tell them anything. They've been to see Dad too.'

'You're in touch with him?'

'Yeah, life's too short to bear grudges, but it's taken all these years before the Salvation Army and my wife made me see that. It held me back from joining up, from making the commitment, but I finally saw the light and I've been in touch with Dad for about six months now.'

'What did he say?'

'He's disgusted that you were bringing your daughter up in a brothel and . . . I'm afraid he said you're getting what you deserve.'

Emma paled, but then a glimmer of light appeared in her eyes. 'Oh, Dick, do you think Dad took her?'

'Don't be daft, of course he didn't. Anyway, from what the police said it sounds like she ran away.'

'But she didn't. I'm sure someone took her. I heard someone lurking in the bushes the night before she went missing.'

'Well, it wasn't Dad, that's for sure. It's more likely to be one of your punters, the sort that likes little girls.'

'Don't you think I know that?' Emma cried, her stomach churning. 'I'm sick at the thought, but we didn't cater for those types. If one turned up looking for a child, he was soon thrown out.'

'Emma, listen to yourself! So dodgy blokes were thrown out, good for you, but you and your daughter lived below a brothel – *your* brothel.'

This was the first time Emma had seen her brother in many years, and she wanted to throw herself in his arms, yet his lack of sympathy held her back. Tinker, her beautiful little girl, was missing, and instead of comfort, Dick seemed to be rubbing salt in the wound. She knew it was her fault, knew that if anything happened to her daughter she wouldn't be able to carry on, wouldn't want to live without her.

'Oh, Dick, you say you found forgiveness in your heart for Dad. Why can't you feel the same way for me?'

'I have forgiven you, Emma, but you wouldn't close the place down. How could I associate with someone who runs a brothel? It would be like condoning it. Surely you can understand that?'

'It's closed now and I live next door.'

'I'm glad to hear that, Emma, but it's a shame that it took something like this to bring you to your senses. I tried to warn you – Luke too. If you'd listened to us, none of this would have happened.'

So Dick thought the same – that Tinker had been taken as punishment. She couldn't bear it.

'Don't you think I know that? Oh, please, just go away, just leave me alone.'

'But ... Em ...'

Emma didn't wait to hear anything else he had to say, and if she hadn't been so exhausted from walking the streets, she'd have run the rest of the way home.

It only took her ten minutes to reach the house. She closed the door behind her and slumped against it, finding that the empty house seemed to mock her. For a brief moment her heart had leaped when she'd seen Dick, and when he had mentioned their father, she had been stupid to hope, if only for a second, that he had taken Tinker. He had never been a parent to any of them, leaving their upbringing to their mother, and almost as soon as she died, off-loading two of the boys on to Alice Moon. He wouldn't want Tinker, having shown no interest in his grandchild since the day she'd been born. Emma staggered away from the door, only just making it to the kitchen where she slumped, desolate, onto a chair.

Another five days passed, days in which Emma continued to walk the streets looking for Tinker. Doris still came round every morning, sometimes joining her on the search, and only her friendship kept Emma going. Doris nagged her to eat, but Emma could barely face food and when encouraged to wash, she would just dash a damp flannel over her face. She hadn't seen Terry, Doris assuring her that he was still looking for Tinker, going out of the borough as his search widened.

When there was a knock on the door, Emma felt a surge of hope as she went to answer it. Dick stood on the step, a woman just behind him and, thinking it was Mandy, Emma stood aside to let them in.

'Hello, Emma.'

As her eyes focused on the woman, they widened in shock. It couldn't be! 'Susan, oh my God, Susan!'

'Oh, Emma, when I called round to see Dad and he told me, I just had to come.'

'I . . . I can't believe it,' she said, clutching Susan as they hugged, unwilling to let her go.

It was some time before they parted, and then Emma took her siblings through to the kitchen, still reeling with shock. Susan looked wonderful, the ugly duckling turning into a beautiful swan. Her short, blonde hair was shining, her skin perfect, with just a touch of make-up, and she was wearing a fashionable suit, pale blue with a short skirt and box jacket.

There was so much to catch up on. Emma learned that Ann and Bella were fine, both still living at home, happy and well.

'Did . . . did you ever get my letters?' Emma asked.

'No, I'm afraid not. We were hurt at first, thinking that you didn't care about us any more. We wanted to write to you but Dad told us that you had moved and he didn't have your address.'

'Oh, how could he?'

'It was wrong of him, dreadful, but you hurt him badly.'

'I hurt him? What about what he did to me?'

'Emma, I know Dad was no angel, and you have every right to be bitter, but he's a different man now. He works hard, hardly drinks, and, well . . . he's been a good father to us. In fact, he went very quiet when the police called to see him, so I'm sure the news about your daughter upset him too. Polly said he's been acting very strangely and he keeps disappearing for long walks, but won't talk about where he's been. Oh, Em, I'm sure he's feeling for you. Can't there be reconciliation? When I go back, if I ask Dad to come to see you, I feel sure he'd be down here like a shot, especially now that Dick tells me that you're not running a . . . a brothel any more.'

Emma sat quietly, pondering her sister's words, but uppermost in her mind was her daughter. All she cared about at the moment was getting Tinker back, her mind unable to focus on anything else. 'I don't know, maybe, but I can't think about it at the moment.'

'Of course you can't,' Susan said, gently patting the back of Emma's hand. 'Is there any news of her?'

'No, none.' Emma choked back a sob. She felt arms around her shoulders, and leaned back against Dick. 'It's my fault, I know that, and like you I think this is God's punishment.'

'Oh, no, Em, you're wrong. I don't think that. God isn't interested in earthly things. They are for our own consciences to deal with. If we sin, we damage our souls, keeping us away from Him. It's our spiritual wellbeing that He cares about. He is a loving God, a forgiving God, and will be there if you turn to Him for comfort.'

Emma began to cry, to sob, and it was some time before she was able to pull herself together. Dick sounded so assured, but she was unable to draw comfort from his words. She *had* turned to God, *had* begged his forgiveness, but Tinker was still missing.

Susan grasped her hand, squeezing it, whilst Dick had his resting on her shoulders.

'How . . . how are Bella and Ann?' Emma asked when she had recovered.

'They're fine, and anxious to see you, but after discussing it we felt that you have enough to cope with at the moment. It's better to wait to see them until Tinker is safely home.'

'And . . . and Dad. He's going to allow it?'

'Yes, of course he is. Anyway, we aren't children any more, Em.'

Emma returned the pressure of her sister's hand, feeling the connection, the ties of blood. Dick and Susan were part of her family, a family she had thought lost to her. *Oh, Tinker, Tinker, where are you? They're your family too, and like me, they will love you so much.*

Dick and Susan stayed for another two hours, and when they rose to leave, Emma clung to them.

'Don't worry,' Dick said. 'We'll be back.'

She forced a smile, finding some comfort in her brother's words, but as she closed the door, the empty house wrapped around her again and she felt more alone than ever.

48

During the months that followed, the weight fell off Emma. In despair, and an emotional wreck, she hadn't been able to cope with the thought of reconciliation with her father, though Dick and Mandy called to see her once a week. Susan kept in touch, ringing her constantly, and Emma spoke to Bella and Ann, but by now Emma hardly ate, hardly slept, and had almost given up hope.

Doris called round regularly, and one afternoon in spring they sat in the kitchen, Emma endeavouring to swallow the tea that her friend had made.

'Emma, you've got to eat, love. Christ, it's beginning to look like you're starving yourself to death.'

'I . . . I'm not hungry.'

'Don't give up, Em. The police still might find her, and Terry's still looking.'

'Is he? I didn't realise. It's been ages since I've seen him.'

'It breaks his heart to see you like this. I think that's why he's staying away.'

Emma said nothing, finding it difficult to summon up the energy to talk. Doris still insisted that she and Terry were just friends, but Emma doubted this was true. When had she finally admitted to herself that she loved Terry? Emma didn't know, but it was too late now. The man had moved on and she didn't blame him. Anyway, she wasn't fit to love, or be loved.

'Try a bit of this soup, Em. Please, love.'

She lifted the spoon, managing to swallow a mouthful, but every time she tried to eat she felt it would choke her. How could she eat? How could she take any sustenance whilst her daughter might still be in the hands of a monster? Or even worse, dead?

'Go on, just a few more spoonfuls,' Doris urged. 'You'll need a bit of strength if you want to hand out those leaflets again.'

Emma managed to nod. Yes, she had pawned more of her things to get them printed and would go out again, but knew deep in her heart that there was little hope now. Dick and Mandy were helping too, using the resources of the Salvation Army but, like her, they'd been unsuccessful.

Emma stared at the bowl of soup, unable to eat any more. If her beloved child was still alive, she'd have been found by now, yet while her body allowed, Emma would continue to look. After that, she wanted only one thing. If she couldn't be with her daughter in life, then she hoped to be with her in death.

'I ain't seen Terry for days,' Doris said, but Emma was hardly listening. 'He's gone off somewhere again, but Gawd knows where.'

Emma closed her eyes, seeing her daughter's face behind closed lids. 'I think she's dead, Doris.'

'Oh, don't say that, love. Of course she ain't.'

Emma didn't answer, and for a while the two of them sat quietly. When there was a knock on the street door, it was Doris who went to answer it, returning with two police officers.

When Emma saw the expression on their faces, the room spun. *Oh God! No! Please, no!*

She became aware of a hand on her arm, Doris holding a glass to her lips, and as her head cleared, one of the officers spoke.

'Mrs Bell, we've finally managed to trace your husband.'

'Horace! You've found Horace? Did he . . . have you found her?'

'No, I'm afraid not.'

Emma slumped, running a hand over her face. 'I told you he wouldn't take her.'

'Your husband was living under an assumed name and that's why he's been difficult to find.' The policeman paused, clearing his throat. 'I'm afraid I have some bad news, Mrs Bell. You see, when we finally traced him, it was to find that he had died a month ago.'

Emma looked tiredly at the officer. 'Our marriage has been over for a long time and, to be honest, I don't care. All I want is for you to find my daughter. Please, isn't there *any* news?'

'No, I'm afraid not. Anyway, Mrs Bell,' he added, handing her a card, 'you may want to get in touch with this solicitor. Apparently your late husband left a large estate.'

Emma shook her head, refusing to accept it, ignoring it when the police officer laid it on the table. Horace was dead, but it didn't touch her. She had no interest in his estate, no interest in money now. The only thing she wanted was to have her daughter back.

Doris showed the men out, returning to sit at the table. 'Fancy that, Em. Your old man's kicked the bucket and it seems he's left a pretty penny. You were daft to burn your money, so this is a godsend.'

'I don't want it. I don't want anything from him.' With a strangled cry she blurted, 'Oh, Doris, when I first saw the expression on those policemen's faces, I thought they'd come to tell me that they'd found Tinker, that she was dead. Do you know what's worse? For a split second I wanted it to be true, to be put out of my misery.'

'Oh, Em, you don't mean that.'

'No, of course I don't, but just for a brief moment I wanted this agony to be over, to know once and for all what's happened to my precious baby.'

'They'll find her, I'm sure of it.'

Emma choked back a sob. 'I'm going out with the leaflets again. There's only been one possible sighting, and that was at Clapham Junction station.'

'That was months ago.'

'I know, but I can't think of anywhere else to try.'

'All right, love. I can't give you a hand today, but I'm free tomorrow. Just finish that soup before you go out.'

Emma managed a small smile of thanks, but when Doris left she pushed the bowl to one side. She then rose to her feet, put on her coat and picked up the last pile of leaflets.

Emma stood outside the station, a leaflet held out in appeal, whilst a high wind fought to snatch it from her hand.

'Please,' she begged, 'have you seen this little girl?'

As had so many others, the man ignored her plea, brushing her aside as he hurried past.

Rain began to fall, small spatters at first, but as

heavy clouds gathered it became heavier, soon soaking both her hair and clothes. It didn't stop Emma. Nothing would. Clasping the rest of the leaflets close to her chest, she tottered forward, thrusting one towards a woman emerging from the station wearing a straight red skirt and pointy-toed shoes.

'Please, have you seen this little girl?'

The woman took it, her eyes showing sympathy as she said, 'Sorry, no.'

'Please, look again.'

The young lady lowered her eyes to the picture, but then, needing both hands to open her umbrella, she shook her head, the picture falling onto the wet pavement. She wrestled the wind to keep the umbrella over her head, her grip tight and knuckles white as she bustled away.

Emma watched her for a moment, but then her eyes came to rest on the leaflet lying wet and forlorn on the pavement. A gasp escaped her lips. The eyes of her child seemed to gaze back at her, rain spattering the picture as though tears on her cheeks. She shivered with fear, vowing silently, *Oh God, I have to find you – I have to*.

She straightened her shoulders, desperation and determination in her stance. Another train disgorged its passengers, and as they streamed from the station she saw a tide of faces. Hand held out, she once again proffered her leaflets.

It was dark before Emma gave up, uncaring that she was soaked to the skin and almost dead on her feet as she trudged home.

The house felt empty, desolate, as she walked inside, the plush décor meaning nothing to her now. She was alone. They had all gone, but it didn't matter. The only one she cared about was her daughter.

With hair dripping onto the thick red carpet and wet tendrils clinging to her face, she wearily climbed the stairs to her bedroom, peeling off wet clothes before throwing on her pink, quilted dressing gown. Tears now rolling down her cheeks, Emma flung herself onto the bed, clutching a pillow to her chest. It had been over three months and she feared the police had given up, but she wouldn't. She would die first and, if anything, death would be welcome.

Why had she had let money become an obsession? It had begun in her childhood – and her iron will had grown from her desperation to lead a different life from the one her mother had suffered. But there was more to it than that. It was men! Her need to make them pay – her need for revenge.

And they *had* paid, and she *had* made her fortune, but at what cost? *Oh, my baby! My baby!* The money was meaningless now. She'd burned it all, given up every last penny, but still they hadn't found her daughter. What more do you want from me? her mind cried, eyes heavenward.

She sobbed, unable to stand the fears that plagued her. She forced her thoughts in another direction. To the past, and to where it had all begun.

49

Emma was drifting, reliving it all when she heard a loud banging on the street door. She opened her eyes, but the room was in darkness and, having no idea of the time, she tiredly climbed out of bed. She swayed, her body so weak now that it was an effort to walk downstairs.

Her hand reached out to switch on the hall light, and then she pulled open the door. No! No, it couldn't be! Her arms reached out, tears spurting, and then her legs finally gave way.

'Mummy! Mummy!'

She was dreaming – she had to be – but as Tinker flung herself down and across her body, with a sob Emma held her. 'Oh my baby! My baby!'

'Come on, you two,' Terry urged, but Emma couldn't let go. She was holding Tinker! It was real!

Terry leaned down, pulling Tinker to her feet,

and then helped Emma up. 'Oh, Terry, you found her! I . . . I don't know how to thank you. Where? How?'

'It's a long story, Em, but it's after midnight and I think it can wait until the morning. The nipper's had a long journey and is almost dead on her feet.'

As Emma gazed at this man, the man who had found her child, her heart overflowed with love. She flung her arms around his neck.

For a moment he held her, but then both pulled apart as Tinker forced her way between them. 'I'm hungry, Mummy.'

Emma spluttered, then she laughed. For the first time in over three months she laughed, clutching her daughter to her with joy.

Terry stood watching them and Emma saw that he looked exhausted. She sobered, feeling a *frisson* of fear. Was Tinker all right? Had she been . . . been touched?

As though sensing her thoughts Terry said softly, 'Don't worry. She's fine.'

Emma's mind filled with questions, but she knew as Tinker pulled on her arm that they'd have to wait. They went to the kitchen, where Emma quickly poured a glass of milk for Tinker before making her a sandwich.

'What about you, Terry? Are you hungry too?'

'No, I'm all right. I'd best be off now, but I'll see you in the morning.'

'No, don't go,' Tinker cried as she ran to his side, throwing her arms around his waist.

He gently disengaged them. 'You'll be fine now and when you've had something to eat, you'll be going to bed. I'll be here when you wake up in the morning, I promise.'

Emma's heart was singing. She had her daughter back and it still felt like a wonderful dream. She wanted to hold her again, to never let her go. 'Terry's right, darling, and I expect Auntie Doris will be waiting to hear the news. Now come and eat your sandwich.'

Terry gave Tinker another swift hug. ''Bye for now.'

Emma's face was ablaze with joy as she looked at Terry. 'Thank you. Thank you from the bottom of my heart.'

'Yeah, well,' he said brusquely, 'maybe you'll eat something now. 'Night, Tinker, I'll see you in the morning.' Then, with a wave, he was gone.

Yes, Emma thought, it was true, she was ravenous, but only managed to eat half a sandwich, her throat constricted with tears of happiness as she gazed at her daughter.

Tinker's eyes were drooping and, with an arm around her daughter's shoulder, Emma led her up to bed in her own room, unable to bear the thought of letting her out of her sight again. They snuggled closely, Emma wanting to ask questions but holding them back.

Tinker yawned, saying tiredly, 'I was glad when Terry came to fetch me, Mummy. I like Uncle Luke, but I wanted to come home.'

'Luke! You were with Luke?'

There was no answer, Tinker had gone to sleep.

Emma hardly slept, tossing and turning. She was burning up with anger, unable to believe that Luke had taken Tinker. Her brother had put her through months of agony. Why had he done it? Why?

True to his word, Terry was at the door first thing in the morning. As Emma let him in she held a finger to her lips. 'Tinker's still asleep.'

They walked through to the kitchen, the questions that had raged in Emma's mind half the night immediately springing to her lips. 'Tinker said she was with Luke. How did you find her? Where were they?'

Terry heaved a sigh. 'It was just a long shot, that's all, and to be honest, I couldn't believe my luck when I found her.' He paused, drew out a chair and sat down. 'I'd searched everywhere, Em, and had all but given up hope. If you remember, I asked Doris to let me have all the addresses in your book, but Tinker wasn't at any of them. That left only Luke, but he was a priest, living in Ireland

and until I had tried all the other avenues, I dismissed him.'

'But why did he take her? It makes no sense. Why did he do it?'

'Religion can do funny things to people, Em, and sometimes they can become fanatical. Luke thought he was saving Tinker.'

'Saving her?'

'We had a long talk, and well, I sort of understand. He spoke about the brothel, of taking Tinker away from sin. He didn't hurt her, Em, and apart from missing you, she was well cared for.'

'My God, I've been almost going out of my mind with worry, thinking the worst, when all the time she was in Ireland with Luke.'

'They weren't in Ireland. It was a wasted journey and when I arrived I found out that Luke left his church a week before Tinker was taken. That aroused my suspicions, but it took me on a right old wild-goose chase to find him. Suffice to say that I had to ask a lot of questions, and there were a lot of people that didn't want to answer them. It seems your brother was well thought of, so well that I was told he had been left a cottage by one of his flock. It wasn't easy to get the address, but there's a certain solicitor in Ireland who ain't gonna forget me in a hurry.'

'Oh Terry, will he report you to the police?'

He shrugged, 'Maybe, but don't worry about it.

I'm out of the country now and he doesn't know my name.'

'And the cottage?'

'It's in North Wales, close to Snowdonia and miles away from anywhere. As I said, Luke and I had a good talk and I found out that he's been watching you on and off for years. He hoped you'd stop running a brothel, but when you carried on he became obsessed with taking Tinker away before she became tainted.'

'Tainted!' Emma rubbed her hands over her face. 'Yes, I can imagine him saying that. He came to see me many years ago, and that was one of the words he used.'

'I'm not surprised. He's got a thing about women. He mentioned his stepmother for one. To be honest, though he seems harmless, I don't think he's quite right in the head.'

'Have you told the police?'

'No, not yet. Look, Em, I know Luke did a terrible thing, but Tinker's back now, she's unhurt, and surely that's all that matters.'

'I'm not sure I, or the police, will see it that way.'

'No, I suppose not, but do you really want to prosecute him?'

Emma first instinct was to say yes, but something Luke had told Terry resurfaced in her mind. Luke had mentioned their stepmother, the sins of women. Had what happened in the past twisted his mind? Had her own refusal to stop running a brothel tipped him over the edge?

'Mummy! Terry!'

Emma rose to her feet, pulling the child into her arms. She didn't want to think about Luke now, or the police, all she wanted to do was hold Tinker and never let her go.

'Well, Tinker, it's about time you got up,' Terry said, smiling widely.

'I keep forgetting, but she prefers to be called Patricia now,' Emma said.

'No. Uncle Luke called me Patricia. He said I'm too big for nicknames now, but I want to be called Tinker again.'

Emma refrained from telling her daughter that Luke had originally picked the nickname, saying only, 'Yes, of course we will. Anyway, I think you'll always be Tinker to all of us. Now come on, I'm going to cook the three of us a nice big breakfast.'

Tinker ran from her arms, scrambling onto a chair, and Emma found her heart singing again. It felt so strange, yet so normal, but there was one person missing. 'Terry, where's Doris? I thought she'd be with you.'

'I gave her a knock, but we had such a late night and she was dead to the world. No doubt when she wakes up she'll be round here like a shot.'

'She must be so proud of you.'

'Proud of me? Well, I don't know about that.'

'You found Tinker and she must be over the moon.'

'Well, she's certainly chuffed.'

Emma turned her back, busying herself at the cooker. Oh, she'd been such a fool, but it was too late. She loved Terry, but he had Doris now and there was no way she'd ever come between them.

The rest of the morning was fraught. Emma rang the police, told them that she had her daughter back, and when they came to the house, Terry had to put up with many questions.

She kept Tinker out of the way, trying to keep her daughter amused, but found a subtle change in her. Tinker had been so loving at first, wanting cuddles, kisses, but now she was becoming belligerent. Emma was puzzled by her behaviour but indulgent, and when there was a knock on the door she found Doris there, beaming widely.

'See, Em, I told you not to give up.'

'Auntie Doris,' Tinker cried, throwing her arms around the woman's waist.

'Hello, ducks,' she said, hugging the child to her. 'Where's Terry?' she then asked Emma.

'The police are still questioning him. Oh, Doris, I'll never be able to thank him enough for finding Tinker.'

528

They walked through to the kitchen, Doris laying a hand on Tinker's shoulder as they crossed the hall. 'I bet you're pleased to be home, love.'

Tinker frowned, and as they drew out chairs to sit down she said, 'Mummy let Uncle Luke take me on holiday.'

'I did no such thing,' Emma spluttered.

'Yes you did.'

Emma's eyes were wide as they met Doris's, and it was she who answered.

'Your uncle took you away without telling Mummy and she's been worried sick.'

Tinker shook her head. 'Uncle Luke said the only good woman was Mary, Mother of Jesus. He read the Bible a lot and made me read it too. He said I've been a bad girl, and that Mummy said I had to stay with him until he made me better.'

'Oh, darling, that isn't true, and of course you aren't a bad girl,' Emma protested.

Tinker suddenly flung herself into Emma's arms, crying for the first time, 'I . . . I thought you didn't love me any more.'

'Oh, sweetheart, of course I love you. You're my precious girl and I always will. I've missed you so much.'

Dabbing at her eyes, Doris stood up, saying she'd make a drink, whilst Emma held her daughter, rocking her in her arms.

50

It was the catalyst that Tinker needed, and over the next few days the child appeared normal, untroubled, and unhurt by what had happened.

It was only eight in the morning when Doris called the following week, Tinker still asleep as they sat in the drawing room.

'Well,' Doris said tersely, 'I know you don't want to talk about it, but I reckon you should see that solicitor. You're still Horace's wife and have a right to his money.'

'No, I don't want it.'

'You may not want it, but you should think about Tinker's future.'

'I've still got this house and I can sell it. It'll raise enough to buy a smaller place, with money left to tide us over for a while.'

Doris shook her head. 'I still think you're mad.' She paused then before asking, 'How did Dick take it when he found out it was Luke who took Tinker?'

'He was shocked – the rest of my family too.'

'It's nice that you're in touch with them again. Now that you've got Tinker back I expect you'll soon see your other sisters, and what about your father?'

Emma was about to answer when there was a knock on the front door. Her eyes widened when she saw who was on the step. It was as though Doris's question had conjured him up. For a moment she floundered, unsure of how she felt, but then she stood back to let him in.

'Hello, Dad.'

'Hello, Emma. I hope you don't mind my calling uninvited, but one of us had to make the first move.'

Emma led him through to the drawing room, still unsure, still full of bitter memories. Doris immediately rose to her feet and, after Emma had made the introductions, she insisted on leaving, saying she'd call back later.

'You need to talk in private, love,' she said as she and Emma parted.

When Emma was alone with her father, she found the atmosphere strained, but then he began to talk.

'I know I ain't been much of a father, but it was the war that changed me.'

He paused, lowering his eyes momentarily before going on to describe what had happened to him, the horrors he had seen. 'I know I was weak, know that other men got over it, but me, well, I turned to booze to drown out the memories. I know it's not much of an excuse, love, but it's all I've got. When I married Polly and we moved to Kent, I gradually came to my senses, but it was a long time coming. I just wish I hadn't made your mother suffer so much.'

Emma found that she too had to lower her eyes. Like her father, she had once turned to drink, living her life in a fog of alcohol until she'd fallen pregnant. Yet her excuse was nothing compared to her father's. God, he'd been through hell!

Still she hesitated, but then her father said the words she had longed to hear and her heart skipped a beat.

'Emma, as I said, I know I ain't been much of a father, and I can't tell you how sorry I am, but I love you, girl. You were my firstborn, and so much like your mother that it breaks my heart to look at you. Can't we let bygones be bygones and start again?'

This was the father that Emma remembered, the one who, when she was child, had sat her on his lap, cuddling her, but he had left, gone to war and she hadn't understood. All she had felt was abandonment, especially as the man she remembered had returned a stranger, one who never showed her an ounce of affection.

'Oh, Dad,' she gasped, her bitterness draining away. 'Yes, I'd like that.'

'Right then,' he said, smiling widely. 'Give me a cuddle and then let's talk about Luke.'

Emma found herself with her father's arms tight around her. They remained like that for a while, but then slowly drew apart.

'The police still haven't found Luke,' Emma said.

'Yeah, I know. How do you feel about that?'

'I don't know, Dad. I've got mixed emotions – part anger at what he did, but I can't help feeling pity too. Terry said he thinks Luke's mind has turned, and that worries me.'

'Me too. And talking about Terry, from what Dick told me he sounds like a nice bloke.'

'Oh, he is, and I'll never be able to thank him enough for finding Tinker.'

'Kidnapping ain't something the police take lightly, and if they catch up with Luke he could go away for years. I can understand your anger, love, but if he ain't right in the head, I think that rather than being locked away, he needs help.'

'I'm just nervous that he's still at large. What if he tries to take Tinker again?'

'I wouldn't worry about that. Luke might be off his head, but he's never been stupid. He's probably miles away by now.'

'I hope you're right, but I still want him found.'

534

'They'll catch him eventually, and when they do, we'll talk again and take it from there. Sufficient unto the day, as the saying goes.'

Emma nodded, and when her father began to question her gently about the brothel she was open with him, spilling it all out, finally saying, 'I was desperate for money and thought it was the only way.'

'Yeah, well, I can understand that, but you're the last person on earth I expected to run a brothel. When Dick got in touch and told me, you could have knocked me down with a feather.'

'Dad, when Tinker went missing, he . . . he told me what you said, that . . . that I deserved it.'

'Oh Christ, I'm sorry, and I didn't mean it, Em. It was shock, guilt, and as soon as I said the words I wished I could take them back.'

'Guilt?'

'Yeah, I was riddled with it. I left London a bitter man, full of self-pity that you wouldn't sell this place to buy a pub. I cut you out of my life, refusing to pass your letters on to your sisters, thinking that you were sitting pretty, when all the time you were struggling, driven to running a brothel.' He raked his fingers through his hair. 'Christ, of course I was full of guilt. I was doing all right in Kent and could have helped you, and if I had, none of this would have happened. Not only that, I gave up my two youngest, and though

I know James and Archie have had a good life with Alice Moon, I should never have let them go, Em.'

'You . . . you've seen them?'

'Yeah, but they didn't really know me. They're big lads now, and it didn't take me long to realise that I wasn't needed in their lives. Alice and Cyril are their parents now, and they're happy kids. Alice didn't want to rock the boat, but she said that when they come of age she'd explain it all to them, and then, if they want to, they can get in touch. It's no more than I deserve and the best I can hope for.'

Emma lowered her head. How could she blame her father? She'd been no better, wanting them to go to Alice so she could find a job, and look where that had led! She could have kept in touch with them, but she hadn't, and now, like her father, she regretted it. 'I know how you feel, Dad, but we've got to put it behind us. Guilt eats you up – look at me, I'm proof of that.'

'Yeah, girl, you look like you need feeding up.'

There was the sound of footsteps, and Emma smiled. 'That's sounds like Tinker. Come on, Dad, it's time to meet your granddaughter.'

Tinker was thrilled to meet her grandfather, the two of them hitting it off immediately.

'Gawd, Em, she's just like you and as pretty as a picture.'

She smiled, her heart light as she watched the two of them getting to know each other, cooking them breakfast, and when her father left it was with promises to bring Bella and Ann to see her. Emma couldn't wait, hugging herself with excitement.

It took Tinker a while to settle after that, but at last she was absorbed in painting a picture, whilst Emma thought about her family. Her heart soared now that they had reconciled, to know that her father loved her. She had no interest in riches now, but did she have the right to deprive her daughter of financial security? For a while she continued to ponder, but then rose to her feet, a plan forming in her mind.

'I'm just going to make a telephone call, Tinker.'

An appointment wasn't easy to arrange, the solicitor's office being in Liverpool, but thankfully they had a branch in London and said they would transfer the papers there. As Emma replaced the receiver, she smiled.

It was a week later and, with Doris looking after Tinker, Emma made her way to the solicitor's office. Of course her friend had been delighted that she had made the decision to accept Horace's money, but if her plans could be arranged Emma imagined Doris was in for a shock. Of course, until she saw Horace's will, she had no idea if her ideas were possible, but her fingers were crossed in anticipation.

On arrival, Emma shook the man's hand, showing him her marriage lines and Tinker's birth certificate. When the formalities were over, she had been handed Horace's death certificate, the cause a sexually transmitted disease. Emma shuddered, knowing how it affected the body and brain, so much so that she had ensured her girls received regular medical checks. It seemed ironic, sad, that Horace had died such an awful death.

The solicitor then patiently took her through Horace's portfolio, and her head had reeled at the amount of money and property he'd accrued.

'Your husband's will is explicit, with the bulk of his estate being put into a trust that will mature when your daughter is twenty-one. He has however added a provision that will allow you to apply to the trust for such expenses she may need, her education for example. He has also left you two thousand pounds and the deeds to his house in Clapham.'

Emma was delighted and eagerly put her ideas to the solicitor. She then said, 'I'm glad that my daughter's future is assured and though I originally intended to say I didn't want anything from my late husband's estate, I'm glad I changed my mind.'

The solicitor raised his eyebrows. 'Yes, well, I'll

be in touch as soon as probate is granted. In the meantime, if I can be of any assistance, please don't hesitate to contact me.'

Realising that the appointment had come to an end, Emma rose to her feet. She shook the man's hand and left the office with a spring in her step. She was thrilled for her daughter, thrilled that she would never know poverty, and with her own inheritance she could carry out her plans.

When Emma arrived home, Doris was obviously itching to hear what had happened.

'Most of Horace's estate goes to Tinker, and that's wonderful,' Emma told her, 'but he's also left me the house and a bit of money.'

'Blimey, that's smashing.'

'I was relieved to find that Horace left me anything, but thinking about it I don't understand why. When he left, Horace acted as though he hated me, and refused to believe that I was carrying his child.'

'Maybe he found out his mistake. Maybe it was guilt, and let's face it, he must have known that Tinker's his. I mean, why else would he leave her all that money?'

'Yes, it's possible, but I don't want the house.'

'You're mad, Em! Think about the struggle you had, how you had to run a brothel to survive, and all because that bastard left you.'

'If truth be known, I was glad when Horace walked out. He may have left me that house, but I hate it now, hate what I allowed it to become, and I don't want to benefit from it ever again. In the meantime I'll accept the money, not that it's a vast amount, but added to the sale of this place, it will ensure that I can manage until Tinker reaches maturity. I can also apply to her trust if necessary, so we'll be fine.'

'Leave it out, love. If you sell next door too, you'll be in clover. Cor, wait till I tell Terry. He'll be dead chuffed for you.'

Emma forced a smile. She was finding it increasingly difficult to see Doris and Terry together, but she had so much to thank them for. Doris looked so happy nowadays, her face bright, obviously thanks to Terry, and now she hoped to increase their happiness. 'Oh, don't worry, I'll sell Horace's house, but the money will be shared out. You'll benefit and, added to your savings, I think it'll be enough for you to buy a little place of your own. The rest is going to my brothers and sisters. My dad's all right, he's got the pub, but I'll treat him to a little something too.'

'A house! Me!' Doris cried, throwing her arms around Emma.

'Come on, don't go to mush,' Emma said. Gently she pushed Doris away and went to the window, seeing Tinker playing happily in the garden. Her heart lifted every time she saw her now, but she still feared for her safety. The cottage in Wales was empty, and until the police traced Luke, she was terrified that his twisted mind might lead him into trying to snatch Tinker again. She kept the house like a fortress and her daughter in bed with her every night, but sleep was elusive, her ears pricked for every sound.

Doris spoke again, dabbing at her eyes. 'I don't know what to say, well, other than thank you, but that hardly seems enough.'

'You've been a good friend to me and deserve it. Now come on, I don't know about you, but I'm worn out and could do with a cup of tea.'

'Yeah, I must admit, you do look a bit washed out and you've got dark rings under your eyes. What's the matter? Ain't you sleeping?'

'Not very well. I'm frightened that Luke will try again.'

'Well the answer's under your nose. Why don't you ask Terry to move in for a while?'

'Oh yes, that would be wonderful, and of course you must move in too.'

'I must say it's tempting, but I can't. I start my new job tomorrow.'

'New job! But that needn't stop you, and I can't see Terry living here without you.'

'Em, I don't know what you're on about. It won't make any difference to Terry, and anyway, I didn't know that I was gonna be able to buy my own place, so I've got a live-in job.'

'But the money is for both of you . . . so you can buy a house together. If you take a live-in job, Terry will hardly see you.'

'A house together! You must be joking. After kipping in his spare room for so long I should think he'll be glad to see the back of me.'

'But . . . but I thought . . .'

'Yeah, I know what you thought; even though I've told you time and time again that me and Terry are just friends.' Doris sighed heavily, obviously exasperated. 'Look, love, when are you going to see the light? There's only one woman for Terry and always has been. It's you he loves. When are you going to admit that you love him too?'

'He loves me? Oh, Doris!'

'Yeah, that's brought a spark to your eyes, and now it's up to you to do something about it. Shall I ask him to call round later? Though I'd like to be a fly on the wall when you tell him how you feel.'

Emma couldn't believe it, could barely take it in. She hugged herself, daring to hope. 'Oh, yes. Yes, please!'

Emma's stomach fluttered with nerves as she waited for Terry. She had put Tinker to bed, read her a story, relieved when she soon fell asleep, and was now applying a little powder and lipstick.

542

At half-past eight there was a knock on the street door and, trembling, she went to answer it.

'Hello, Em,' Terry said, his forehead furrowed. 'I don't know what this is all about, but Doris said you want to see me. She also said that I had to wait until the nipper's in bed.'

Emma found herself suddenly shy. 'Yes, that's right. Please, come in.' And with her face flaming, she kept her back to him as they went through to the drawing room.

'Doris said you're not sleeping because you're worried that Luke might show up.'

'Yes, that's true,' Emma said, 'I'm frightened he might try to take Tinker again.'

'Well, worry no more. He's been caught and is in custody.'

'What! How do you know?'

'Because I've kept in touch with a copper who tipped me the wink.'

Emma sank onto the sofa, her emotions all over the place. Luke was in custody, locked in a cell, and though she felt relief, she also felt her heart going out to her brother. He had taken Tinker, and it had been terrible, but he had acted out of a misguided love. He hadn't wanted Tinker tainted and now Emma knew he was right. She wouldn't have been able to protect her daughter for ever. One day Tinker would have found out how her mother made money, and how would that have affected her mind? If Luke hadn't intervened, she would have just carried on, obsessed by money, running the brothel until it was too late.

'Oh, Terry, will I be able to see him?'

'Yeah, but not until he's charged. He'll go before a magistrate in the morning, and once officially charged he'll be transferred to prison pending his trial. You'll be able to visit him then. Mind you, I'm surprised you want to see him. I thought you'd want him locked up and the key thrown away.'

'I felt like that at first, but not now. In fact, I want to do all I can to ensure his release. Luke must have been out of his mind to do such a thing and he needs psychiatric help, not prison.'

'Yeah, I think you're right. But don't worry, I'm sure they'll realise that, especially if you speak up for him in his defence.'

'Oh, I will, and I'll find him a good lawyer too.'

There was a small silence, Terry filling it by saying, 'How's Tinker?'

'She's fine, but missing you.' Emma paused, trying to pluck up courage, taking a deep breath as she quickly added, 'And I'm missing you too.'

'Well, that's nice, but you ain't running a brothel now and don't need me. Doris said I should call round because you'd be telling me something I want to hear. What is it? Have you got some other sort of job for me?'

Emma lowered her eyes for a moment. She had

rebuffed this man, sacked him, and knew that any move would have to come from her. Would he still want her?

She rose to her feet, trembling as she moved towards him. 'Oh Terry, I've been such a fool. You see, I've known for some time how I feel, but I thought it was too late . . . that you and Doris were together.'

'Nah, me and Doris are just mates.'

'Yes, I know that now.' She was close, looking up at him, and as their eyes met she whispered, 'I love you, Terry.'

For a moment he froze, but then it was as if a light switched on behind his eyes. 'You love me? Are you kidding?'

'No, I'm not kidding,' she said, smiling widely. 'Now are you going to give me a kiss, or what?'

He did more than kiss her, he swept her up into his arms, spinning her around and around until she was dizzy. Emma clung to his neck, her heart full. Instead of fear there was joy now, joy at being in his arms. He was her man. Her bear of a man. Her Terry.

Read on for an exclusive extract of Kitty Neale's
Family Betrayal

PROLOGUE

Nervously, the woman approached Drapers Alley. She had been told that all but one of the houses was empty, yet still her heart thudded with fear.

Had her informant lied? Yes, it was possible. Many years had passed, yet there was still venom – spite aimed at her family – locals who wanted to see her, and them, brought low. For a moment she froze, wanting to turn and flee, but she had to risk it – had to tell her mother the awful truth.

Taking a deep breath to calm her nerves, the woman entered the narrow passageway, skirting the iron bollard that barred all traffic other than those on two wheels. The sign was still on the wall, the ally's name, but now her eyes widened. Her father and brothers had ruled here, no one daring to enter their domain without permission, but now the 'D' in Drapers had been crudely painted out. Instead of Drapers, it read Rapers Alley. Yes, rape may have been one of their sins, it was certainly possible, yet worse had been done – much worse.

The fact that the name had been defaced was all the proof she needed that they had left, the tension at last leaving her body. To one side of the alley a towering, dirty, factory wall cut out light, the atmosphere dim and foreboding. Above the high wall the upper floors of the factory were visible, lined with a myriad of mean, grimy windows. Though it had closed many years ago, it was a building that, from childhood, had dominated her life, appearing to lean over the alley, visible as soon as she stepped outside the front door. She hated it, had longed to see grass, trees, but unlike her nephews, she hadn't been allowed the pleasure of playing in the local park.

Her eyes avoided the factory building and the horror of what would be found inside. Instead she looked to the left and for a moment paused to take in the small row of six, flat fronted, workers houses. They appeared smaller, shabby with neglect, yet the first in the row, number one, stood out as different. This was her parent's home, one that in fear of her life she'd been forced to flee.

She crossed the narrow, cobbled alley, her gaze fixed on the house, and at the same time a ray of spring sunlight pierced the gloom. Like her, it had dared to penetrate the alley where it momentarily sparkled like a jewel on her mother's window. Was it a good omen? Did it mean she'd be safe? God, she hoped so.

The brass doorknocker and letterbox gleamed, but instead of smiling, her lips thinned. Now that her mother was alone, she'd expected her to change – to no longer be obsessed with housework. Her mother had dusted, polished, swept and scrubbed every hour of the day, excluding any opportunity to show her children an ounce of affection.

For a moment she hesitated outside the street door. What if she'd been lied to? What if her mother wasn't alone? *Come on*, she told herself, *show a bit of spunk. You've come this far and nobody would have dared to call it Rapers Alley if they were still around.*

Her hand slowly lifted to the small, lions head knocker, and after rapping three times she involuntarily stepped back a pace.

The door slowly opened. 'Is it really you?'

'Yes, Mum,' she said, and seeing the smile of welcome on her mother's face her eyes filled with tears. What she had to tell her mother would break her heart. She stepped inside, her eyes encompassing the small, immaculate living room and the past, one that until recently she has tried to forget, came flooding back.

551

CHAPTER ONE

Drapers Alley, South London, May, 1962

Dan Draper was fond of relating the tale of how he'd found the alley, and on Saturday morning he was doing it again as he sat facing his youngest son. Dan's pug nosed face was animated, his huge, thick, tattooed arms resting on the table.

Chris Draper at twenty four years old is a replica of his father, with light brown hair and grey eyes. He has his father's tall, beefy build, both of them six feet in height, but so far his nose remained unbroken, his good looks intact. 'Yes, you've told me, Dad' Chris said wearily as he cut vigorously into his rasher of crispy bacon.

As though he hadn't noticed the interruption, Dan carried on, in full sail now that he'd started. 'I'd had a few beers too many and my bladder was fucking bursting. It was sheer chance that I cut into this alley for a slash. You could have knocked me down with a feather when I saw the name. Blimey, it was like fate, and not only that, I saw the potential straight away. With narrow entrances at both ends, cut in half by the bollards, the only thing that can get through is a bike.'

'Yeah, I know.'

'This alley is as good as a fortress.'

Chris nodded, hardly listening as his father rambled on. He looked at Joan, his mother, seeing her hands were busy as always as she polished the brass ornaments. She appeared distant, unreachable, but Chris was used to this. In his childhood it had upset him, but he was a man now, not needing displays of motherly affection, or so he told himself. She was a tiny woman, two inches less than five feet tall and as usual aroused his protective instincts. 'Are you all right, Mum?' he asked.

It was his father who answered. 'Of course she's all right. Why shouldn't she be? Now then, where was I? Oh yes, there was only one house empty in the alley at the time and I had to tip up a back hander to get it. Gawd, despite homes being in short supply, you should have seen your mother's face when she saw it. I thought she was gonna have a fit, though I must admit it was a squash to fit us all in.'

'Yeah, I remember.'

'It was even worse when after giving me five sons, your mother dropped a girl.'

Chris heard his mother's tutt of displeasure but she said nothing, giving up on her husband's coarseness years ago. Chris looked around the immaculate room, knowing that the outside of the house bore no relation to the interior. In their line of business it would give the game away to flaunt their wealth, yet even so there was every comfort that could be accounted for. Against one wall sat a deep red, velvet sofa with gold tassels along the bottom hanging just short of the Wilton rug. To one side of the small Victorian fireplace there was a matching chair, but Chris's eyes were drawn to the radiogram, which thanks to his mother, looked as shiny and new as the day his father bought it. With a small table and four chairs in the centre, the room was crammed to the rafters, yet from the brass fender to the ornaments, everything was sparkling. When they had first moved in, there hadn't been a bathroom, just an outside loo, but his father had solved that problem by building an extension, one that took up half the yard. Chris smiled. He hero worshiped his father, admired how clever he had been when installing the bathroom, one that held a secret that only the male members of the family were aware of.

'Oye! Are you listening to me or am I talking to myself?'

'I'm listening, Dad.'

'Right, well, we ain't done bad by Drapers Alley. Over the years, when your brother's got hitched, I saw off the neighbours and with a few more back handers I made sure they got their empty houses.' Dan leaned back in his chair, smiling with satisfaction. 'It's all Drapers living here now, other than your cousin Ivy, but she was a Draper before she married that short arsed git.'

Chris had to grin. It was true. Ivy had married Steve Rawlings, a bloke whose head only came up to her shoulders. Mind you, with her looks she was lucky to get anyone to take her on. Ivy was the odd one out and could only be described as ugly. She was tall, strong, with a round, flat face, piggy little eyes and thin, mousy coloured hair. The trouble was, Ivy had an ugly personality to match and Chris would never understand why his father had secured a house for her in the alley.

There was a clatter of footsteps as Petula ran downstairs before bursting into the room. 'Dad, can I have some money? Elvis Presley's latest record is in the charts and I want to buy it.'

'I gave you a quid yesterday.'

'Please, Dad,' she wheedled.

Chris knew that Pet would get her own way. She'd been born when he was ten, and after all sons, she was his father's pride and joy. At first he'd resented this, but gradually, like all his brothers, they had fallen under their baby sister's spell. She had been a beautiful child, and even though she was now a gangly fourteen-year old, it was plain to see that as an adult she'd be stunning. Pet's hair was almost black, sitting on her shoulders and flicked into an outward curl at the ends. With vivid, blue eyes, a cute turned up nose, full lips, and slightly pointed chin, her features were in perfect symmetry, but so far Pet seemed to have no idea how pretty she was.

Petula continued to beg and as usual, she won, Dan putting his hand in his back pocket to draw out a ten shilling note. 'All right, but this is coming out of your pocket money.'

'Thanks, Dad,' she cried, 'I'll be back soon.'

'Hold on! Eat your breakfast first and I don't want you roaming around Clapham Junction on your own. Chris can go with you.'

'Dad,' she whined, 'I'm fourteen years old and I'll be fifteen in December. I can look after myself now.'

'You'll do as I say.'

Petula pouted, but her father's tone of voice had hardened and she knew better than to argue. She went into the kitchen, returning with a box of cornflakes. The pout was still there as she poured herself a bowl, but with her naturally light hearted personality she soon brightened when Chris winked at her.

'I want to buy a record too so I might as well

come with you,' he said, his tone placatory.

Pet smiled, then saying, 'Dad, there's a dance at the youth club tonight. Can I go?'

'What time does it finish?'

'At ten o'clock.'

'Yeah, you can go, but one of your brothers will meet you afterwards to walk you home.'

'Oh, Dad, there's no need for that. It's less than a fifteen minutes away. I'll be fine on my own.'

'You'll be met,' he insisted.

'None of my friends will be escorted home. I'll be a laughing stock.'

'It ain't safe for you to be wandering the streets at that time of night, so either you're met, or you don't go.'

Pet scowled, saying no more as she quickly ate her breakfast. Chris finished his and they rose simultaneously.

'Right, we're off,' he said. 'See you later.'

'Yeah, and keep an eye out,' Dan warned. 'Don't forget we've got a meeting at the yard later. I want you there by eleven.'

'I'll be there. Bye, Mum.'

Joan obviously hadn't heard, locked as usual in her own world, but nevertheless Chris still offered a small wave. As they stepped out of the alley and turned into Aspen Street, Chris swiftly looked both ways, but other than a few kids playing there was no one in sight. Nowadays he knew it was unlikely that there'd be any trouble, but even so he was cautious. With the enemies they'd accrued it was prudent to be vigilant, but with Petula straining at the leash for a bit more freedom, it was becoming a problem. They did their best to keep her in ignorance of why she needed protection, yet it couldn't last much longer. She was growing up and they'd need to come up with some sort of explanation. He'd have a quiet word with his dad later, but in the meantime Chris continued to keep a look out, more so when they traversed a few more streets and reached Lavender Hill.

Half way along the hill, past the Town Hall, the Police Station loomed and glancing at it, Chris's smile was wry. The Drapers were notorious and had once been thieves, but careful planning had ensured they had never been caught. The entrance to the alley wasn't wide enough to accommodate a police car, but they'd been raided on foot a couple of times, rozzers pouring through the gaps at both ends of the alley. Of course the police had found nothing and it was unlikely they ever would, the Draper family out foxing them every time.

C.I.D had a go at the yard too, but once again all they had on show were building materials and perfectly kept account books. Chris smirked. Drapers Building Merchant, the family business, a good front and good cover that served them well. Chris hoped it would continue to do so, especially as nowadays they had a more lucrative sideline, one that was out of the borough and more likely to attract the attention of the Vice Quad. So far they'd been lucky, the business well concealed, but they were ruffling a few feathers and were always at risk from their rivals.

'What record are you buying?' Pet asked as they reached Clapham Junction.

Chris's thoughts had been wandering, his sisters chatter only eliciting grunts, so now he floundered for a reply, 'Er . . . The Young Ones.'

'Not Cliff Richards and the Shadows?'

'Yeah, that's it.'

'Cliff Richards isn't bad looking, but he isn't a patch on Elvis.'

'I'm not buying it for his looks. I rate his backing group, especially Hank Marvin on guitar.'

They turned into the entrance of Arding and Hobbs, heading for the small record department at the back of the store, which at nine thirty in the morning was almost empty. He eyed the assistant, liking what he saw, smiling as he and Pet approached the counter. It wasn't much fun being Pet's minder, but if this girl was available she'd be the ideal cover. She was young, pretty, and the sort of girlfriend his family would expect him to have on his arm.

Dan Draper eyed his wife as she bustled around. Joan was showing her age, but when he'd married her she'd been a stunner, a bundle of dynamite. Now though her hair was greying, her faced lined, and the firm body he'd once gone mad for, now resembled a little round ball. Still, she'd been a good wife, keeping her mouth shut and not asking questions. As if aware of his scrutiny she met his eyes, her hand involuntarily patting her tightly permed hair.

'You spoil that girl,' she said.

'Leave it out, Queen. I only gave her ten bob.'

'Petula should earn it instead of having it dished out every time she bats her eyelashes at you.'

'Don't be daft woman. She's only fourteen so how's she supposed to earn it?

'For a start she could give me a hand around the house. It's about time she leaned how to cook and clean.'

'The boys didn't have to earn their pocket money, so it shouldn't be any different for Petula.'

'They didn't get the amount of money you throw at her.'

Dan's lips tightened. He wasn't going to stand for this. Joan did alright; her housekeeping allowance large, giving her little to complain about. He treated her right, saw that the kids showed her respect, but he was the boss, the man of the house and she'd better remember that. 'If

I want to treat my daughter now and again I will. Now for fucks sake shut up about it.'

Joan paled, but did as she was told, whilst Dan picked up the daily paper. He turned to the racing page, studying form before picking out a couple of bets. Nowadays he could afford to lay on a good few bob and a satisfied expression crossed his features. Since they'd got into this new game, things had looked up big time. The money was still rolling in, and though at first he'd had reservations about getting into this line of work, he was glad that his sons had talked him round.

Yes, his dream was closer, but glancing at Joan he wondered how she'd fit into his planned new lifestyle. In the near future he was determined to retire – to hand the reins over to Danny Junior, his eldest son. A nice house in Surrey beckoned, one with stables for the horses he intended to buy. Instead of a punter, he'd be an owner, mixing with the elite, looked up to and respected. Petula would love it and instead of hiding his wealth he would be able to dress her like a princess. She'd be away from this area and the riff raff, mixing instead with the upper echelons of the racing fraternity.

Joan went through to the kitchen and Dan heard the tap running, the clatter of plates as she washed up the breakfast dishes. Housework. All his wife thought about was housework. How the hell was she going to adapt to living in a big house, with cleaners paid to take over her role? Huh, Joan would probably insist on doing it herself, making a fool of them when they entertained. The trouble was, she had no class. Joan was a born and bred Battersea girl, and, unlike him, she had no interest in rising socially. He heaved a sigh. At least Petula would fit in. He'd made sure his daughter spoke well, paying for her to take elocution lessons from an old biddy in Chelsea. Yeah, Petula could mix with the best and he'd just have to keep Joan in the background.

Dan rose to his feet, passing his wife to go through to the bathroom where he locked the door behind him. Involuntarily, as always, his eyes went straight to the hiding place. Joan cleaned in here every day, but had never discovered its secret. If she didn't twig, then the police never would. Only the boys knew and he trusted them to keep their mouths shut, his married sons knowing better than to blab to their wives.

He washed and shaved before taking the money he needed from the secret cache, returning to the living room with it tucked into his back pocket. 'Right, Queen, I'm off. I'm going down to the yard.'

Joan was busy as usual, just nodding an acknowledgement and as Dan stepped outside, he paused to look up and down Drapers Alley. It felt like his – his kingdom, and in some ways he'd regret leaving it. He patted the money in his back pocket, mentally calculating. It was for stock, more bricks and cement, enough to keep the yard ticking over, but there'd be enough over to place a few bets. The other business was thriving and maybe they'd have to increase productivity to keep up with the demand. It was lucrative, but with five sons and Ivy's husband wanting their share, they needed to push harder.

Dan passed through the narrow entrance and around the corner to his lock up garage, opening the door to climb into his Daimler car. There was a powwow today, his eldest son coming up with a way to increase the coffers. Dan grimaced, disliking the rough plans his son had outlined. It would be too risky. They'd be treading on competitors toes, but he'd wait to gauge his other son's reactions before vetoing the idea.

For a moment he smiled. Christ, if Joan knew what they were up to she'd have a fit, but there was no chance of her finding out. How the daft cow thought the builders merchants made enough money to support them all was beyond him, but as long as she carried on living in a world of illusions, that was fine by him.

CHAPTER TWO

Next door, in number two Drapers Alley, the eldest son, Danny, his father's namesake, emerged from the bedroom. He was the tallest of the family at two inches over six foot, and his almost black hair was tousled; his mouth open in a wide yawn, but even this didn't detract from his looks. Danny is handsome, a charmer, with large, sultry dark eyes and full lips. A scar on his cheek, the relic of a knife fight, didn't scare off women. If anything the scar added something, a hint of danger that complimented his rakish charms.

'Christ, why didn't you wake me,' he moaned as he walked into the kitchen.

Yvonne, his wife, poured him a cup of tea, saying shortly, 'I didn't know you had to get up for work today.'

His eyes darkened with anger – sure that he'd told her there was to be a business meeting that morning. 'Shit, I'm sure I mentioned it, and if I don't get a move on the old man will arrive before me.'

Yvonne pushed a cup of tea towards him, her hazel eyes avoiding his. She was tall, her height emphasised by the below knee pencil skirt she was wearing with a crisp, white blouse tucked in at the waist. Her brown hair was immaculate as usual, and her make-up freshly applied. When Danny first met Yvonne in 1954, she reminded him somewhat of Wallace Simpson, with the same elegant manner and style of dress. However, unlike the sophisticated woman who had captured a King, Yvonne showed her true class as soon as she opened her mouth. Like his mother, she was Battersea born and bred, her diction letting her down and sometimes grating on his nerves. Even so, he'd been instantly smitten, but as the years passed she'd grown so thin that the woman he'd once been attracted to, now resembled a stick insect. Nerves. Huh, she was supposed to be suffering from nerves, but he knew the real problem. She wanted a kid, but though they'd been trying for seven years, the skinny cow was barren. Not that it bothered him. As far as he was concerned his life was fine without brats cramping his style. Of course Yvonne didn't know that, the daft cow thought he was as keen on the idea of a family as she was.

Danny picked up the cup, gulping the tea before

565

hurrying through to the bathroom. He had to get a move on or his father might talk to the others before he arrived, putting the kybosh on his ideas. After running water into the sink he splashed cold water onto his face, deciding to forgo a shave, but he still smacked a handful of Brut after-shave onto his cheeks. It was a big day today. He hoped his brothers would back his plans, but with the old man against them, maybe he should have approached the boys individually first. Danny cursed his lack of forethought. Yet surely his brothers would see the sense of it? Surely they'd see the potential and for once go against the old man. Yes, there'd be risks, big ones, but the rewards could be vast and a way out of Drapers Alley for all of them.

He returned to the kitchen, drank a ready poured second cup of tea, and grabbing a slice of toast he held it between his teeth as he tucked his shirt into his trousers. 'See you later,' he then called, leaving the house without a backward glance.

Yvonne watched her husband leave. There was no kiss goodbye, no quick hug of affection, and as the street door slammed behind him she desolately went upstairs.

In the bedroom she picked up the shirt that Danny had discarded when he rolled home after midnight, but as she lifted it to her nose to sniff it, tears stung her eyes. It reeked of cheap perfume, confirming her suspicions that Danny was playing away again. How many affairs had she put up with? Yvonne had lost count, but each and every time he'd assured her it would be the last. She was a fool, a mug, an idiot for believing him, but loving Danny so deeply she couldn't bear to leave him.

Oh, if only they'd had children, and though there was still time, after seven years of marriage she had lost hope. She knew Danny resented it, knew that he envied his married brothers with small families, whilst they remained childless. He blamed her of course, said she was barren and he was right. Maybe that was why he kept having affairs. Maybe if he got another woman pregnant, he'd leave her! Yvonne slumped onto the side of the bed, giving vent to her feelings as tears rolled down her cheeks.

Ten minutes passed before Yvonne was able to pull herself together. She then rose to her feet, throwing the shirt into the laundry basket. She had to get a move on – had to make sure every-thing was clean and tidy in case her mother-in-law popped round. Joan had high standards, ones that Yvonne fought to match, always looking for her mother-in-laws approval.

She made the bed, and though it was unlikely that Joan would see it, Yvonne made sure the sheets were tucked in as tightly as a hospital bed, pillows plumped and the pale blue quilt, shaken. She then dusted the furniture, making sure the blue, enamel backed brush set on her dressing table, lay in perfect symmetry.

A glance in the mirror showed red, puffy eyes, and fearful that Joan would see them, Yvonne ran downstairs to the bathroom, splashing her face with cold water. Danny had left a mess, one that she quickly tidied, folding the discarded towel before placing it neatly on the rail. Like Joan's, this bathroom had been an added extension shortly after she married Danny, and Yvonne was proud of it. To her, after her parents outside toilet and tin bath in front of the fire every Friday night, having a bathroom was sheer luxury. Her eyes saddened. She still missed her mother, mourned her death after a long fight with cancer, and couldn't remember the last time she'd seen her father. He had disapproved of Danny, forcing her to choose between them. It had nearly broken her heart but she couldn't give Danny up, and, as an only child, losing her father had been hard to bear.

It was a half hour later, the kitchen and living room immaculate when there was a rap on the letterbox. The door opened, Joan poking her head inside to call, 'It's only me.'

'Come in, Mum. I'm in the kitchen,' Yvonne called back as she arranged her best porcelain cups and saucers. Not for Joan thick china. Carefully pouring boiling water into the matching teapot, Yvonne plastered a smile on her face as her mother-in-law walked in.

There was no fooling Joan Draper, the woman frowning, 'Have you been crying?'

'No, of course not,' Yvonne protested. Christ, Danny would go mad if she complained to his mother. Quickly finding an excuse she stammered, 'I . . . I've got a bit of a cold, that's all.'

'You want to look after it or it could turn into bronchitis.'

Why anyone would want to look after a cold was beyond Yvonne, but then again a lot of the things that Joan came out with sounded daft to her. They weren't religious, but Joan insisted on eating fish on Fridays, and the routine of house-work was the same. Washing on Monday, rain or shine. Ironing on Tuesday, in fact every day had a designated task. The woman was like a little beaver; always busy doing something, so it was a wonder she took time out every day to come round for a cup of tea. If anything Yvonne found her mother-in-law a bit of a Jekyll and Hyde char-acter. Meek when her husband was around, but of sterner stuff when he wasn't. 'Do you fancy digestive or garibaldi biscuits?' she asked.

'Digestive, please,' Joan said, but then her lips tightened. 'Chris has taken Pet to Clapham Junction. Dan gave her the money to buy a record, but I wish he'd stop spoiling the girl.'

Yvonne knew that her mother-in-law was wishing for the moon. Dan Draper was a hard man, and despite the fact that his son's were adults, he ruled them all. Only Petula saw his soft side, and it was true, the girl *was* spoiled. Thankfully, so far it hadn't ruined her character, but if she ever had to face the real world she'd be ill prepared. Petula had been cosseted and sheltered since the day she was born, wanting for nothing. Mind you, it wasn't only her father who treated her like a little princess. Her brother's were as bad, all of them over protective when it came to their little sister.

Joan's eyes flicked around the small kitchen but it didn't worry Yvonne. Every surface was shiny and clean, everything in its rightful place, the woman unable to find fault. She picked up the prettily laid tray, carrying it through to the sitting room where they sat at the table.

Joan hated tea-leaves in her tea, so holding a strainer over the cups, Yvonne carefully poured. She then added milk from a matching jug, a spoonful of sugar from a matching bowl, and with a spoon balanced in the saucer, she handed it to her mother-in-law.

'Thanks,' Joan said, but then added abruptly, 'Linda's pregnant.'

Yvonne stiffened. Linda had married Danny's brother, George, less than a year ago and they now lived in number five. He was her least favourite brother-in-law, quick to violence, but she couldn't help a surge of envy. Married for such a short time, but already a baby on the way. Oh God, it just wasn't fair. She struggled to pull herself together, forcing a smile. 'That's nice, but is it definite? She hasn't said anything to me.'

There was a pause as Joan lifted the cup to drink her tea. She then said, 'Linda knows it's a sensitive subject so maybe she doesn't want to hurt your feelings.'

'Once she starts showing, she could hardly hide it.'

'Yeah, that's true. Oh well, I suppose I'll have to get my knitting needles out again. This will be my forth grandchild, but It's been a while since I've had to make any matinee jackets.'

Yvonne felt a wave of desolation. It was as though her mother-in-law enjoyed rubbing salt into the wound – but why? She tried to be a good wife, kept the house immaculate, and though she and Danny remained childless, Joan had other grandchildren to love. Huh, love, that was a joke. When did Joan ever show any of her grand-children an ounce of affection? Yvonne shook her head, saying sadly, 'I envy Linda. I want a baby more than anything in the world.'

Joan leaned forward to pat the back of Yvonne's hand, her voice soft, 'I know you do, love. Don't worry, it still might happen.'

Tears welled, Yvonne blinking wildly to stave them off, but Joan rose to her feet, saying hurriedly, 'I'd best be off. Thanks for the tea.'

Before Yvonne could respond, Joan had gone, and she was left sitting at the table, amazed that her usually cold, undemonstrative mother-in-law had actually shown her a little sympathy.

Joan almost ran into her front door, closing it quickly behind her. Gawd, she had almost brought Yvonne to tears and that was the last thing she wanted. Of all her daughter-in-laws, Yvonne was the only one she had any time for, and she could guess the sort of life Danny led the poor girl.

Joan wasn't a fool, she knew her eldest son's faults, knew he was a womaniser and was amazed that he'd managed to hold onto his wife for seven years. She knew that Yvonne longed for children, but was tempted to tell her what a thankless task motherhood was. She had hoped that after five sons, things would be different with Petula, but instead, like the boys, she galvanised towards her father. Maybe things would have been different if she could have shown them affection, but found it impossible. Her own mother had been a cold, undemonstrative woman, bitter at being a single parent with the stigma it carried.

With a sigh, Joan picked up a duster, absent-mindedly flicking it over furniture she'd already polished earlier. Her own mother had been a dirty woman, their home a tip, one that was looked down on by their neighbours. During her infrequent attendance at school, Joan had been called a smelly cow and at first hadn't understood why. It was only as she grew older that she learned about hygiene – learned that her mother's method of rubbing a damp flannel across her face every day, the body untouched, wasn't enough. Her first bath had been a revelation, the water almost black, but from then on she had gone to the public baths once a week, relishing the feel of being clean from top to toe.

When she'd married Dan Draper, Joan had been determined to be different, to make sure that her home was always immaculate. At first it had been easy, but as the babies came along it took every minute of her day to keep up. One by one the boys had been born, filling the place until it felt they were bursting at the seams. Then, just when she thought her child bearing days were over, Petula had come along and though she hated to admit it, Joan was filled with resentment. She'd had enough of babies, dirty nappies, broken sleep, but she'd hidden her feelings, leaving most of Petula's welfare to her father and older brothers. It had been a mistake, the child spoiled, fawned on, but it was too late to change things now. If she so much as opened her mouth in criticism, Danny shot her down in flames, his daughter able to do no wrong.

'We're back,' Chris said as he flung open the door. 'I can't stop. Dad wants me down the yard.'

'I thought it was your Saturday off,' Joan said.

Chris looked surprised at her interest. 'Yeah, but there's some sort of business meeting and Dad wants me there.'

'It's the first I've heard of it.'

'He mentioned it earlier but you obviously weren't listening.'

'What's this meeting about?'

Chris's eyes became veiled and Joan knew she was wasting her time. When it came to the business, she was always kept in the dark, but in truth she preferred it that way, berating herself now for asking questions.

'I'm not sure what it's about, Mum,' Chris said, 'but no doubt Dad will put you in the picture.'

'Yeah, and pigs might fly,' Joan told him.

He grinned, turning to leave. 'See you later, Mum. Bye Petula.'

'Don't call me Petula. You know I hate it.'

'It was Mum who named you after Petula Clark,

574

her favourite singer, not me,' and on that note, Chris closed the street door behind him.

'It's a daft name,' Petula complained.

Joan ignored her daughter, instead going through to the kitchen to boil a kettle of water. She would scrub the doorstep before getting the Brasso out to polish the letter box and door knocker. With any luck it might inspire her daughter-in-laws to follow suit. Yvonne was the only one who had good standards, the rest slovenly cows, and it was about time they pulled their socks up.

She heard Petula thumping upstairs, followed by music, the sound of her daughter's new record filling the house. She was growing up, fifteen in December, and no doubt already interested in boys. Not that she'd have much luck meeting any, especially with her father and brothers keeping her under close guard. The time would come when Petula would rebel, and for the first time Joan felt a twinge of pity for her daughter. The girl couldn't win - it would be a losing battle. Any man who came near her would soon be chased off.

By the time the kettle came to the boil, Petula was playing the record again, and Joan closed her eyes against the sound. Every time the girl got a new one it was played repeatedly until Joan felt like screaming. All right, Elvis Presley had a good voice, but by now she knew all his songs off by heart. Her ears pricked. What was this one? *Good Luck Charm*. Well, it wasn't bad, but hoping to get away from the racket, Joan filled a bucket with the hot water, adding a generous amount of soda before going outside to tackle her doorstep.

'All right, Mum,' a voice called, and Joan's eyes flicked sideways.

Sue was standing on her doorstep and Joan hid a scowl. This was her least favourite daughter-in-law. Like her, Sue was diminutive, but the resemblance ended there. With peroxide blonde hair and a huge bust, the girl looked a bit like the up and coming star, Barbara Windsor, and knowing this Sue played on it, emulating the actress's gyrating walk and style of dress. Joan shook her head against the sight of Sue's tight, sheath dress, her bust thrust out in front as she wandered closer and her hair so thickly backcombed that it looked like candyfloss.

'Bob left early for the yard,' Sue said. 'He said something about a meeting. Do you know what it's about?'

'You know better than to ask me that,' Joan snapped as she dipped her scrubbing brush into the water. 'I'm cleaning my step and it's about time you had a go at yours.'

'Why bother? The kids are in and out every five minutes and will only muck it up again.'

Joan's eyes flicked along the alley. 'Where are they?'

'I gave them their pocket money so they've gone straight to the sweet shop to spend it.'

No sooner had Sue spoken than the two lads came careering into the alley, their skinny legs pumping, with Robby at six years old in pursuit of his younger brother.

'Mum! Mum!' four year old Paul yelled. 'Robby's trying to nick my sweets.'

'No I'm not,' Robby protested, skidding to a halt beside Joan.

'He is, Gran,' Paul insisted, making sure that though she was kneeling, his grandmother was between them. 'He's got his own sweets, but he's after my gobstopper.'

'Look, it's up to your mother to sort this out, not me,' Joan protested. 'I've got work to do so bugger off and leave me in peace.'

'Yes, come here boys. After all, you can't come between your grandmother and her housework.'

Joan looked daggers at Sue, but her daughter-in-law ignored her, dragging the boys inside and slamming the door. Joan shrugged, unconcerned. When the boys had been born her daughter-in-law had expected her to baby-sit, but she'd soon nipped that in the bud. She'd told Sue that she had no intention of looking after her kids whilst she went out gallivanting. Huh, she'd done her stint, had six kids, and wasn't prepared to start all over again. Joan wrung out her cloth, her mouth grim. Sue resented it, didn't like her, but Joan didn't care. The feeling was reciprocated, their animosity only held in check for Bob's sake. On the surface the marriage appeared fine, but Joan doubted her son was happy. With Sue for a wife and his house a tip, how could he be?